THE MAKING OF GHOSTS

A NOVEL

BOOKS BY THE AUTHOR

AUTHORED BOOKS

The Psychoanalysis of Symptoms
Dictionary of Psychopathology
Group Psychotherapy and Personality: Intersecting Structures
Sleep Disorders: Insomnia and Narcolepsy
The 4 Steps to Peace of Mind: The Simple Effective Way to Cure Our Emotional Symptoms. (Romanian edition, 2008; Japanese edition, 2011)
Love Is Not Enough: What It Takes to Make It Work
Greedy, Cowardly, and Weak: Hollywood's Jewish Stereotypes
Haggadah: A Passover Seder for the Rest of Us
Hollywood Movies on the Couch: A Psychoanalyst Examines 15 Famous Films
Personality: How it Forms
The Discovery of God: A Psycho/Evolutionary Perspective
A Consilience of Natural and Social Sciences: A Memoir of Original Contributions
The Making of Ghosts: A Novel

CO-AUTHORED BOOKS   (with Anthony Burry, Ph.D.)

Psychopathology and Differential Diagnosis: A Primer
    Volume 1. History of Psychopathology
    Volume 2. Diagnostic Primer
Handbook of Psychodiagnostic Testing: Analysis of Personality in the Psychological Report. 1ˢᵗ edition, 1981; 2ⁿᵈ edition, 1991; 3ʳᵈ edition, 1997; 4ᵗʰ edition, 2007. (Japanese edition, 2011).

EDITED BOOKS

Group Cohesion: Theoretical and Clinical Perspectives
The Nightmare: Psychological and Biological Foundations

CO-EDITED BOOKS   (with Robert Plutchik, Ph.D.)

Emotion: Theory, Research, and Experience
Volume 1. Theories of Emotion
Volume 2. Emotions in Early Development
Volume 3. Biological Foundations of Emotion
Volume 4. The Measurement of Emotion
Volume 5. Emotion, Psychopathology, and Psychotherapy

THE MAKING OF GHOSTS

A NOVEL

HENRY KELLERMAN

BOOKS

Published by Barricade Books Inc.
185 Bridge Plaza North
Suite 309
Fort Lee, N.J. 07024
www.barricadebooks.com

Library of Congress Cataloging-in-Publication Data

Kellerman, Henry.
  The making of ghosts : a novel / by Henry Kellerman.
    p. cm.
  ISBN 978-1-56980-468-1 (alk. paper)
  I. Title.
  PS3611.E435M35 2012
  813'.6--dc23

                                                          2011049106
          ISBN:978-1-56980-468-1

        10 9 8 7 6 5 4 3 2 1
    Manufactured in the United States of America

For
Linda

CONTENTS

PRELUDE

BOTTLES UNDER THE BED

Wishing is ubiquitous. This means we are all wish-soaked creatures. The problem is that only infrequently do we get these wishes met, too many damn variables that we can't control. Even if a wish is met, it's not always met exactly when we want it. And even if we get it when we want it, the wish is usually not met to the fullest measure. In the end, wishing is both ubiquitous and peripatetic—now you see it, now you don't.

And my impossible wish—to retrieve Katie—reflects my absolute die-hard protest that past events can't be changed. That's my disgusting fight with the world. It's a rectification crusade. For sure, injustice cannot, must not, be stronger than rectification! My insistence is that past events, at least, can be questioned, challenged—doubted. It's my refusal to give in. Get back what you lost. Rectification must triumph; it must, without fail, prevail over injustice, and the so-called immutable past be damned. The world cannot be constructed so that events that shatter the lives of people turn out to be more powerful than that which is vital to us. Of course I know better, but then again, I'm fighting it.

So, the whole thing is about retrieval.

And lo and behold, I now needed to invoke what I believed were my rectification powers so that along with Katie—Sebastian, and then Billy—could be rescued. Retrieve! Seek and ye shall find! And that's it. But all this protest of mine brought me to my knees. But not to pray. It was the weight of it all. And the story started like this.

It was ten years ago that I published a book on dreams and nightmares. While writing that book I stumbled upon a citation to a tract on dreams written by a medieval monk by the name of Sebastian of Livorno. This monk, in turn, referred to the work of St. Augustine on demonology and dreams. The reference implied that the monk had developed a deciphering method that he was using as a path to understanding symptoms as well as his own dreams. Good God. Before Freud? It's exactly what I'd been struggling to put together—a method to unravel and cure, yes, cure, psychological symptoms. Imagine the possibilities! People with symptoms of the psyche, like irrational fears, sexual dysfunction and other such symptoms that no one can explain through physical causes, would be subject to cure—through the talking method. And I wondered, had this monk hit upon the synthesis so that a method was revealed that showed the way to dissolve, neutralize, suspend, and basically cure the symptom?

In trying to ascertain whether any other citations to Sebastian existed, I devoted a weekend to researching it in the hospital library, housed in an austere brick building on the sprawling Brentwood (N.Y.) Hospital grounds, the mental hospital where I was a psychologist-consultant in two departments. The hospital library was a good place for me to work because it was usually quiet—actually unoccupied, even desolate—and I was planning to search the psychological, psychiatric, and psychoanalytic literature on the web for any clues that might lead me to publications by Sebastian, this medieval monk.

It was a blistering hot day in late July and while I was at it, I was also going to search for any pre-20th century material on dreams and nightmares, especially as these would be related to how psychological symptoms like fear of heights were formed. I was hoping that material would turn up at least from the 12th century on. But as I sat there starting this search, a commotion from the hospital grounds directly outside the reading room and adjacent to the hospital outdoor swimming pool, rippled into the library. A few seconds later, one of the social workers stumbled in Zombie-like.

"Billy Soldier drowned in the pool. He's dead."

Staring, she listlessly slid into the chair next to me. It was just before noon, and apparently Billy had been face down in the pool—probably all night.

"A couple of attendants fished him out. He was blue. Dr. Kruger called the police. I'm sick."

I didn't feel sick, but I was shocked. It rang a bell—like a body blow. Maybe I did feel sick. I liked him. Everyone liked him. Billy may have been the most popular patient in the hospital, and was well known for having that savant ability to name the day of the week on which you were born merely by having your birth date. This fact of his death suddenly gripped me, and I was fixed for the next few seconds on that fact. Then I thought, "blue" meant he'd probably drowned the previous evening and been in the water all night. It was an outdoor pool enclosed by a high cyclone chain-link fence which was always kept locked, except, of course, when staff members used the pool. It was not a pool for patients, and everyone would be wondering how Billy got in. No patients in the hospital had keys to locks. That never happened.

Billy was going on eighteen. He'd been hospitalized since he was a kid, probably about seven or eight, diagnosed with autism and mental retardation. You see, it wasn't enough that he was autistic. The fates had to make him retarded as well. But I knew that was bull. Billy was not retarded, and it didn't matter what the official chart said. "No known relatives" is what it said. "Parents killed in automobile crash, child only survivor; no siblings, no visitors." That's what it said. Billy was alone.

Autism—a brain anomaly that keeps the afflicted in a socially alienated state for life. Some, however, are really bright and can do genius things. These are the savants—numbers geniuses, musical wizards, and so forth. Billy, however, in addition to his autistic state, also tested in the retarded I.Q. range. That was official. In spite of that, we all knew that he had talents as well as an interesting intelligence and that's why some of us—certainly I—were sure he was not retarded. Definitely not! But, it was Dr. Kruger who had him tested—the great Dr. Kruger, Director of the hospital—and that was that. For the past four or five years the hope of many in the hospital had been that Billy would be released. I felt differently because even if he wasn't severely limited mentally, how would he care for himself? With what money? Under whose supervision? So for the only time that I can remember in our professional relationship, Siegfried Kruger and I did in fact agree: Billy Soldier would probably be better off in the hospital—permanently.

Kruger had him doing what was considered simple jobs. Billy would tally property items of chronically ill patients. You know, sixty shirts in this pile and thirty wrist watches in that, and eighty suitcases here, and fifty sets of keys there, and seventy-five wallets, and on and on. The secretarial staff knew that Billy was meticulous in his record keeping. Meticulous! His mentally-challenged I.Q. score could have resulted from some organic brain damage or from a partly weird understanding of social relationships. Because of this so-called weird understanding of how people react to one another, Billy may have given odd responses on tests that then showed up in his lowered score. Technically, this psychopathology is considered morbid functioning that lowers scores on tests. But was he conventionally retarded? No.

Absolutely everyone was going to be devastated by his death. I never came away feeling untouched by his vulnerability, his innocence, his sweet nature. Here's the heartbreaker. Billy seemed always to be proud of his job and was entirely obsessed with his counting and cataloguing. It was all he talked about. Repeating it. Constantly keeping track of the time so that he wouldn't miss a second at his little broken-down desk in the property office. Each morning after breakfast, there he'd be—waiting at the door for maintenance department personnel to unlock the property office building. He'd be earnestly inching toward the door, especially at the moment it was being unlocked.

As we exited the library, two police cars and an ambulance were pulling into the hospital complex. The detective, Steve Stroud, about mid-forties and about six-foot three, introduced himself. Then he pointed to his partner, Joe Grillo, also about mid-forties but a half foot shorter. They both immediately engaged Dr. Kruger at the scene of the crime. Crime! That came out automatically. A large crowd was gathering, and patients and staff began milling around the police cars and the ambulance. I was standing alongside Dr. Kruger and both detectives, glued to their conversation. Stroud, the detective doing the talking, looked directly at me, and Kruger, not missing a beat, introduced me.

"Dr. Kahn, how do you do?" Stroud said matter-of-factly.

I nodded and automatically said, "I just heard about it." Stroud took it in, hesitated, looked at me and turned back to Kruger. I guess I felt I had to prove my innocence. In any event, right there in front of everyone Stroud kept talking to Kruger, not even asking him to step inside. Kruger answered each question in an objective manner. Then both detectives and Kruger started walking toward Kruger's building.

* * *

"Every symptom is bottles under the bed."

That's what I told him. It all started with a phone call about Josh. It was the indomitable Dr. Charles Granger, psychiatrist extraordinaire. I was always fond of him, this lumbering friendly giant. We met when I was an intern psychologist at Kings County Hospital in the mid 90's and he was an outstanding psychiatric resident. We hit it off and kept in touch, seeing one another every year or so. My wife, Katie, and I visited Charley and his wife, Josie, at the birth of Josh, their only child. Over the years, whenever I phoned Charley, Josh would sometimes answer the phone, and he and I always had things to say to one another. We would laugh, and it was easy.

"Glenn, I've got a problem. It's Josh. He's got a symptom."

I could hear him taking a breath.

"Like what? What makes you say it's a symptom?"

"Well," he said, "I was getting dressed the other day and I noticed he was putting bottles under the bed. I said, 'Josh, what are you doing?' He hesitated and then he said it: 'I'm putting bottles under the bed.'

"I asked him what he meant and he said that he liked putting bottles under the bed. He told me that he gets a funny feeling in his stomach, and when he puts bottles under the bed, the funny feeling disappears."

"Okay," I agreed, "he's got a symptom."

Charley told me that in questioning Josh, the kid confessed to having had this urge to put bottles under the bed for a while now and that it was getting worse all the time. Charley didn't call me at the outset because he felt the psychiatrist colleague on his ward at the hospital could take care of it, as he said, "one, two, three." As it turned out, the psychiatrist said that Josh's symptom was too dense, too complex, that medication was the only cure. That psychiatrist then consulted Dr. Siegfried Kruger who said he would have to see Josh twice a week for about a year in order to cure him.

What a joke. Kruger loved the moniker Siggy because he thought people would associate him with Freud, but no one called him that. We were both affiliated at the same psychoanalytic institute and had also worked together for many years at Brentwood. Kruger was senior to me in age by about fifteen years, and of course in position, but the adage about age and wisdom clearly missed the boat with him. Charley had no way of knowing this, but Kruger couldn't cure Josh of anything if either of their lives depended on it. When we first worked at Brentwood, Kruger was in charge of one of the wards. There was nothing going on in the ward in terms of therapy, so I suggested we form the patients into groups and get them talking to one another. To that, Kruger said, "That's not possible," and with authority added, "Don't you know, talking is catching!"

Talking is catching! Can you believe that? He wouldn't permit patients to talk to one another because he apparently believed they could toxify, contaminate or infect one another, perhaps releasing airborne pathogens and allowing them to float freely and waft into all available olfactory orifices on the ward so that patients would adopt and even swap symptoms. So, rather than talk, these patients would sit on the ward and while away the time. We had a huge fight over that one and neither of us forgot it.

Charley must have instinctively disregarded Kruger's opinion as well as the other psychiatrist's.

"So I'm calling you now. What do you think?"

"C'mon, Charley, not to worry. It's a symptom and it'll fall. What you have here is aggravation not trouble, and you know I know the difference!" For sure, he didn't want to answer that, and, of course, he didn't answer it. I repeated: "The distinction's important. Right?"

I followed by telling him that in my opinion the symptom was not dense at all; it was not at all impossible to understand and it wouldn't have to take a year to clear up. Then I got that mildly sinking feeling thinking, "Here I go again, saving someone, promising it'll be okay, plain and simple. What if it won't be okay?"

As a matter of fact, when Charley was describing what the psychiatrist and Kruger had told him, I even had the audacious thought that it might take all of about ten minutes to get into the symptom, to really decode it. For a while now, when someone was suffering with a symptom, especially a painful one, I found myself getting belligerent towards the symptom, indignant towards it, even righteous.

* * *

Kruger's office was something to behold. Warmly lit, spacious, two area Oriental carpets, walls lined with oak bookshelves filled with psychiatric tomes, a large mahogany desk, leather chairs. What I always wondered was how Kruger had gotten into the faded, sepia colored framed picture on the wall behind his desk. It was a photograph of a psychiatric congress circa late 1950's and included a contingent of about a dozen men huddled together at the front entrance of some ornate building. Immediately recognizable were Carl Jung, of collective unconscious fame among other things, and Sandor Rado, famed educator in psychoanalysis. I also identified Ernest Jones, one of Freud's biographers. Kruger was the only young adult in the picture.

Of course, whenever Kruger held meetings at his office, everyone was impressed with the richness and comfort of the place. No doubt the detectives Stroud and Grillo felt the same way. And Stroud said it: "Quite a place."

"Yes," Kruger replied in the muffled manner befitting someone who needed to be seen as beyond reproach, as an elder statesman.

"Tell me, Dr. Kruger," Stroud said, "what about this kid could have gotten him into the water?"

Kruger stated he really didn't know and then started telling him Billy's story, relating that he had given Billy simple and odd jobs that would offer him an occupational therapeutic experience since, of course, without this Billy would just be "vacant." For the first time, Detective Grillo intervened and asked Kruger about Billy's symptoms.

"You know," Kruger continued, "autism is this private inner world."

"You mean," Grillo said, "that the autistic person only relates to himself and that no one can really know what's going on inside? I guess like Dustin Hoffman's 'Rain Man?'"

"Yes, that's it exactly," answered Kruger.

"So," Grillo continued, "if a kid like that decided to jump off a building or even go for a swim at night, no one would know? No one would know his motive?"

"Yes, of course," answered Kruger. "It would only be known to him. He would have no need to tell anyone. And that doesn't mean he would be concealing anything from anyone. It's not that it would be a secret. The same logic that applies to you or me would not operate with him. He doesn't, or rather such people, do not live in a world of dialogue or interactive communication. It's one way, not two ways, so if he decided to swim, he would, I guess, try it—somehow."

There was silence for a few seconds and the detectives just stared at Kruger. They seemed to feel satisfaction in learning about this exotic and weird kind of mind called autistic. Grillo broke the silence.

"Dr. Kruger, what sort of symptoms does an autistic person have? I mean, let's take Billy. What were his symptoms? I mean, specifically."

"Oh, yes, he had many. He would perseverate — that is, he would repeat the same behavior or say the same thing over and over. Sometimes he would rock in his chair. At other times he would concentrate on the time of the day and keep worrying about it, even though no one else could figure out what his concern was. All kinds of self-defined things like that would happen. Oh, yes, if he decided to do something, he became determined and single-minded about it. And if his path to this goal was blocked, he would become very anxious and begin to panic. And at these times, his brow would get wet with perspiration, his breathing could become labored, and his heart rate would speed up. It would be the onset of what we call an anxiety attack. So, yes, he had many, many symptoms. If I thought more about it, I could probably enumerate several others he had that just don't come to mind at the moment. I've known him since he was first brought here. I've seen just about all of his symptoms — the usual posturing oddities, speech problems, and eye contact problems — at least those that he displays in public. But I'm sure it's not different in private, either."

"Dr. Kruger," Grillo continued, *"I can see this is a pretty large hospital. How large is it?"*

"We have 45 buildings, our own post-office, a laundry, and even a farm. The patient population is about 8,000, down from a decade ago when we had 13,000. About 50 or 60 years ago one of these hospitals housed 18,000 patients. It's not like that now, but nevertheless, as you say, it's quite large."

The detectives gathered as much information as they needed and told Kruger they would wait for autopsy results before classifying the case. As they were about to leave, Grillo mused that Billy seems to have had a whole raft of symptoms.

"You know," Grillo said, looking to Stroud, *"the kid really was loaded with this crazy stuff. Saying things over and over and, uh, all the other things."* Then turning his attention to Kruger, Grillo wondered: *"You know, as you say, this place is so large, with so many patients, uh, I was wondering why Billy, who had so many symptoms, was allowed to wander around the grounds. I mean, couldn't that get out of hand?"*

"Oh, no," Kruger explained, *"Billy was not ever wandering. He was only interested in his job of counting. That's all that mattered to him. So over the years, he would go from his building directly to the property office, and if*

anything deterred him from that trajectory, he could go into that symptom I mentioned of anxiety and sweating. As you said, Detective, the boy had many symptoms. I can tell you that everything about him was either about his symptoms or happened as a result of his symptoms."

The detectives moved to the door. Stroud gave Kruger his card and told him that they would need to talk some more after the pathologist's report came in.

"By the way," Grillo interjected, "my condolences on Billy's death. I can imagine how you feel. You knew him a long time." Kruger nodded, paused, then said:

"No matter how many years' experience I have, it never fails to amaze me that any person could have almost nothing but symptoms in their personality."

On the way to the car, Grillo looked up at Stroud and said:

"Drowning is a symptom?"

* * *

It was always hard for me to talk to other psychiatric professionals about symptom cure because it was frequently obvious to me that they knew next to nothing about it. I was becoming tired of being patient, tired of being respectful, humble, deferent. But with Charley it was different. He was not pretentious, and as far as I was concerned, he had a first-rate mind. He and I had been friends since we'd gotten into a discussion about the purpose of psychoanalysis and psychotherapy. We were at an all- hospital Grand Rounds case presentation, with fifty or sixty of the staff attending. After the presentation everyone spilled out into the reception hall. Charley and I continued to talk about what we'd heard in the meeting, debating the goal of therapy.

He said, "Look, the job of the analyst is to analyze, to reduce anxiety, change the neurotic pattern, and cure the problem."

I said, "Charley, with one exception, and one exception only, we don't really cure anything!"

He stiffened. At that point I decided to lower the boom and calmly said, "Charley, now listen carefully, I don't want you to miss this. You ready?"

He nodded, making it plain that he was indulging me.

"Okay. Here I go. The only goal of psychotherapy—the only goal—is to help people struggle better. We can help them work on conflicts and struggle better with these conflicts. Struggle better! Everybody hear that?

And that's it!" And I paused. "That's the best we can hope for. Peereeod! You don't cure life."

He tightened more. You see, I didn't know Charley very well then, and in general it's hard for me to suffer fools gladly. The problem for me was that it turned out he was no fool. And as sometimes happens, I regretted my attitude, especially when someone turns out to be a truth seeker, like Charley.

He didn't skip a beat, and ignoring the belligerence, arrogance, immaturity, impatience, or whatever the hell it is that gets into me sometimes, he said:

"Okay, what's the exception?"

"Charley, the only cure thing we do is symptoms. We can actually cure symptoms. Not that anyone can really detail a standard way of doing it. We like to think we know about it, but the truth is, we don't. We're all really flying by the seat of our pants even though we actually do know parts of the instrument panel. And even with that, still, only because of a series of interactional permutations associated with the therapy, symptoms actually get cured. If we're successful, everything else is helping the patient to struggle better—no more, no less. There's no such thing as eliminating anxiety. You may as well stop breathing. Happiness is 'iffy,' man—here today, gone tomorrow. Charley, we need to talk about wishes. We're all carrying bundles of them. And they figure into symptoms. But for now, as far as I'm concerned, if we talk about cure—that's for symptoms and symptoms only."

"Well," he said, "what about intransigent symptoms. We always see those. What about those? You think some miracle medication without side effects is in our future?"

I thought, Good question, Charley. "As a matter of fact I do."

Charley relaxed, smiled, and said it was interesting. Starting to walk down the hall, he turned, gave me a see-you-later wave, and called, "By the way, what exactly did Freud say about symptoms?" He emphasized the *did*.

I shouted down the hall, "Before we get to Freud, what's the most important emotion in life?" I started listing: "Love, joy, fear, anger, guilt, shame?"

He stood there staring at me for a moment and disappeared.

Charley and I would talk a lot after our first encounter. His parting question was relevant because Freud's formula for curing symptoms was incomplete, even though he said that at least the narrow focus of psychoanalysis was to alleviate symptoms, to cure them. He gave us many insights: consciousness is curative; a symptom, like a dream, reflects a wish; and many others. But a systematic code to unlock the symptom was absent. There was no legacy of a standard sequence of axioms reflecting ironclad rules of the psyche. No such legacy. Perhaps only the monk Sebastian had some of those principles, and he predated Freud by five hundred years. But now, as far as Josh was concerned, the onus was on me, not on Charley or Freud, and definitely not on the monk.

In my phone conversation with Charley, I set up a session for Josh on the assumption that the kid would agree to see me at my office. As it turned out, Josh called to say he was busy with school and would call me sometime later. But later turned into several phone calls and postponements. Even though I knew he was friendly toward me, nevertheless, he was obviously resisting our meeting. It was too bad because I already had half the symptom unraveled just by connecting what I knew to Freud and what I suspected about Sebastian's discoveries—utilizing basic principles of mind and psyche. Of course I also knew that Josh's postponements represented his resistance to knowing something. It's an example of how resistance in therapy is the first line of defense in supporting repression—an attempt not to know!

Then I got a call from Charley, who asked me to continue to call Josh and in that way encourage him to come in to see me. It was actually several months later that Josh finally agreed. But Charley also had something else on his mind.

"Glenn, I thought about what you said—the symptom thing? Well, listen to this. I've got a patient who's a pathologist. He started getting an intrusive thought about viewing corpses. Then he felt a need to actually do it, and now he is in fact doing it. The obsession became a compulsion, and he's acting it out. Every night he returns to the lab and looks at these dead bodies, some of which—or is it some of whom—are in various stages of dissection. As far as I can tell, he doesn't touch them—yet. It's weird."

"Not really, Charley. No symptom is weird. None! Every one is bottles under the bed—every one. It's the code, Charley. With the code, every symptom breaks down."

"So you've got the code—my body watcher can be cured?

He was silent for a moment and then summed it up in typical Charley fashion.

"You got a title for the book?"

Over the years I accumulated fragments of the symptom code through my clinical experience and postdoctoral work in psychoanalysis. Like other analysts I had a standard Freudian fund of knowledge. Yet the synthesis—the unlocking of the symptom code—really came from Sebastian. And notwithstanding the immediacy of Billy's death, as well as the unlikely discovery of a bona fide split personality at the hospital—where we actually begin is in the mystery and unlocking of the symptom code.

BOOK 1

SYMPTOMS

· 1 ·

No Writing

The reference to this arcane work by Sebastian of Livorno identified him as a monk who preserved illuminated manuscripts and was influenced by St. Augustine in the ways of introspection. Apparently this monk kept diaries of his experiences — mostly of his dreams and nightmares. He also wrote treatises on life, marriage, relationships in general, and the derivation of basic principles on the functioning of the psyche. His works were translated into English in the late 19th century, but not made available for general circulation. The only citation to Sebastian's work that I could find was included in a clinical paper by the Italian psychiatrist, Aldo Fiscali, who had researched all the material on dreams that predated Freud. Fiscali cited the work of Sebastian of Livorno and referred to the monk's self-analysis, his work on dreams, and his work on symptoms. Fiscali also reported that with respect to his dreams, the monk kept a detailed narrative that traced his thinking about a multitude of elements of these dreams.

This was the work I wanted.

But I also wanted to see the books and accounts that Billy Soldier kept. I was told that they were copious, and I had this inkling — maybe it was a wish — that Billy's books would tell me something about his death. So here I was searching for the works of a 15th-century monk as well as a 21st-century autistic drowned boy.

I learned in my research that Sebastian's works were in a Vatican archive that contained only sealed manuscripts considered by Vatican authority to be important and sensitive. Banned Hebrew texts of the Inquisition, for example, were under lock and key in this archive, which was rumored to be located under the Vatican, no less, in protected and insulated vaults, deep within the catacombs in an intricate arterial network. That got me curious. But I was also disturbed by what had happened that morning—the death of Billy—and by the nagging thought I had that those detectives were going to question me. I realized I was worried about it even though I knew I had no information that would be of use to any investigation. I knew my sense of worry—maybe dread—was also, Katie.

I thought about the Vatican archive, under lock and key. And then I pictured Katie's gravesite. The earth on top. No key. And then I did what I always do. I shake out of it. So I flashed to the hospital pool—under lock and key. And then I thought it had to be that Billy considered his notebooks to be important, even precious. And finally I remembered that it was common knowledge that sensitive manuscripts housed at the Vatican library, also considered to be important, included early Coptic, Arabic, and Ethiopian works, as well as the ancient Hebrew manuscripts. In fact, it was well known by historians and church scholars that after the Vatican library was constructed in the mid-to-late 16th century, the church hierarchy dispatched an army of priests to all parts of Asia and Europe, the purpose of which was to purchase, beg, borrow, or steal, every important document relevant to church activities of historical importance. These documents were then added to the Vatican collection and many were sealed, probably to protect various nefarious church involvements of the past. Recent estimates pegged the number of works in the Vatican library—those both sealed and public—to be between one and two million items. And what I wanted was, of course, sealed.

Fiscali's research indicated that in his dream introspection Sebastian was able to identify and even categorize his reactions to his own dreams. Fiscali reported that Sebastian apparently was able to differentiate between his need to think about his dream with no interference (even from himself) and a very different need that would overtake him occasionally, to interpret and to talk to another about his dream, this in the face of his vow of silence. According to Fiscali, Sebastian had no doubt that his dreams were infused with essence. He quoted Sebastian: "I see the deeper structure to the dream. The depictions that we experience are not what the dream is about, or is not what is beneath. I have begun to see the beneath."

Fiscali also stated that there were occasions when Sebastian did not want to interpret his dreams. Rather, at times Sebastian would only want to drift in his thoughts and not analyze them at all (an early reference to stream of consciousness, or free association?). Sebastian also reported a host of discoveries about his own personality from his work on these dreams.

I was absorbed, I would say even compelled, actually suddenly obsessed with the idea of examining Sebastian's diaries. At first, I was only considering the single entry, that reference I stumbled upon in my research. And then it struck me—I wanted them all. There was something about Sebastian. I needed to see all of his manuscripts.

*   *   *

Of course the day's events stirred it all up. Billy led directly to Katie. I distracted myself by wondering if Sebastian could do what none of us could—systematically cure Josh of his bottles and Charley's pathologist of his corpses. And then I thought, what about Billy of his autism? While I knew many good and well-trained analysts who could analyze the symptom and eventually cure it, most would base the treatment on a three-or four-or even five-year psychoanalysis where, because so much material is covered and so many interpretive permutations take place, the better odds are with the cure. But systematically cure the symptom? No. No one could do it.

Since the reference to Sebastian's work cited in the original abstract I had found suggested he had compiled a list of the constituents that contributed to the formation of psychological symptoms, my curiosity and my anticipation of what was on that list almost ran away with itself. Could Sebastian, I thought, have formulated an understanding of symptoms and their vicissitudes so that sufferers of symptoms—all of us—could ourselves do the unraveling of the symptom? For me, the possibility of this kind of discovery seemed phenomenal. I felt that it might get me back to the conferences and liberate me from the din. It's what all scientists seek: the ability to identify what is important and what isn't, and what is elegant, inspiring, intelligent, useful, and beautiful.

I made calls to the academy of medicine, sent an overnight letter to the chief librarian at the Vatican and one to Yale Theological Seminary.

No go. Then it hit me. Jean Kaye. Over the years Jean had unearthed several incredible citations for me for books I was writing. She was unusually resourceful and seemed to be able to establish the provenance of any manuscript. But could she get this manuscript?

My friend at Yale Theological, a tall, somewhat stooped elderly professor of hermeneutics by the unlikely name of Vlad Strebovinich, called me with the information that any illuminated manuscript, or any manuscript for that matter, held in the Vatican archive is impossible to see without special dispensation from the highest Vatican authority. He paused and then said it also might require special "dispensational compensation."

"Vlad, in other words, you're telling me it's a payoff. Like organized crime. Vlad, I don't want anyone killed. This is scholarship, not international intrigue."

The fact was, however, that I actually was beginning to feel drawn into an intrigue. I heard myself. I said I didn't want anyone killed. Billy. And in my mind—Katie. I made that call to the Academy of Medicine and sent my letters after I had settled down from the shock of Billy's death. Immediately after Billy was found and after the ambulance took the body and drove off, I then returned to the library thinking I could get back to work. Of course, I couldn't. Thinking of Billy, and trying not to see Katie, I shook it off by looking to the monk. It didn't work and I headed for the hospital cafeteria for a cup of coffee and an apple turnover.

The cafeteria was in the basement of one of the buildings. I usually tried not to eat there as the food seemed to take on a distinct odor, and even taste, of hospital. Sure enough, the whole place was buzzing about Billy. I sat with Tommy Gersh, my psychologist colleague, and we spent a half hour speculating about what had happened to Billy—from accidental drowning to suicide, to some prank that turned into death. As I was about to head back to the library, Tommy said:

"Glenn, there's another possibility."

"Yeah, like what?"

"Murder," he simply said.

"Murder?" I repeated with a question mark/exclamation point. I guess I was naive about it probably because to me the hospital environment was a place of healing.

"Yeah," he said. "The range is from accident to suicide to a prank that went awry to murder. Don't rule it out." I looked at him and even though, earlier, my thought was, "crime," I think, still, my eyebrows must have said, "Whoa." As I started walking away, he raised his decibels: "And don't think those detectives aren't considering it."

Then, walking away, I thought, "These detectives are going to investigate a life, Billy's life, a quasi, bizarre, almost-life. And despite the undeniable fact that he was the most popular patient in the hospital, nevertheless, he was as an illusion is to real life. Not that he was an illusion to those around him. He was the illusion looking at us. And for most of his life he felt ignored, shunned, invisible—a ghost."

* * *

Vlad Strebovinich and I had met only very recently and we both felt quickly comfortable with one another. We happened to meet when I was retained as a psychological consultant to examine an elderly gent who had been committed to the hospital because of bizarre behavior and a variety of symptoms. Vlad was a friend of this patient, and was visiting him when I arrived. He and the patient had met in the Bergen-Belsen concentration camp in 1944. Vlad's friendship with this patient seemed to be a highly unlikely one. When they met at Bergen-Belsen, Vlad was a lad of 15, intending, even at that age, to become a Christian theologian and Meyer Lerovitz, who had achieved early fame, was a Jewish communist poet in his early 20's. Vlad was incarcerated because he was a courier for the underground, and Mr. Lerovitz because of his three crimes: Jewish, communist, poet—in that order.

I was called in on the case because Lerovitz mostly spoke Yiddish, in which I was fluent. His main symptom that got him hospitalized combined a major depression and delusional thoughts with an impotency problem. Despite his more than eighty years, he had been sexually active with his woman friend, who was in her seventies.

Kruger had asked to see my treatment plan for this elderly Holocaust survivor, Meyer Lerovitz, whenever it was ready. My sense was that he hated the idea that I had been called in on the case (though my fluency in Yiddish made it difficult for him to object), so he was asking for my plan only to assert his authority. Was he really going to improve the plan or contribute something new or valuable, or was he still burning about another, rather dramatic encounter we had had a couple of years earlier?

It was at a Grand Rounds meeting with the entire staff present—about 30 or 40 people. Dr. Kruger had declared that symptoms were actually few in number and have, more or less, all been identified. I challenged him on that one by raising my hand and calling out that recent findings have concluded that although there were an indefinite number of symptoms, they could all probably be listed by a few categories—but that again, the point is that there are indefinite numbers of symptoms. Then he challenged me as he had several times before, and each time I felt he really wanted to embarrass me. So far, he was partially successful in letting everyone know he was boss and I wasn't. That was okay with me in terms of my not being the boss, but it was not okay with me that his tone and attitude were obviously and clearly meant to at least discredit me.

"Perhaps Dr. Kahn can estimate how many symptoms there are and also elucidate our patient's symptom-meaning right here and now?" And with authority, Kruger emphasized the "right here and now."

I didn't want to do it because it was about to become evident that Dr. Siegfried Kruger was living in a fantasy world thinking that what he first learned about psychopathology decades ago was all there was to know. In addition, what he was doing in challenging me was what he's done many times in the past that truly embarrassed, actually shamed people even to the core. Yes, there was a sadism about him—like when he once put a female psychiatrist on the spot. She was very bright but had a difficult stutter. Kruger, in a small meeting on the hospital ward which I attended, and with about six or seven other staff members present, brazenly and inappropriately confronted her about her stutter. Rather than respecting her and addressing her as Dr. Fowler, he said something like, "Beatrice, you know you don't have to stutter. Just close your eyes and think of the word you want to say." And he said it with an effusive smile as though he was only having her best interest at heart. But as he uttered that sentence, the entire room froze. People stopped breathing, and everyone was obviously embarrassed for Dr. Fowler (whom we all liked) and horrified at Kruger's crass insensitivity. It was absolutely evident that Kruger did not at all have Dr. Fowler's best interest at heart. It was sadistic, nothing more, nothing less. Beatrice, Dr. Fowler, fled the room. She just couldn't take what apparently she felt was the shame of it, the severe awkwardness of it, and the sheer embarrassment.

And now, about two years later Kruger felt he could do it to me by challenging me in what he felt was something I couldn't really answer or handle. But I was going to do it—first for Beatrice, and then secondly for me. I was going to take his challenge. At this particular Grand Rounds meeting, Dr. Fowler was sitting in the back of the room, where she always sat. I spotted her and I think she saw that I looked at her. I even think I might have sent her a subtle smile. I thought that perhaps I shouldn't do it because I had the thought, "Revenge is mine sayeth the Lord."

But, I couldn't help myself. I started.

"Well, there are symptoms associated with the respiratory system, skeletomuscular system, nervous system, sensory system, reproductive system, circulatory system, dermatological system, and digestive system; and specifically, we have throat clearing symptoms, hyperventilation, pain in joints, tics, auditory hallucinations of an infinite variety, hallucinations of each of the remaining senses, edema, psoriasis, nausea, purging. We have phobias of all sorts, and phobias within phobias, as in agoraphobia or the fear of open spaces, where a person might be fearful of entering a stadium, and then this same person deteriorates further so that the trip to the stadium becomes difficult, then it becomes difficult to leave the lobby of the building, then to leave the apartment, then in the end the problem is in leaving the bedroom itself. With such an agoraphobic symptom, the person's perimeter in life becomes more and more circumscribed, to very small areas like the perimeter around the bed, so that finally even getting out of bed becomes the difficulty. There are also the common phobias like claustrophobia and acrophobia. Then there are the idiosyncratic symptoms, like the obsessive ones or those involving intrusive thoughts, and we may ask, how many obsessive symptoms can there be? Or how many intrusive thoughts can there be? And of course the answer is, an infinite number."

I paused and sensed that Kruger thought I'd finished. But I hadn't. "Idiosyncratic symptoms can include anything under the sun, like impotence, nail biting, compulsive masturbation, and even fear of doorknobs. Symptoms are even ecumenical and certainly, perhaps inescapable. We all have them. I have them." I paused and looked at Kruger. "Even Dr. Kruger has them. The patient presented here today has an especially interesting one at that because it helps us distinguish between a symptom isolated from the rest of the personality, in contrast to one that infiltrates the entire personality so that rather than only being an aspect of the personality, the symptom becomes the personality. In this case what we are looking at is not so much a symptom as it is the anatomy of a psychosis."

There was silence in the room. Kruger was sitting almost stone-faced. He thought I had finished. He hoped I was finished, but I wasn't. What we knew was that the patient was a man in his 50's who was a cracker-jack salesman in the men's department of a well-known clothing shop. Although he was the single most productive salesperson, he had a serious problem that everyone who worked with him knew about and which they all considered crazy. It *was* crazy. This man could do everything required of him as a salesperson except commit anything to writing. He refused to write sales slips and actually paid other salespeople to do it for him even though he was literate and could, in fact, write well. Yet his consistent mantra was: "No writing!"

Again, I wouldn't stop. I continued:

"This man became exceedingly paranoid and what we see along with the paranoia is an agitated depression. Now, why was he not writing sales slips? The answer, I believe, concerns some profound fear he had and, I'm sure, still has, that if he writes anything at all it will incriminate him in some imagined crime. Now here's the rub. He knows he really didn't do anything wrong but is gripped by this obsessive, all-consuming feeling that, in fact, he did do something wrong, and more, that this wrongness will be revealed should he write anything. He is afraid that if he writes any-thing down in black and white, he won't be able to control his impulse to confess, so that what he writes will turn out to be his confession. He most likely has what is considered a pseudomania or enosiophobia. It's basically considered to be a shame psychosis. Thus he is entirely guilt-ridden and this guilt has permeated his very being. You see, deep down, at the core, he feels himself to be completely imperfect, incomplete, inadequate and inferior, and is furious—that's the key word, furious—about this self-assumed inferiority."

Now I announced that I was going to speculate. "I'm speculating that because of the chronic nature of the symptom characterized by his rumina-tion and obsessive focus on his ostensible guilt, all of it presumably reflects some basic rage against a specific person in his life, probably in his child-hood—I would guess, his mother. This rage is like a wish to kill. Usually people can have such wishes, but they are harmless and remain on the level of wish, in the form of fantasy, and even with respect to figure of speech. In this man's case, I believe the original wish was very intense and he didn't have the resilience to see it as different from behavior. In his mind, thinking became equivalent to doing. Ergo, guilt. He feels he's killed some-one—his mother, perhaps—even though he knows it isn't so. But the feeling prevails and triumphs over what he actually knows. In his experience, knowing has very little power, while feeling is compelling. Therefore, not writing keeps him in a guilt-free state. Unconsciously, he has convicted himself of murder."

I knew I would be accused of gross inferential, circumstantial, and even irresponsible theorizing here. But again, I didn't stop, primarily because I felt I was right, and secondarily I guessed that no one would have an explanation as extravagant as the one I was proposing—especially as I was proposing it with what I considered to be, of high probability truth. And third, this one was for Beatrice. It began to feel that I had taken the entire Grand Rounds away from Kruger, but again, I continued.

"Because the entire syndrome is so chronic and so pervasive, any kind of psychotherapy without medication is doomed to failure. We are dealing here with an ambulatory character psychosis in only partial life-long remission.

"This case is especially instructive because it shows us the difference between a symptom that can be cured through talk therapy—a symptom that doesn't swallow the person whole—and one that indeed takes over the personality entirely so that person and symptom become indistinguishable. What we have here is an example of the latter.

I finally stopped. I had been so absorbed in my research on symptom formation that it was all at my fingertips. I knew Kruger was embarrassed and for whatever reason, in order to soften Kruger's embarrassment, I suggested that a good project might be the development of a dictionary of symptoms based upon the few organ systems of the body such as skeleto-muscular, nervous, sensory, respiratory, and so forth. That took the spotlight off Kruger and put the discussion back in the arena of symptom psychology and the patient at hand.

But for sure, Kruger never forgot it

So, because he was the director of the hospital, and because here we were, back to our patient at hand, Meyer Lerovitz, I would have to honor Kruger's request and submit to him my treatment plan for Meyer Lerovitz. And here we were, back to symptoms. Mr. Lerovitz was riddled with symptoms, including one that took the cake: he was terribly troubled about the holes that he felt he had all over his body. Real holes—all over his body! But regardless of Lerovitz's considerable distress, Kruger didn't care a hoot about Lerovitz; this was his chance to undo his defeat at my hands at that Grand Rounds meeting two years earlier when I did my soliloquy. And now, Kruger was going to show me that his was the last word in the treatment.

I knew without a doubt, that I was going to have to manage Kruger in order to make sure that Lerovitz would be properly cared for and could go home — symptom-free.

· 2 ·

HOLES

My cell phone went off. Detective Stroud was asking, if possible, to see me at my private office. At first I didn't understand why he specified my private office. I mean he could have suggested his office or my office at the hospital. I couldn't help feeling I was a suspect. I agreed on the spot but then realized I had never given him my cell number.

Not only was Stroud tall, he also had good looks. Movie star looks. What you would expect a successful detective to look like. He arrived promptly, with his partner, Joe Grillo. Grillo was of average height, maybe five-foot nine or ten, about 165 pounds. It was clear. Stroud was number one, Grillo number two.

At first Stroud did all the talking, and despite the fact that I motioned to the chairs, we all stood for the first few minutes.

"I'll be frank. Detective Grillo here thinks it was deliberate. Someone's dirty work. Personally, I'm not sure. We've gotten the preliminary pathology report but we'll know more later. It's incriminating. No doubt about it. No water in Billy's lungs. That means he was dead before he hit the water. But, it's a big 'but.' Sometimes that's not foolproof. I mean, once in a while people get fished out and there are no signs of a struggle, but water is in the lungs. You see, when someone accidentally falls in or is pushed, they'll try to breathe. And the struggle will affect the muscles in the neck and the shoulders—and the middle ear will also shows hemorrhaging.

And there are other things like stuff in the lungs and the lips. But if the person is dead first, then no air in the lungs. No one's trying to breathe when they're dead. Know what I mean?"

I nodded, but it hurt. He continued. "But since it's not completely foolproof, I'm not completely convinced. What do you think?" He emphasized the *you*.

"Well, I'll tell you, it never occurred to me that it could be murder."

When the word "murder" came out, there seemed to be a deafening silence in the room. "It never even occurred to me that it might have been a prank gone haywire. I just assumed it was an accident. But a colleague of mine pointed out it could be these other things."

Stroud immediately asked for the name of the colleague and I told him it was Tom Gersh, suddenly feeling that I had implicated Gersh. Then Stroud got to the point.

"How well did you know Billy?"

"Sort of," I said. "I'm a consultant at the hospital. I'm there only on average of about a day and a half each week. Sometimes a bit more or less. I consult on difficult cases in the clinical department, usually on diagnosis, and I'm involved in research. So over the years, yes, on second thought I guess I saw him a lot."

"So whadya think of Billy's diagnosis?" he asked.

"Like I once told Dr. Kruger, I never thought Billy was mentally retarded. Mentally challenged, yes. But that's because he was autistic and autism affects functioning on I.Q. tests. But in other ways like in math, the kid was a savant—a genius. But I think his true diagnosis is, or rather was, what's known as Asperger's Syndrome. That's a high-level autism. Like that lady who constructs strategies for the slaughtering of cows, I think it is. You know, she figures out the most efficient and most painless way of doing it."

And then I tried to recall her name. It was on the tip of my tongue. "Temple Grandin," I blurted out. "That's her. Temple Grandin. Billy was a little like her."

Then Grillo pointedly asked:

"Knowing the kid, you think it was an accident? I mean could he climb that fence? And would he want to go swimming?"

That last question cleared it up for me. I felt for sure, Billy wouldn't want to swim at all. I'm not sure why, but I definitely felt Billy didn't swim.

"No, come to think of it, I really don't think Billy was a swimmer."

Stroud came in. "Now this Asperger thing, why wasn't that his diagnosis?"

"I think it should have been," I said. "Billy also showed some signs of psychosis. You know, he rocked and was extremely rigid in his attitude. So I'm not really clear about it. The truth is, there may not be a simple diagnostic picture here. But retardation? No! But Dr. Kruger's findings are different. Dr. Kruger had Billy tested over the years and the diagnosis according to test scores puts him in the retarded category. Now you have to understand, the state would require him to leave the hospital if he scored higher. And if anyone is cognizant of that, it's Dr. Kruger. But over the years I've seen the test scores and they confirm Dr. Kruger's diagnosis of autism with retardation. Despite that, I've never considered Billy to be retarded—not in the real sense."

They had me there for what seemed like an hour and were frequently highly specific in their questions. I felt challenged. Grillo kept pushing me on the diagnosis.

"What," he asked, "do you remember about the size of his head? Was it in proportion to his body? I've heard in these kinds of cases that the head is kind of different. I asked our path guys and they said Billy's head was perfectly normal in size."

In a way I felt Grillo was measuring my head, my knowledge, my skills. "Well," I said, "in autism, head size is not a significant aspect of the diagnosis although head size starts smaller than average but then accelerates and becomes slightly larger than average. I think you're talking more about something called Rett's Disorder. In Retts, the basic problem is a deceleration of the head's circumference, and this happens, more or less, between the child's fourth and fifth years of life. So at that point the head is smaller. But that's not what Billy had. Size problem for Billy was maybe in his brain, maybe inside the cranium—not the cranium itself. So whatever it is you're looking for, you won't find it if you're looking for Rett's Disorder. That's for sure."

I thought that would do it, but Grillo stated that they needed me to go over test results with them. They said they would call me about it and that they also wanted to discuss test results with Kruger. On the way out, Grillo turned and said:

"See, Doc, every detective is a psychologist with a point of view of how and why things work. Me, I like to speak the guy's language. Nobody, I guess, spoke the kid's language. I don't care much about other things. Just speak the guy's language and I'm in. So speaking in tongues, you might say, is my usual way in. We'll be in touch." When they finally left I mused, Grillo number one, Stroud number two.

After they left, and standing there alone in my office I thought, "Yeah, autism is a foreign language. And no one ever spoke Billy's language or to Billy in his language." Grillo, of course, was right. It's not only important, it's actually crucial to be able to speak someone's language.

*   *   *

When I began the first consultation with Meyer Lerovitz, we were sitting opposite one another in a small office on the ward. I told Mr. Lerovitz who I was and why the ward attendant had brought him to the office, all in Yiddish, of course. He was a slight, short man who was unshaven, but I felt he was comforted by the fact that I could speak his language. Billy never had that kind of comfort. But I reasoned that Billy's need for contact was at best, underdeveloped, and at worst, highly limited.

I had known that Mr. Lerovitz's communism was of the idealistic type but that reality had sobered him big time. Everyone knew what Stalin had done to those Yiddish writers, and so Meyer Lerovitz's ideals had been permanently compromised by those lying Red Fascists.

He said, "Ir redt Yidish zeyer gut." (You speak Yiddish very well.)

"Yo, ikh red Yidish, un ikh bin gekumen do haynt tsu prubirn aykh tsu helfn." (Yes, I speak Yiddish, and I came here today to try to help you).

"Ir zayt do goboyrn gevorn?" (You were born here?).

I answered all his questions. My parents were immigrants, arriving here in the 1950's—from Ukraine to Romania to Canada, to here. Yes, I was born here and grew up speaking Yiddish at home with a grandmother who spoke no English. We then talked about his work, and he told me he was particularly interested in literature produced by people of the Holocaust. He said that despite his own modest fame as a poet, the publication of a book of women's poems of the Holocaust, that he helped publish, was the single best thing he ever did.

I tried to shift unobtrusively to the work at hand, and with that, Meyer Lerovitz, the human being with all sorts of worldly problems, not Meyer Lerovitz the idealistic poet, launched into a flurry of stories regarding his children, his woman friend, work and so forth. He didn't seem depressed at all. Not one bit. Yet he suddenly said:

"Ikh bin azoy depressed dokter, az ikh hob zeyer a shlekhtn gefil in boykh." (I'm so depressed doctor that I have a very bad feeling in my stomach). When he referred to his stomach, he pointed downward toward his genitals and not his stomach. And he pointed to his genitals again when he referred to his stomach again. Clue number one.

Apparently, something bothered Meyer Lerovitz that caused his impotence. The bad feeling in his stomach is understood psychoanalytically as a displacement upwards (meaning that the problem was down further and not in his stomach). He described his active sexual life with his common-law wife, and of course regretted his current condition.

Knowing about all of his symptoms, and speaking to him in Yiddish, I told him that I understood he thought there were holes in his body.

"Yes," he quickly answered in Yiddish, "Ikh hob lekher iber mayn gantsn layb." ("I have holes all over my body.")

Here we had a bona fide body-delusion symptom. This man actually had the belief as well as the sensation that his body was full of holes. Holes you could see through. I felt like asking him, 'If the Nazis couldn't put holes in you, who could?' It was clear that this delusion was connected to what he called his depression as well as to his pointing to his genitals when referring to his stomach. But it also occurred to me that my question about the Nazis was actually a good one. Who was the now-Nazi that caused his current conflict? His symptoms didn't materialize out of the clear blue sky. That you can be sure of. Here was the crucial question. It had to be a person. Someone got into his guts.

By the end of the session I knew that he had an only son who was highly successful. The week before his hospitalization, Lerovitz had called his son and asked him for a small loan because he ran short for the week. Apparently, he had called at an inopportune time, and his son, apparently in a busy moment, dismissed the phone call out of hand, not even attending to what his father was saying. Lerovitz felt humiliated, embarrassed, quite shamed. Within a few days his sexual functioning ceased. Then came the bad feeling in his stomach, then the holes, and then the depression.

I told him we were going to cure him. No more bad feelings in his stomach, no more holes, no more sexual problem, and no more depression. This was a man I could not let suffer. There I went again, promising he would soon—very soon—be as good as new. I decided to do some social work and asked for his son's phone number and permission to call. He resisted, but I persisted.

*   *   *

It was at that meeting with Lerovitz that I first ran into Vlad, who was visiting him. Vlad and I also had a lengthy conversation, in which he filled me in on aspects of Lerovitz's history that had not been noted in the chart. When the interview ended, Vlad and I drove back from the hospital together. It was a long drive and we had a chance to talk. He was so erudite that I had assumed he was one of those Christologists who believed in Jesus the man; no, he believed in Jesus the God and in the resurrection. I expected him to at least think that Alfred North Whitehead's incomplete God was interesting, but no, he didn't. At that point I thought I might have more in common intellectually with Lerovitz and that Vlad was more aligned with, let's say, Isaac Bashevis Singer, who also believed in resurrection. I told him I had trouble with Auschwitz and the fact that God didn't attend. He said maybe God did attend. I took the position that every question in life is answered at Auschwitz and illustrated it with the question:

"How do I know there is no such thing as levitation?"

I answered my own question.

"Because no one ever levitated over the barbed wire at Auschwitz."

Vlad agreed. It was not possible to argue with him—only to seek and find a discussion. As Professor of Hermeneutics at Yale, he, of course, was quite interested in interpretation and in fact had written extensively on psychological subjects. But there in the car he was more interested in Meyer Lerovitz's symptoms.

"I'm sure we can erase the entire syndrome," I told him. "Holes, impotence, stomach and depression. If I bring the son in for a consultation, then we'll avoid a long hospital stay. They'll straighten it out themselves."

"But what do you make of the holes themselves?" he asked.

"The holes are easy. We all have wishes to be empowered, adequate, whole. Get it? Whole. WHOLE. Not HOLE." I spelled it "And Lerovitz used the word 'hole' both in Yiddish and in English. So he knows what 'whole' means, and he knows what 'hole' means. In this case, when he felt inadequate—after being humiliated—the feeling of needing to be whole turned into a feeling that there were holes in his body. As soon as his son apologizes and they patch it up, he'll be symptom-free, you know, free of holes. That's a bet.

"You see, for our friend Mr. Lerovitz to develop this array of symptoms, he really had to swallow a lot of anger. When he expostulates it or dissolves it, then he'll be just fine, especially when he realizes that it's his son who is the anger-culprit here. I'm sure his son will also gladly grant his request. After that the symptoms will begin to disappear. Then Meyer will not have to rely on the tricks of the unconscious — hole and whole — and he will be able to feel *genuinely* whole."

As it turned out, the son did visit, profusely apologized, and gladly satisfied his father's request. After his son's visit, Mr. Lerovitz's hospital stay lasted just three weeks and he was discharged, symptom-free. Several years later at the age of 92, Meyer Lerovitz died in his sleep.

*   *   *

The business of 'hole' versus 'whole' became my thinking shorthand when diagnosing inadequacy problems. I began referring to such problems as, "Lerovitz Holes." And so, in thinking about Billy, I realized that he had a huge Lerovitz Hole. I felt his autism reflected a large and profound hole. But then I thought that if my diagnosis of Asperger's was right, then there were parts of Billy's makeup, his cognitive map if you will, that was not simply whole, they fell in the genius range. His mathematical ability and his record keeping, for example, were great. And then it hit me. Asperger types usually become very ownership-minded about whatever it is that grips them. It could be collecting stamps or coins or pieces of colored vine or whatever. It could even be record books of items tallied in the property office.

And that's what Billy Soldier had. He had books and books of perfectly recorded data in columns and rows with black and red markings. Without any prompting he would freely tell people, "Dr. Kruger says my records are very good." Many people at the hospital heard him say it just that way, repeating it: "Dr. Kruger says my records are very good."

Billy repeated that sentence to me more than once over the years. So what's the big deal? Well, the deal is that I never mentioned it to Stroud and Grillo. It never even occurred to me. And they never asked me about it. About what? About where these books are. That's what. I'll bet no one knows. I realized that for me there was never any doubt. Billy was an Asperger. And he must have had what we might call these Asperger possession imperatives. So that means he had those books stashed. No doubt about it. I'll bet not even Kruger knows where they are.

In a way, trying to recover those record books of Billy's was like reaching for Billy himself. Those books had consumed him. He loved them. In the moment of the thought of reaching for Billy, without necessarily consciously wanting to, I shifted to Katie, quickly shook it off, and then to Vlad.

Vlad had begun to send me his papers to read and would ask for my comments and editing suggestions. I thought, "Well, I'm going from Billy to Vlad, and it's about what they were writing—and then Sebastian, and what he was writing."

*   *   *

Vlad had a solid professional relationship with Jean Kaye. At the psychoanalytic institute, a rather industrial-looking, 10-story stone structure in a commercial district in New York City, the library was housed way in the back of the building. There, among the thousands of books and journals covering all of psychoanalysis, psychiatry, psychiatric social work and psychology, was Jean, an unassuming, intelligent, self-assured lady in her mid 60's. We became friends out of a common interest—books—and, of course, my two published books lived there. I always wondered how she was able to obtain any and all information whenever I needed it. It seemed that whomever she called gave her what she wanted. I spent a great deal of time in the library, and when I was preparing a manuscript for publication Jean and I would be in contact a lot.

Jean was regularly consulted by librarians in many fields, including theology. She was personal friends with the chief librarian at Yale who referred Vlad to her as someone who had a great deal of experience in unearthing long-lost journals and monographs. So when I asked Vlad about some possible route to Sebastian, he acknowledged knowing certain people at the Vatican and then mentioned Jean at my library. Small world.

· 3 ·

NO CHEWING

The investigation into Billy's death must have been on hold, really on a back burner. Now it was late December, and I hadn't heard anything about Billy's case and hadn't spoken to the detectives. It gave me plenty of time to talk to Katie, though. Plenty of time. It also took that much time before we got the first of Sebastian's manuscripts. The manuscript had been scheduled to arrive on three different occasions, but each time the delivery was canceled. Finally, all signals must have connected because without warning, virtually in the middle of the night, and right before my vacation, we got the first manuscript. Vacation canceled. It's never a vacation anymore, anyway.

*   *   *

It happened in the middle of the night. The figure of a large, hooded man, face covered with a kerchief, moved swiftly through the hospital grounds. He selected a large key from a number of keys on a chain, unlocked the door to the women's dormitory and deftly entered. There were eight or nine beds arranged around the room in a large, open dormitory. The women were all asleep, but it wasn't quiet because of the uneven cadence of breathing. The hooded figure could have done damage to any number of these patients and in any number of ways, but instead he walked past the beds and directly to the back of the dormitory toward a tiny office off the back vestibule. The purple flickering of the TV set in the tiny room was accompanied by low-volume applause coming from the set.

In a loud voice, unhurried and unworried about anyone confronting or attacking him, he began to wail:

*"**I am Jericho!**" And with that both attendants—one male, one female—engrossed in their TV program, were startled out of their collective reverie and in a split second were half out of their chairs when Jericho smashed the male attendant with a hammer-like object wrapped in a rag, knocking him out cold. Motionless, Jericho stared at the female attendant, who slowly sat back down. Jericho continued to stare at her, then turned and, walking boldly, headed for the front door. By this time all the women were sitting up in bed, and a few started shouting. Jericho exited, never bothering with the women and apparently not at all disturbed by the commotion that by this time had reached a crescendo.*

*   *   *

"It's a good coincidence that your vacation was canceled, Dr. Kahn." It was Grillo. He was on the phone asking me to meet him in the hospital infirmary. No commotion there. There he filled me in. The attendant was being treated for concussion. He could have been killed, but the blow was slightly off.

"Well, Dr. Kahn," Grillo continued, with Stroud observing, "what can you tell us about a guy who, in the dead of night, enters a women's ward—everyone asleep—ignores the women, and before he leaves, announces out loud that his name is Jericho and then knocks out a male attendant? You know, doesn't touch the women—including a female attendant. I mean psychologically speaking. What can you tell us about him—psychologically speaking? We're asking you as a consultant. Let's forget for a minute that it might have been some revenge thing. We'd like you to think about some other, let's say, psychological angle to the thing. And this on top of Billy!"

"You haven't been around in a while," I said. "We've all been thinking about Billy's death, but none of us have heard anything about the case."

"Not to worry," Grillo continued. "We've been working on it without letup. We've actually been investigating most people at the hospital. We're not finished with it by a long shot. But now tell us, any psychological angle to this attack on the women's ward that you can think of?"

I wasn't sure what to think. It seemed strange to me that they seemed to be treating the Billy Soldier situation in such a perfunctory manner. But I tried to focus on Grillo's question. At first I thought just what Grillo had said. Some kind of personal payback. A private "revenge thing," as Grillo put it. But they wanted me to turn into a forensic psychologist, which I wasn't.

"Like you say, the first thing that comes to mind is that he had a grudge against the attendant," I said.

"What's the second thing, Doc?" Grillo asked. "We want something psychological. Emotional."

"The second thing," I slowly responded, "is that he was jealous of the attendant. You know, with all the women there, because he wasn't interested in hurting the women. Maybe he wanted to protect them out of some paranoid idea that the male attendant had some private agenda about them. Like he may not have liked the idea that this attendant had access to them when he didn't. But I feel silly making these wild guesses. It's all armchair speculation. Well, maybe he felt a kind of possessiveness. I don't know."

"No, no," Grillo said. "It's helpful. In other words," he continued, "this guy named Jericho likes women."

"Well, if you want to speculate like that," I said, "then I'd say, yes. From what you've told me, that's it. But I'm not sure it's just that he likes women. It would certainly be more complex than that. Some kind of oedipal mother thing. Like a mother obsession or something. But that would only be part of it. You know, loving mother? Another part would be hating mother. You know," I said, "it's psychoanalytic."

"Oh boy," Stroud instantly said, "a mother psycho job! A drowned kid and a mother psycho job — and all at the happy farm."

After a moment of silence, Grillo thanked me.

*   *   *

Richard, Jean Kaye's husband, was in on it. Now we had three crates of Sebastian's manuscript, each page sealed by two sheets of fine plastic panes. Richard handed me one of the panes. As fate would have it, my first contact with Sebastian was not the beginning of a story but the middle. I only had part of it. He was describing what sounded like a contemporary anorexia symptom. Reading in dim light I was fascinated by his opening paragraph:

> This child of eighteen looked twelve. She was emaciated, skeletal. Yet she appeared not to be depressed and spoke amiably. She and her mother conversed intimately and with interest in one another. They spoke in hushed tones as, of course, was appropriate. The mother indicated that her daughter was a robust baby and then, suddenly, at some point became uninterested in food. I thought, uh oh, could be another mother psycho job, as Stroud called it. But Sebastian was focused. He asked the young lady to describe her experience of eating, to which the mother preempted, "No chewing, she hates to chew." Then Sebastian described the daughter's rendition of her no-chewing symptom, which she ended by saying she only liked to drink.

It was then that I sensed I was starting in the wrong place and handed the pane back to Richard. I wanted to begin at the beginning. I would deal with this entry when I reached it in the sequence of Sebastian's writings. But I could tell already that I was reading about a classic eating disorder occurring in the 15th century. Good Lord, I thought, did Sebastian understand the arrangement of inner forces that ultimately resulted in a girl developing anorexia?

Here we were in the mid-15th century—the middle ages, for crying out loud—the time of demonology, promoted by the church. Control people by frightening them. Keep people from feeling any kind of personal power. Aquinas reinforced the notion of a psychology-free soul, assigning secondary status, even begrudgingly, to an inner life. The general notion promoted by the church was that if you experienced a psychological problem, it was the devil.

The original abstract I came across indicated that Sebastian the monk was influenced by St. Augustine, who was, in certain respects, an anomaly for fifth-century thinking. His *Confessions* contain all sorts of implications of inner psychological motives. Thus, in a positive sense St. Augustine was aligned with Aristotle, Socrates and Freud in wanting to understand the process of emotion. In a negative sense, he believed in physical punishment and, along with Aquinas and especially Luther, comprised an intellectual axis ultimately perhaps justifying inquisitions of any stripe.

The operation of emotion. I'm always asking people what they think is the most important emotion. And I think I know the answer. Of course, it's a challenging question. I wanted to see what Sebastian said about it, if anything, because without the answer to that question, I'm convinced the key to unlocking the symptom can never be found. For sure, that's a vital part of the code. Dare I say, I may have discovered it.

Perhaps because Sebastian the monk demonstrated an introspective bent in the superstitious and primitive 15th century, volumes of his writings were apparently under lock and key. Why? That was the question I had asked Jean weeks earlier, and it was that question, one concerning freedom of thought and expression, that galvanized her to break the rules and get me Sebastian. Could it be that the tradition of introspection and concern with inner forces of the personality, championed by history's great thinkers, was also augmented by Sebastian? Were there discoveries that Sebastian had made about the psyche that have gone unnoticed and unread for more than 500 years? Discoveries that perhaps not even Freud made?

Before I had a chance to think it over, Jean informed me that the bust of Freud in the vestibule on the seventh floor of the psychoanalytic institute/ outpatient clinic had been destroyed. Two bullets were found in the statue. Someone with a gun had been in the building. The theory was that it must have been a patient who was furious at his therapist, his father, Freud—all the same. My first thought was a silencer. Someone in the clinic with a silencer.

*   *   *

We were all standing around the statue in silence—looking at it. It was just like the crowd standing around the ambulance and police cars at the hospital. All of us standing around. Shrinks, secretaries, patients. Looking at the fractured statue. Then, as we were all talking, in walk detectives Stroud and Grillo. And whom do they spot first?

"It wasn't me." That was my reflexive response the instant our eyes met.

"You're part of this clinic?" Stroud asked.

I nodded. Grillo humorously chimed in, not realizing it was a serious question, "And Dr. Kruger, he's affiliated here, too?"

"Yes, he is," I said. "He's a big shot here, too."

"Don't say 'shot,'" Stroud quipped.

We talked a bit and I explained what kind of clinic it was, what my position was, as well as Kruger's. I don't know why, maybe it was how they were listening, but I got the feeling that the detectives already knew that we were affiliated with the clinic but were pretending they didn't know. But I proceeded and quickly tried to explain the idea of transference—that in some person's mind, anger toward a father could be transferred to the therapist or even a bust of Freud, the father of psychoanalysis. I emphasized "father."

"Okay," Stroud said. "But I can't get over it. You and Dr. Kruger here, too." Grillo, on the other hand, was more interested in the phenomenon of transference.

"This transference thing I suppose can kick in, in a real way, huh?"

He obviously knew that was a self-evident truth, but he asked it, I think, just to keep me talking. So I naturally accommodated him by confirming the fact of transference.

"Okay," Stroud said, "we're going to have to examine all staff time sheets and all time schedules of doctor/patient sessions, and all the names of the patients and any other scheduled appointments, whether they were kept or not. We need to see who was in the building, more or less around the time the shooting took place."

Stroud looked directly at me. "Basically, the men in blue should be here first, but we were assigned. And no one's even been shot. Just a statue. Where's the head of the clinic?" His unintended pun was too much and I laughed.

"I think you want to speak to Dr. George White," I said. "He's director of clinical services and he's here full time."

They were both looking at me and Stroud said, "We'll talk." I nodded. Of course, I already felt guilty, and I hadn't done a thing. The entire building was then combed by four men in blue who had accompanied Stroud and Grillo. Security was set up so that henceforth, all those entering the building would have to sign in and out, registering the time as well as their destination within the building. It felt dangerous.

* * *

That night, after contemplating all that had happened, I felt I had to stop focusing on these police incidents. I needed to concentrate on Sebastian the monk. At first, before we ever got the manuscript, Jean was reluctant to pursue the matter. Not that she had never managed to have anything spirited out of the Vatican, but she said it was nerve-racking and possibly dangerous. She added, however, that there was a small contingent of rebels there and that she would see what she could do.

The way Jean referred to these subversives hinted at the presence of a mole at the Vatican archive. A mole! I learned the details much later, when we were threatened with a law-suit. The fact was that among all of the staffers at the Vatican library, there had always been a group of libertarians dedicated, often covertly, to facilitating the free flow of information. The latest of these democrats was Father Leonard Boyle, who had been appointed prefect and began immediately figuring out how to open all the files. He didn't know that an underground railroad was already operating. Boyle was educated at Oxford and specialized in Latin paleography—deciphering medieval tracts. Of course, when the church hierarchy got wind of what he was up to, he was unceremoniously dismissed. Cardinal Alfons Stickler, in commenting on Boyle's so-called extravagance in digitizing manuscripts, actually said something like there was no money for culture, only for religion. Boyle's tenure had been a breath of fresh air, and his departure was depressing to scholars who needed access to Vatican materials.

But Jean had access and it was out of the blue that she called me to say that a reading of Sebastian's manuscript could be arranged. The condition was that we could only view the work in dim light. These were 100-year-old English translation copies, faintly printed and at some later point in the century treated chemically, so that the print fades if bombarded with high energy photons as in the intense light emissions of copy machines. In other words, no scanning or duplicating, as in Xeroxing.

The other condition was that we would get the delivery by courier at 8 A.M. and it had to be back on a plane at Kennedy airport by 8 P.M. that same day. My guess was that the materials needed to be replaced in their vaults before anyone knew they were missing. Jean said to expect about three hundred pages of manuscript. In other words, I would have to read three hundred barely legible pages in dim light — about thirty an hour. She also said it was only about ten percent of Sebastian's work.

According to those figures, Sebastian actually produced somewhere near three thousand pages — certainly more than ten standard volumes. The good boy in me, the one my mother arranged for me to be, thought, "Well, I've got to get ready, get enough sleep and focus. Can't be tired. It all depends on me. We can't copy anything. The instructions are clear. Read without tampering. Just read it and send it back. No one else should see it after you read it. Send it back to its dark, airless, unforgiving fate — its vault. Don't let it breathe."

The other me who wants to drink life, destroy injustice — and get Katie back — that me thought, "Hell, no! Copy it! Open it! At any cost, do not send it back without retaining a copy. Stenographers and a photographer with high-speed film. That should do it. I'll read. That's one. A photographer with high-speed film. That's two. And two stenographers. That's three units. We should be able to get it all. Call it a heist." I didn't care. I've always wanted files to be open. Open them all — the Kennedy assassinations, the King assassination, Malcolm's, and let's see Sebastian's stuff, too.

It happened. The manuscript was delivered in the early morning on a cold December day. The psychoanalytic institute was just awakening. Jean had coffee and sandwiches prepared and Richard, her husband, was on the phone arranging for transportation to Kennedy for the manuscript's 8 P.M. Alitalia flight back to Rome. We could leave the building before 7 P.M. and still make it to Kennedy in time.

Wouldn't you know, it started snowing at about 10 A.M. Jean closed off the back room of the library, set me up with a desk and table, and pulled down the shades to dim the light. Jean's assistant, Lil, was appointed to handle all the day's activities in the outer library.

And now it all got stirred up: first the body of drowned Billy, and I was questioned; then the attack on the attendant, and I was consulted; then the shooting of the statue, and I was there too; and now I'm probably getting involved in something illegal and again I'll probably, no, ultimately and almost certainly, be a suspect. And with this one, rightly so. Jean said:

"Glenn, what's the matter? You're staring."

Then I told her all about Billy, Stroud and Grillo and how I was feeling.

"Guilty?" she exclaimed incredulously. "You've never done anything wrong in your life. And you're not starting wrongdoings with this sort of thing here, either. Goodness, drowned! An autistic boy." Then she snapped out of the horror of Billy's drowning and became all business. "Glenn," she said, "I know you're thinking Katie, but we've got a job to do. Now let's do it."

So despite my depression and divided and cumulative anxieties, I went ahead and invited two top-flight stenographers to join us — Rita, my secretary at the institute for three years and a crackerjack, and Jilliana Rodriguez, a twenty-five year old whiz with a pencil. The photographer, Ted Jackson, came loaded for bear: Leica 50 milimeter with a 1.2 lens calibrated to pick up the image on each page. With the combined efforts of Rita, Jill, Ted and me, I believed we had a chance of putting together a faithful copy of Sebastian's entire manuscript.

And then I had several quick thoughts. First, I thought that when we put it all together I would meet Sebastian. Sebastian would be talking to me. It would be like I retrieved him. No, it's not resurrection. Resurrection means dead, then alive. It's more that I need reappearance. And I need it for more than one reason. But second, I heard detective Stroud's six foot-three presence, and Grillo's ten-foot pressure, saying to me, "Did you steal manuscripts from the Vatican?"

· 4 ·

THE LILTING ROOM

First they wanted to see me at my office, now I was escorted to theirs. Stroud, with me at his side, strode in. Grillo, leaning back in his chair, had his feet up on the desk. He was thinking something but interrupted himself and greeted me. Stroud intruded.

"Joe," said Stroud, "you're thinking. Dangerous." Grillo ignored it.

"Doc, the truth is," said Grillo," I don't think I can work on anything except the autistic thing at the hospital. I know what you're thinking. It's an obsession. Anyway, it's too coincidental and it's, uh, I guess, crazy."

I was actually listening to and watching Grillo carefully because I wasn't really sure why they wanted me there. Was I a suspect? Or worse, was I their chief suspect? I did know I was nervous about it. And I thought, "What's he mean, 'coincidental,' and 'crazy?'" Then Grillo launched into a kind of summary of events.

"You see," he started, "first the kid drowns. Then you tell us the kid's diagnosis is wrong. Right? Then the attack by a hooded masked guy giving himself a name, and he doesn't touch any of the women, and you tell us he's got a mother thing. On top of that, lo and behold, we're at a clinic where a statue got assassinated, and who do we meet there? The K's, you and Kruger! But easy, Doc, you're not being accused of anything. It's natural for anyone to feel accused, and usually even guilty, in this kind of situation."

He was right about that. And how! And what did he mean by "this kind of situation?" He was on a riff, talking non-stop. And I was feeling even more awkward in the sense of guilt because he wasn't giving me a chance to respond. So, in addition to feeling guilty, I now also felt mute—and powerless.

"Definitely," Stroud chimed in. "There's no accusation here. We like you, Doc, and we trust you. We're just reviewing the whole thing and we thought you should hear it. You know, maybe you'll come up with something that could be interesting. Because, like Joe says, there's something a little nutso here—a killing, a shooting, and an attack."

"Yeah," Grillo piped in. "The kid that's drowned is doing some kind of record keeping. And that's bananas because Kruger says he's retarded. How could he do record keeping when he's retarded? And where's the records? We can't find 'em. But anyway, you, Doc, say, 'No, he's not retarded.' And then Kruger, on top of it all—you know, after saying the kid's retarded—calls him a math whiz. And then you explain it all by bringing in this Asperger diagnosis where the kid, it seems, can be everything, maybe retarded, not retarded, autistic, not so autistic. But Kruger never mentions Asperger. Why?"

I was about to answer that but Stroud then picked it up. "The pool is locked. How'd the kid get in? Climbed the fence? Not a chance. We can't prove it, but we know someone unlocked it and brought him in, and that's how he got in. The kid was a math whiz, not an acrobat. You know? People may be thinking maybe he climbed it, but we know it didn't happen that way. We know what it was, and an accident isn't it. And he didn't just fall in. We know someone dragged him there, carried him there, whatever the hell happened. Maybe Jericho. Wouldn't it be something if Jericho was being treated at the clinic—or, what is it, the institute—and someone at the hospital was the shrink? That we have to check out. You're not treating Jericho, are you, Doc?"

"Are you serious?" I almost belligerently said. "I don't know a thing about Billy's death, and, no, I'm not treating anyone with the name of Jericho!"

"Easy Doc, we know that," Grillo continued. "Just a formality. We have to ask the question. By the way, another formality: Do you own a firearm?"

"Absolutely not," I answered. "No."

"Right," Stroud said. "We know you're clean, Doc. Not to worry. But we want you to help us put it all together. You know, like you helped us understand that the guy hated his father so he shot the statue. That was a good one. We didn't get anywhere with it, but we know in the end it's gonna be important."

"So maybe," Grillo ping-ponged in, "it was the same guy then who loved his mother and couldn't take it that the attendant had all those women to himself so the attendant was like his father. See? So he attacked the attendant. So maybe it was like he was attacking his father. And then the same guy could be the killer of the kid."

"You're doing psychology," I said. I actually just timed it so I could slide it in before either of them continued. "Looks like you don't need me," I added.

It was Stroud's turn. "You know, Doc, its gottta be someone at the hospital who did it. But we know that sooner or later other channels will pop. Okay, we know that. It's gonna get more complicated. Know what I mean?"

Of course I knew what he meant. But what did he mean? I felt the whole thing was strange. Even though they tried to reassure me, nevertheless I was rattled by it. Maybe it was a variation on the good cop, bad cop theme—like, for example, good cop, good cop. Maybe they wanted to give me a false sense of security. Or could it be they just wanted my help?

*   *   *

The evening before our crates were to arrive, Jean had called me with some strange news. When she went to my desk to retrieve some papers—the airline fax we'd gotten and other materials—they were missing. She couldn't understand what could have happened since she had left the papers there several hours earlier thinking I would stop by and review each item. What she didn't know was that in contrast to the Vatican library—an environment in which guardedness was the cultural ethos and where there was a mole, a person who facilitated the free flow of information, albeit secretly—here, where the cultural ethos was characterized by an openness, I knew there was a person who was an obstructionist, one who had at other times rifled through papers, intercepting important materials to keep them from reaching their destination.

One such incident involved a review of my first book. The reviewer called it a "tour de force." That review disappeared from my desk. Someone at the institute—no doubt a member of the faculty and clinical staff—seemed to be competing with me, even though I never knew a race was taking place. I surmised that he (I was sure it was a he) probably was non-productive with big wishes, a grandiose type reaching for prestige but never really contributing anything valuable or new. Whoever he was, he was fundamentally, I felt, a petty mind. I had my suspicions. Siegfried Kruger? But I wasn't worried because whenever the obstructionist struck—and it occurred several times over the years—I always managed to rectify the situation.

As soon as Jean told me the papers were missing, I assumed the mystery man had gotten wind of what looked like important goings-on and once more was trying to undermine something that he was not part of. I told Jean not to worry. I thought of other possibilities besides Kruger and fixed on the chairman of the department of psychiatry, Ralph Bird. Dr. Bird had a fairly good reputation, but was actually not very productive and never published, though for some strange reason—perhaps his aura—he was occasionally referred to as a scholar. Yet, I felt in my heart of hearts that Ralph Bird was basically benign, the type who would not get involved in sabotage. The bottom line, though, was that the airline fax was gone.

At the library the next day, again I told Jean not to worry, but again, in truth, I was already worrying. I had this unsettled feeling that we needed to shore up our departure plan, but there was too much going on and Richard seemed to have all bases covered. Every so often, when there were no visitors to the outer library desk, Jean's assistant, Lil, would come to the back office door and I could hear her loudly whisper, "Jean, is everything all right?"

Jean would answer from our side of the door—also in a whisper, "Yes, he's reading."

From time to time Jean would say to me,

"Glenn, it's 11....Glenn, it's 12:30....Glenn, two and a half hours to go. . . ."

And now here it was. Sebastian was describing how he went about analyzing his dreams. He reported a recurrent nightmare which he called "an incubus." Although he didn't identify it as a nightmare, it was clear to me that that's what it was. He said that whenever he had this dream, he would awaken in a fright, and he had it several times when he was a young man. Even now, many years later, he remained curious about it. The dream, he suggested, seemed more like a fragment of a larger scene.

> In the dream I was sleeping, and sometime in the middle
> of the night someone was trying to enter the house. At
> first I began feeling a bit distressed and then the intruder
> began breaking down the door. As the intruder was be-
> coming more successful, I became more frightened until
> the door was completely broken into. I was terrified. I
> cried out and awakened, finding myself sitting up.

I remembered a patient I had treated who had more or less the same
dream. He began to feel closed in when his girlfriend decided they should
marry. Immediately thereafter he had the Sebastian nightmare. Someone
was trying to break into his house. As the door was broken down, he awakened in terror, moaning, "Help." His eyes widened when I pointed out
that one aspect of this dream was probably an expression of pressure he was
feeling about his girlfriend entering his life in a more permanent way. We
talked about this dream for some weeks. Then he had the same nightmare.
This time, when the intruder broke down the door, the patient dreamed
that he leaped out of bed and challenged the intruder. Fists clenched, he
said, "C'mon, I'm ready for you!"

His terror had been vanquished really because he was better able to acknowledge his anger about being pressured. He married. In contrast, Sebastian's terror had not been vanquished. I understood Sebastian's dream also to mean that
the intruder was his own anger threatening to surface. It became clear to me
later that indeed, the intruder was, in fact, Sebastian's anger directly related to
his father's death. I thought, "I can't get away from death." I felt cursed.

Interpretations about Sebastian flooded me. As I was reading I was also
trying to visualize his face. Even as a child, I seemed to be able to tell what
someone was feeling by their facial expression, gesture, or just general body
language. I suppose that's how I could diagnose Billy Soldier's problem as
Asperger's and not simple autism. Subtle gestures and postures were always
for me X-rays that enabled me to see something deep within the personality. It was kind of like an eidetic empathy.

I hit upon a passage where Sebastian discussed different ways he would
think about his dreams:

> I notice a difference in my thinking about the dream
> while lying rather than sitting upright. I also wonder

about my need to be understood by another person. At
times I feel an urgency to declare to another, meanings
that I feel are relevant. Other times I crave companionship or need dialogue. Then again, I also want only to be
alone in solitude and think. I know I am more than one
me and must learn more about my inner person. There
are no demons. Of this I am certain. There are only inner
tensions. The psyche.

Here, Sebastian was revealing his metapsychological understanding by
simply reporting his sensations and thoughts. I ruminated that he had clas-
sical psychoanalytic leanings—he noticed his stream of consciousness while
lying down and felt a desire to find interpretation. Yet he also noted the
narrative, descriptive level of the dream while sensing a more richly textured
and detailed underpinning. He was actually moving from surface to depth
as a psychoanalyst would, and further, he interpreted ego before id—that is,
he was interested in the dialogue before getting to the impulse of the emotion. And his quest for dialogue revealed an interpersonalist dimension to
his thinking, while his constant reference to his emotional connectedness to
others and what it meant defined his need for people, even though he was
a monk. Finally, he sensed a multidimensional self, nowadays called a self-
psychological view—personality variation while sustaining self.

Now, for the uninitiated this all may seem esoteric. But for someone
like myself, steeped in the theoretical and clinical soup, Sebastian's obser-
vations could be described as nothing less than staggering. Here was an
amazing precursor to late 20th and early 21st century life—a foreshadow-
ing of thinking to come hundreds of years later.

*   *   *

Secretaries seem to know everything. A call from the institute director's secretary located me in the library. Jean took the call and then reluctantly interrupted my immersion in Sebastian's theoretical and clinical
network—his manuscript.

"Glenn," she said. "a message from Dr. White. You need to call Dr.
Kruger at the hospital immediately." I hated to do it but stopped reading
and made the call.

"We've got a problem," Kruger said. "Apparently sometime around 6 A.M. this morning, still dark out, a man stood outside of the solarium and exposed himself to the windows of the female side of *J* Building. He must have first made a racket because many of the women were awakened and saw it. Also, the two ward attendants, Betty Scanlon and Tonya Robinson, and the night nurse, Nancy Ryan, all saw it. Before they had a chance to call security he disappeared. It was the second exhibitionistic act this month. I'm calling you because after reporting the incident to our detective friends, they asked me to inform the entire staff. They'd like to have all of us here this afternoon. You know, this happening after Billy's death and the Jericho attack and all."

I was conflicted. How could I say no? But I couldn't, no, wouldn't leave my reading of the manuscript. "The hell with them," I thought. Then I had the further amusing flash: "Who the hell would want to expose himself on a cold December morning? I mean, if you want to expose yourself, shouldn't you do it when it's warm, or at least warmer?"

"By the way," Kruger continued, "no one can identify his face, but they all agreed on the description of his penis. They said they didn't have time to see his face."

I guess that said it all. Exhibitionists really know where people will look first. I told Kruger to tell the detectives that I simply couldn't make it and I'd call them the first chance I got, either the next day or the day after that. Kruger tried to imply that this would be considered insubordination, that is, putting my needs first and so forth. But I wasn't having any of it. I just said, "Sorry."

"By the way," he again said. "He was wearing lipstick. Two of the women managed to agree on that. They were sure of it because it was glistening they said, just the way wet lipstick would look. But they only remembered the lipstick, not his face."

*   *   *

I tried to get back to the reading, but my emotions were a bit jangled by the interruption. I didn't know if I was angry at Kruger, Stroud, or Grillo, or even Jean. But I couldn't help thinking, first, about Billy's drowning, second, the attack on the attendant, third, the shot statue, and now at the hospital, a fourth incident—an exhibitionist wearing lipstick, no less. A male transvestite exhibitionist?

I told Jean, no more calls except clear-cut emergencies. I took a deep breath, mused about what I thought of as Reading Interruptus and got back to Sebastian's first section on dreams. In a sentence or two I was reinvolved. What he did was to crystallize for me a lot of clinical fragments that were not always easy to put together in the form of an elegant principle, and his conclusion had the unmistakable ring of truth:

> In the scores of dreams that I have tried to analyze, the emotion in the dream begins to make sense whenever I connect it to a person. Furthermore, I seem to feel better when I am able to identify who the person is that connects to the emotion. I am beginning to consider this phenomenon regarding the connection of emotion to people to be a reflection of some immutable psychological law that reveals emotion as a conduit to the true meaning of the dream. Thus, if I want to understand my dream, I must follow the emotion.

Sebastian conveyed the authority of received wisdom. I could feel it. His postulate related to one of Freud's principles of dream interpretation, which holds that emotion in a dream is that element of the dream almost entirely immune to disguise. For many years now I, too, have seen that emotion always connects with people. It would appear to be a simple principle, but in reality, it's a detail that is usually overlooked. Now, reading Sebastian's treatise on dreams and emotion and seeing his certainty about the connection of the emotion and the person, I began to formulate a new principle. As I thought about it, it not only made perfect sense, but, I believed, also had profound implications. This principle or, as I am calling it, this axiom is: *All emotion takes an object.*

The term "object" refers only to a person. It never means a table or a chair. Can an emotion be an emotion if it doesn't connect to a person? Can it just hang there, as in virtual state? For me the answer is a conclusive, resounding no! An emotion must be connected to a person if it is to be realized as an emotion. I thought, "See, there are, in fact, hard-core principles in this so-called soft science of ours."

I've tried all the challenges to this principle. None works. So, as I now tell all my colleagues who ask: "Always look for the *who* when emotion is involved. Do not dwell on the first question too long—that is, 'What happened?' Identify the *who* and you'll satisfy principle number one of the psyche: *All emotion takes an object."*

I applied this principle with a patient who was a college professor. His was another problem with the fear of commitment. His physical equilibrium in the classroom would be affected by his girlfriend's need to marry. If she was expressing this desire only moderately, he would enter his classroom feeling only uneasy. If she mentioned marriage, he would feel derealized, as in an existential disconnect, and the classroom would begin to lilt. Then he would hold onto the desk for stability.

Whenever that happened he evidently was repressing his anger and then popping the lilting symptom. The patient thought the symptom was caused by some virus. Then he attributed it to the fact that his aged father was ill. Then he thought it might be a result of other guilts. These were possibilities, and some were even interesting, but none were right. The pursuit of any or all of them would never have had the slightest effect on the symptom. This particular anger was not about the virus or his father. It was about his girlfriend. When he became conscious of the anger/symptom connection regarding his girlfriend, he could actually help himself, as it were, in camera—a concrete affirmation of Freud's principle that consciousness is curative. But—and it's a big but—we may now see that this principle, whether or not Freud himself fully understood it, means that consciousness refers to connecting the person—the "who"—to the emotion. Furthermore, perhaps, just perhaps, the emotion that always needs to emerge into consciousness is *anger.* Ergo, principle number two of the psyche:

Unconscious anger always refers to a "who" and, with respect to symptom cure, must become conscious.

I could almost hear Sebastian thinking American lingo: "Now remember, the emotion in your gut must connect to the person—the *who*—in your head."

*   *   *

The cemetery again. Always the cemetery. Going, standing, talking. I have to tear myself away. Talk about connecting through emotion! And it always connects to the *who*, in my head. And of course, the *who*, is always

Katie. People tell me one never gets over it; never gets over the loss, the sense of abandonment, the helplessness of it all. But in my case, it's not a matter of getting over it. In my case, it's a matter, in the first place, of it not computing. How do you ever get over something you haven't accepted? Is my will to retrieve her, that is, to rectify the event, stronger than the actual event itself? And even in my talking to her when I visit the cemetery, doesn't that prove that the fact of her so-called demise—as a fact—may be incontrovertibly factual? My answer is that her absence is what I refer to as a so-called absence. This all means I'm negotiating with coincidence, with happenstance, with connection and misconnection, and with plain high-probability simple mistaken identity. In the meantime, I'm sustaining us in our so-called intangible relationship—until such time as. . . .

· 5 ·

The Brilliant Hallucination

So people connect through emotion, and all emotions connect to people. But how does that apply to autistic kids? The emotion doesn't do the same thing for them—or does it? Is emotion the intangible glue for autistics, too? And what about Jericho? Who connects to his rage? What's his world of relationships like?

It's precisely what Sebastian was considering in the manuscript. He began to actually examine the world of relationships. At first, I thought that the principles that governed relationships four to five hundred years ago certainly would be different now. But as I read I began to think that perhaps the principles that governed relationships back then really are not too different now. And my afterthought was that perhaps they're not at all different now than they were then. Sebastian was giving me the sense that relationship rules—I'm calling them principles—may be immutable, no matter the era and perhaps even no matter the evolutionary age. And then I thought, "abandonment." Billy was abandoned. That's one of the key issues of relationships that can hurt: abandonment, vulnerability, helplessness, and, on a larger scale, even genocides of the helpless—and I'm one of them.

If you consider geological or glacial time, you realize that we are only a split second away from the Neanderthal sensibility. So to call Neanderthal man primitive, and then think of ourselves as civilized, is perhaps to deny reality. Remember, the Spanish Inquisition took place about five hundred years ago. It was barbaric, primitive. Then we jump ahead to our supposedly more civilized time, and we see how far we, as thinking and feeling people, have progressed. Ask Meyer Lerovitz that question. He'll tell you. He'll tell you that abandoned people who are then helpless can be parsed, and killed. Murdered. The making of ghosts.

So the extent to which the mentality that created the Inquisition is different from the mentality that created Meyer Lerovitz's concentration camp torture is a ratio that might also be applied to the difference in the laws of relationships between people then and now. And I would say that these equations are probably exactly the same in every respect today as they were five hundred years ago. Is it reasonable then to think that the principles of relationships that determined happiness or disappointment for the Neanderthal also apply today? The answer, I believe, is yes. Does this apply to people like Billy? Again, I think the answer is yes. It seems to me that relationships are either successful or not, depending on whether individuals interact the right way or the wrong way. The right way generates a deepening of trust and yields that important ability to struggle better, and perhaps even a chance to achieve a decent measure of general gratification. The wrong way produces disappointment, rejection and bad feelings. I believe this was just about as true for the Java ape man, for the medieval population, and for people like Billy, as it is for us.

*   *   *

To this point, it had to be that Billy Soldier also had relationships. This fact became clear to me, to Stroud, and to Grillo at the same time. It was while we were talking to Nurse Secora at Kruger's hospital. It started with another call I got from Detective Stroud. It was 10 A.M. and he wanted to meet me at the hospital, "in about an hour" he said, "if possible." As it turned out, it was possible, and even if it hadn't been, I would have made it possible, especially since I had already turned him down when I was involved in the marathon reading of Sebastian's manuscript. So there we were, talking to the head nurse of Billy's ward, Velma Secora.

For whatever reason, the detectives invited me to sit in on their questioning of Nurse Secora. I didn't know her very well as she'd only been in the job about six months. I might have encountered her seven or maybe eight times at the most, but because of her voluptuous figure, she was a standout. Apparently, the detectives had called Secora in advance and arranged the meeting. They also may have informed her that I would be there because she wasn't at all surprised to see me.

Grillo took the lead. "What can you tell us about Billy? Did he have anyone he was close to?"

She was terse. "Another kid." Grillo paused, leaned a bit toward her as though to say "and . . . ?" but Secora just waited.

"Could you tell us about this kid?" Grillo continued.

"His name is Edward. He's fifteen years old. You might say Billy's best friend. But he's autistic. Quite primitive."

Both Grillo and Stroud looked at me in a way that told me we were all thinking the same thing—namely, how in the world do autistic kids have best friends, or even, how do they have friends, period. Secora suddenly added, "No Asperger's there—Edward was autistic."

The detectives looked at me again. This time, it seemed, entreating me to clarify.

"Well, could it be," I said to her directly, "that really, it was Billy who was Edward's best friend? I mean, I could see Billy helping Edward in certain ways, but I can't quite see it the other way around."

"Yes, that's more accurate. Billy took care of him in little ways," she said.

"Wait a minute," Grillo said. "I thought these kids have no empathy?" Looking at me, Grillo continued, "Doc, you told us that the whole autistic thing is considered a disorder of not being able to feel for anyone. Isn't that right?" And not waiting for an answer, he takes out his notepad, flips a few pages, studies it and finds the place. "Yeah, here it is. You said, 'Autism is also a disorder of empathy.' I have it right here. And you quoted a specialist in Asperger's who called autism a disorder of empathy, meaning that the guy can't imagine how another person feels or how it might feel to be in the other guy's shoes. Right?" Again he didn't wait for an answer. "So," he continued to Secora, "how was Billy able to have empathy for Edward?"

"I don't really know," she said. "The fact is, however, that Billy did help him. Yes, Billy helped him and that no-name cat. He cared for both of them."

I interjected here and explained that in Asperger's, individuals can be helpful to others and sometimes helpful out of simple social understanding, and not necessarily out of pure empathy. I said, "It's kind of seeing what has to be done and doing it." Then I explained that given his intellect and talents, and even though he may not be a sky-high Asperger savant-type (for example, someone who's a professor at a university and who could be the world's greatest expert in, let's say something like precious gems), I believe that despite the psychopathology of his Asperger's, he was definitely able to assist others in any number of ways, and not surprisingly, without any self-consciousness whatsoever.

Grillo took that speech and segued into a simple question.

"Maybe Billy was on some drugs—wasn't he on medication here?"

"No," Secora said. "Billy was drug-free. It was Edward who was on medication."

Stroud, for the first time, initiated a comment to Grillo. "Take down the medication." He looked at Secora. Without consulting her chart, Secora knew exactly what the medications were.

"Edward took Risperdol and Buspar," she said. For some reason, rather than getting more of an explanation from the nurse, both detectives looked at me as if to ask what these medications were for. I quickly summed it up for them. The Risperdol was an anti-psychotic drug also used for the control of agitation and emotional eruptions, the Buspar, for anxiety. So apparently, Edward was both explosive and probably depressed. Grillo was tenacious. Cueing me, he wanted to know more about the eruptions.

"Eruptions," I said, "belong to a relatively new diagnosis called Intermittent Explosive Disorder or IED. Edward can become overly excited, even violent at almost any time and usually no one can tell what caused it. There's just an overall sense that the patient gets frustrated and then erupts. Autistic thinking is so private and so weird that frequently it's virtually impossible to tell what caused the eruption."

And as I said that, I flashed to the principle of the psyche intimated by Sebastian the monk—that all emotion takes an object and that the object is always a person. I realized that thinking about what caused the eruption misses the point; even with autistics, looking for the *who* can hit the target, while looking for the *what* might miss it. Then, as if actually on cue, an eruption on the ward shifted our attention to the nurses' station, where several autistic patients began creating some turmoil.

The ward consisted of two long corridors that criss-crossed with the nurses' station, with single rooms along the corridors, each for one patient.

At any given time, these rooms were usually unoccupied because most of the patients were sitting on chairs in the main area around the nurses' station. The radio was constantly playing, and patients were either singing or talking—sometimes to no one in particular—so that it was never silent on the ward. And it was here that we had a coincidental enactment of intermittent explosive episodes involving several patients. One started throwing objects off the nurses' desk—a dangerous sign because such a patient could trash a room in record time and create a stampede of explosive chaotic behavior in others as well.

Nurse Secora raced over to her station, was joined by two ward attendants, and they immediately separated all the participants. One of the patients was being physically restrained by one of these attendants, and Secora, in a precise manner, instructed him to strap the patient onto a restraining bed. We all followed. In a minute or so, Secora and the attendant exited. She called him by name—'T'—more accurately, by initial, and thanked him. 'T' was a formidable figure. He was as big as Stroud, girth as well as height, but muscled, not simply large. He looked at us, nodded, and walked out. It was all calm.

Grillo asked Secora, "Was Edward anything like that?"

"Yes," she again tersely answered. "Edward had trouble with almost everything."

"Did that affect his relationship with Billy?" Grillo continued.

"No, it didn't. Billy had a calming effect on Edward. Actually, Billy was always being very calm with Edward and also calming Edward. Billy was also very calm with the cat that wanders around the grounds. Sometimes Billy would take the cat into his room, sit on his chair and pet the cat. Billy loved the cat. No one ever named it. The cat had no name, but Billy cared for it whenever he could."

It ended there. Nurse Secora went to her station and Stroud, Grillo, and I walked to the front door of the building. Their car was parked directly in front of the entrance. As they were about to drive off, Grillo leaned out of the window.

"By the way, we haven't mentioned this, but the coroner's report on Billy's autopsy indicates bruises on his legs and arms. He was manhandled. Billy was drowned, murdered." It was a shock. I heard Tommy Gersh's voice in the hospital cafeteria, suggesting murder. Billy was murdered.

I instantly thought that Billy knew his killer although I didn't know why I had thought it. After a couple of seconds I realized that it was the difference between autism and Asperger's that led me to the thought. I realized that in simple autism only meager eye to eye contact exists, sustained conversation is rare, emotional reciprocity is limited, idiosyncratic language is evident and a lack of spoken language frequently characterizes the disorder. Thus before such a person would get the point about being in the process of death, it would be over. The suffering wouldn't be different, but the cognition might and whether true or not, it seemed that because of this, the terror might not hit as quickly. In Asperger's it's not the same. The prosody part of speech in Asperger's changes things. This prosody part involves issues such as rhythms of speech, intonation, rate of speech, volume, and inflection, and there is not the major assault to cognition the way there is in simple autism. The point is that Billy must have known exactly what was going on. Correctly or not, I surmised, therefore, that he had experienced maximum terror.

I felt dazed at what Grillo had just told me, and I shifted to Katie—to how I was sure/hoped she couldn't have suffered because she, let's say, disappeared, wasn't there. Thankfully I was distracted by Tommy Gersh, who came running and waving. Hurriedly, he told us that the exhibitionist had confessed. He was being questioned by one of the psychiatrists in the ward of the Probation Building—where patients are given their first chance to leave a locked ward and gain freedom of the hospital grounds.

The four of us rushed over to Probation. As we walked in, Dr. Eugene Alexander, the attending psychiatrist, was questioning a man who seemed obviously chronically disturbed and who must have been in the hospital for years. His clothing was baggy and unpressed, his body odor was, let's say, distinct, but the startling fact that I think hit all of us simultaneously was that this man was at best about five foot six inches tall and decrepit-looking, while the exhibitionist was reported to be over six feet tall and strong.

Standing around Alexander were two attendants, Betty Scanlon and Tonya Robinson, and the night nurse, Nancy Ryan, all of whom had witnessed the exhibitionistic act. And the funny thing here was that these women were shaking their heads "No" while the patient was trying to convince everyone "Yes." Suddenly the patient dropped his pants, and there he was, stark naked from the waist down, half erect, and with an obviously small penis — at best three inches. We were all surprised, and the women stopped shaking their heads as everyone stared at his penis. Then the women again began shaking their heads from side to side again, signaling "No."

Nancy Ryan started it: "No fireman's hat."

Then Tonya Robinson took the cue and without skipping a beat, she said, "And it's not long enough. That guy was about six feet five inches tall and had a big package there — long." To which Betty Scanlon quickly and seriously added, "And wide. Real wide."

Most of the men in the room felt a bit awkward but Stroud was trying not to laugh. He didn't feel awkward at all. I then looked at the patient. He had this weirdly inappropriate smile on his face. Then I looked at Tommy and shrugged my shoulders as though to say, "How'd this guy ever get to Probation?" He was obviously still quite delusional. Dr. Alexander then motioned to Betty and Tonya to help the patient with his pants and to escort him to the nurses' station.

As we walked out, Grillo gave me a quizzical look. I anticipated him.

"No self-respecting normal neurotic exhibitionist would ever do it that way. Only someone psychotic would do that. He's obviously schizophrenic. That weird smile. He's probably still experiencing delusions and hallucinations."

Grillo said it was illuminating.

*   *   *

But what I wanted illuminated was the surprising, hopeful relationship between Billy and Edward. I remembered what Sebastian had written about relationships. So, I decided to go back and reread my notes on Sebastian's criteria for mate selection and spousal roles, in order perhaps to distill some nugget of an insight about those boys, even though they were not mates or spouses. And the fact of Billy's death was rattling me because I myself was resisting the feeling of helplessness, of hopelessness.

It was Sebastian's "System of the Psyche" that he discussed. I was curious whether Sebastian actually wrote "psyche" or whether the word was updated in contemporary language when the manuscript was translated. This "system" is akin to a "Psychological Immune System" — a system that needs to be held in abeyance in order for people to bond. He said that when this system awakens, people begin feeling dissatisfied, and that only courage to talk about such dissatisfactions can ensure a deepening of bonds. He stated that suppression of dissatisfaction can lead to feelings of revulsion, or even underlying hatred toward the partner.

I felt this was important. To put it a different way, Sebastian was intimating that that which attracts can also be that which kills. And of course, we see it in couples all the time. The passive one marries the assertive one. After a while the fighting begins. Now the assertive one hates the other's passivity, while the passive one now hates the entitlement of the assertive one. Hence: *That which initially attracts you, is that which can eventually kill you*—kind of like the gradual emergence or even the sudden appearance of an allergic reaction—psychological though it may be.

My first association was that maybe that's what happened to Billy. And I flashed to the moment Richard handed me another pane of Sebastian's manuscript when I caught a glimpse of a fragment of a sentence. The word "hallucination" caught my eye.

I thought: "Sebastian's talking about a hallucination that someone had in the 15th century." It was irresistible so I copied it verbatim.

> She was poverty-stricken. The woman of about forty appearing sixty or older. Considered of substandard intelligence. Sheltered for two decades in the sanitarium. In this refuge the mother and brother visit each week. She was not fettered or in any other way physically restricted. She had been exceedingly dependent on her mother. The mother, who was aged, died suddenly, and shortly thereafter the daughter became despondent and hallucinated. She would be observed talking to air. The physician, a member also of the court, described this unfortunate woman to me as an example of forces able to enter the personalities of the vulnerable. I inquired as to whether he had ever conversed with her at length, or did he feel it was at all even possible to do so? "She was not able to develop her thoughts," is how he answered. I inquired further as to whether he could remember anything at all that she might have said. Proudly, he described her query to him. Referring to her mother's death, she said, "Oh,

please, tell me, does this mean I am caring for myself now?" And the physician responded by telling her that yes, she was, indeed, now an independent person. He confirmed this position by indicating that her brother would need to transfer her possessions from the mother's home to the sanitarium. The physician then remembered something the brother had told him. He said, "Her brother mentioned that in all of their growing-up years he knew that even though she was not able to understand or grasp ideas as well as others, that there was always a reason for things she said and did." And, he added, "Sooner or later I would see the reason."

Sebastian instantly saw a connection between what the woman had asked the physician and her subsequent hallucinatory symptom. He then went on at length about the death of the mother and how painful it must have been for the daughter to have sustained such a profound loss—surely perceived as an abandonment. He further speculated that the case contained rich implications for the study of mind; that is, that even though the conscious mind may seem, or even be, injured, what is beneath with respect to emotion and purpose may still be sound. I couldn't help but wonder whether it could also be true of Billy.

I contemplated that what Sebastian meant was that consciously you may be mentally challenged, but in the unconscious, where feelings, impulses, and intuition reign, the existence of mental retardation may not even be possible. No retardation beneath; that is, in the beneath exist only normal emotion IQ's. A compelling thought indeed, especially the idea that people like Billy or even Edward are liberated in the unconscious where emotions are tropistic, having only a single mandate and outside of civilization: fear means flee, anger means attack, sorrow means cry, and so forth.

In any event, the physician, in an attempt to reassure her and convince her that she was making progress, obviously did not understand the woman's purpose for asking the question in the first place and therefore missed the point entirely. She needed her mother *not* to be dead! She needed not to be abandoned. And she got her way. Sebastian unraveled the meaning of the hallucination. He simply said:

She reverted to an imaginary sensory existence and began talking to her mother. The hallucinatory experience was not random. By reverting to this more regressed state, she was able to retrieve her mother, thereby realizing her wish and at the same time proving her physician wrong. Her mother was not dead, and she, the daughter, was indeed still dependent, and not, as the physician stated, independent. Thus the patient empowered herself and had no need to be angry. Her possessions, therefore, could remain at home, with her mother!

I had the thought that this IQ-challenged woman was ingenious. She successfully subverted her mother's death by reversing the process so that her mother went from ghostliness to animated life. But then I got the sinking feeling that I, too, am delusional by insisting that Katie merely disappeared and that at some point I would find her.

I shook out of the thought by asking myself whether any of it applied to Billy and Edward? Maybe they communicated in the same way—in some delusional or hallucinatory-like code. In some code that if we're smart enough, we may be able to understand. Maybe it involved reversals, like this woman did in developing her hallucination that brought her mother back to her.

Yes, reversing the process! I'm wishing it all the time. No one's caught me talking to the air, but I do. It's not hallucinatory and I'm not psychotic. But I'm trying to do something—insisting in a way that logic says is impossible. But other than Deborah—my former supervisor who became my shrink—it's the only thing that gives me relief.

Relief! Sebastian definitely understood the meaning of that lady's disturbance. He knew it was the only thing that gave her relief. He actually called her symptom *"The brilliant hallucination."*

· 6 ·

PANIC ON THE BRIDGE

"Like I said, Deborah, I went to the cemetery looking for relief. I think it's my favorite place—I mean it. Being here with you is comforting, but the gravesite is my place. So, standing there like I've been doing now going on over three years—can you imagine that, more than three years—as usual, I just talk to her. Bring her up to date. This time I did both—in my mind, and out loud. Both ways, and even in the same sentence. Then—and this happens a lot—I find myself standing there, not saying or thinking anything. Just standing there. I don't even know for how long, but I know a lot of time passes.

"Deborah, you're the only shrink I know that cries."

"Someone needs to cry, Glenn. I guess I'm crying because you're not. You don't cry because you're stubborn, and you're ready to fight even God. You won't accept it. I know that's not hard for you to hear, because it probably makes you feel good—validating how you feel. If I said it the other way—like you need to accept the finality of it—you'd instantly find a way to distract yourself, avoid taking it in, go on to something else—yes, and get angry."

We sat there in silence looking at one another. I knew it was her art that enabled her to slip it in without it making me angry, or without it challenging me head-on. Then she almost impulsively said, "The truth of it is that I admire you for it, and I don't think I should even say that."

Then I cried. Covered my face with my hands. We both sat there, choked.

But I still needed to tell her what I talk about when I'm there, or rather actually what I say to Katie in what could be called, or maybe is, my dissociated state. Even though they never knew one another, I've come to feel an affinity between Katie and Deborah—so much so, that when I sometimes say "her," I almost feel that it doesn't matter whether it's Katie or Deborah that I'm referring to. It's pretty clear—I've made it so that I can almost, almost feel Katie's presence via Deborah. I create channeling. Whatever works.

"You know, Deborah, I've already told her about Billy and the monk—a number of times. Now, there was no one else there so I talked audibly to her. I kissed her name on the headstone. Sometimes I kiss my hand and place it on her name on the headstone, and sometimes I actually kiss her name on the headstone with my lips. This time I kissed her with my lips.

"Katie, hon, it's me. 'Hi.' I love saying 'Hi' to her.

"I'm feeling terrible about Billy, and I'm identifying with the monk. He lost his father and I can tell it was impossible for him to deal with it. Like me—I can't deal with going home and you're not there. You gotta come back. You can do it. But I also wonder if this is putting too much pressure on you because maybe it can't be done. And now I'm desperate because I never believed in all this kind of hocus-pocus, and I still don't, and yet, even in the face of it, I still want you to come back. You have to come back. You can do it. You're so talented, so capable. If it can be done, you can do it.

"Then I became silent, but in the next moment I realized that I implied that maybe it can't be done, so I added 'You can do anything that they say can't be done! You can break through!'

"That, Deborah, was easy for me to think, even though I feel the desperation when I talk to her like that. But it makes me feel good because for the moment I can believe that it could be possible—not maybe that it could be possible, but that it *could* be possible. I know it's obsessive and even grandiose—and thank goodness for delusion!

"But now comes the hard part. Usually, even after a half hour I still can't leave. At some point I walk halfway to my car, about fifteen feet away on the side of the path near the gravesite, then quickly turn and retrace my steps to her. It always happens that way, and I always kiss the headstone again. Then after a while I leave—head bowed, but not at all out of reverence. It's so as not to see anything—just the ground. When I get to the car I feel a shift in my consciousness, an altered state, almost as if I, and time, are on, or in, two different dimensions. Next thing I know, I'm on the highway. I never turn on the radio.

"The truth is, I understand all the connections here, and no, I'm not crazy. All that literature on the normal grieving process, Deborah, on the details of bereavement—throw it all out. But on the basic phases of bereavement, the wishes and so forth, it's probably right."

"You mean everyone does it their own way."

"Right. Everyone does it their own way! When my friend Hank's sister died at the age of 23, late at night when no one could see her, his mother would dance a slow waltz around the room with her departed daughter's picture in her arms. One night, two other friends of ours and I spotted her doing it. They made some joke about it. We were adolescents. It was very long ago. I never forgot it. I was the one who didn't laugh. I understood it. Even then. Now I'm doing the same thing. I'm dancing with Katie's picture, but instead of dancing with her picture, I'm practically living in the cemetery, talking to her. And I couldn't care who feels what about it."

"That last tack-on is your anger, Glenn. It's your way of handling it. And your anger is your defiance. It's your defiance of what is said to be irreversible."

"I hate that word, Deborah. I won't say it. Refusal! That's my word. And I hate the word 'denial,' too."

"You've internalized her, Glenn. So she's with you."

"That's exactly right. I carry her with me. Otherwise it's incomprehensible. The only deciphering I can do is the relief that melts over me when I imagine that she'll be there, at home, when I arrive. I'll walk in and they'll tell me it was a mistake. She was actually in a hospital, in a coma, but now she regained her memory, and everything's okay. I'll just sit with her day and night, and not let her out of my sight."

"You're crying again. You don't have to cry, Deborah; be sure that this fantasy makes me utterly happy. It's better than any medication."

"Can't help it, Glenn. Of all the connections we make, your own sense of it led you to the only reality that works."

"That's it. That picture, the reality I make myself, saves me. I'll just sit with her day and night, and not let her out of my sight. Whenever I think about it—well, I know it's even more than a wish. It's the only thing that matters."

*   *   *

Actually, the hospital mess saved me. Whenever I even thought about the hospital with all that was going on—a murder, a violent attack, an active exhibitionistic male transvestite—I definitely did not understand the connections, if there were any. But I realized a shift had taken place in me that was pure Pavlov. In a way I was relieved whenever the image of the hospital came into mind. And my anxiety there at the hospital also helped because I was feeling accused. I guess it was a self-imposed accusation. And it did the job. It actually distracted me from my Katie-agony!

I was suspicious about why the detectives had brought me in for the Nurse Secora interview. Did they actually expect me to put something together? Put what together? How was I going to put a murder of an Asperger kid together with someone exposing himself to women, along with a rage attack on an attendant presumably to protect women! And what about the shooting of the statue at the institute? That's the kind of puzzle, the kind of code, that needed far more deciphering than I could ever do.

In contrast, the very first time I would get a chance to put the symptom-code together occurred when Jean, Richard, and I were arranging to get the crates with Sebastian's manuscripts repacked and back to the Alitalia freight terminal by 8 P.M. Jean said we would be met by a person who has had experience transporting this sort of material. I guess that meant that some courier was going to babysit the crates.

But there was a surreptitious counterpart playing itself out simultaneously. The problem was that at the institute/clinic where the statue was shot, in the basement, where those on the maintenance staff have their lockers and where the mail room is located, Tyrone and Manuel, whose job it is to pick up all outgoing mail from faculty and clinic therapists' boxes and deliver incoming mail and memos to those same boxes, were about to perform one of their thieveries. It all came out through a secretary who had discovered them opening her private mail. She reported them to Dr. White, head of the clinic, and he called a meeting to discuss it all. The investigation lasted some weeks, and then Tyrone and Manuel finally implicated Dr. Kruger in all kinds of things. "Good God," I thought at the time, "Kruger was in it now!" This occurred after a staff consultation with a patient who had a whopper of a three-day migraine.

Tyrone was a medium-sized black man in his mid-30's who was entirely unassuming, someone who could get lost in a crowd. Whenever he picked up or delivered something from or to an office, he was in and out. Manuel was a shorter Hispanic man, also in his mid-30's. Except for the usual salutation, neither of them spoke to faculty or clinic staff during these forays.

The detailed story they told Dr. White included a step by step reenactment. Manuel, looking for Tyrone, walked into the mail room where many people were milling around doing various things associated with keeping the clinic moving. They needed to distribute yellow pads to offices, supplies to administration, sort mail, work the various machines—Xerox, postal. A busy place. Apparently, Tyrone told Manuel that Kruger wanted the fax and folder on my desk.

They told Dr. White that Tyrone, indeed, was carrying several pieces of mail and inter-office memos meant for my in-box. Tyrone had entered my office by passing through my secretary's cubicle, placed the mail and memos into the in-box, and simply picked up everything lying on my desk. Everything was exactly where he was told it would be, and he walked out. Instead of taking the elevator down, he took the stairs.

Tyrone and Manuel finally put the finishing touches on it. They laid it all out. Kruger engineered it all. I had the thought that Kruger would have been well suited to run a sanitarium in the middle ages. As a matter of fact, one of the psychiatrists who worked at his hospital once told me that Kruger kept locked files on all his employees, keeping everyone on edge as though he had something on them. It was ominous! That story jibed with my sense that he was deceptive—somewhat gregarious on the outside, but within, ridden with envy. Talk about autism! He was an egoist of the first order, morality and intellect devoted rather exclusively to aggrandizement and self-interest.

And that was how Kruger had access to all sorts of information. Stealing!

*   *   *

But of course, we also had a caper to pull off. We tried not to break stride. The Alitalia freight terminal was our destination. It had been snowing the entire day and the streets were dirty and slushy. When I had finished the last page of Sebastian's manuscript, and after Ted, Rita, and Jilliana had also finished with it, Richard placed it carefully in the third crate. The other two crates had been completely repacked. By this time Ted was exhausted. Jill, on the other hand, seemed exhilarated. I was bleary-eyed. I sat back for a moment, looked around, and realized that we had done it. I could tell that Ted and Jill also sensed we had successfully reproduced the entire three hundred pages, assuming, of course, that I could fill in the material that might not have been properly caught by Ted's camera or that might have gotten jumbled in Jill's and Rita's steno pads. Yet I wasn't worried about Jilliana and Rita. Ted was a hope, though he felt confident. My greatest concern was whether I myself could faithfully reproduce the gist of the three hundred pages I had read. Not counting three or four brief rest breaks, a quick sandwich and coffee for lunch, and some note taking, it had taken me most of the day to read it all. I would say I also consumed, all told, about an hour drifting in my thoughts while I was reading. Sebastian was proposing connections between various psychological phenomena, and it was all fascinating to me. My stream of consciousness catalyzed by this marathon read would take me the better part of three days to fully process. It would only be when I metabolized it all that I would feel normal, as if something had lifted.

Then it happened. I hated it for its inconvenience, but although it was a surprise, I connected the dots and suddenly the light bulb lit up. I knew it. Dammit! About forty-five minutes before we were going to leave, Richard called the commercial van company to alert them that he was about to leave to pick up the van. They told him the reservation had been canceled earlier that day, and that no other vans were available. Jean asked how that could be, and I reminded her of the missing folder from my desk. The reservation confirmation fax for the van was one of the missing items. It was only later that we learned from Tyrone and Manuel what had really happened.

The canceled reservation caused a panic. Jean was beside herself. But Richard, usually the supporting actor to Jean's lead, sprang into action and went for the yellow pages. Hertz, Avis, National, Budget, Enterprise—he called them all. No vans in our immediate area. That took ten of our precious minutes. Then Richard located a one-man mover who had a beat-up, makeshift station wagon, truck-van or whatever the hell it was. The vehicle looked like a Dr. Seuss creation. Let's call it customized. The owner was a Pakistani who apparently had a vision for his new business, and to this end had remodeled an old station wagon and put a second story on it. By the time the driver arrived it was 6:45 P.M., and we had an 8 o'clock rendezvous at the airport. It was going to be close, but even that was wishful thinking. I got a sinking feeling that there was no way to make it and that we were going to be stuck with the goods.

Richard was eagerly awaiting him in the street. The driver double-parked while we all started loading the crates one by one into the back of his vehicular contraption. I must admit, I admired his ingenuity and industriousness and mused that here was an example of the American experience. An immigrant from a far-away land and culture, and he's inventing ways of making a living. Little did I know what we were in for.

Our Pakistani friend started driving. New York City with snow and traffic on a cold Friday evening when people are leaving the city is not the easiest drive, especially since, as it turned out, he wasn't, to say the least, the best driver in the city. Standing there on the slushy, snowy street, Rita, Jill, and Ted all motioned a little wave and watched us soberly as we slowly pulled away.

We hit the East Side Drive at 7:05. Soon we were on the Triboro Bridge; there was still an outside chance for the 8 P.M. deadline at the terminal. But then it struck. Here it was, a major anxiety attack. The driver began sweating. His hands were wet, he was hyperventilating and I could tell his heart was racing. I had the thought, "panic on the bridge."

In a quaking voice he said, "I must stop here. I cannot go over the bridge."

I didn't move a muscle, just watched. We were now stopped cold on the Triboro Bridge with a so-called moving company driver who couldn't drive on a bridge. Jean, of course, like any normal person in such a situation, predictably said, "What's wrong?"

The driver steered the contraption to the extreme right-hand lane. This meant that cars would have to go around us, and everything on the bridge slowed down. With a quivering voice and a perspiring brow, he said, "I always have trouble on bridges. I never go on bridges. Many years ago in my country I was driving over a bridge and it happened. I must breathe the cold air."

He rolled down his window and began taking deep breaths, permitting the cold air and wetness to revive him. He told us he'd been driving in the city for five years and that he always avoided bridges. He never went anywhere that required driving over a bridge. Then he added, "also tunnels." In other words, here was a driver who got panicked on bridges and claustrophobic in tunnels. And in our hour of need we got him. Again, Jean asked the relevant question, "Well, why did you take this job if you couldn't get us there?"

His answer was simple, but in the meantime Richard wasn't saying anything. I guess he realized that the driver was about to answer that question with the obvious—that in Richard's haste, he never told him we were going to Kennedy. The driver thought it would be a moving job from one part of Manhattan to another. Richard then confirmed that in the confusion and alarm of trying to get some transportation he had only focused on getting the driver to the clinic thinking he would then give him our destination. And not giving the driver a chance to ask anything, Richard had quickly gotten off the phone.

I was taking it in stride, but realized that it was like a muscle tear. In those first split seconds there's no pain, but you know that the brain is about to get the message and dispatch the signal—pain. In the meantime I was calm, perhaps because Jean was the one feeling it all. She was my proxy for being worried. And she was really seriously worried that the crates could not be returned in time for their reincarceration, and that this snafu could place—would place—someone in jeopardy. She was in despair and in an out-of-character comment said, "I'll give you fifty bucks more but you have to let me drive." Trembling, the driver began shaking his head from side to side. "I am afraid. I have no insurance on the truck."

And Jean, again predictably said, "What, no insurance?!" and shot Richard a look. An argument between them was about to erupt when the driver complained of light-headedness and said he was nauseated. Of course, he was the architect of his own dizziness because he continued to hyperventilate.

Basically, I wasn't terribly sympathetic with the driver or with Jean. Without even planning it, my priority, as it turned out, was my relationship with Sebastian. Second, was this nagging feeling that detectives Stroud and Grillo were shadowing me, suspecting me, tailing me, developing a dossier on me, and for all intents and purposes, reaching into my life. I knew they had all my phone numbers though I hadn't supplied any nor had they ever asked for any. That was disconcerting. Ostensibly, they were taking me into their confidence. It was that feeling of doubt that clued me in that I was definitely still paranoid about the whole thing. So here, with respect to my concerns, our dilemma on the bridge came in a distant third. Yet I did, in fact, also have that sick feeling about missing the flight. Clearly, I was going to be involved with the daunting task of getting three wooden crates marked "Fragile — Glassware" to their point of origin without shipping them through normal channels. And again, I could hear Grillo saying, 'We're investigating Billy Soldier's drowning at the hospital and you work at the hospital; we're investigating the shooting of the Freud statue at the clinic and we find that you also work there and that it's your statue. Now this. You're involved in stealing and smuggling too?"

So I was still very much with Sebastian, and Billy, and Stroud and Grillo, much more than I was in that crazy contraption of a moving van. But then I came back to earth. Here was my plan. I was going to take what Sebastian had conveyed to me, pair it with what I'd already discovered about symptom cure, and amalgamate all of it with what Freud taught us about symptoms. In this synthesis, this explosion of theory, I was going to cure this man's panic. Cure it! Right there and then on the bridge. And I started to put it all together right in the middle of a snowstorm, right in the middle of a traffic jam on the Triboro Bridge, and right in the middle of this man's anxiety/panic attack. With his head still out the window poised to throw up, I called to him.

"Sir."

It was the first word I had uttered since we left. I tapped him on the arm. Infirmly, he turned and looked at me.

"Yes?"

"I think I can help you. I'm a psychologist." I pointed to my head. "Uh...a psychoanalyst...a person who does the psyche business."

Shivering and quivering, in heavily accented English he breathlessly began his story.

"Ahh, a doctor. Oh yes, please ask me questions. I will tell you anything you want to know. But it never before helped. In my country I saw a doctor but he didn't help me. Then two years ago it was very bad and I was sent to see a doctor for the nerves, but he, too, didn't help. He gave me pills, but the pills were not good for me. They made a bad thing, you know, for my wife and me, you know."

He was self-conscious about relaying this information because Jean was in the car. He was obviously referring to some antidepressant medication that had interfered with his sexual functioning to such an extent that he was forced to discontinue its use.

In the middle of the snow storm with cars going around us, with his window open and his face wet with perspiration and snow, sitting in this increasingly freezing contraption, he began in short bursts, to describe various other examples of the kind of treatment he had received. It took him time to convey each episode because he was stammering and kept catching his breath. Essentially, he was prescribed a cognitive-behavioral regimen in which various treatment personnel tried to desensitize his fear through the use of a number of tasks including having him fantasize a gradual approach to both bridges and tunnels.

For the most part, and philosophically, I guess I had what might be considered aversive feelings about this kind of logic-therapy. For me, the main point is that knowing is better than not knowing, and far better than repeating a mantra ad infinitum or trying to be talked down from a fear. The mantra can effectively mesmerize in a given circumstance, but it probably won't prevent another episode from occurring; it has no value in the building of a solid fund of knowledge about one's life, one's feelings, one's motives, conscious and unconscious. Furthermore, it's practically impossible to reason with irrational fear. Why? Because it's never about the fear. Never!

In any event, they couldn't cure him. Nothing worked. Whatever the reason, I like to think that it takes two people to do therapy, one of whom — ideally the therapist — should understand what is going on. In his case, neither he nor his therapist seemed to know how to proceed; neither understood the first thing about the symptom, and no one even considered the possibility that the driver's fear of the bridge was not the issue at all.

Now it was my turn, and I relished the chance. It was quiet in the car, reminding me of those lucid moments called peak experiences. Jean and Richard were intrigued and perhaps a bit transfixed by my calm implicit promise of cure. The truth was that I saw it — the whole thing — and I knew what to ask. My sense of it was that no one had ever treated a symptom the way I was about to, following a set of principles and axioms about the psyche and its role in symptom formation. No rummaging around for things to ask. No panic on the part of the therapist. No, "Oh God, where do I go from here?" This was not going to be buckshot. It was all going to be aimed.

*　　*　　*

Velma Secora ran out of the trailer, but he was already in the car aiming and screeching out into the road. She tripped over three or four of the rabbit cages strewn in the path that he had deliberately knocked over. Rabbits were scrambling to regain their balance within the cages. He saw her in the rear view mirror. Velma regained her balance, stood, and brushed the dirt from her dress. She tried to see the car but it became a blur in the distance. In the car he was ranting at the top of his lungs.

> ***"I am Jericho, you bitch. I will fuck you up. C - U - N - T!***
> ***I will tear your fuckin' heart out. I will fuck you up.***
> ***You hear that? You hear that? B - I - T - C - H !"***

He was speeding, shouting, and cursing at people and cars as he was passing them. He spotted a jogger and instantly swerved the car just enough toward the jogger that the guy lunged for the farthest point on the side of the road toward the foliage. Then Jericho righted the car, cursing all the way.

> ***"I will kill you, mother-fucker. Kill you!"***

He was angry, enraged. He steered the car to a makeshift road off the highway, parked it away from sight, took an axe from the trunk and stormed into the woods.

Jericho waited. He was motionless, but in response to bird calls he shifted his eyes from tree to tree. He held the axe in a throwing position, like a tomahawk, and it was obvious that he was going to aim it and that some animal was about to get it.

After some minutes a rabbit appeared. With no hesitation and with one swift throw, he sent the axe flying through the air, end on end, and caught the rabbit on the run, striking it directly on its back and practically splitting it in two. His wish — his need — was to kill that rabbit, and he did it. He was angry, in a rage before he killed it, and now, after it was destroyed, in one more outburst, he screamed:

"I got you! Split you!"

He was calmer. Felt better.

* * *

I was quickly thinking through all the principles of symptom-cure that I was about to apply. Aiming it was on my mind. First, it occurred to me that Sebastian had answered my main question in the way that I had gradually, over the years, begun to see it myself. *What's the most important emotion in life?* It's the question I originally asked Charley. In a great insight, Sebastian said it was *anger.* I thought, of course the cliched answer would be love. I suppose it's the humanistic answer, perhaps the theological answer, and almost certainly the prevailing psychological answer. But it's the wrong answer! Derivatives of the wishes include love, hope, prayer. Wishes are so ubiquitous and so characteristically thwarted; love is also just as frequently adumbrated, unrequited, unmet, disappointing, fading, illusory. So, we're always flirting, with the consequences of not getting our wishes met. Which emotion is instantly generated when the wish is not met? Always the answer is anger. Why? Because when a wish is thwarted, we experience a disempowerment—we feel helpless, like in feeling abandoned. The question then becomes one of understanding why anger is the natural reflex to such disempowerment. Sebastian knew why. He put it this way, in his usual way of stating a proposition:

> "Becoming angry is the only way to feel reempowered
> when one is either helpless, made to feel helpless, or in a
> state of frustration over thwarted wishes."

And that's the key. *Anger is a reempowerment!* What we do about it once we get angry will determine whether or not we get a symptom. This is the touchstone for the first law of symptom formation: *Where there is no anger, there is no symptom.* This really refers to suppressed or, in Freudian terms, repressed anger. Thus: *Where there is repressed anger, not only will there be a symptom, there **must** be a symptom.* And it all hinges on whether the wish is met or thwarted. If it's met, no anger. However, if the wish is not met, then with the resulting anger repressed, and the wish sustained, a perverse form of the wish will appear as a symptom.

When this became clear to me, I realized that Sebastian had the more powerful theory with respect to symptoms than even Freud. So, the frustration of wishes leading to anger is what figures most in life. Love is beautiful, but anger is the power lever.

Anger! That was it, and I knew it. It was not love, not disgust, not acceptance or expectation or surprise or sorrow or joy, or even shame or guilt, and it was definitely not fear. Our driver was angry and didn't know it. That was it! He thought it was fear. Doesn't panic equal fear? But Freud originally told us that it could not possibly be fear. According to Freud, "behind the fear is the wish." That was a big one, a revelation of major scientific importance. If Freud had never said anything but that, he would have gone prominently into the pantheon. Behind the fear is the wish. That means there is something that the fear is concealing—something much more basic, profound, and sometimes even horrifying. And anger is it. That's at the core.

Now I knew that to cure this man's symptom I had to consider four elements: the wish, the anger, the *who* toward whom his anger is directed, and finally the doing of something related to the original wish. If I get those four, his symptom cannot live.

My next thought was: *All emotion takes an object.* Josh was angry at someone! Ditto for the body watcher. Meyer Lerovitz was angry at his son.

Our driver was angry at someone.

* * *

Armed with these principles, I proceeded with this systematic attempt to unravel our driver's panic symptom. I tried to think systematically. *A symptom means repressed anger*—thus his panic tells us he's angry. *All emotion takes an object*—then he must be angry at someone specific. *No wish will be denied*—his panic is the wish perversely realized. I couldn't start out by asking him who the *who* was, because the repressed anger and its target person would be outside of his awareness. So I needed to begin in a much more non-threatening place such as when this bridge/tunnel symptom first appeared. How many years ago was it that he first experienced panic on a bridge?

It took him some time to relate that entire pivotal first event. He summarized it by telling us that five years ago, when he was a taxi driver in his country, he was in the middle of a bridge and got his first experience of panic. He then quit driving. It was only in America that he decided to start a moving business though he would not accept any clients going from borough to borough. When he realized he would be going over the Triboro, he got terribly nervous, and before he knew it the panic became overwhelming. The most important fact that emerged was that the symptom had first occurred five years ago. My task now was to try to identify what was going on in his life then, because I knew that the person toward whom he was angry was connected to that time and place of his life.

Who was the *who* five years ago? That was the most important question. Without my asking he said, "I got married five years ago."

· 7 ·

Standing on His Head

Meanwhile, at the hospital, it became common knowledge that since Billy Soldier's death, Dr. Kruger had been feverishly going through his own files, his office closets, his secretary's desk and even Billy's room in the autistic ward. Kruger made no bones about it. What he was looking for were the property building records kept by Billy and registered in books and lists. The problem was that although it was known that Billy did in fact have these records, no one ever really thought about where he stored them. What we did know was that Billy treasured them. And now, according to Kruger, they were missing. He had questioned everyone, asking people whether they had seen the records or knew of anyone who might even have them. He questioned Nurse Secora at her building, and while he was there also questioned several attendants. The consensus was that Kruger was losing it. He was frantic.

As I walked into my office at the hospital, there waiting for me was Tommy Gersh, who was sitting and talking to Gail Forester. Mrs. Forester was about 50, friendly, always pleasant, and efficient. She liked Tom and me and would talk to us whenever we were anywhere near her office. When she heard us but couldn't see us, she would pop her head out of the office and invite us in, sometimes offering us tea. For whatever reason, she always called us Dr. Kahn and Dr. Gersh, and we always called her Mrs. Forester. She'd been a civil service employee for many years at the hospital and for the past two years she'd been Dr. Kruger's secretary. The moment I entered she said, "Oh, Dr. Kahn, I'm so glad to see you." She was visibly upset and looked at Tom. Nodding to her and looking at me, Tom urged her, "Go ahead, tell him."

"It's Dr. Kruger. He's out-of-his-mind nervous. He's pulling papers out of drawers. He can't find his books and he can't find Billy Soldier's lists and he actually accused me of either misplacing them or worse. And he didn't apologize. Just stormed out of the office. I'm very angry about it."

At least, I thought, she's aware she's angry and not attributing her state of mind to being upset — that code-phrase for being angry.

"She came to me," Gersh said, "also looking for you."

"I only wanted to talk to the two of you."

"Well, what else happened? Anything else?" I asked.

"Yes. Dr. Kruger just now, about twenty minutes ago, went to *G* building looking for Edward, the autistic boy."

G building, of course, was the area of the hospital reserved for autistic patients. Billy had lived there, and Edward had been there now for several years as well.

"And Dr. Kruger was very angry," she continued. "We all know that Edward can't talk. I'm afraid Dr. Kruger will expect him to answer questions about Billy's lists and books. Just the tone of Dr. Kruger's voice could upset Edward."

I assured her that the professional staff wouldn't let that happen, but just in case, I told her that Tom and I would go over to "*G*" and make sure Edward was not under any pressure from anyone. Relieved, Mrs. Forester thanked us and on the way out indicated that she was thinking of reporting Dr. Kruger. I had the thought that she wouldn't know how to follow through on that one because my hunch was that she would want to report him to the director of the hospital. Trouble was it was Kruger who was the Director.

Tom and I rushed over to "*G*." As we entered the building, Nurse Secora and 'T' were walking toward the main doorway together. They ran right into us and without blinking, Nurse Secora stopped, gestured ever so slightly to 'T,' and he walked out.

"Yes, before you ask, Dr. Kruger was here and he wanted to question Edward. I think he realized how ridiculous that was, so instead he looked all over Billy's room, which was sealed by police tape. He unlocked the door, and I regret to say, slid under the tape and entered the room. Then he searched Edward's room. It's good that Edward was in the hall because if Edward had seen it he would have become quite agitated. After he left, I immediately straightened the room."

We told her that that was good thinking and assured her that we were not going to talk to Edward. What we wanted was just to look in on him. She hesitated, but the fact that we were implicitly deferring to her authority seemed to soften her and she nodded.

Another attendant was there supervising the ward. Edward's door was open. We kept our promise and didn't disturb him. Walking past his room we saw him singing to himself, standing upside down at the headboard. He was standing on his head.

*   *   *

That reminds me that I had almost stood on my head in that contraption of a moving van, but that no, I hadn't been able to keep my promise. I couldn't cure him on the spot. Our driver, for cultural reasons, was not able to discuss various issues connected to his symptom, not the least of which concerned his sexual functioning. With Jean there and with the windows open and the freezing air penetrating the customized contraption, our driver was frozen in more ways than one. I told him we could meet at my office—no charge—and he appeared to believe me when I indicated that I understood his symptom. I realized I had a 2 P.M. opening the next day and he readily agreed. As I was telling him that he would have to permit Jean to drive because he was simply not able to, Jean had already opened the driver's door. She helped him out of the car and into the back seat. Then she got behind the wheel and aimed straight for the far side of the bridge. Our driver didn't really understand what was happening because he was at a forty-five degree angle, half lying down in the back seat, with me propping him up.

When we finally arrived at the airport, our prearranged person was nowhere to be seen, so Jean's hope-against-hope that he might have waited was dashed. We were already forty minutes late, and Jean recognized the futility of the situation.

Driving back to the city, Jean made the decision not to take the tunnel, feeling that the Triboro was still the lesser of two evils. We all felt that the driver would never be able to tolerate the tunnel. It may have been moot because his symptom probably awakened only when he himself drove, not when he was a passenger.

All the way back I kept wondering how we were going to get three wooden crates marked "FRAGILE, GLASSWARE" to their destination. We arrived at Richard and Jean's West Side apartment, and Richard and I unloaded the crates and took them up in the freight elevator. Jean said she had to give her Vatican contact the bad news. Next, I drove our driver home, thirty blocks north to 107th Street, and made an appointment to see him the very next afternoon. I then paid him for his, shall we say, efforts. At first he refused, but after I insisted he accepted. I then cabbed it home.

Before I slid into bed I took a tour of the apartment. I looked at Katie's paintings all over the apartment. I'd forever been smitten with her work. She always had her finger on the pulse of what was important. Never interested in nonsense. I just liked the way she inhabited the world, and her paintings were nothing less than wonderful.

* * *

At 2 P.M. sharp the buzzer rang. The driver didn't comment at all about the office. He wanted to be cured of his panic and he went right to it.

"You see, I knew you knew I could not talk about my sexual problem with the lady present in the car. But now I will tell you anything you want to know."

"Of course, now we'll be able to talk about it," I said. "But first, you know I don't even know your name. We were in such a hurry last night and with all the difficulty, we never exchanged names. So let me tell you my name. I'm Glenn Kahn."

"Oh, what a coincidence. My name too is Khan."

"Is that right? How do you spell it, with an h-a or an a-h?" I asked.

"My name is spelled K-h-a-n. I am Ayub Khan. I am Pakistani. Sihk. Not Muslim. I know Americans think we all in Pakistan are named Muhammad. And it is true. Maybe seventy-five percent, maybe even more are named Muhammad. My best friend he is named Muhammad Syed. And you, too, are named like me — Khan?"

"Well, it sounds the same, exactly. But it's spelled differently. You have the h before the a and I have the a before the h. I am Jewish."

"Ah, I know all the doctors are Jewish," he said; "I believe in peace for everyone."

"Okay," I thought, "me too."

I liked Mr. Khan, and as I thought about the previous night, I admired his entrepreneurship, his energy, his striving. I shifted back. I reminded him that the last thing he mentioned was that he got married five years ago. He immediately told me it was difficult to marry, because, even though he loved his wife, and even though they did "a lot of loving," he couldn't quite bring himself to leave his family. He said the idea of marrying made him nervous.

"But you married her," I said. He nodded, Yes. "And soon after you married, you had your first attack on the bridge?" I asked.

"Yes, yes, that is the way it happened."

I thought that perhaps I now understood the genesis of the symptom and its operation for the ensuing part of his life. It seems that his wish was not to be married, even though he loved his wife. She persuaded him, forced him, cajoled him, frightened him, convinced him, stampeded him, whatever it was, into the marriage. He had, I believed, a serious case of separation anxiety. He may not have been ready to leave his family. Most likely, he wasn't ready to leave his parents, probably his mother. He didn't like getting married, especially while he was ambivalent or worse, while it was against his will, or perhaps better said, against his wish. And it made him angry. Angry toward whom is the question, and the probable answer is angry toward his betrothed. He couldn't express it to her, so he repressed it. And in that repression, he popped a symptom that in an ingenious but perverse way represented his original wish not to be married. Namely, he got anxious on a bridge. A bridge represents a construction that enables two bodies of land to be connected—perhaps a perfect symbol for the union between two people. Without the bridge, one body of land is disconnected from the other, but with the bridge they connect. A connection in contrast to the wish for disconnection or unconnection. It's what could have done it. Let's call it a conflict.

So, Mr. Khan's panic on the bridge may have represented his original wish not to be connected, committed. Being unable to cross the bridge, therefore, grants his wish not to be connected. Hence the Freudian proposition: *in the psyche, no wish will be denied.*

I decided to explain it to him. Since I knew that our therapeutic contact was going to be extremely short term—perhaps just this session—I decided to try to give him a sense of the theoretical map. Not that I thought it would be, content-wise, therapeutic. But I did feel it would forge more of an intellectual bond between us and that this alliance would be the therapy with the longest-term effect. He listened intently and then said something that astounded me. He wanted to know how the wish got translated into the symptom. He asked, "How does the wish travel from your mind to your symptom?"

I answered him directly. "I usually think of it as a little talk between what you wish and the anger you feel. The angry feeling says: 'I'm going into the unconscious mind—deep down.' I explained that it was the part of the mind not known to us.

"And the wish says: 'I need to go, too.'

"The angry feeling then says: 'Hop on.'

"And so the wish hops onto the back of the anger and into the deep mind they go, so deep that you don't even know they're there. Then the symptom comes out. The symptom is the wish, but looking different. The angry feeling stays forgotten, but keeps pouring fuel into the tank of the wish/symptom. However, as soon as we *see* and *feel* the anger, the fuel stops pouring, and that's when the symptom stops."

He then said that at no time in the past five years had anyone ever shed any light on his problem, and he agreed that mine could be the answer to the puzzle. I told him that he needed to tell his wife that his expression of dissatisfaction did not mean he didn't love her. That sort of discussion was the "doing" he had never done. I then thought:

"Speak it," Freud said, "otherwise it well be reenacted."

"Have courage to express your dissatisfactions to your partner," Sebastian said.

We actually met twice more during which time I tried to help him talk about his separation concerns. We also discussed the *who* behind the *who*—that is, his relationship to his mother representing his dependency. I suggested that being angry with his wife may have been more convenient than examining his relationship with his mother.

He kept wanting to engage me in theoretical discussions about psychology. I have seen many patients over the years. Some have the courage to look, others don't. He did. He also knew I respected him, and this too, helped. He even said, "How long, years in school, to be a psychologist?"

Was Mr. Khan's symptom cured? Time will tell. I think, at worst, we undermined it. But I was confident that he would be able to struggle better, ultimately defeating the symptom. To struggle better—isn't that the crux of everything? It occurred to me one day in an epiphany: *The goal of psychotherapy is to struggle better.*

I was pretty confident in Mr. Khan's struggle-program, but again, not in mine. I wouldn't work mine out because for me there was nothing to work out. My only solace was in the plan of finding her. So I continue to resoundingly defeat life's irresistible force, always there, lobbying for me to acknowledge it, to work it out. The obstacle is the presence of that proverbial paradox: that immovable object—me!

· 8 ·

A KILLER MIGRAINE

At the hospital, Velma Secora was struggling into her perfectly fitted nurse's uniform, standing behind the open linen closet door, only partially obscuring her from view. She was not at all bothered by the glances of autistic patients to her state of undress. This full-bodied, abundantly endowed woman was also being observed by attendant Carl Emory. Standing there in bra and slip and knowing he was looking at her, she continued to slowly roll up her stockings, leg propped on a stool. Emory then precipitously walked away as he noticed 'T,' Tino Vescaro, the other attendant, entering the ward. Vescaro stopped in his tracks, barely catching Emory's exit while Nurse Secora was buttoning her last button and closing the closet door. Even though Tino was not witness to the entire scene, he was absolutely certain as to what had just happened. And knowing Velma, he was also absolutely certain that as far as Velma was concerned, what had happened was not at all unusual.

*   *   *

I had a 7:30 P.M. meeting at the clinic. An emergency session had been set to deal with an unusual case of migraine. A man of sixty had been referred to the institute's clinic because his internist as well as a consulting neurologist could find no evidence, clinical or laboratory, to attribute the migraine to anything physical. They were both certain that the migraine was psychologically based, so they naturally sought consultation from our institute personnel—specialists in understanding and treating emotional and psychological disorders.

I needed to be at the clinic in any case because Jean had informed me that she and Richard had the three wooden crates transported back to the institute's library and had them stored in the back room under lock and key.

I still had a full day ahead of me. I had a meeting at Brentwood Hospital at noon, and then, finally, my meeting with Josh and his "bottles under the bed" at five, and then really finally, my 7:30 P.M. "migraine" consultation at the institute/clinic.

At Brentwood, the admissions building where new patients were housed was always at full capacity. A dozen patients at least, two nurses and two attendants on duty on the nine-to-five shift and after that, only one nurse and one attendant till the following day. With psychologists, social workers, and psychiatrists conducting therapy sessions in the three treatment rooms, making rounds, checking charts and medication regimens, having meetings in the conference room, and arranging for everything to work smoothly, and, in addition, recreational therapists, occupational therapists, transfer agents and various other personnel in and out of the place, the admissions building was a very busy place, indeed.

* * *

In contrast, sandwiched between the admissions and autistic "G" wards, was an abandoned section of the building. Entrance was gained through a locked door on the ground level within each ward, each adjacent to the nurse's stations. No one gave this desolate section any thought. It was shabby, dark, empty. We all knew it was condemned and that the stairs leading to the second level were unsafe. What almost no one really knew, was that this unused dark section did in fact retain electric power. It could be lit. And it also had running water. The bathroom was in a terrible state of disrepair, but the sink, tub, and toilet were still functional. The fact was that the electrical work as well as the plumbing were all still hooked up within the entire building. This extension had been condemned, obviously because of a crumbling infrastructure, yet apparently no one took the time or, had the interest to complete the dismemberment.

The questions were how Kruger managed to get in there without being seen, and what was his interest there in the first place? Actually it was easy since Kru-

ger had the keys to everything. Then there was the simple approach to the night nurse, Ms. Van Dame. He had done it many times before, and naturally it was in her interest to keep it quiet. He again told her he was going to work all night and that she could go home. And Kruger offered the attendant the opportunity to take one of the rooms and spend the rest of the night sleeping there. As he had responded many times in the past, the attendant was grateful and off to sleep he went. Thus, with Van Dame gone, the attendant dead to the world, the door to the upstairs patient rooms locked, and the door from the showers to the upstairs also locked, and after locking the front door to the admissions building itself, only then did Kruger enter that domain of darkness. Windows weren't a problem because they were boarded.

Unlocking the door and entering this dark world, Kruger made a bee-line through the foyer directly to one of the couches in the middle of the living room. He upended the pillows, directing the narrow beam of his flashlight on what he expected would be under the pillows. Nothing! He then leaned all the way down, aiming the flashlight under the couch itself. Nothing! He repeated this with each object of furniture in the room and carefully scanned the other rooms as well as the bathroom. Gone! Then he hesitated, reviewing it all. He remembered telling Billy to store the books under the pillows. Now it seemed that Billy had changed the hiding place. He recalled how Billy had started it.

"Dr. Kruger," Billy said anxiously. "It went over a hundred thousand dollars." He repeated it, as was his way. "It went over a hundred thousand dollars. You said it would never get to a hundred thousand dollars. I hate it. I hate it. You said."

Kruger had been alarmed. He felt it as a direct assault. Billy had never confronted him that way. Now Billy's panic was forming and so was Kruger's. But Kruger was afraid that Billy could lose it and maybe scream or even become violent. Kruger tried to remain calm.

"Billy," he said, "that's only because both necklaces sold for more than we figured. But my idea is to have them returned. Then we'll subtract the six thousand so that the grand total will be ninety-five thousand and not the not-good number."

Kruger knew not to name any number over ninety-nine thousand. Billy wouldn't be able to handle it. So Kruger started repeating a number several thousand less than ninety-nine thousand. "Ninety-five thousand, Billy. Ninety-five thousand. Okay? You see, I'm promising. Ninety-five thousand."

No. This was not luck. Kruger knew. "Ninety-five thousand" over and over until Billy, staring at him constantly, slowly began to relax. Knowing full well that Billy was obsessed with never reaching the hundred-thousand number, Kruger found the perfect strategy to disarm the panic, though he never tried to analyze the 'why' or 'who' of it. The fact was that Billy couldn't tolerate hearing that number, one-hundred thousand. For Billy, it was life or death.

And here was Kruger going over each detail of their conversation about the books and where to keep them. The only way Billy would assist Kruger in this bookkeeping was if he, Billy, could keep the records of all transactions, of all goods sold. And Kruger knew that it wasn't that Billy was keeping an eye on him or was insidious or surreptitious. No. Kruger knew very well that it was Billy's innocence within his pathology and nothing else. Kruger didn't have to worry about Billy as some mole or undercover agent. Furthermore, and most importantly, Kruger needed this employee who was indentured by law to, more or less, be permanently under Kruger's care—to work full time on this little project of theirs, which was making Kruger a rich man. Money didn't matter at all to Billy. Kruger got Billy whatever he needed—candy, snacks, sneakers, nothing of consequence. But Billy's need to maintain meticulous records was of a firmly anchored, unshakable, obsessive nature, and it coincided with Kruger's heist of many possessions stored in the property office. Kruger needed Billy as a full-time person to monitor the operation and to keep careful records of the loot. And Billy was perfect. Pity those back-ward patients whose possessions were pilfered. They were not going to leave that hospital so soon. Kruger would make sure of that. We're talking years, decades. If they didn't die there and were eventually released, they wouldn't have the slightest memory of what had been in their possession at the time of their hospitalization so many years earlier. And if someone did remember? So what? Goodbye.

So this is how Kruger's corruption seriously impacted the patients at the hospital. In effect he was taking their lives away by keeping them incarcerated because of his own nefarious purposes—essentially turning them into something other than viable people. Kruger created a miasma, relegating people to the netherworld. Ghosts!

Now we had a dead Billy on the one hand, and a frantic Kruger on the other. But connecting Kruger to Billy's death was another story. As for Kruger, his tenacity in searching for Billy's books now became his only imperative in life. He became infused with an Asperger-like obsessive spirit. Keep those books away from those detectives! But no matter what he did or where he searched, he couldn't find the books. They weren't in Billy's room or, for that matter, in Edward's room. And now, even in this crumbling domain, the books were nowhere to be found—not even behind the fireplace frame. He reluctantly exited this virtual place, locked the door, and checked the ward. The attendant was snoring.

At about the same time, a drama was beginning to unfold at the psychoanalytic institute/clinic. Kruger's henchmen, Tyrone and Manuel, were at it again. Kruger had gotten wind of the goings-on and instructed them to get into that locked back library room to see what was in the crates. They could have easily done this if they hadn't been interrupted by Jean, who returned after work to retrieve her tennis sneakers from her bottom desk drawer. When she asked them what they were doing there, Manuel, cool as a cucumber, answered that there was a leak in one of the floors above and that they needed to see whether any water damage had occurred to the ceiling. Jean unlocked the door, everyone looked at the ceiling, where of course no water damage was visible, and they left the room. As Jean locked the door, she told them the room should not be entered by anyone, for any reason, and that she would hold them personally responsible if that instruction wasn't complied with. Jean could be tough.

* * *

Jean told me that her Vatican contact, through a series of complex maneuvers, had managed to obscure the fact of the missing manuscript, and that a plan had been set into motion to get the crates back. She was relieved, and had been on the phone all that day formulating a travel strategy. We agreed that I would remain after the migraine presentation and we would discuss it then.

Finally, after leaving the hospital where I attended a nonsensical meeting, I arrived at my private office ready to see Josh about his bottles under the bed. It was close to 5 P.M. and I knew he would be prompt. I was pretty clear as to what Josh and I would talk about, and I knew he would be open. Josh was a mature, poised, and really bright eleven-year old. My only problem, which would take me a few minutes to navigate, was to shift my focus away from Billy and the hospital, and toward Josh and my therapy work with him.

Like his dad, indeed, Josh was prompt to the minute. I felt we could take care of this symptom in record time because I already understood, going in, some of the major dynamic underpinnings: one, that he was angry; two, that it was at someone—probably mother or father—and, three, that the symptom represented his wish. What that wish was we'd have to discover. What I did know was that the wish was visible in the form — the perverse form — of putting bottles under the bed. My job was to identify the target of his anger — the person — and elicit enough information from him so that I could help him crystallize, and then verbalize, the actual original wish. It would be important for him to be able to see that he, in fact, did have a wish, and to know specifically what that wish was. It would also be important to make the symbol understandable, to help him see that bottles under the bed related to a specific feeling — anger — about a specific person, and to some issue with that person. For me it's fascinating to anticipate that the symbol, like bottles under the bed, can be observed actually to be reconstituted so that the original form of the wish is revealed. Of course, to achieve this objective would require Josh's cooperation, interest, and, most importantly, his willingness to say things that might be embarrassing.

I had told Charley when he originally called to ask for my help that we were dealing with aggravation, not trouble. And I meant it. Despite the fact that Josh was becoming more and more obsessed with the bottles symptom, I knew that this sort of unique, exotic, odd, and highly condensed symptom actually could be knocked out with one well-placed hammer shot.

Josh was a big kid, built like his father. He told me that for the first time the symptom was beginning to scare him because it was happening all the time. He confirmed what Charley had originally told me — that at first it was occasional, then more frequent, and now it was taking up a lot of his time and he could no longer control it. I asked him how it started and he told me that about six or so months earlier he started feeling funny in his stomach and that he started collecting bottles and putting them under the bed. He said that when he did that, the bad feeling, like magic, disappeared.

What I needed to do here was to pin down the pivotal event that had occurred six months earlier in order to locate the *who*. Josh then spontaneously began telling me how difficult the symptom was to live with. He said that at first it was only happening once in a while, but that he started worrying about it when it was happening every day. Finally, he would even lie in bed and couldn't get to sleep because he would be thinking about it then, too.

Now story details were pouring out. After a while I steered him back to the beginning, when he first felt the bad feelings and hit upon the idea of curing them by putting bottles under the bed. The beauty of it was that Josh and I together were going to penetrate his unconscious. Perhaps a daunting task, perhaps not.

"Josh, I want to know a little more about when you first got the funny feeling and then got rid of it by putting bottles under the bed."

"Well, like I said, it was about six months ago and it just happened."

"No," I thought, "it didn't just happen." These things don't just happen. Nothing psychological comes out of the clear blue sky. There's no such thing as a phantom psychological symptom. Every symptom has a pivotal event that contains a person. Every one! When it comes to symptoms there are no visitations from the other world. There are no auras, devils, levitational forces, reincarnated residues, psychic crystal ball phenomena, ESP, talismanic curses, past-life regressions, channeling, rebirthing, astrological references, or anything else of this new-age stuff. Once the code of the formation of the symptom is understood, all hocus pocus is reduced to ashes.

I've always known that there was such a code. I began to detect it years ago in my clinical work. Freud confirmed my intuition, and Sebastian's discoveries enabled me to put it all together. At first I was astonished. I had synthesized it and I just looked at it. It was then that I finally knew what the physicists and theoretical mathematicians mean when they describe how beautiful some theoretical structure or model is, and even how the beauty of it begins to confirm for them the validity of the structure.

Knowing the symptom-code enabled me to direct Josh from any vantage point of his story. I knew exactly what to ask and where to go.

"So, Josh, what happened about six or so months ago? I have a hunch you might know about it already. You know, sometimes something happens and it affects you. And sometimes you remember it. Maybe something that upset you?"

He nodded, looked at me for a moment, and then told me that his parents had a big fight and threatened to divorce. His father's threat to divorce his mother is what stayed with him, while he felt his mother's counterthreat was only made in self-defense.

As he was talking I noticed that my identity suddenly shifted from a specialist determined to help Josh, to a stalking killer who was single-mindedly focused on assassinating the symptom. And I felt the symptom knew it! Now I began to focus on the *who*. Mom or Dad? I was almost certain it was his father, but I wanted to make sure.

"Josh, tell me, whose bed do you put the bottles under?"

I had not assumed I knew which bed it was. So far, we had been talking for less than ten minutes. I remembered that Kruger said it would take a year of twice-a-week sessions for the symptom to be cured, and that the hospital psychiatrist had said the symptom might turn out to be too dense to be handled without medication.

"My parents' bed. Right from the beginning, I always put the bottles under my parents' bed."

Now I was about to get the all important *who. All emotion takes an object.* I reasoned that when Josh told me under which side of the bed he placed the bottles, I'd have it. I knew he never placed the bottles in the middle. It would either be on his father's side or his mother's. I was looking for the singular object his emotion took.

"Under my father's side," he said quite naturally.

"Always?"

"Yes, only under my father's side."

His father was definitely the *who*, and now my job was to determine why that was so. For that answer I needed to examine further details surrounding the bottles. It was obvious to me that the bottles were heavily symbolic. But about what?

"Josh, what kinds of bottles go under the bed? I mean, are they big or small or a certain kind of bottle? You know?"

Again he answered easily.

"They all have to be medicine bottles, or about medicine," he said.

It then hit me like a locomotive—straight on. I had it. I understood the entire process of his symptom formation and I understood it in detail.

Josh needed his parents to stay together. It was his wish. When they threatened to divorce, he felt his world would be shattered and he became terribly frightened. That was what he was conscious of. Underneath, however, he was very angry, and the anger was directed toward his father, not his mother. Why? Because he believed his mother loved his father but that his father probably didn't love his mother. And the fact that it was his father who was threatening the integrity of Josh's world made Josh feel all the more angry.

What about the symbolism of the bottles? Medicine is to cure. Josh put medicine bottles under his father's side of the bed so that his father would be cured. Of what? Of not loving his mother. Then, of course, his father *would* love his mother and there would be no divorce. Josh's world would be salvaged, his sense of security protected, and his wish for his family to remain intact, met. Then, and only then, would he no longer harbor anger. And so each time he put bottles under the bed, all the funny or bad feelings disappeared because in his wish, the symbolic medicine would rise through the mattress into his father's corporeal being. Josh kept curing his father over and over again, so that each time he did that he also cured his own anger and hence, no symptom.

That was it. The definition of funny or bad feelings will probably always mean angry feelings. That was one of Sebastian's key discoveries and revealed just how sensitive and keen were his powers of observation. This allows us to understand that Josh's bad feelings were unconscious angry feelings translated into consciousness in the form of a funny-feeling stomach. And I explained it to him with the full expectation that it would cure him. But, I had an additional plan that involved the final "doing" component. I told him I wanted to see the three of them together—him, his father, and mother. He first hesitated, then we talked more about it, and then he agreed.

I was convinced we had penetrated this symptom and were about to entirely erase its power. Josh would forever be free of compulsively putting bottles under the bed. No more funny-feeling stomach.

We had reached the answer in all of about twenty minutes but he wanted to talk more. We wound up talking about the tensions of life. I told him that sometimes tensions are more serious, sometimes less serious, and that the objective in therapy, as in life, is to struggle better. I remembered that Freud said it differently—he mused that the objective in psychoanalysis is to turn real misery into ordinary unhappiness. My take on it is that active struggle can get to be interesting.

Josh left the office at about 5:40, having spent slightly less than the usual forty-five minutes. He did a great job at the session and, for sure, no longer felt lost. I still had more than an hour before I would consult with the other specialists at the institute's clinic on the patient with an extraordinarily severe migraine.

* * *

Talk about having been lost. It was Stroud who uncovered the fact that the hospital didn't even have records of Billy's origins—no birth certificate, nothing. He and Grillo were interviewing everyone they could get their hands on at the hospital as well as institute/clinic in their ongoing investigation into Billy's death, the violent attack of the attendant at the hospital, the shooting of the statue at the clinic, as well as the exhibitionist's display. All told, they had interviews scheduled for perhaps sixty or seventy people: doctors, patients, other staff and personnel. They were hoping that something would turn up. And so it did.

Grillo's bent was to dig deep in each interview, but that took too long. What was needed here was an intimidator, someone who was not going to fool around. Shake it up and let's see what falls out. In this case, the Grillos of the world weren't as efficient as the Strouds. And indeed, it fell out.

Stroud had his man. He was interviewing Carl Emory, the attendant who was supervising the ward when Tommy Gersh and I were looking in on Edward. Stroud was telling everyone he interviewed, including this attendant, that if anyone knew anything about Billy Soldier's activities but didn't report it, and more especially if such information was ultimately important in the understanding of Billy's murder, that he could assure them that he would personally see to it that that person was indicted for aiding and abetting, and further, that he would use his considerable influence to insist on jail time. And Stroud never smiled during these interrogations.

With that lead-in, Carl Emory just spilled. "The thing was," he said, "and I don't even know if this figures in, but the thing was that Nurse Secora was always interested in Billy. She would even visit him on Sundays, but it wasn't considered a visit because she was the chief nurse. I had nothing to do with Billy. It's just that I noticed it. I saw it. I mean I used to think: What's she doin' with Billy? I mean she's not his mother or anything. And she's a nurse. I never saw that sort of thing. It never really happens that someone on staff looks in on a patient on Sunday. Never happens."

Emory stopped but Stroud knew there was more. Soberly, Stroud said: "What else?"

"I saw Secora put her arms around Billy. It wasn't like a love thing, like hugging. It was more like she was holding him, her whole body against his body. 'T,' he's another attendant, saw it too. Man, he got mad when he saw it, like, like he was another person. But the funny thing was he didn't act like he was mad."

Stroud didn't let him breathe. "Exactly what was the conversation between you two?"

Emory took a second. "You gotta remember, I'd been on the ward less than a week. They transferred me from Recreational Therapy to Nurse Secora's ward. It's only temporary till they appoint another attendant. Then I'm going back to R.T., uh, I mean Recreational Therapy. So I didn't really know Nurse Secora or 'T' or Billy or Edward or anyone. But I couldn't help noticing Nurse Secora. I mean, c'mon, she's comin' at you with that body. You gotta notice it if you're alive. Know what I mean?"

"C'mon," Stroud insisted, "what was the conversation?"

*"I said to 'T' something like, How'd ya like to be in **her** arms?"*

"And?" Stroud prompted.

"And 'T' just stomped off. He hasn't said a word to me since. If you ask me, that guy's as strange as some of the patients. As a matter of fact Secora's even more strange than he is. The way she uses that body, that's no accident. There's no one that doesn't wanna make a move on her. No one! Yeah, and the way she would hold the kid. And the kid would just stand there. He wouldn't move a muscle."

And that was that. Stroud had something. What it was, he didn't know. But he did know it was important. And he got it in record time. Emory was his fourth interview out of eleven people assembled in the waiting room awaiting their turn. Stroud was happy. He assured Emory that he appreciated his help.

Stroud immediately called Grillo over.

"Joe, I think I got somethin'."

*　　*　　*

I took care of some administrative work, then headed over to the institute/clinic, and still arrived about forty-five minutes before the meeting. Before long, most of the consulting group had assembled—about eight other staff clinicians, plus Dr. Kruger, Dr. Bird, and me. Dr. White, the clinical director still had not arrived.

As we milled about and socialized, it startled me to see Detectives Stroud and Grillo standing there holding their coats. They spotted me and asked to talk. I became nervous, almost instantly realizing that beneath my nervousness they were making me angry. The problem was that I couldn't feel the anger. I could only feel my anxiety. Why the hell was I anxious? The answer I gave myself was that they were making me feel guilty about something I had nothing to do with. I obviously didn't kill Billy, and had nothing to do with the defaced statue. But I thought, what they don't know is that I'm receiving stolen manuscripts. I could reason that I was angry because they were making me feel a little helpless. Whenever I saw them, I could feel myself trying extra hard to be smart, on my toes. It was clear to me that I was trying to be strong in the face of obvious greater strength. But why was I comparing strengths? I didn't do anything, for crying out loud.

"Dr. Kahn, we happened to be in the neighborhood and decided to see if you were here. We need to understand something about split personalities and we came across your article on *Multiple Personality as Symptom*."

I instantly had the thought: They think I'm a multiple! They think I killed Billy and don't realize it because my other personality did it. Of course, that was ridiculous.

"Okay, how can I help? By the way, why are you interested in multiple personality? And how'd you get to my paper? Or better, *why* did you get to my paper?" I paused, then quickly said, "Mind if I ask?"

I thought: "Man, I came right out with it."

"No, not at all," Stroud said. Grillo was watching us. I had the further thought that Grillo tended to be introspective, to consider things carefully. I guess it was the way he was observing us. Maybe observing me. "Well, it's like this," Stroud said. "You see, we've been asking people both here and at the hospital, like colleagues of yours, all sorts of things. You've been singled out as the one with the biggest interest in symptoms. So we're just checking everything out and Joe here got one of your reprints on this multiple personality business, so we're interested in it."

"But why?" I asked. "What do you want to know about it?"

"We're interested in the whole idea of the different emotions in the separate personalities. Like in one personality the other doesn't know what the first one did. Like could one of the personalities commit a crime and the other doesn't know it? I mean we do hear about this from other cases and the movies and court trials. You know?"

Now I got it. "So Billy might have been murdered or rather killed, whatever, by someone who doesn't realize it because one of the other personalities did it, and since I wrote the paper, naturally you'd ask me about it. Right?" I didn't wait for an answer. "And of course, I myself might be a multiple and not even know it. Right? So that I'm a prime suspect in the Billy murder. Right?"

Hooray, I felt. My anxiety was gone. I noticed it instantly. The way I said my piece sounded like I was angry. And I noticed that, too. My anger was freed. How about that? And, of course, no anger, no anxiety. My symptom was gone because my anger got unrepressed and expressed directly to the *who*. The amazing thing to me is that I didn't even know it was happening until after I did it.

"Hey, Doc, c'mon, calm down. We can understand why you feel that way. Most people feel guilty when they're questioned. We notice it all the time."

That was Grillo talking. The consummate detective. He'll nice you to death and then he'll nail you.

"Okay, Doc," Stroud said. "We were really wondering if you thought anyone on the staff or especially any patient in the hospital, maybe on Billy's ward could be a split." And he continued. "You see, we think if that was the case, the split part that came out would be the aggressive personality. Is there anyone that's being treated for split personality at the hospital or at this clinic that you know about?"

I was thinking that that was really grasping at straws. Man oh man, what was going on here?

"I haven't seen a multiple either here or at the hospital in about two or three years. Every once in a while we get one. But not for a while now."

"Doc, the truth is," Grillo continued, "that in your article the thing about the three personalities got me interested." Stroud then jumped in: "So what about that aggressive part, Doc?"

What they were referring to was the basic structure of the split or multiple personality. In my paper I had outlined this basic structure as containing distinct personalities: in the several cases I've seen, it was all the same—there was a normal one called the host, an aggressive one, and a sexual one. What they were saying is that someone at the hospital could be such a split or multiple personality. It was obvious to me that they liked this lead because it could tie the whole case together with one suspect. The host (so-called normal person), wouldn't know that there were any other surrogate people in him, and therefore, wouldn't ever know what these surrogates were doing. However, each of the other two, the aggressive and sexual, would, indeed, know of the presence of one another as well as of the host. In this way, the murder of Billy, the attack on the attendant, and the exhibitionism, all at the hospital, and even the shooting of the statue at the clinic, could be pinned on one person. And since I wrote the paper, then I couldn't help but feel that they must be suspecting me—no matter what they said.

"You know, Doc," Grillo said, "my favorite part is the *why* of it. It's a great psychological strategy. Because the person can't admit to having sexual feelings or feelings of violence, then they make themselves into three different people—one for the normal part, one for the sexual, and one for the violent one. It's nuts, but I guess they think it's better than nothing." He paused. "So, Doc," he continued, "is there anyone you know that could fit that description, like not being able to put together the aggressive and sexual parts with the normal part?"

"Listen, guys," I answered, "do you really think a multiple personality type is operating here? Let's get real. And by the way, it's now called a dissociative identity disorder."

"Well," said Grillo, "we're checking everyone on staff here and at the hospital, so we're asking questions. And we get information about the likes and dislikes and special interests of these people. And you've published articles on the subject, so we're asking about it. It's nothing incriminating. By the way," he continued, "you mention that when these splits shifted back to the normal personality after an episode of either one or the other two, they sometimes complained of headaches. Is that in the majority of cases?"

"Look," I said, "the headache is just another symptom that shows the person's wish. The wish in such a person is to be whole. You know, to accept that the different parts are normal to have. You might say the person is *aching* for that to happen, to be normal—to have a normal head. So the person is aching for it—as in head-*ache*. Get it? The symptom is the wish, so that the headache is the wish to be normal—whole."

Again, there was a pause. "I was thinking," Grillo said, "do you know anyone who gets headaches or complains of headaches a lot? I mean here or at the hospital. "

"Okay," I said. "I have to admit, it is, in fact, an interesting hypothesis even if it is far-fetched. And it is far-fetched. Very far. And to answer your question, sometimes it's a headache, sometimes fatigue, and sometimes the person has what we call a smile of denial. Kind of like an awkward smile." Then for a change I did the pausing and waiting. Grillo was also pausing but Stroud broke the silence and just thanked me for my time. We said our goodbyes, but we also knew it was just intermission.

At that point, so help me, Dr. White, the clinical director, forty minutes late, walked into the room to announce that the migraine patient had not been ready up to that point but was ready now. Trying for humor, he said, "Anyone for headaches?"

* * *

The meeting was called to order by Dr. White. He told us the patient, Mr. James Dunbar, had an unrelenting migraine in its third day, was unable to sleep, and on top of that, it was hard for him to stay awake as well. The migraine was so bad that the patient asked to be put under general anesthesia, which of course the internist was not going to do. All neurological tests were negative. He was a man of sixty, married with no children, and partially deaf.

The patient entered, walking slowly and somewhat stooped. He was apparently trying to prevent any physical jostling of his body. Dr. White made the introductions. Dunbar, about a stocky five-foot ten, was holding his head with one hand and motioning with the other from his ear, around his eye, and across the top of his head. Dunbar whispered, "I have to speak softly and I can't move too suddenly. I have a terrible vise killing my head, my ear and my eye. It won't go away, it won't stop." He told us the headache medication didn't help and that he had this kind of migraine twice before in his life but could never figure out what caused it. He said it also made him nauseous.

Dr. White went around the room giving each consultant a chance to question the patient. Of course, everyone had something to ask. Feigning sensitivity, Kruger started it. He asked Mr. Dunbar whether any of these attacks would suddenly disappear if he got some good news or if an event was taking place that he enjoyed. Mr. Dunbar answered no by slowly and slightly moving his head.

Typical Kruger alchemy—entirely irrelevant. I was embarrassed just to be in the room with him. Ralph Bird shot me a look. Bird had his faults, but he was knowledgeable about diagnosis. Kruger was saying that the migraine was a hysterical symptom and that there were times when it could be hard to distinguish between malingerers and hysterics. For that matter, it's even harder to distinguish between malingerers and paranoids.

Dr. White did not pursue it. No one in the room seemed to give Kruger's question the slightest credence. My colleague, Sully Polite, leaned over to me and, through clenched teeth, said, "Non compas mentis. The guy is blotto."

By the half hour point we had determined that Dunbar was born almost entirely hearing challenged and not partially deaf as the chart indicated. Everyone in the room noticed that his speech was awkward. We also learned that he was in financial straits and could not afford the lifestyle to which he and his wife had become accustomed. He told us he was depressed and that he felt everything was falling down around him.

Dr. White felt encouraged because he thought we had located the source of the problem. Depression was the diagnosis, his financial difficulty, his tension, and his hearing problem exacerbated it all. There was a buzz in the room, everyone talking at once. White called for order and actually thanked Dunbar for coming in. He told Dunbar that we would discuss a treatment plan and convey this plan to his internist immediately. With that, my iconoclastic psychiatrist colleague with the ponytail and unlikely name of Dr. Sullivan Polite, interrupted White and practically insisted that Dunbar stay a while longer. I agreed with Polite and said so. It was my first comment. I knew Dr. White was way ahead of himself. White then asked Dunbar to wait in the anteroom.

This was a perfect example of a problem I'd become aware of in understanding a case. Even trained clinicians frequently have difficulty seeing that the information they've accumulated is too general. In order to get to the real issues, you must have *details*. And, of course, the important redundancy is that *details had to be specific*. It takes a certain kind of concentration not to assume that you have the details just because the information sounds good. Since I'd been focusing on symptoms for some time now, I'd become especially attuned to instantly identifying what was specific and what wasn't. And I'd come to realize how difficult that is. What are the operative details, the linkages, those concatenations that trip the lock? And, furthermore, what are the steps that don't trip the lock? What Dunbar had told us at each juncture was general, not specific. There was no way anyone could help him cure that migraine with the information he had given us. The devil was in the details, and we didn't have that devil.

We knew he was born almost completely deaf. How are we going to use this information to help him? Second, we knew he was in financial straits and could no longer afford his lifestyle. What lifestyle? Is he being deprived of something important with respect to lifestyle? The fact that he was depressed didn't give us the slightest idea of how to understand the migraine either. So what we got was—nothing. We were lost. A dozen professionals there, and as far as I was concerned, nothing happened.

I had many questions to ask Dunbar. I wanted to pursue them either there or in private consultation. If nothing happened here, I would nominate myself. Yet, I was also plagued by my sense of urgency about meeting with Jean and Richard later, and hearing anything new about Sebastian's materials.

Happily, Sully Polite recommended we bring Dunbar back for a more in-depth interview with a smaller team to further track his symptom. White agreed and without asking, appointed Polite, me, and himself. The three of us talked it over and regrettably I asked to be excused, explaining that I had a prior important meeting that I now had to get to. I asked that Sully conduct the interview and White agreed. I told Sully to round up the usual suspects in Dunbar's life—at the most, four or five people in anyone's life—and see if he could get Dunbar to talk about the one with whom he might be angry. I also suggested that he try to ascertain Dunbar's basic wish. My hope was that merely talking about his symptom in relation to these variables might in itself help Dunbar dilute the symptom. Therefore, Sully knew to look for the anger and the *who*. I also told Sully that in treating migraines the patient may suddenly feel something like tectonic plates moving in his head. If that should happen it will most likely signal the breaking-up or loosening of the migraine. The crux of the matter rests in making the unconscious conscious. In all such cases this means that anger is made conscious, especially toward the *who*, and becomes a powerful factor in the cure. It's about the moment of truth when the anticipated actual disappearance of the symptom is realized.

I thought: "Good luck, Sully. Good luck, White. Good luck, Dunbar."

· 9 ·

THE BODY WATCHER

They were all on the ward. Patients all over the place: 'T' escorting two of the children to the play room; an occupational therapist holding the attention of several of the other autistic children; two administrative secretaries talking at their desks; people coming and going and, Carl Emory assisting Nurse Secora at the linen closet. She had him hold some bed sheets which, on her tippy-toes, she was collecting from the very top shelf of the closet.

As she stretched directly in front of Carl reaching for the sheets, he didn't know what to think. Was she giving him a signal? He felt she was being seductive and he was immediately turned on. Every time she stretched and then added another sheet to the growing mountain in Carl's arms, she aimed an unmistakable, direct, lascivious smile into his face — head tilted down, eyes looking up at him.

They were only partially obscured by the door to the closet. So after several of these apparent come-ons, Carl moved a step closer to her, answering her ostensible cue. He thought she then answered him by brushing up against him, her breasts grazing the length of his arm. She then turned away from him and ever so slightly leaned back against him. He remembers the perfume and the intoxicating bouquet of her hair.

No more guessing. He was in it now. He freed his right arm by resting the weight of the sheets against the inside of the closet, still holding them with his left arm and supporting the weight also with the side of his body. He then reached around her with his freed right arm and drawing her in, felt and then caressed her large and protruding breast.

Just at that moment, 'T,' returning from the play room, froze in his tracks. It was the second time he had seen them suspiciously together. Secora knew it would happen. She timed it. She then wheeled around and, glaring at Emory, shouted:

"How dare you! How dare you!"

Carl was startled. Bewildered. He knew what was happening was nuts, yet looked around as if to say, "I didn't mean it," or, "I didn't do it," or, "I'm sorry," or, "I'm not sure what happened—I thought you wanted me to." Carl saw 'T' staring at them. Glaring was more like it.

Nurse Secora backed two steps away, shook her finger at Carl and said: "If you ever touch me again I'll bring you up on charges of sexual harassment. And I could do that right now. You apologize to me immediately."

Carl was accused and pronounced guilty before he could say anything. He looked to 'T' for help but instantly realized that was not a good idea.

"I'm sorry, Mrs. Secora. I'm sorry. I thought. . . ."

"What do you mean you 'thought!?' And it's Chief Nurse Secora," she bellowed. "Do you understand? Say it," she commanded. "Say ' I'm sorry, Chief Nurse Secora.'"

She had him. And 'T' was watching. 'T' could be a witness—would be a witness.

"I'm sorry, Chief Nurse Secora. You know, uh, it'll never happen again."

He looked toward 'T,' who, without saying a word, was now walking out of the ward. With 'T' still in earshot, she demanded: "Why are you turning your head away from me? Look directly at me when I speak to you. Do you understand?"

She now held the power of his job over his head, and that's really what she was threatening. He knew it. But he also saw that Secora's response was way over the top. So he sensed that this was something else. And then it hit him. She was being commanding, like a dominatrix. That's why she was ordering him to say this or that—exactly! That's what it felt like. Her real objective was to make him obey—more specifically, to make him feel like obeying. He even knew that if Chief Nurse Secora didn't have that sword of Damocles over him, he could possibly feel turned on by it all. It dawned on him. If he did what she said and went along with it, maybe, no, definitely, he would then get all of her. At some point in her domination, she would capitulate and permit him access. He decided to be eager to listen to her. He was going to obey her.

"Chief Nurse Secora, I am definitely sorry." She wasn't forgiving. 'It wasn't good enough,' he thought. And then he remembered how she wanted him to say it, exactly. He wasn't saying it exactly. With his fear receding, he said it exactly—and eagerly:

"I'm sorry, Chief Nurse Secora."

* * *

Jean and Richard were eagerly awaiting me. The library was dim, with only the lights in the front room lit. Jean burst out immediately, "What in the world took you so long? That was an interminable meeting. We've been waiting on tenterhooks."

"Is everything okay? I take it the crates are gone?"

"Gone? You should have seen how they went. First of all, as soon as we got home I called my contact at the Vatican. It was 6 A.M. in Rome. He created some mutational event in order to get the crates back undetected. And he didn't want me to ask him about it, so I didn't. Richard and I originally met him at the Vatican ecumenical library meeting and he struck me as being such a dedicated person."

"Jean, what happened?" She was talking a blue streak.

"I'm getting to it. And we have a tremendous surprise for you. But it's your turn to be patient. We're so excited. He was the one who asked us to get the crates back to the institute. A panel truck marked *York Seminary* pulled up and out poured six priests in full regalia—collars and all. Two for each crate. They were in and out in seconds. Then one of them handed me this note."

Jean gave me the note to read. It was typed on plain, unidentified stationery.

> Jean, S.'s Diary No. 1 will be delivered to you at the institute tomorrow 9 P.M. New York time. It's the first of six. Please be careful with it. I'll have it picked up the next day at 9 P.M."

The note was not signed. I looked at Jean, who was wide-eyed and smiling. Richard was equally excited. Apparently, Sebastian had a number of diaries and we would have the first one for twenty-four hours. Richard sat down and in uncharacteristically bravado fashion said, "We're involved! We are involved!" He accented the second syllable.

But Jean noticed my mood. "Glenn, what's the matter? I've been meaning to tell you this—I think some medication could help."

She was probably right about that, but at the moment I was actually happy about the news. We were going to get Sebastian's diary. But again, my mood was first chronically affected by Katie, and secondarily by Stroud and Grillo. What I hadn't said to Jean was that I was concerned with what felt like police circling me and making the circumference smaller and smaller.

"It's the whole thing at once, Jean. Katie, Billy, our little escapade, and to add to it those same detectives were here earlier tonight about the bullets in the statue. You know? And who do they spot first?"

"Now look," Jean said. "You're not a naive person, but you are innocent!"

"How do you know I'm innocent?" I said. "Maybe I'm a dissociated identity disordered, split, multiple personality, and I don't know it?"

That stopped her. It looked like she thought I was being funny, but she wasn't sure. Anyway, she disregarded me and we agreed to a 7:30 P.M. meeting the next day, more than an hour before the diary was to be delivered.

We talked about it all for a few minutes, but it was only after she asked me how I was coping with the Katie situation that, without thinking, I blurted out that my obsession with Katie meant that I was actually angry at her; she wasn't careful crossing that street. And it's that exact anger that keeps me from sinking into a permanent despondency while at the same time fuels and permanently locks my obsession into place. Yes, I indeed understood it.

My mood lifted.

* * *

Rita phoned at ten o'clock the next morning.

"I don't know what you did last night, but the instructions you gave Dr. Polite were, according to him, indispensable. He said they worked beautifully and by the time the interview ended the patient's migraine had actually subsided. Dr. Polite and Dr. White are telling everyone in sight. Dr. Polite said he would call you. He said the *who* was Dunbar's wife. Now everyone wants to talk to you about their patients. Dr. Gerard called asking for a consultation on a patient of his who wakes up in sweats—he said usually twice a week. Then Dr. Sherman called about a patient of his who has strangling fantasies. He apologized to me for being so specific but felt that if you knew exactly what the symptom was, you would understand his urgency and call him right back. Then Dr. DeLuca called. He has a patient with 'a holding symptom' is how he put it. And he said she becomes mute. As I hung up with Dr. DeLuca, the phone rang again and it was Dr. White himself. He has a patient who is obsessed with death and would like to talk to you about it."

I told Rita to return each call and ask whether they wanted me to consult with them over the phone or actually see the patients. Then I hung up the receiver and shifted to Rita's list: sweats; strangling; holding; and, death. I thought: "People never fail to amaze me."

* * *

The amazing thing was that at the hospital someone had managed to gain entry to the abandoned section of the admissions building—to that dark, remote off-limits place. It was a man. He was stark naked. His penis was conspicuous and even in the dark, and despite its flaccid state, seemed large. He was about six foot-three or four and appeared to weigh about two hundred or so pounds. He was sinewy and muscled. He pushed the fireplace frame out of its position to reveal a little vestibule-like closet. Articles of clothing were hanging over boxes that were stacked on top of one another. It seemed that he was putting on nylons and smoothing them out on his legs. Then he slid his arms into bra straps and stuffed the bra cups with some material. Hanging there in the closet were blouses, dresses, and sweaters. He was stroking them. He began to apply makeup—first, some kind of cream, spreading it evenly over his face, then another substance over his face, and then lipstick and rouge. He then wiped the facial cosmetics off and after taking all that time dressing as a woman, he put his pants on over nothing but skin, put on his work-shirt over a blouse he had selected, and tied his boots.

It was early afternoon, not long after lunch. Everyone was around. All the while in the ward outside that room, several autistic children were noisily active. At one point Chief Nurse Secora went to the far side of the corridor to supervise some patients. 'T' was nowhere to be seen. At about the same time, in the dark room, the man replaced the fireplace frame to its original position and went to the door, opening it a crack. He could see several of the autistic children as well as Nurse Secora at the end of the corridor. Striding out of the darkness and into the ward he blithely exited the building. He was a large man transformed into a statuesque Amazon woman but then cross-dressing to look like a man.

* * *

Arriving at the office at about noon, I only had three sessions on my calendar including Josh and his folks. It would then be about 4:30, and I would catch a quick late lunch and head for the institute/clinic and Sebastian. As I reached for the phone to call Rita and begin my consultations with sweat, strangling, holding, and death, my cellphone rang. It was Ted. He was excited. He told me that only three plates were problematic although some words and phrases were still readable. Everything else was good. He also said Jill confirmed that we got it all.

I was electrified. I felt the challenge was winnable. I felt confident that I could reconstruct any of the fragmented passages Ted referred to because I had read it all.

"I'll tell Rita to set up a meeting for the three of us," I said. "But before that happens I'd like Jill to transcribe everything you have."

I was rolling now. I dialed Rita. Before I could say hello, she was all over me.

"The phone is ringing off the hook. Dr. White wants to know if you can present your work at the next staff meeting. It's in two weeks. He wants to print notices and..."

I timed it so that I could cut her off. "Tell him okay. Two weeks is fine."

She must have timed me because before I could continue, she said that Dr. Sherman urgently needed to speak with me. He answered Rita's call on the first ring.

"Glenn, thanks a lot for calling. I think it's an emergency, and I'm worried about what this guy could do." Sherman told me that his patient, a 45-year-old man, who had never acted out any serious behavior, was in bed with a woman when he suddenly felt he wanted to strangle her. Then he couldn't function sexually, became agitated and depressed, and in what seemed like a split second, he dressed and was out of the apartment heading for a cab. He then called Sherman in distress.

The patient told Sherman that this woman he was with was talking about her previous relationship non-stop and that the patient was bored to tears about it but sat there and listened. Sherman confirmed my hunch that the patient had strong narcissistic impulses. I told him the patient was probably having a solipsistic episode. "Narcissistic impatience is what it means," I said. "Bored really means angry." I explained she was not talking about him so that he wanted to tell her to stop talking about others because that's what was making him angry. He couldn't tell her to stop and he suppressed or repressed his anger. The anger was then directed to the self and he popped a symptom—an intrusive thought of strangling. The intrusive thought represents his wish for her to stop talking about herself and others and begin talking about him. He's not really in danger of strangling her. His problem is that he can't get her to talk about him. So as soon as she starts talking about him, no more symptom. The strangling thought is just another way for him to say "stop talking," or "shut up" or more accurately, "shut the fuck *up!*"

That basically was it. Rita was back on the line. I reassured her that it went well. Rita thought she was my mother. She then tried Dr. White, who wasn't in, and then Dr. DeLuca, who was.

When DeLuca got on the phone, he was off and running. He told me the patient was a woman with a holding symptom. "Mutism—sometimes can last two or three days," he said. I'm pretty sure you want to know that the *who* is her husband."

I suggested she might be angry at her husband and the holding is her protest against him. After some more discussion, I told him my guess was that when he stops withholding, then so will she.

Rita was back. "I've got Dr. Gerard. He's waiting for you."

"Glenn, I got this man who wakes up two or three times a week drenched in sweat. Soaks everything—sheets, covers. His wife has to change him *and* the bedding as he lies there bewildered." He didn't have to say much more because it washed over me like an epiphany. "The wife sounds like an angel," I said, "but I'll bet she's the *who*. She may be giving him a hard time about something and so he can't get what he wants. Like he's angry and sweating bullets to get whatever it is he wants. Get it? His wish is for her to stop making him sweat, *sweat* being the operative term. So you tell me, what's her problem?"

"That's it," he said. "The guy is desperate for a family and she wants to wait, to do it in her time, if at all. That's it."

And that was it again. Rita was back, but I told her I couldn't do more.

* * *

Carl Emory did everything Velma told him to do. And he looked forward to work every day. Supervising him from the nurse's station on the ward, Velma issued instructions which Carl unfailingly obeyed. He was deferent and courteous to a fault. But Chief Nurse Secora was never appreciative. Instead, she was stern with him, and in an obvious way. But he didn't care. Because with him, it was all pretense. He was biding his time, all the while pretending to be obedient. He made her feel that she was in control, when he knew that it was he who really had mastery over the whole act.

*Only one thing bothered him. It started a couple of days after the incident at the linen closet. He began masturbating. Compulsively. And only with the image of Chief Nurse Secora as his fantasy. All the previous fantasies that had excited him, were no longer interesting. He also knew that if he had someone to talk to, like a therapist, he would wonder whether he really had control over the situation, or whether Chief Nurse Secora was in some way **actually** in control. What he knew for sure, though, was that he liked calling her Chief Nurse Secora, even to himself. He knew that that excited him. So, who was in control?*

'T' saw it all. The thought that Carl was sharing time and space with Velma filled him with jealousy and rage—emotions he denied having. But he longed to do something about it! He didn't want it to be the three of them. He wouldn't let that happen!

* * *

The three of them. I ushered them in—Charley, Josie, and, of course, Josh. I started out by reviewing the deal—that it was okay for everything to be discussed. Although it was a bit awkward at first, when we all started to talk, it became natural.

I then carefully spelled it all out, essentially telling them that Josh got worried about a possible divorce, the result of which was the symptom of putting bottles under the bed. "The bottles were medicine bottles to cure you, Charley," I said. "Josh felt you were going to divorce Josie—and he postponed calling me for an appointment because he really couldn't face putting it all in words."

"Josh, Dad and I aren't getting divorced! We love each other," exclaimed Josie.

Charley kept nodding in the affirmative, and Josh kept looking over at him. Charley indicated he didn't know how Josh had gotten the idea about a divorce, but Josie remembered and recounted the event. Then Charley remembered. Josh looked at me. I shrugged my shoulders as though to say, "I told you that was all there was to it."

In the end, Josh was relieved, especially now, since he had heard it directly from his parents. Since the entire conflict—including his anger toward his father—was made conscious, I was certain he would never be putting bottles under the bed again.

Everyone was happy. Charley said he wanted to talk about his body watcher, but that he would call me later. I told Josh I wanted him to call me just to check in. As they left, Charley gave me his great big smile and Josie hugged me.

After my sessions, all the phone calls, and the excitement of the previous days, I was beginning to feel a bit spacey. It was almost 5 P.M. I decided to call Rita because I knew I still had to speak to George White before meeting with Jean and Richard, and, of course, and most importantly, actually seeing Sebastian's diary.

*   *   *

"I've got him on the phone now," Rita said.

"Glenn, hello. I'm sorry I couldn't get back to you sooner."

White immediately summarized the case of a sixty-year-old woman obsessed with death, overcome with anxiety, and trying to manage insomnia. We talked a while and White indicated that this patient was constantly complaining about her husband. It became evident that she had become very angry at her husband because he had declared bankruptcy. I guessed that her anger was translated into her obsession with her own death reflecting a more basic unconscious wish, for his. That was the key. White then felt he had a theme to work with.

I quickly buzzed Rita again. Before I had a chance to say anything she told me she had Dr. Granger on the phone. "Last call," I thought.

Charley said he couldn't talk with Josh and Josie there. We chatted some and then he said, "Okay, what do I do with my body watcher?" He gave me a thumbnail sketch of the case and mentioned a conflict this doctor, who was his patient, was having with the chief of service at the hospital. I told him I was weary and could only conjure up one idea. It concerned the conflict — the probable anger at this chief of service, who I was guessing was the *who*.

"Let's say he was angry with this departmental chairman and wished him dead," I said. "Then he represses the anger and acts out the whole thing by repetitively looking at corpses. It could be that the wish is for the *who,* this chief of service to be one of the corpses. He keeps repeating the act of finding this person as a corpse each time."

We talked a bit more. I could tell he wanted me to get in there with my sleeves rolled up but there was really nothing more I could do, especially since I had had them rolled up even before we started to talk. I told him, "Charley, remember, every symptom is 'bottles under the bed'. Every one!"

I told Rita no more calls. Then I reviewed the consultations I'd already done: sweats, strangling, holding, death, bottles under the bed, and the body watcher. I began contemplating my three psychoanalytic patients I still needed to see. First was the tenor, whose stage fright I'm beginning to understand as a psychosexual identity problem in which unconsciously he's angry because he believes the audience will look at him and see a woman. Next, the passive-aggressive patient, who tells me she wants to be my fantasy "life-partner," and stay in therapy with me forever; she doesn't yet know that unconsciously it's really her wish for me to predecease her — she wants me to die first — a fantasy in which she waits me out and in that way gets her revenge — passive-aggressive, passive type, all the way. Finally, the patient who is obsessed with Mario Puzo and Francis Coppola's Godfather saga, but is unconsciously really wishing to be all-powerful himself in order to justify his rage at his father for making him feel so helpless.

Clinically, that would be enough for the day. At 6:30 my treatment day would be over. In a few hours I would be in possession of Sebastian's diary: the diary of a monk who lived five hundred years ago. Although it had been translated at the end of the 19th century, this diary had never been critically read. Now it had to be spirited across a continent and an ocean to get to me, and the gravity of it boggled my mind. I knew that at the end of the 19th century or at the beginning of the 20th, Fiscali, the Italian psychiatrist, had already gotten access to Sebastian's scientific material and had it translated. The identity of the original translator was a mystery. I was curious about whether his translation would faithfully reflect 15th century syntax. The main point however, was that I was grateful to be getting the translation at all. And the topper was that this was Sebastian's diary—his life.

I headed over to the institute/clinic.

· 10 ·

Doubled Over

*Detectives Stroud and Grillo were hard at work following the remote pos-
sibility that a multiple-personality type might be connected to Billy's death.
They reasoned that since my study on multiple-personality/dissociative identity
disorder had gained so much notoriety, the hospital where I consulted would
be a place where multiples might gravitate. They decided to check on the two
major headache centers in the city because I as well as others had noted that
headaches frequently appear when multiples morph out of the alternate personality and into their host identity. The first was at the Cornell Medical Center.
They began by checking for names of anyone in the program at Cornell who
also worked at Brentwood, Kruger's hospital.*

*The answer was negative. Then Grillo and Stroud paid a visit to the Head-
ache Research Project, an experimental program using biofeedback, relaxation
techniques, and visual imagery designed to alleviate several of these headache
conditions.*

*The detectives were lucky there. Three names of employees at Brentwood
appeared on the screen. Each of these employees was visited and questioned.
The last of the three was Tino Vescaro, 'T.' Too good to be true.*

*They quickly found him. Like Stroud, he was strong, tall, handsome, muscular.
Stroud standing eye to eye with 'T' was a sight. Stroud launched right into it. "Mr.
Vescaro, you remember us?" It was more an assumption and less a question. "We
interviewed Nurse Secora a few days ago and you were on the ward then."*

"Yes, sir," he said. "Sure I remember you."

"We're making inquiries about people who get headaches. We know you visit the Headache Project for treatment. Is that right?"

"Yes," he said, "I've been going there since the project began, about three or four months ago. I saw their ad for subjects so I called them. I've had a bad history with headaches. Since I was a kid."

The detectives tried to squeeze out some connection to any odd behavior, but came away feeling that he was "a real innocent guy," as Stroud said to Grillo when they were driving away. "Yeah," Grillo answered, "but neither of us can shake the feeling that it's an amazing coincidence that he works on Billy Soldier's ward, can we? Now, c'mon man, that's too much. We got somethin' here. It's just a matter of time."

* * *

I took my time and decompressed as I walked slowly to the institute. I got there at 6:30 and went directly to Rita's office to see how many notes she had left for me. The institute was also a psychotherapy clinic, and the corridors and waiting rooms on all the floors, especially in the early evenings, after work, were about the busiest times.

As I walked in and moved toward the elevators, the new procedure hit me. There was now a uniformed guard posted in the lobby. He asked me to sign in, and I instantly had that bad sensation. I felt the influence of Stroud and Grillo. Then, of course, as would be expected, the unusual happened. As I approached Rita's office on the seventh floor, there was a man standing in a doubled-over position right there in the corridor. It was only natural for me to ask if he needed any help. He squeezed out the "no" in a tone that conveyed his stomach was in knots.

"You're okay?" I asked him again.

"Are you a therapist?" he responded. "My therapist is twenty minutes late. I don't know what happened to her. She's never late."

I confirmed I was a therapist and that he might want to check with the bursar as to whether his therapist had left a message. I asked if he was in pain. He told me he was, but then shifted to his story.

"I think I need a male therapist," he said. "This is something that's not easy to talk about with a woman. Maybe you could be my therapist?!"

I told him that when a patient had a problem with a therapist, it was customary for it to be addressed directly with the therapist. Before I had a chance to explain it further, he started.

"I get doubled over all the time. It's about beautiful women, you know — built. When I see one in the street or anywhere, I feel like someone shot me in the stomach. It's so fierce that it doubles me over."

Again I told him I really couldn't get into this, and that he'd need to speak to his therapist about it. He disregarded me and whispered, "It's tits. They get me right in the labonza. Know what I mean? The minute I see one of those real sexy types — you know, I just double over. It's like getting shot with a shotgun or something. And it hurts. I've gotta tighten my stomach muscles to get over it. What the hell is it?"

I knew. But still, I couldn't get into it. I asked for his therapist's name and told him I'd talk to her about it.

"Okay. But don't say 'tits' to her. Say I said 'breasts.' But between you and me, breasts ain't it. It's tits that does it to me. And you know that blonde secretary with the big ones down the hall? Well, she just walked past me right before you showed up, and look at me. I'm all messed up."

Psychoanalytically speaking, for a man with this kind of problem, to possess a woman with such a pronounced bust line was the equivalent of feeling adequate. More than adequate — to be admired. And that's the "something else" in the equation. "Large" is the operative term here. I would reveal its further meaning from a psychoanalytic understanding when, and if, he and I worked in the therapeutic session. In any event, the wish is met albeit in perverse form, as the symptom (doubled-over pain). It's a displacement upwards and what that means would be revealed to him as well as we worked it out.

"Listen," Doubled-Over said, interrupting my reverie. "When you speak to her tell her I like her but I need to see a male therapist. I mean between you and me, I can't say shit to her. I mean I can't use words. I can't say fuck or anything. Know what I mean?"

*   *   *

Tino was afflicted in the same way. Velma had breast power over him, and he wanted to possess her. Only Velma's acceptance per se, would make him adequate. That and having some woman, some Velma equivalent, see his penis and admire him. Now, however, he felt the pressure of Carl Emory's presence in Velma's orbit. And the thought that Velma would be interested in Carl was enough to send Tino into the woods again. But rather than doing that, he obtained Carl's address and, for a week, on and off, and from some distance, watched Carl's house. Just watched when Carl came home and when he left. He was checking Carl's every move, and he was doing it for a reason. He wanted some special personal time with Carl.

* * *

Finally, Rita's office. I checked the bulletin board where she posts my notes, looked over a few things, and left. Now it was time to meet Jean and Richard. I felt unusually calm in the face of this imminent and special personal time with Sebastian. I would treat the diary with the utmost respect. Sebastian was very real to me.

Through the auditorium to the back of the building, I saw the lights were on and that meant Jean and Richard were already there.

We began chatting. Jean then predicted the diary would arrive exactly at nine. We had over an hour to wait, so we phoned for sandwiches and coffee. They were eager to hear more about our non-driver on the bridge and whether or not he had shown up. I told them that he did indeed show up and that we had a fruitful session. A few minutes later a gentleman appeared at the library door and stood at the threshold as if about to ask a question. Jean couldn't believe it was our courier because we still had almost an hour to go. But it was him. He was wearing civilian clothes and I say that because my hunch was that he was a priest. One of the rebels.

"I believe I'm early. Are you Ms. Kaye?'

Jean was excited. "Yes. Please come in."

She was about to introduce us when our courier interrupted her and said, "No need, please. I've been instructed to deliver this to you and now I must leave."

He handed Jean a small package, nodded to us, bowing ever so slightly, and left Even before we could thank him. I thought, "He never even asked to confirm who we were. There was not even a password or something."

But we had it! Sebastian's diary number one. I carefully unwrapped the package. Not parchment. Plain paper. About fifty pages, pen-printed. I thought that the original would have been in Italian or Latin, but I was wrong. Sebastian was from Spain.

* * *

The first page was dated March 31, 1494. His first sentence was,

> Two years to the day. I am away from the horror. It is gone. Ester, Alba, will I ever see you again? I will never speak. I cannot speak. I do not want to speak. I would say to people, "Do not hate." But now I hate. My Spain is a country for murderers. These are not mere castigators. They are torturers. Perhaps only in this monastery is Christianity free of the Devil. Two years of death, prison, hiding. All of Europe is poisoned. Spain, the worst.

It was slowly occurring to me. I said to Jean, "Could you find the dates of the Spanish Inquisition?" She looked at me and hurried into the back room of the library where all of her reference volumes were stored. I thought, "Two years to the day. That would make it 1492. Columbus. What have I uncovered here?" I continued reading.

> Like father, many killed on the quemadero by the Ferrers. We should have fled. It was too late. I thought my hidalgo station would be useful to the king and save us. It didn't matter. They sought my counsel. No matter. We were powerless. They took them, and imprisoned me. I am forever cursed with the screaming that I now continuously hear in my head: Confess! Confess!

Of course I had no idea who the Ferrers were. The quemadero meant "stake," and "hidalgo station" a man of the royal court. Jean came running in. "March 31st, 1492 was the exact date of the expulsion law for the Jews of Spain."

Two years from the date of Sebastian's first entry—to the day! Jean continued, "The date of the formal establishment of the Spanish Inquisition was 1478."

"Yeah," I said, "and it was established by that so-called Royal couple Ferdinand and Isabella and directed by that twisted Torquemada."

"Royalty," I thought. "What a joke!"

"His wife may have been burned at the stake," I said. "You would think I would know how to live through that, but I don't." She didn't answer.

We looked at one another for a few moments when suddenly the thought rushed at me, and I said it out loud:

"Sebastian the monk was a Jew!"

BOOK 2

RELATIONSHIPS

· 11 ·

PARENT AND CHILD

What the hell was I getting into? Now it's some killing during the Spanish Inquisition? But there it was. His name was printed on the cover of the diary: Sebastian Arragel. Apparently the translator was faithful to the letter and translated not only exactly what was written, but also exactly where in the manuscript Sebastian had written it—in this case his name on the cover. I gave Jean some terms from the diary to look up. In the first few pages of the diary the words "hidalgo" and "quemadero" were repeated and "auto-da-fé" was also cited. Later on the word "grandee" was also untranslated, but I knew that "grandee" meant a high-ranking member of the royal court.

Jean was ahead of me. She was already looking up the Spanish Inquisition in an encyclopedia from her reference room. "Auto-da-fé," literally "an act of faith," was defined as "the ceremonial sentencing and execution of an alleged heretic." I had known about the auto-da-fé, in which Jews who had converted were put to the test. If they actually burned at the quemadero, the stake, it "proved" they were lying, and their conversion to Christianity was false; if they didn't burn, their conversion was genuine. "Man, oh man," I thought, "I guess all the conversions were false."

Jean continued reading aloud while Richard and I listened quietly.

"Burned alive one at a time at the stake with hundreds, perhaps thousands, witnessing." She skipped a few lines. "Then burning many simultaneously. Six men and six women were burned at the quemadero on February 6, 1481, at the first auto-da-fé."

Then I saw it. As Jean was reading I was also glancing through the diary. On one of the pages Sebastian was noting his duties at the court. In an entry dated 5 April 1494, Sebastian's notes dripped with irony and agony.

> Summoned by Isabella to conduct diplomatic translations in Italian with a courier of the Media family in Florence, the vital region of Italy. He had been on a clandestine mission to Castile. In the afternoon both with the British Magistrate from London and the French Trade Minister who complimented my fluency to the queen. Later that evening summoned again, simply to be assured that she appreciated, as she said, my "golden facility with languages." Two days later, in desperation, access to her vanished. Did she know my predicament? It was then that I was accused by that scoundrel, that pestilence—Modesto Ferrer. Modesto. A name that bore no resemblance to the character of the person. Mendacity would have been a more suitable name—shouting at me in that dungeon. My life stripped. Ester gone. Alba. Oh, my child.

I was strangely calm. It was a sang-froid moment. Then I thought, "You cocksuckers!" I guessed that Ester was his wife and Alba his daughter. And I was gripped by the name Alba. I remembered Tennessee Williams's *Camino Real*, in which the name Alba, meaning daybreak, tells us the play is about hope. And yet Williams gives us a play about relics, people as traces, residues, rather more like shadows. Ghosts!

I quickly scanned the diary and began to understand his situation—that he was a linguist, and, amazingly, an official translator for Queen Isabella and I assumed also for the king. Sebastian was indeed high up in the court.

I asked Jean to duplicate all the pages on the Spanish Inquisition and to print out selected material from the Internet. I needed to read whatever history I could on the Inquisition. I needed to appreciate the diary as fully as possible.

I knew that the urgency I was beginning to feel was driven by my instinct to try to save the three of them, however futile that effort would be some five centuries later. I could sense the helplessness, the terror, they must have felt. And then out of the blue I flashed to Billy. What terror, what utter helplessness he must have felt. And of course, Katie. Gone in a split second. And here I am, palpably feeling the urge to save them all—and, of course, desperately insisting that if at all, I could retrieve Katie.

My sense of urgency to read about the Inquisition was a gestating rage, fueled by the thought of people helpless against their imposed fate: people subtracted from themselves. Now I was focused on Sebastian as well as on Billy. Both were plundered because they could be. Katie—out of the blue—hit by a meteor! A random traffic-event-meteor. But Billy. Who knows? And Sebastian—definitely not random. No accidental situation there. It was premeditated malevolence by an unholy alliance of depraved so-called royalty, and to say the least, a church body composed of profoundly sanctimonious anti-Christ Christians (whether they knew it or not)—miscreants, really.

*   *   *

Talk about rage. 'T' was boiling about Velma and Carl, but it didn't compute with his conscious self; that is, he felt angry, but didn't really know it. He tried discussing it with Velma, but it came out as a plea. He wanted her to stop talking to Carl entirely.

"You don't need him. You have work to do on the ward."

But Velma dismissed his concerns. "Now, Tino," she said, "you know very well that I love you first. But Carl was bad and he needs to learn how to behave. You know how I had the same problem with you? I know you remember, Tino. Now you're much better because you listen. And you can already see that Carl is better now, too. Don't you see that, Tino? He's listening more. And, Tino, you're whining again and whining means that you're already expecting not to get what you ask for. Now stop it."

Her tone was gradually changing. At first she pretended it was all nonsense. Now she was becoming stern. "Should I say it exactly, Tino? All right then. Carl is more and more under my authority. Under me! Is that clear enough?" She paused and then suddenly softened. "But you'll always be number one, Tino. The very best one."

Tino stood there in the trailer not knowing what to say.

"So, Tino, as usual, I will decide how to handle it. And we know that handling it can be a very delicate issue. And we also know that my way of

handling it is just what Carl wants. Just what he needs. Now, Tino, I have work to do."

And with that, Tino was dismissed.

Tino hastened out of the trailer, deliberately kicking over some of the rabbit cages and creating a commotion among the dozen or so rabbits in these cages. He drove off, screeching out of the gravel yard. He had much work to do.

*   *   *

We closed down the library. I had much work to do. I would spend the next few days reading all of Sebastian's material. I would also review the history of the Spanish Inquisition, and most importantly, I could pore over Sebastian's diary.

On the way home, I asked the cab driver to turn on the overhead light so I could read. I browsed through the diary, fixing mostly on names: Torquemada; Vincent Ferrer, referred to as a Dominican friar and, I thought, probably related to Modesto Ferrer; a friend named Luis Vives; frequent references to Moses Arragel, perhaps his father; and, Abarbanel. Other references that caught my eye were "illuminist," "chamber," "burned my tongue," "slaughter," "Alba bible," and the title, "Parent and Child."

For some reason, it was the "Parent and Child" reference that caused me to stop and read. Then I knew why. Sebastian was talking about the child who couldn't eat and the mother who insisted on answering all questions addressed to her daughter. Actually, I remembered from his manuscript that the "child" was in her late teens; she hated to chew and only wanted to drink. I had considered it a fifteenth-century case of anorexia.

Sebastian mused about the mother, who was inherently, albeit seemingly unconsciously, collusive in her daughter's symptom problem:

> She will not let her breathe or grow. The mother must control everything. The child clings. I have learned the child was left to be cared for by servants while the mother's whereabouts were unclear. When asked, the mother was not forthcoming. The child must be angry with her but can only experience the attachment not the fury. The mother professes concern and yet abandoned the child for the day, only returning at night. My suspicion is that some

nefarious pursuit called to her. I believe the child will only eat when she experiences her mother's interest, not merely her control. The immediate task is to enable the mother to accept the possibility of this proposition and not incite her rage, her fleeing. It has occurred to me that the concept of family illness is one that needs to be considered. It would be an illness of the psyche of the ostensible patient, in this case the child, along with a social difficulty arising from conflicted relationships within the family. Clearly, this unfortunate child is the identified patient. Yet I believe there is a more germane patient, one who can be considered the actual patient. In this case, I believe the fulcrum of the problem is the mother. Thus, I am beginning to understand that the definition of "patient" can be ambiguous. I see a principle forming regarding such problems in families. Perhaps there is always an apparent patient and an actual one. The not-eating symptom manifested in the child may be actually composed of mother/child interaction and in no sense can be attributed solely to the child. With regard to this case, if one insists on the identification of a sole patient, who then, other than the mother/child dyad, could it be? Yet, surely any direct depiction of this mother's alleged complicity in her daughter's problem would be instantly rejected, and moreover such an implication could create havoc for me.

I stopped reading. The driver glanced at the rear-view mirror, saw me gazing, and asked if he could turn off the overhead light. I nodded. But I immediately remembered a case I had treated some years ago of a nineteen-year-old woman that bore a remarkable resemblance to the one Sebastian was considering. The salient issue in the case I treated concerned a strong attachment between father and daughter that was sacrificed by the father when he went to work in the mother's business. At that time the patient was only two or three years old. We were able to reconstruct her feelings about his sudden disappearance as her primary caregiver. She said, "I stopped eating when he went to work. I was left with baby-sitters. I felt: 'Only when he returns will I eat.'"

I called my case one of quasi-anorexia because the girl was quite thin, but unlike anorectics, she hated her appearance and wished she were normal. In classic anorexia, gazing at one's reflection and always seeing "not thin enough" is probably a translation from: "I feel the anger is still there — it's not gone!" Getting ever thinner is then a repeatedly failed attempt to eliminate the anger. And it never ever works because getting thinner has no real relation to eliminating anger. This is the kind of symptom that can swallow a person whole so that the symptom becomes the personality. That kind of symptom that can just about vanquish the personality was not as germane to my case, but I could see that it definitely corresponded to the case Sebastian was considering.

Thus, I believed that Sebastian had been on the right track and understood the essence of the problem. He sensed his patient was in the middle of a family pathology which he called a "difficulty." Unfortunately, he didn't have the psychoanalytic technology to proceed with the treatment. Furthermore, he was hinting at the presence of some danger to himself were the mother to feel accused for causing her daughter's problem. Given the state/church-sponsored hate climate toward Jews at the time, if this was Sebastian's concern, it was more than likely justified.

* * *

In the darkened cab I was again flooded with the feeling that I needed to read it all immediately, yet knowing there was so much ground to cover. What began as curiosity about an obscure citation in a clinical compendium turned out to be serious business. This was not something I could take lightly — the Spanish Inquisition, a harbinger of the Holocaust. And I had access to the diary, the first of ten or more volumes, of a Jewish hidalgo of the court, close to King Ferdinand and Queen Isabella.

This entire drama miraculously deflected my guilt complex regarding the relentless presence of Stroud and Grillo, who were contacting me intermittently and causing me considerable tension. Because of Sebastian's ordeal and my anger about it, the ever-present Stroud/Grillo voice in my head that was accusing me and saying, "Dr. Kahn, what have you done?" was actually gone. And although my reflex was to share everything about Sebastian with Katie, I caught myself and realized that instead, it was going to be Danny Margolis who hears it all.

Danny was a very good friend of mine, also Jewish, a brilliant biochemist and extraordinarily fair-minded. It was said that his work on DNA structure and the brain merited a Nobel and that someday he might get one. We met in graduate school and remained close. Over the years we've shared many discoveries and ideas. I was also eager to talk all of it over with Vlad. I realized from what I had already gleaned from the diary that Sebastian was terribly persecuted. It didn't matter that he was a hidalgo. He was a Jew and was stripped of everything, including his family. I thought about the auto-da-fé. Burnt corpses. Again, death!

Sebastian may have physically survived, but it was clear that he was emotionally devastated. The one phrase that stuck with me was his reference to a "burned tongue." I assumed that it wasn't a metaphor—that they actually burned his tongue. I closed the diary feeling upset, which I knew was nothing more than feeling angry. But then as we approached my building, I always felt grateful to be entering this peaceful, persecution-free zone, imagining, of course, that Katie was there—waiting.

* * *

Carl Emory was walking to his car. It was quitting time at the hospital, and everyone was rushing to their cars, eager to get home. But 'T' was suffering terribly, really devastated with the knowledge that now, each day before Carl went to his car, Velma would closet him in a room with her for several minutes.

"If I feel he's listened, and if I feel his attitude was good, then I might let him tell me how he feels about me. But he must tell me the truth. I can tell if it's not the truth, Tino. You know I can tell. Then he can say whatever it is that he feels. Whatever. Then I won't scold him. I'll just listen. And then we would see."

That's how she ended it: "And then we would see." And then we would see what? Tino had to imagine what that meant. So Velma was simultaneously controlling Carl and tyrannizing Tino. Because Tino, after hearing "And then we would see," could think of nothing else but that. He was tormented by it, imagining Velma and Carl in some kind of closeness, perhaps in an embrace. Sexual intercourse wasn't the issue. It was the electrifyingly erotic, possessive thought of someone else merely touching her. That's what had Tino in an unrelenting grip. He was entirely controlled by it—by her voice, her inflection, her authority. He hated Carl.

Carl was followed home. At about 8 P.M., Carl left his house and drove to a diner. He ate alone. Almost an hour later, he left the diner. Jericho was waiting for him at the hedges adjacent to the garage. Carl's little house was enveloped in shrubs, greenery, flowers. But Carl never got a chance to enter his house. Waiting there was his fate.

Jericho, hooded, was holding a weapon wrapped in some kind of rag. Could've been an axe or a hammer or some other heavy object. Carl didn't know what hit him. And Jericho had no need to announce anything, to exact sweeter revenge by explaining why he was doing this. He just wanted to end Carl. Nothing more, nothing less. With one stroke Jericho knocked him down and out. Then he leaned down, took a lipstick from his own jacket pocket and carefully painted Carl's lips with it. He made sure that the lipstick covered more than the defined area of Carl's lips. Trampy-like.

"Got that one from Veronica," he thought.

Reaching into Carl's back pants pocket, he removed Carl's wallet. Then Jericho let it out. He stood, and with arms raised to the sky and head and body stretching the same way, Jericho screeched at the top of his voice:

"AAAAAHHHHHHH."

*   *   *

It was 11 P.M. sharp. I sighed deeply and entered the apartment. If anything could help me make a transition from the rage I felt, it was this palatial, ornate, seven room apartment, with the ten and a half-foot ceilings, moldings and archways and Katie's paintings everywhere. A private healing gallery of beauty: plants and flowers, accents of green. The whole thing was a painting. We were both living in a painting. Now I'm living in the painting, alone—and looking for her, really expecting to see her.

Before I had a chance to put my papers down, Rita was on the phone, a bit concerned that I hadn't answered my messages. I told her not to worry and that I'd be canceling everything for the weekend. I knew I wouldn't be able to concentrate on anything but Sebastian. She told me that Jean had messengered me a six-hundred page, two-volume edition on the Spanish Inquisition.

· 12 ·

THE SELF

Tino was sitting in Kruger's waiting area outside Kruger's office at the hospital. Kruger opened his door and motioned for Tino to enter. He began with a tease of a question, knowing full well that Tino wouldn't be able to answer it.

"Well, Tino, were you out last night doing certain things?" Tino was bewildered. He wasn't actually sure what the answer to the question was, but he knew that it was at such times that his concentration wasn't good.

"I think so," Tino said. "You think so," Kruger said accusingly. "You think so? Well," Kruger continued, "was it to hurt someone because you couldn't hold it in anymore, or were you, shall we say, in costume?"

Tino was staring. Whenever Kruger put it to him directly that way, Tino would just stare. "Now look, Tino, we both know why you're here. We have to get to who you really are so that we can cure the headaches and the other things. You know, so that you don't have to do all those things that you do. But of course you're not sure about it. Are you?" A rhetorical question. Now Kruger became more deliberate in his inquisition. "Well, Tino, I want to know. Did you find the books that Billy was keeping for me? They weren't for you, and they weren't for your mother. You know that. Those books and records were for me and me alone. I think you or Velma might have them."

Tino was grateful that Kruger focused on Billy's books. Those questions were easy for him. It was the other questions about who he was and where he went that were impossible and made him squirm.

"Dr. Kruger, I don't know anything about the whereabouts of those books."

"But you knew that Billy had books and records that he was keeping. And so did your mother know. Isn't that true?"

"Yes," Tino answered.

"And if you don't have them then you're both looking for them? Isn't that true?"

"Yes," Tino complied.

"So," Kruger intoned, "if she gets the books, then she has a certain power. Doesn't she? Just like she has that power over you. And she does have that power over you." He paused for some seconds. "No matter, because I'm going to free you, Tino. I'm going to free you of all that torment. No more headaches, Tino. No more head pounding, no more pain in your eyes, no more needing to be in a completely dark room, Tino. Velma can't help you cure the headaches, Tino. But I can. And you know I can. Because I'm going to unlock the symptoms, Tino. The code to unlock the symptoms, Tino — I'm getting it, and we're going to unlock all the compartments, and put them all together so you can be one person, Tino. You'll be only one self, not more, not others."

Kruger would overwhelm Tino with this kind of barrage, including repetition of his name, direct references to Tino's "problem," as well as innuendoes about who Tino really was — what kind of self he was. That's how Kruger would put it. He would say, "Tino, what kind of self are you?" When Kruger was like that, Tino would become a citizen of some unknown place, not able really to identify himself. It was the apogee of a virtual state, where there was an almost complete subtraction of Tino's consciousness; where his physical being felt grotesquely misshapen — a pretzel — twisted.

"Where is she looking for the records?" Kruger demanded. Tino was awed by Kruger. He depended on Kruger to cure his headaches, and he found that although he would space out several times during a session, when it was over, the feelings actually would be better. It gave him hope that he could be rid of the head-pounding. He never knew how Kruger was helping him, but he knew he was.

Of course it was obvious how Kruger was helping. Despite Kruger's sadism, the fact that Tino's apparent identity problem and his complex relationship with Velma — obviously the root of the problem — were merely alluded to was enough to lower the tension level. Through it all, Kruger's so-called treatment apparently enabled Tino to experience some semblance of a catharsis.

"She's looking for the books all over the ward," Tino answered. "Does she have you looking for them as well?" Kruger followed. "Yes," Tino said. "Okay,"

Kruger continued, "if, or rather, when, you find the books, you must return them to me. Is that understood?" Then, and only by implication, Kruger laid down the gauntlet. He always did it by implication. "You'll bring the books to me, Tino, because I will cure the headaches forever. I will make you into one person, one self, Tino, and I will never reveal anything about, shall we say, your previous habits. And this little project of ours, Tino, will be just between you and me. If you tell your mother about it, she will leave the hospital, just like she's left other places whenever you got close to knowing certain things. So if she leaves here, you can't get better. And I want you to get better, Tino. Only your normal whole self, Tino. You understand? None other."

Tino knew what Kruger meant. He felt that Kruger was his only chance to be free of those vague, yet terrible sensations he would harbor of feeling either homicidal or sexually desperate. He wasn't really sure about them and, of course, never talked about them, especially not with Velma. He could only talk about them with Dr. Kruger because it was Dr. Kruger who had first jogged Tino's memory. It had happened when Kruger found him one night in the condemned, dark room, dressed as a woman. After that, it was only a matter of time before Kruger also personally experienced Tino's rage, directed at him, right there in the good doctor's office.

The words were ringing in Tino's ears: "Only your normal whole self, Tino. You understand? None other."

* * *

"Well, Glenn," Deborah said, "can you be the whole person?"

She didn't say "a" whole person. Rather she said "the." She's like that. Very subtle. It keeps it a little away from being too in the present tense, or like an arrow to the heart. So the way she says it is not devastating. She knows I'm sensitive to the slightest nuance, so she does it ever so gently. It's her touch. It's what I like about her and it's a rare gift. She's considerate, perceptive, and plainly smart.

"No, not anymore," I answered. "But I don't care. I just don't care. I look at women and I keep saying to myself, 'Nope, doesn't looks like her.' And I still talk to myself—and sometimes out loud. Yes, I still talk to the chair."

"I thought you would say that," she said. "You don't give up."

"I don't actually see her sitting there," I continued, "so it's not a hallucination. But I imagine it. I've also thought that I actually may not be able to ever leave the apartment—I mean sell it—because I feel her presence there. But when I think more about it, it occurs to me that I could maybe, eventually sell it. I'll just take her with me, simple as that. But then I think, No. That's how I keep driving myself around and around."

"Everyone handles things their own way," she kindly observed.

"My way is I control myself with my head, but I relate to her with my heart, and in that way, believe it or not, my heart feels loved. I also imagine that her heart feels loved, too. Sebastian said that if your heart feels loved, it's one of the cardinal criteria of mate selection. Imagine that? He called it mate selection. I always tell her I love her and that I'm not going to permit us to be condemned to some dark place.

"Now here's the obsessional, perverse stuff—definitely the nutso stuff. It's hard for me to say this.....but at times I get a peaceful feeling knowing that she's in one place—at the cemetery—so that I always know where she is. In some crazy way, that thought seems to help me. But then I move away from it because suddenly it upsets me."

"Glenn, I'm not exactly crying, but I'm glad time's up."

"Good. Because my salvation is that I can shift to other things—almost on a dime. And with all that's going on, I've got a lot to think about—even though they all take me to my personal Inquisition. I've got a lot of reading to do concerning Sebastian's situation. At least for a time, I'll be distracted from my own agony in order to learn more about his—about *his* Inquisition. I'm very identified with Sebastian, Deborah. Because, like him and Ester, with Katie it was the ecstasy, and without her it's gone."

*   *   *

Resting on the center of my desk and occupying the remaining surface to the left, were two volumes on the Inquisition that Jean had sent me. A crisp copy of the diary was on my right; I had had the original duplicated, page by page.

I was reading the diary as though I had found a strange, yet familiar being—a ghost. I was about to resuscitate a ghost. I began to feverishly check various references that Sebastian made to events and people. The diary was actually a record of Sebastian's ideas and experiences, the reportage of his life. Only about half the time would he indicate the date. Gradually I realized that he was recording events that occurred mostly in the years 1481, the time of the first auto-da-fé, and eleven years later, in 1492. The diary had evidently been written in 1494, two years after the expulsion of the Jews from Spain. I deduced that he left Spain empty-handed, as departing Jews had all their possessions confiscated. The confiscated possessions were taken by the church and the noblemen of the court, who enriched themselves. Sebastian must have had stacks of books and marvelous cultural artifacts. After all, this man was a civilized human being, obviously a person of value living amidst the so-called elite, the court/church society.

I was apparently daydreaming this drama because in my reverie I imagined Katie walking in to ask me something, and in my mind I started speaking to her. It was my way of audibly talking to and answering her without attributing it to an aged dementia seen in people who talk to themselves.

"I think I've distilled some of the bare bones of Sebastian's life from sections of the notebook. He was born about 1442—thirty years after the agitation against the Jews began. Vincent Ferrer, a Dominican friar, was an uncle of the guy who destroyed Sebastian. In the early part of the fifteenth century Vincent Ferrer led an army, really a rabble, and killed thousands of Jews. And this was before the Inquisition. I've pieced together various dates, Katie, and I see from the diary that Sebastian remembered making his first entry about a week after the first auto-da-fé, which would be about Feb. 13, 1481, because the first auto-da-fé happened on Feb. 6th."

Then I snapped out of it because, I guess, the enormity of these events occurring to Sebastian pulled me out of my personal quemadero. I was guessing that this was the pivotal event that motivated Sebastian to keep notebooks and diaries in the first place. He must have been rudely awakened by the accelerating horror unfolding around him.

The downstairs intercom rang. A minute later Ted rushed in with exciting news. "Glenn, look, here it is!"

I leafed through three hundred and eighteen pages of the newly typed manuscript. It was impressive—Sebastian's work in perfectly readable form.

"There are only four pages that are difficult to read," he said. "Otherwise we got everything. One in the first third, two in the middle, and one at the end. I put page markers down for you. They just came out cloudy in my work, or incomplete in the notebooks. You can see a few words here and there."

He turned to the first one, and I knew exactly what was missing because Sebastian was using a fascinating thinking device. The only visible words on the page were in a section called "The Line." I remembered that when I originally read it, I took my time and reread it on the spot because I knew "The Line" was a simple, yet in its simplicity, an elegant and original piece of thinking.

Instead of tackling the two volumes before me, I now turned my attention to Sebastian's manuscript, masterfully reconstructed from Rita's and Jill's shorthand and Ted's photography. I wanted to tell Ted about "The Line," but he quickly turned to his second marker and told me he was concerned because it wasn't just one page or even part of one page — there were almost two full pages that were unreadable. Again, this was easy as I remembered Sebastian's discussion completely. The two pages concerned his analysis of individuals who are supersensitive to feeling blamed and will overreact to the slightest suggestion that they've done something wrong.

"Don't be a textbook example of Sebastian's point here, Ted. You guys have done a fabulous job. I'm not worried about every word. But in this case I can reproduce almost exactly how he put it. He said, 'These sorts hear whispers as screams.' I remember liking the phrase 'hearing whispers as screams,' thinking it really captured the essence of the alarm reaction."

"So you think blanks don't really matter because you've got it?" Ted asked.

"Well, definitely these first two," I said.

And as I was about to ask him to turn to the last page in question, he was already there. "Here it is. Only the word 'perception.'"

Here too, I knew what it was. Sebastian was discussing the difference between objective perception and perception based upon personality needs. When I first read this passage, it reminded me of the social psychological studies published in the early 1950's in which this same point was used to derive the concepts of selective perception and perceptual defense — the first meaning you see what you want to see; the second meaning you don't see what you don't want to see. From a psychoanalytic perspective, these are components of the defense mechanism of denial. I now had it all and reassured Ted.

And it was true. We now had it all. The manuscript, the diary and a couple of solid historical volumes on the Inquisition. I felt I could work on this material uninterrupted for the ensuing three and a half days, till the end of the weekend, and hoped that then I would be in a good position to understand Sebastian as well as the social context in which he found himself. I was also beginning to think more seriously that I needed to introduce Sebastian to the world.

"You know, Ted," I said, "I'm beginning to think I'm going to need to convene a conference to introduce Sebastian to the world. I'll have to talk to Jean about it because I don't want to reveal anyone's cover at the Vatican. This stuff 's too important to remain cloistered. As far as I'm concerned, at this point, in terms of what I know about him, I believe that Sebastian could be considered the first psychotherapist. He alludes to treating that anorectic girl and understood the larger problem. I think people around him valued him for his wisdom. Sagacious is the word. He was actually treating people—in the Middle Ages—when demonology reigned and the church practically prohibited real thinking. My feeling is that he knew he was in hot water because of it."

Ted looked over my shoulder at the manuscript and then stepped back. He said, "The first real therapist, huh?"

"It looks like he was treating clinical conditions based on what he understood about the self. It's like he had a developing theory and was looking for a technology that corresponded to the theory so that he could treat people. I think he was risking his life doing it. The whole thing's amazing to me."

Ted hesitated and then said, "What about 'The Line?' What does 'The Line' mean?"

"You know," I said, "a heuristic or mnemonic device is a way of meta-phorically understanding or remembering something. Sebastian visualized a line. He noticed that it's quite normal for people to slip behind this line for a welcomed breather, some relief. It's a place to restore your equilib-rium and take that breath before you step out again in front of the line. There, behind the line, you become a specter of yourself. The main point he made was that to be in front of the line was to be in a place of real-ity—a doing place—and not in a place of rumination or withdrawal. In front of the line, no procrastination. Procrastination is behind the line. My take on it is that in front of the line one procrastinates later." Ted repeated my little joke.

"Sebastian said that the normal imperative is for people to slip ever so slightly behind the line, even several times a day, and then, just as suddenly, to step right back out in front of it again; that is, we all need some alone time and we actually all get it, even though it's accomplished in a way that's so subtle that we ourselves don't notice it."

I paused and looked at Ted. I realized I was actually practicing my speech for some future conference to be convened on behalf of Sebastian and his discoveries.

"And, Ted, I've also noticed this same withdrawal phenomenon, but I didn't attach it directly to the psychology of the self. Sebastian called it 'necessary moments of withdrawal.' And he also said that slipping behind the line need only be a hint of a slip—hardly noticeable to others. For him, real pathological withdrawal consisted of staying several paces behind the line and for long periods of time. I started to think that living behind the line is essentially the relationship of the self to the self."

With that, the phone rang. To my chagrin it was detective Stroud.

"I'm just letting you know," he said, "that one of the attendants, a Mr. Tino Vescaro, a.k.a. Secora, that's right, the nurse's son," he quickly added, "has been getting treatment at a certain headache clinic in the city."

"Why are you telling me?" I asked.

"We've decided to keep you posted on our progress as we go along," he said.

I thought for a moment and braved the elements by saying, "I guess that means I'm not a suspect."

"Right," he said, and humorously added, "so far. We need to know more about him. Do you have any special information that would be useful? Like something about his history? I mean, he did work on Billy's ward. That's just too much of a coincidence."

"The answer is I haven't got the slightest bit of information on him. I've seen him around on various wards, but never really had any contact with him."

"Okay," Stroud ended, "we'll be in touch. By the way, regards from Joe." I knew he meant Joe Grillo. Was I starting to like these guys? Did they like me? I felt that maybe they trusted me. At this point, my paranoia about my possible complicity in Billy's death was gone. I felt some relief as I hung up the receiver.

Again, I was startled by the phone. It was Doubled Over's analyst. She reminded me that we had met at an administrative meeting at the clinic. After we talked a bit, she thanked me for agreeing to take the case. This was a good stopping point, and Ted needed to leave. I thought I could work for another five or six hours.

*   *   *

I opened the diary to a section on some history of Sebastian's persecutor. Here Sebastian's writing combined a personal account within a historical narrative:

> Modesto, the grand nephew of Vincent Ferrer the murderer of Jews, was Isabella's trusted lieutenant from Castile. The Ferrers were instrumental in uniting Ferdinand and Isabella, and Modesto Ferrer was rewarded with Court appointment and title. In this union of Ferdinand and Isabella, Spain was thus consolidated. Like the ignominious Ferrers before him who were responsible for father's death, this Ferrer, Modesto, hated me, and I feared would not hesitate to destroy me. Then he did destroy me. He was the worst of *The Familiares*, the worst spy. It was Modesto Ferrer who accused me. And it was Modesto Ferrer who had me imprisoned and tortured. The accusation concerned my crushing of a crucifix. A spurious charge. A lie! But it was enough.

The entry stopped there. Elsewhere in the diary I found another reference to Modesto Ferrer in which Ferrer accuses Sebastian of doing doctor's work. Ferrer wanted to know by what right Sebastian took on such honors. Sebastian's friend, the poet and philosopher Vives, was standing nearby and answered. He told Ferrer that he personally knew Sebastian did not hold himself out as a doctor, but that people respected Sebastian's good sense and it became a habit for them to request an audience with him for all sorts of problems they were having. In this section of the diary, Sebastian states:

> These interviews consisted of concerns regarding marital difficulties as well as descriptions of odd bodily symptoms. I do not understand why they sought my counsel.

Ester would tell me it was because they respected me. Perhaps it was because they knew I was conversant in several languages and took that to mean I could understand things. They even brought me their dreams. I was familiar with Shmuel Ben Hofni's work on dreams. It was Ben Hofni, also a Jew, who was the first to inspire me to look at my own dreams.

I thought, as Ester did, that they simply respected him; everyone could see that he was obviously a person of extraordinary ability and intelligence. Ferrer, I guessed, was beside himself with rage that a Jew should be held in such esteem.

I made a point to look up Shmuel Ben Hofni and found that he was, along with Sebastian, a renaissance man in the Middle Ages, a Jew who wrote tracts on dream interpretation almost two hundred years before the Renaissance.

A book from Jean arrived, entitled *The Origin Of The Inquisition In 15th Century Spain*, by Benzion Netanyahu. One thousand three hundred eighty-four pages. I knew the name, of course. Benzion Netanyahu was the father of Lt. Col. Jonathan Netanyahu—Yoni—the Israel Defense Forces commander of the Entebbe raid who was killed during the rescue of those hijacked Jews in Uganda. He was also the father of Yoni's brother, Benjamin Netanyahu, the Prime Minister of Israel.

Now I felt I was in the midst of Israeli history. I had a strong need to meet with Danny. He would be as absorbed in it all as I was.

· 13 ·

SPOUSES

Over to Rockefeller University. It had been just announced in the New York Times that a new Nobel prize winner in biochemistry had accepted an appointment there. Rockefeller now housed eighteen Nobel laureates. Dr. Daniel Margolis was popular there and many thought that sooner or later he would get one, too.

Danny was a specialist in DNA research and brain development. As it turns out, I, too, was interested in DNA and had for some time now been working on what I considered to be the inevitable connection between DNA structure, the immune system and emotion, and, of course, linking it all with my specialty—symptom formation. Danny's work, however, was hard-core experimental stuff while I was doing what scientists usually call thought experiments—speculation and theoretical possibilities. But I shared my thinking with Danny anyway, and he taught me a great deal about the structure of DNA. Even Freud underestimated the role of biology and certainly the role of chemistry in the formation of dispositional tendencies of emotion and personality.

Danny loved this sort of analogizing and we did it all the time. Through my research on the structure and difference between the apparent circular versus the actual transformational shape of small human groups, I had proposed that the macro-universe was shaped as a hyperbolic paraboloid (like a figure eight). Danny thought that was an important proposition and he mused about some future time when we would read that indeed, some physicist had discovered that the universe was shaped in the form of a hyperbolic paraboloid. As it turned out, the eminent mathematician and physicist Sir Roger Penrose, at Oxford, was now suggesting that because the universe is a low-density one it is therefore also of negative spatial curvature; that is, saddle-shaped, which is like a hyperbolic paraboloid. His theory appeared several years after I had published my speculation about such a shape. Danny called me with the news about Penrose's focus. He was excited and said they would have to include me in the discovery.

In any event, Danny and I had a standing luncheon date on a once-a month basis. This had been going on uninterrupted for many years now, starting sometime during graduate school and continuing during our post-doctoral work—his in molecular biology, mine in psychoanalysis.

*   *   *

"It's now more than twenty years ago. I was about three or four and I'd been in that institution for a while already. It was for kids without parents. Like an orphanage. Then she took me. The state would pay these people to take kids and raise them, I guess. When I got there, there were three little girls, and it was a small house. I remember one of the girls, name of Dierdra. She was shy but she was cute. She was blonde. Velma didn't like her. She didn't exactly scold her or anything, but she wasn't nice to her. The other two were twins and at first I couldn't tell them apart."

"How long had you lived in that orphanage or whatever it was before you got to Velma?" Kruger asked.

"I don't know," Tino said. "Maybe forever before that. All I know is that they told me I had no parents, that they had died. But I knew there was something wrong with that story because I do remember, I think it must have been my father. I was very small and he was always falling and bumping things. Now I think it was because he must have been drunk a lot, or maybe he was really sick with something. I don't know."

"Okay," said Kruger, "continue with how Velma got you."

"She worked at the place and like I said, the state paid her to take kids to live with her. They did it with a lot of people. At that time she always had three at a time. They would stay for months or something and then leave. I was the only one that kept staying. And I was the only boy. She only had girls.

I remember the first day I ever saw her in that place. Yeah, it was called a children's shelter. Anyway, when I first saw her I fell in love with her. She was so beautiful. And she still is. I smiled at her but she didn't smile back. That scared me. I thought I did something wrong and that she wouldn't like me. But she did like me. I would sneak looks at her. Her body was very good. It was beautiful. I know that sounds funny, like a little kid having those feelings, but even then, a lot of the times when I would be in bed at night and thinking about her, I would get, you know, hard. In the house, the twins had a little room to themselves, and they slept in one bed and Dierdra slept on the couch. The only other place to sleep was in the main bed where Velma was, and that's where she put me. Next to her in bed. That's where I slept."

Kruger interrupted him. "Were you sexually excited by her then? Like you said, getting hard."

"Yeah, that would happen almost every night of my life."

"Go on," Kruger said.

"She adopted me and was my mother. She's the only mother I ever had. She told me to call her mother, so that's what I always did."

Kruger backtracked. "What do you mean you would get hard every night of your life? You mean in bed with Velma? Are you still in bed with Velma, even now?"

Tino hesitated because Kruger made it sound bad.

"Well, you know we live in a small trailer and there's only one bed to sleep in so that's where we sleep."

Kruger's next question was obvious.

"So did you two ever have sex? I mean, was there love-making or touching? You know? Is there?"

"Never!" Tino exclaimed. "Velma never lets me touch her that way. To this day."

"So you got hard because you wanted to touch her but you couldn't?" Kruger added.

Then Tino burst forth with his confession.

"Yes, but I did touch her and I still do. But she doesn't know it. She never caught me. It started when I was small. I could tell when she was in a real heavy sleep. I could tell by her breathing. I was dying to touch her. I would lean over and smell her first. Her back. I could smell her back. I even started smelling her legs and, then, you know, I took a chance and started smelling, you know, in-between her legs. And I got used to the smell of it when I was young. I do it whenever she lies in bed over the covers. When it's warm. I move very slowly and lean from my side all the way down and smell it. Sometimes I touch her there and sometimes I touch her on top—you know—but only with one finger. Like I point the finger and press it down only a little."

Tino gestured with his finger as he described the touching.

"I would even get hard before bedtime because she always walks around in her underwear. Like in her bra and panties. I can see everything."

"Wait," Kruger announced. "Did she do that when you were a boy, too, or only now?"

"Oh, no," Tino said, "she always did it that way. She was never ashamed and told me not to be ashamed, either, because she said it was like wearing a bathing suit. Nothing to be ashamed about. I thought she was so beautiful."

He stopped. Kruger sensed there was more, and his own voyeuristic impulse was now hard at work as well.

"Go on, Tino. This is important. What else? You must have had thoughts about doing more with her. What did you want to do? Did you want to do something more?"

Tino knew exactly what he meant.

"When I was a kid, sometimes I would cry because I couldn't lie on top of her and hug her. I just wanted to kiss her all over. And I used to get so hard then. I thought it was the most anyone could want something. She has those beautiful—on top, you know—and her skin smells so good. I'm in love with her and I always was in love with her. That's what I think." He hesitated. "It's what I know."

Kruger wouldn't let go. "Tino, you mean she never covers up her body at home when you're around?"

"Oh, no. I always see her that way. She tries for me not to see her naked but I have. A lot of times."

"Did you do yourself—you know—thinking about her?"

"Sure, oh yeah. All the time. I've been doing that all of my life. But I hide it now. She used to catch me doing it and she got disgusted at me for it, especially since she told me not to. One time she caught me and forced me to finish doing it right in front of her. I didn't know what to do. But she told me I had to do it right there with her watching. So I did. But it took me longer with her there watching. I think I was scared she would send me away or something. But she sat down on the bed and told me to finish it and that she was going to watch while I did it. And she watched until it worked, and it all spilled into the paper towels. I always try to do it in paper towels."

"And how old were you when this happened?"

"I was about thirteen. But I was already doing it for a few years. I'm sure it's because I was tall and strong. She always told me I was handsome and strong. She said, 'ahead of your years.' I was shaving when I was about twelve years old. And before I was twelve, she would sometimes let me hold her in bed even though she usually wouldn't let me even touch her. She'd only let me once in a while and I never knew if she would or not. Sometimes it was when she said I was good and sometimes it was when she said I was bad. And sometimes, she gave no reason. She just let me. But after I was twelve, about the time I started shaving, she stopped letting me."

Tino stopped. He seemed to have lost his train of thought. Kruger noticed it immediately and reminded him of what he was talking about.

"The first time it happened was about then. I was ten or eleven and we were in bed. She was fast asleep and I was jerking it and squeezing it and trying to bend it. It was giving me a great thrill. I was doing that with one hand and I wanted to touch her with the other hand, like I would always do, like with my finger. I did it. As soon as I touched her with my finger, the explosion happened right into my undershorts. It was the greatest thing that I ever felt. But I was scared. I didn't want her to know about it so I snuck out of the bed and I went to the back yard and took off my underwear. And then I smelled it. And I knew as soon as I smelled it that it belonged to the same kind of smell that Velma had between her legs. Not exactly the same but I felt like it belonged to it. I wiped myself off with the underwear even though it was messy with that stuff and then I buried it using my hands to dig the hole. It was the middle of the night and I was standing there naked in the dark. I snuck back in and washed my hands and feet and my other stuff in the bathroom. Then I put on clean shorts and tiptoed back to bed. She never knew anything. And you know what? A few years later, it was a long time later, I dug it up and dumped it in someone's garbage away from the trailer."

"Tino, I want to get back to what happened after you ejaculated—exploded with that stuff—and she was watching you?"

"Well, when I did it to the end, she said something like, 'Okay, are you happy now?' I don't remember anything after that. She never said anything about it again."

"Did you ever do it picturing her sitting there watching you do it?"

"I think so," Tino said. "I think I started to picture doing it with other people watching too. I think it got me real hot."

Kruger knew he was hearing the genesis of one part of the split—exhibitionism in the flesh. He knew that Tino wasn't sure of these memories—an indication that Tino's personality had already fragmented.

"How were you in school? Did the sex and getting hard happen in school, too?"

Tino hesitated.

Kruger repeated, "I said did it ever happen in school, Tino? Like with girls?"

"I never went to school," Tino said. He waited. "She kept me home and she was the one that taught me how to read and write and do my arithmetic and stuff."

"You never went to school?" Kruger again repeated incredulously.

Tino shook his head.

"Tino, we're getting close to the end of the session. Is there anything else I should know? You've told me a lot of important things, so if you left something out maybe you should get that off your chest, too. You know, secrets aren't good."

"Well, there is just one more thing. It's that after Velma watched me doing it, maybe I started smelling her clothes and not just her body. Then, when I knew she was at work and wouldn't be home, I think I started putting them on. I even smell her shoes. It gives me a good feeling about being in the house. But I'm not sure about it."

And Kruger was now certain that he was hearing about the birth of Tino's cross-dressing, transvestism. "I see," said Kruger. But he knew he didn't see. He knew he still didn't see the core mechanism involved in the actual crystallization of these symptoms though it was probably staring him in the face.

*　　*　　*

I remembered high school. That's what I haven't told Deborah about. I always love to tell that story about how we were in the same class. Yet, even though that vivid memory keeps staring me in the face, I keep forgetting to tell it to her. It's because these other urgencies come to mind first.

It was 1983 and we were at the High School of Music and Art, in New York City. The school was located on top of the park in Harlem on Convent Avenue adjacent to City College. It was then called "The Castle on the Hill," and it was the last year before the school merged with the High School of Performing Arts and they became LaGuardia High School with its new location adjacent to Lincoln Center in Manhattan. The "Castle" was a solid academic school with exquisite programs in music and in art. Katie's specialty was art, mine was music. But she was also as musical as any of the music students. And she was positively stunning. But we only knew each other casually then. After we graduated, I lost track of her. Everyone knows how that happens. Then about a decade later we re-met at a party, and I knew that was it. We danced close and I could smell the natural bouquet of her body. And it sent me. I liked everything about her, and I remembered that in high school her painting was special. And now, now at the party, I had her.

We sat and talked all night. At the first sign of light we slept for about five hours and then together woke at about the same time. It was in my apartment. We felt we'd been together all of our lives. Then we made love. We've been making love ever since. Even now, we're together. That's what I'll tell Deborah: Even now we're together.

But to distract myself I shift to the real now. Thankfully, I'm always busy working on a book. As it turns out, that's what really saves me. I bury myself in my books. And this weekend it's all Sebastian's stuff.

* * *

It was now after my long weekend of scouring the diary, the manuscript, both volumes of the Inquisition, and Netanyahu's tome, as well as giving Stroud and Grillo complete access to me. Even though I was feeling safe with them—at least for the time being—nevertheless I was only thinking of meeting Danny.

On the Rockefeller University campus I had the sensation of tranquility, where you could think, write, teach, pursue whatever experiments you were doing. Wherever we went on the campus, Professor Daniel Margolis was known. When I called him and told him what I was up to with Sebastian's material, we decided to meet at Rockefeller.

I told him all about the Billy Soldier tragedy and that the detectives were following a lead about the possibility of a multiple personality involvement, and were using me as an expert. I began to talk about Sebastian and the Inquisition. Danny wanted a refresher on the Inquisition. Who started it? How long did it last? I started by telling him that I was only concerned here with the Spanish Inquisition, but that the Inquisition took place all over Europe and even in Central and South America.

All directed by the church. As far as the Spanish Inquisition was concerned, I gave him a quick summary: that it was officially established in Spain by King Ferdinand and Queen Isabella in 1478 as *The Tribunal of the Holy Office of the Inquisition,* with a document of Pope Gregory IX called constitution Excommunicannus; Tomas de Torquemada was its Grand Inquisitor; that carrying it out was the duty or *honor* primarily of the Dominican friars; that twenty years later the use of torture was legitimized by—and I told Danny to get ready for this name—Pope Innocent IV; and, that the killing went on and on.

The priests had so poisoned the Spanish people with anti-Jewish hatred that pogroms became a normal occurrence. Of course, the expulsion of Jews was held in 1492 (a date, of course, that Danny recognized, and that most schoolchildren learn is a happy and good date); and, that it was only in 1834, six centuries after it started, that the Spanish Inquisition was finally abolished. In reality however, the church and royalty tortured and killed Jews for much more than these six hundred years. In fact, even at the end of the 14th century, predating the Inquisition, four thousand Jews were killed in Seville alone.

"Primitive, Danny. All primitive."

"Absolutely," he said. "Murder in the first degree and no one got punished."

"Punished?" I said, "They all became enriched!"

"So," Danny said, "let's walk the campus."

It was cold, but we walked to the far side of the campus above the East River.

"What's in the diary?" he asked.

I started at the beginning and told him the entire story—who Sebastian was, his station in life, his family, my epiphany about him being the first psychotherapist.

"Sebastian was dealing with the barons," I said. "It was the barons who ruled the estates, and they made the deals with the church."

I told him about the Ferrers and reminded him that Marranos, or "pigs," were conversos—that is, Jews who had converted when given the choice either to be baptized or die. Then I explained the auto-da-fé, and that got to him.

"What I discovered from the diary was that Sebastian, whose surname was Arragel, was descended from Rabbi Moses Arragel and that it was

Moses Arragel who translated the famous Alba Bible into Spanish. Moses Arragel was his great-uncle. Sebastian stated that his daughter's name, Alba, was indeed the link to Moses Arragel's Alba Bible." Then I told him what I myself didn't want to know. "Here it is, Danny. They had him in a dungeon. Tortured him on the rack. The rack and screw. But they didn't kill him like they did the rest—they garroted people. With him, they made a blood exception. They took a hot poker to his tongue and burned it."

Danny didn't blink. He said, "What happened then?"

"Well, afterwards, I guess they just let him go. He talks about a vow of silence, and describes his trip from islands on the Spanish coast to the Livorno region in Italy. I traced it on the map. In terms of contemporary maps, I believe he went from Malaga to Valencia on the coast, to the islands of Palma and then Corsica. Because of his illuminated manuscripts, his fame had preceded him. At first, before he escaped, he was hiding amongst the *Illuminists*, these reactionary mystics who followed a Sister Isabella de la Cruz. They were fanatical conversos trying to be purer than pure. He felt it would be the last place in the world where anyone could find him. He was particularly afraid of Modesto Ferrer. He tried to find his daughter but no one could tell him anything about her. I don't think he ever found her. He became a non-person with no influence. You know what a non-person, is Danny?" I didn't wait for an answer.

"A ghost!"

He nodded.

"Danny, Sebastian writes about feeling plagued thinking that Alba might be alive, somewhere suffering, and even said that if that were to be the case, he wished her dead. Danny, I'll show it to you. He just says her name, 'Alba.' I could feel his agony. He says that then she would be in a state of manes, which is something like the venerated state of a dead person."

"What else?" Danny asked.

"The illuminated manuscripts—Sebastian actually created a Passover Haggadah and it was the Haggadah that got him into trouble. In the court they branded him a 'Jew's Jew.' That's how he put it.

"But he was impoverished, by this time living in a monastery in Italy, not able to speak and not able to return to Spain. Apparently he discovered that his wife, Ester, had, in fact, been killed. That one kills me," I said.

Danny knowingly nodded, and suddenly began a process—actually more like a riff. "I know why they burned his tongue. Because his life was language. Talking. They hated that he held private information, that people confided in him, and that people respected him. So they silenced him—turned him into what they considered to be an incorporeal being."

As he said it, I knew he was right. The meaning of the whole thing was obvious now that Danny had put it out there. His genius was to see what most didn't. Then he said he was feeling a bit spaced-out which in shrink talk is called "depersonalized." I think Danny had to migrate to this state of mind in order to manage his anger at the whole thing.

Then his light bulb turned on again, and he said, "Glenn, you know that article of yours on multiple personality is a perfect parallel with this Inquisition business. The church is really entirely multiple, split, fractured, and even maybe schizo. On the one hand you've got a mother church telling its participants to be good, honest, even innocent. At the same time, mother church tells its parishioners to renounce aggression and to control sex. So what happens? While many parishioners try to do good, and be good Christians, the church goes ahead and constructs an aggressive, out-in-the-open Inquisition—no less a genocide—against Jews.

"On the other hand, priests themselves go ahead and act-out all this sexual perversion stuff, you know, the sexual molestation of little boys. You really think these thousands of molestations by priests only began in the 20th century? Nonsense. It's been going on for two thousand years; hundreds and hundreds of thousands of sexual molestations of different boys, and also over and over with the same victims, for over twenty centuries.

"So there it is," he continued. "An innocent church body manipulated by mother church while simultaneously gestating severe aggression on one side, and sexual acting out, on the other. See?" he almost ended, "the church is a perfect example of a split personality."

Actually, it was a pretty good parallel indeed. In the multiple personalities of individuals I had treated, the innocent host personality acts as the parishioner who is split off from anger and sexuality. But the anger and sex are acted out by the church officials anyway, and basically the parishioner doesn't get it. It's not consciously registered. It's all manipulated, arranged, engineered, and choreographed by mother church. In other words, if it were an individual, the mother would manipulate the son, and then the son, without knowing it, would act out aggression on the one hand, and sex on the other. The net effect is that the good son, the good parishioner, feels innocent because he doesn't even know what the hell happened.

"Jesus," he ended.

At that point I was about to describe a portion of Sebastian's final few pages of the diary, which it seemed to me would confirm what Danny had just summarized. But he stopped and turned to me, waited what seemed like a second too long, and said he needed to talk to me about something personal. I instantly had the thought that it may have been triggered by what I had previously told him about Sebastian in one of our phone conversations. Sebastian had related the touching story of his contact with a member of the court, who confided that he was desperately in love with a prominent married woman, also a member of the court. This woman was warm and loving to him, while his wife, as he put it, was cold-hearted.

I didn't say it because Danny was about to tell me his personal thing, and I could feel myself tense up. I could see this wasn't easy for him, that he was about to confess to something like an affair, or else something equally critical. It certainly was going to be important because of the way he suddenly shifted from his very interesting theory of the church as a classic multiple or split personality, to another something that seemed very personal.

* * *

Carl Emory was in the hospital on the critical list. It was now three days since his attack and he had not yet regained consciousness. When it was Emory's turn to be scheduled for Stroud's interrogation, Nurse Secora told him that Emory had not been to work for the previous three days. She assumed he was ill.

After making some inquiries, Stroud discovered where Emory was. He'd been found unconscious by a neighbor, soaked in blood, wallet gone. The other astounding fact, reported in the notes by the police at the scene, was that he was wearing heavily applied lipstick. Stroud immediately conveyed these details to Grillo and, in a split second, guessed that Emory was the exhibitionist at the hospital and maybe even Billy's killer. "Too coincidental," Grillo answered. "The guy worked on Billy's ward, for cryin' out loud. Billy's killer doesn't get killed—he kills!"

They sprung into action and started inquiring about Emory. They spoke to everyone on the ward and did some random interviews with others at the hospital as well. Then they began piecing it together. It was a rumor about Velma Secora and Emory.

"Was Emory a special friend of yours? That's what people are saying," Stroud said. Without a blink Secora answered that they worked together and that she was his immediate superior on the ward. "But, there was nothing else," she said.

Ignoring her statement, Stroud asked a direct question. "Nurse Secora, were you involved with Carl Emory in a romantic or sexual relationship? Like were you having an affair? And that's not a trick question. Just needs a simple answer. Yes or no?"

"That's ridiculous," she again immediately responded. "It's true that Carl sought my counsel on various personal matters in his life and would, how shall I put it, usually comply with my wishes. He never gave me any trouble on the ward. As a matter of fact, I never heard him say no to anything. He was entirely cooperative and went out of his way to assist me in any number of things I needed done."

"Well, how about here on the ward?" Stroud asked. "You know, it's kind of strange. Billy Soldier is murdered, then there are attacks on attendants, first at the hospital and now outside the hospital. That's too much. And almost every-thing seems connected to your ward."

"I wouldn't exactly call it my ward, and almost everything doesn't mean everything," she said, trying to obliterate Stroud's implication that she was somehow connected to it all.

Of course, she knew. When she heard the news about Carl, she instantly knew that Jericho had tried to kill two birds with one stone. He would get rid of Carl, thereby ending the Chief Nurse Secora/Carl Emory liaison, and at the same time protect Veronica by blaming the exhibitionistic behavior on Carl. No doubt—Jericho was a force.

Velma knew she could control almost anyone, but not Jericho. She could influence even Veronica. But not Jericho. And she knew why she couldn't con-trol Jericho. She knew that Jericho hated that she was so ungiving. She knew that Jericho wasn't buying her implicit promises— "Do as I say and perhaps then you can have something you so desperately want." She knew that Jericho was enraged solely because she, Velma, was stingy, tightfisted with her feelings, and even more, with her body. She controlled everything around her with the promise of that beautiful body, but only delivered at her own will, leaving her subject not knowing why. And, of course, Jericho knew she was keeping Tino in abject agony and at the same time in intense delight.

And Velma was perfectly aware that Jericho had complete access to Tino's psyche and that he, Jericho, experienced firsthand how she had managed to usurp that psyche, conquering Tino's libido and his entire wish-system and essentially then owning him. He personally experienced her full grip around Tino's psyche. He felt how she would squeeze it whenever and to whatever extent it suited her, or at other times stroke it, or even better, promise to stroke it. And the killer, so to speak, was that Jericho knew he was the direct product of Tino's permanent state of arrested development. And here is where Velma knew she had him, because Jericho was actually in a quandary about his own existence. They both knew that were it not for Tino's susceptibility to Velma's manipulation, Jericho positively could not exist.

And both Jericho and Velma also knew that this was where Velma had leverage. If she wanted to, she might be able to cure Tino of his problem, release him, thereby forever ending Jericho's existence. And there was the leverage; there was the rub for Jericho. To be or not to be—the essence of Jericho's ambivalence.

So Velma did, it seem, actually have some sway with Jericho, especially because of this existential ambivalence of his. Velma also understood that Jericho was an eye witness to her powers—her entry into Tino's mind. She could tell that it was Jericho, in the process of becoming, who experienced firsthand how she rearranged the forces in that mind so that Tino no longer had any say there whatsoever—and Jericho watched as she began doing it to Carl Emory as well. Then when she was in the process of vanquishing Carl's psyche, she started her dominance patter. She made him beg for everything, just as she did with Tino. So even though Jericho was essentially unafraid of Velma, nevertheless, he knew she could influence things—profoundly.

But Jericho also knew that the psyche was even stronger than Velma. Velma could rearrange the forces of Tino's mind and enslave him, but she couldn't erase his sex or his anger. The best she could do was accomplish the handiwork of division. Thus, Tino still had his sexuality and his anger, but in order to express these feelings, he became fragmented, compartmentalized, parsed. He became three people. On the other hand, Jericho knew that he too, was the mark of Velma's power. She could not be defeated even by two men and a woman—only circumvented. And when she had Tino at the edge of despair—longing for her but deprived, then Tino himself created the monster. In this case, Jericho. Thus the monster always produces the monster. Velma, ultimately through Tino, gestates Jericho. Pure psychopathological incest!

*And don't think Velma didn't know how Jericho felt about it all. She got it directly from Jericho himself because from time to time, when she searched through Tino's bureau, she would come across either Jericho's or Veronica's diary notebook. And she realized several things: that both of them, Jericho and Veronica, kept diaries; that because both of them were out of her reach, she couldn't prevent them from keeping these diaries; that the next best thing was to have access to these diaries; and that she could monitor what was happening with Tino by tracking the contents of the diaries. She was also aware that Tino wanted her to know all of this because, either in the persona of Jericho or Veronica, he would occasionally neglect to return the diaries to their secret place. Obviously, Tino, through his other two, his alter personalities, **wanted** her to know, albeit unconsciously. That was his power—his only power over her. "See, you can make me different, but you can't make me less because I **can** be angry, and I **can** be sexual." That's what Tino was saying whenever he would forget and leave the diaries in his bureau drawer. But alas in the end, Velma was really stronger than all of them. They were all in orbit around her, not the other way around.*

And Stroud thought he could get her on some simple, basic, straightforward question regarding relationships that either she or others were having with one another.

Was he kidding?

* * *

And now Danny was about to give me his personal odd variation on this same theme of relationships.

"It's Ruthie. Sebastian's story opened the floodgates. I have to tell you, Glenn. I've wanted to, but I guess it was my pride. I've never told anyone except a shrink I saw for a few sessions last year. He told me to leave her. I left him instead. Here's the question I've been asking myself for a lot of years now, Glenn. Is it better to love, or to be loved? What's your answer?"

"Danny, my rule is to never answer those kinds of questions because it's obvious that the person is not saying what's on his mind. So what's on your mind?" Danny then described his relationship with his wife, Ruthie, as an emotional wasteland. Apparently she could not express warmth and was, at best, sexually modest. He used many synonyms for "modest" and I had the thought that Ruthie may have been living behind *The Line* in withdrawal. He said she was either immune or allergic to affection.

"She's really dead. Wraith-like. Sometimes I feel like a victim of shunning behavior," he said. "But I can't give it up. I'm stubborn." He paused. "I gradually noticed that she really has trouble giving, but then it hit me, Glenn. It was staring me in the face but I couldn't see it." And then he said it. "She's always angry. That's why she can't give. She can only show love when something, no, maybe someone, is hurt, or like an animal is hurt. Yeah, like if it's a wounded animal."

I believe he actually understood it. Ruthie could only respond to weakness. So I said, "You know, Danny, you're very strong; that might be hard for her."

"The funny thing," he said, "is that I married her because I think I wanted to rescue her. Now I know about rescue missions. In marriage, don't go on rescue missions. What does Sebastian say about that?" he declared. Danny thought it was a joke but I was right there. "It's funny you should say that, Danny, but it's no joke because Sebastian had a postulate on that in his manuscript. He said: 'Relationships have an algebraic function. A positive multiplied by a negative always yields a negative.' And, Danny," I said to him, "not only that, but it may be that in order for any marriage to be sustained, at least one of the partners has to be able to suffer inordinately."

"And how," he practically shouted. "She also has a kind of mantra. It's what I call a 'won't' mantra. It doesn't matter what the question is, the answer is always 'no.' I won't go here. I won't do this. I won't sit, I won't stand. It's all 'no.' But she's an honest person—never lies, and I mistook that for truthfulness. It actually took years before I began to realize that her being true to herself is not the same as her being right. Then I realized that she would be this way with anyone. She would find a reason to be negative with anyone. Oppositional. She can't ever be wrong. I've come to think that it may also be an acculturated gender difference between men and women. Men can't deal with humiliation, but women manage it better. But women can't be wrong while men manage that better." He paused, and continued:

"Now, here comes the hard one. I've recently imagined that Ruthie dies. Either she's hit by a truck or dies of some natural cause."

I felt whomped in the stomach, but in his own agony it never occurred to him how that related to me. Unself-conscious, he kept on going.

"I know it's a wish on my part and that I must be real mad at her. I want to be free of her. But the funny thing is that I can also picture my own death, and I don't really care about it. In either case, one of us gets to be free. Of course then I worry because I don't want anything to hurt her." It must have hit him because, again without pausing, he said, "I really hate saying all this to you, Glenn, because of Katie. As a matter of fact, I'm suddenly realizing that that's where I got the idea." I nodded.

Then he told me that he recently attended a conference at Stanford University. When his plane landed he called Ruthie, and when she answered the phone, he said, "I've either got good news or bad news. I've arrived." The point is that I'm unhappy. I didn't care whether I made it or not.

"I think you're a bit depressed, Danny. Maybe defeated is more accurate. And by the way, many couples have that same fantasy about each other. I hear it in my office all the time. Why do you think that in the marriage vows of most cultures is included a 'for better or worse' statement? You think it's because all relationships always get better? As you know, Danny, relationships are hard work. No doubt."

"But you and Katie worked on it," he said quietly. "I admire and envy it."

I felt myself blink but then asked him about other women. He gave me a litany of reasons why he hadn't. But he admitted to one recent incident that was an almost. He didn't go into it and I didn't pursue it. I told him, "Danny, with Ruthie you've been the uxorious prototype — uxorious meaning excessively or exceedingly devoted to one's wife. But things change, especially with all that disappointment. The rhapsody goes."

He looked at me for what seemed like a long time and said that the talk was helpful. I told him that I felt he had courage. I then told him what I also had said to our Pakistani van driver: "Freud once said, Danny, that if you don't speak it, it gets reenacted instead. And one of the other early shrinks added that if it's reenacted enough it becomes your fate. You can begin to feel that your destiny is to suffer this way. To be deprived. To be punished. That's why Freud said that the unspeakable must be spoken. And not only spoken — it must also be heard as we're doing now."

We were out on the campus for the entire conversation, and now we were both cold. We headed back to his office, and he made some tea.

I wondered whether he and Ruthie ever talked about their estrangement, thinking that they probably never did. He surprised me.

"Only when we're in bed."

* * *

Velma was nuts! They were in bed in their trailer. It was getting late. Before she turned off the lights, she needed to talk to him, but in a way that would not antagonize or in any way prompt him to run out again screeching away in his car. And, of course, she knew how to pacify him. On her part it was a supreme sacrifice of the rules. She'd discontinued their intermittent physical contact when Tino's hormones started coursing. Now she was going to give Tino his wildest dream, knowing that in exchange Tino would give her anything she wanted. Anything.

"Tino, I know we love each other. Come, lie with me on my side." Tino suddenly stared as though almost in a fugue state. "Come here, Tino. Lie in my arms. It's okay." Tino moved to her, sliding over and curling himself up with his head in the crook of her arm and his legs pulled up to his stomach. A larger-than-life man in a fetal position.

Feigning innocence, she asked, "Is this okay, Tino?"

"Yes," was the whisper.

"Okay, Tino, you may stay like this until I finish telling you what I've been thinking. Then if you don't run away and you've carefully listened, and if you're still here when I finish, then I'm going to let you stretch your leg out and put it over mine. I think you would like that. Is that right, Tino? You would like that?"

Again the whisper was "Yes."

"All right, Tino, I thought you might be cooperative, and I see I was right, wasn't I?" She didn't wait for an answer. "Well, then, let's see. I know you know that Carl was almost killed. We both know Jericho did it. Well, at least I know. Jericho was smart enough to put lipstick on Carl. Carl's no transvestite. Jericho was protecting Veronica that's for sure, isn't it? Good, Tino, you're still here, lying here and listening, so I'll continue. Now, Tino, you're too jealous of Carl. You hate it when I'm alone with him so often. I know you, darling boy. I hurt you badly. But you should have known, Tino, that as far as I'm concerned, Carl can't compare to you. You've got to be careful and control things better because if Carl dies, Dr. Kruger will know that Jericho did it. You see, Tino, I'm aware that you tell Dr. Kruger everything you know about our situation. But that's okay because he just might be able to cure your headaches. He can't do anything to us because we've got plenty on him. But, Tino, Jericho is completely out of control, and I want you to control him better."

Velma assumed that Tino, as always, was getting uncomfortable hearing that kind of material. And of course she was most aware that he wasn't budging. At that point Velma took Tino's arm and placed it across her stomach so that now she arranged it so that Tino was holding her—had that beautiful coveted body that she knew he so craved, and about which, all his life, he felt a proprietary sense.

Tino was now smelling her, breathing her in. She was permitting it.

She knew he didn't quite understand it all, but she was banking on the proposition that his unconscious was hearing it and that her aphrodisiacal power would be stronger than all of the forces of Tino's psyche.

"So, Tino, I want you to try with all your might to control both Jericho and Veronica." Tino really didn't know any Jericho or Veronica, but again, there was no response from him. Usually, references to Jericho and Veronica, or "those others" as Velma would occasionally refer to them, could confuse him because it meant that people were telling him he wasn't really himself. At these moments he would usually stare into space. He could only talk to Dr. Kruger about it. But, here it was that Velma was indeed being listened to.

Velma paused and said, "Okay, Tino, okay? Say yes."

The whisper came again. "Yes."

"Good. Now you may stretch out your leg, Tino. You have been excellent. Here now, put it across mine. I know you want to." There was no response. "Don't you?"

"Yes," was the whispered response. But as soon as Tino stretched his leg out, and put it across her thighs and her legs, she felt his body instantly and erratically shudder. And as usual it was premature. "Tino, Tino," Velma effusively said, as she reached over and turned off the lamp. "I know it's because you love me so."

In this veiled dark of the night, Veronica lay there smiling.

* * *

We sat at the table near the window with the silk-shaded lamp that always gave off a soft, warm glow. The tea was comforting. We talked about this and that when he suddenly said, "Looking at Ruthie used to go right to my heart, now it stops in my eyes."

I was trying to help Danny mostly by just listening, but this comment of his about his eyes and heart prompted me to go to Sebastian. "Listen to this gem out of Sebastian's notes," I said. The excerpt was from a passage written by that high-ranking member of the court who had a mistress and who sought Sebastian's counsel, swearing that his cold, ungiving, withdrawn wife drove him into extra-marital love. "I've been carrying this passage around with me," I said. "It's actually a lament." I unfolded the single sheet of paper and began to read:

> Here is the best way I can say it: She is bright, so whatever she says seems to interest me and therefore, my mind is stimulated. Second, she is beautiful. Very. So my eye is nourished — always satisfied. Three, she is honest and has integrity, so her soul is pure, and I admire that. Here is the problem. Her behavior is without grace. She is cold and austere. She cannot give. She will never take my hand — we do not embrace. She will never greet me. So my heart — my heart is starved. Recently in rare freezing weather she was shivering, and put her arm in mine and pressed herself close to me. She kept her whole shivering body tightly against mine as we briskly walked. It took us a short time to reach our destination and it was the only time in our many years together that I felt deeply loved — even though I knew she was only cold.

Without skipping a beat Danny said, "Well, that's me. On the dot. What are the — what is it, five points?" He thought for a moment and said, "mind, eyes, heart and soul — that's four."

And I said, "Behavior — that's five."

"Right, behavior," he answered.

"And," I continued, "behavior is the most important. It's not what you think, or feel, or pretend that counts. It's what you do, and what you don't do. Past is prologue," I told him. "But in any event, 'doing' is the operative term. And from experience, you feel Ruthie's not doing the right things. And for you that's a killer."

Danny suddenly shifted. "The funny part of it is that Ruthie was never my obsession. I don't think I'm obsessed with her per se. I'm obsessed with the fact that she abandons me emotionally and that's what I can't accept. That's the obsession. Believe it or not, I think I've figured out what my stubbornness is all about. It's about my mother. She was always very loving, but I can distinctly remember when she first went to work. I was two or three years old. I remember feeling abandoned. I also remember resenting it. I date my stubbornness from that point. It's like I won't give up until she returns. I'm playing this out in my life. I'm stubbornly waiting for her to come to me, and I won't give up till she does. My problem is that she never came back."

I remembered Sebastian's young woman with anorexia and my own patient who wouldn't eat, both feeling abandoned.

"Okay," he said. "You know, I told you there was something that didn't happen recently? Well here it is. When I began consulting here at Rockefeller, we had a lab assistant who worked three doors down on this corridor. She was about twenty-five or twenty-six so obviously I was a lot older. She was beautiful. Now why did I get obsessed with her? Well, she wasn't just beautiful. She had that smile, that same receptive smile. It floored me. Let's put it this way, if she would have given me more cues, I definitely would have had the affair. She was the only one who could have broken my resistance. I'm still bereft over her. She worked here for about four months and then, poof, gone. She promised to visit but never has. I still think about her, and when I check my messages I look for her call."

He became silent and was staring. Then he visibly relaxed a little and said, "You know, Glenn, talking about it is making me feel better. Maybe it's a eulogy. I'm actually better than I was. Maybe it'll only kill me sometimes rather than every day."

Now I was silent. It was curious to me about why I hadn't become more upset when he told me his Ruthie-being-killed-by-the-truck fantasy. I thought it's because of that head and heart business, where you manage yourself with your head, but others with your heart. So, my head kept me in control—almost detached—but my heart went out to him, even though for me, my emotional anesthesia prevented my heart to go out to me.

But all the while he was telling me about Ruthie and what she wasn't able to do in their relationship, I was comparing, remembering Katie. He said lots of things about Ruthie, none of which were good. She couldn't give, wasn't warm, didn't approach him sexually, and generally hadn't ever really understood him—or maybe anyone else for that matter. But Katie, oh my God. Katie was just the opposite. But then when I say "was," I'm immediately regretful. I need to obliterate the "was." "Is," is the present, not the past. "Is," is. It's not, "was!" When I go through this struggle with what I consider to be a so-called reality, with this "was/is" semantic horror, I feel as though I'm 100 years old because I feel weary and wasted—washed over with stress. It happens instantly. My only out is to shake it off by focusing on something else, on someone else. So, I turned to talk to Danny, knowing, however, that I was really referring to myself.

"Okay, Danny," I said, "I hope you're not in danger of getting post-traumatic stress. It's the universal diagnosis at sixty, but like me, you may be precocious. You feel better because we've been hanging for a couple of hours. Talking and feeling understood is always stronger than the resistance, so you feel better. But feeling understood is never stronger than the pathology. So the underlying anger's got to be analyzed. Right?"

"Cindy," he said. "Her name is Cindy." He paused again. "Two things, Glenn. First, we both know the receptive smile is my mother's."

"Yeah," I said. "The smile's got my attention, too. I think analyzing it will definitely lead to the mother lode—pun intended."

"Two, what other shrink can I talk to except you?" We both looked at the clock. It was already 3 P.M. We got our coats and headed for the door. He put his arm on my shoulder as we walked out, and, as always, he walked me halfway down to the gate.

We waved as I walked further down the hill and toward the gate. I was not feeling great. Then, as he was walking back up the hill to his office and was about to disappear from sight, I tried again to shake out of it and I yelled to him, "Danny, think about this one: What's the main task in life? What's the main task?"

· 14 ·

DOCTOR AND PATIENT

What's the main task in life? These words were still ringing in my ears as I pulled up to the building housing the autistic ward. I had been called in by Detectives Stroud and Grillo, who had been questioning everyone in sight. This included patients as well as staff. They finally got to Edward — for the third time. I arrived after they had tried to get something out of him, but as they later reported to me, Edward wouldn't cooperate. The truth, the sad truth, was that Edward couldn't cooperate.

Chief Nurse Secora would usher each patient into the ward psychiatrist's office for questioning. Edward was the last one. Stroud and Grillo tried to be as patient as they could. They sat with him and Stroud carefully said, "Edward, let's talk about Billy again." But that was not a good approach. Actually, there was no good approach. After some time, Edward dropped out of the chair and to his knees, crawled to the corner of the room and started banging the floor with the palms of his hands, screaming, "No, no, no, no!" Then he jumped up and upended the chair. Stroud, Grillo and Secora surrounded him and managed to restrain him until 'T' and another ward attendant took over, put restraints on him, and finally carried him to the isolation room. And of course, wouldn't you know it? I guess it had to be said. And Stroud was the one who said it to me later: "That's what you call the rubber room, right, Doc?" I didn't respond.

"What's the problem?" I followed. "Well," Stroud continued, "we've been here most of the day interviewing everyone in sight. We're hoping someone saw something." He stopped. "And?" I asked expectantly. He then proceeded to describe the scene with Edward and asked what I thought about it—especially the "nos."

"Where is he?" I asked. Stroud pointed to the isolation room. I peered into the little non-shatter glass window in the upper center portion of the door. There was Edward, motionless, asleep on the bed. "They gave him medication," Grillo volunteered.

"Quite frankly, I haven't the vaguest idea about the 'nos.' But I'll tell you this, no matter what anyone says about the random illogical nature of autistic communication, I don't believe it for a second. For my money everything is caused by something. It's not random and it's definitely not irrelevant. The trick, and maybe it's an impossible one to accomplish, is to take whatever communication is there and decode it. In this case the communication is an angry and probably anguished 'no, no.' Now, what does it mean? Because I'll bet dollars to doughnuts it means something." Then I described what Sebastian said. "Sebastian, the monk who I'm studying now and who lived about five hundred years ago figured that no matter how strange the communication is on top, underneath everyone is intelligent. I think he meant that nothing is without its cause. If you understand the cause, you'll have a better chance of understanding the communication."

"Well, then," Stroud instantly chimed in, "what if we assumed that the kid actually saw something and the 'nos' are his way of remembering but not telling what he saw, or something like that? Know what I mean?"

"No, no," said Grillo, "it's more likely that he's telling us to leave him alone—no more, no less. Whatdya think, Doc?"

"Could be either, but there's no way of knowing which is right—at least at the moment."

"But," Stroud said, "wouldn't it be a kick in the head if the kid actually saw it go down, but can't or won't verify it?"

With that, Grillo, without even looking at either of us, moved silently to the door. He stepped out into the corridor and face to face with Nurse Secora. She had been asked to leave the room earlier, just as I was entering. Without anyone saying anything, she volunteered, "I was waiting here in case you wanted something else."

Grillo thanked her and made it clear that she should return to her station. "That's a creepy chick if I ever saw one. She had her ear in this room. I felt it," he said.

They didn't discuss it further. Stroud told me that Grillo felt the odds of no one having seen the murder was slim to none. Their job was to find out who saw something and what it was they saw. At the moment, Edward's "nos" were all they had but again, they didn't know what those nos meant. Stroud suggested the possibility that Edward just didn't like them or was afraid of them. After all was said and done, the detectives had no relief from the pressure on them to find an actual witness and not a "maybe" one.

*   *   *

Grillo was tenacious and he believed in details. A man after my own heart. Stroud, on the other hand, was more interested in simply getting someone to confess. He put pressure on people. Good thing he wasn't around during the Inquisition. Grillo had his eye on Velma. He didn't like her snooping, but he commented to Stroud about her voluptuous figure in that nurse's uniform. When we had finished talking about Edward, the detectives made it clear that they had no further need for me and turned their attention to Nurse Secora. They asked to speak to her privately.

"Nurse Secora," Grillo started. "We know, of course, that Tino Vescaro is your adopted son."

"That must be a felony" she parried.

Grillo ignored the chance of a possible antagonistic repartee. "We also know he's being treated at the Headache Project."

"That one must be a misdemeanor," she again countered.

Again, Grillo didn't bite. "To your knowledge has he ever acted like he wasn't himself—like, you know, like something possessed him?"

"If you're getting at whether he's a split personality or something like that, the answer is no. Tino is a perfectly normal person. He suffers with terrible headaches and so he needs treatment for it. He's had the condition for a long time."

The more they questioned her, the more clipped she became until she was answering simply yes or no, right to the point. Grillo was impressed with her intelligence, but he didn't trust her.

"I just want to know two things," Grillo continued. "First, have you ever known Tino to be violent?" He headed her off by saying: "Don't answer that

yet. The second question is more personal. So you can answer both together. We'd like to know if you've ever noticed any unusual sexual behavior on his part?"

She quickly interrupted him. "Oh, no! Now you're trying to implicate him in that exhibitionistic display at the hospital. First it's the murder of Billy Soldier and now it's Tino as an exhibitionist? Oh, no. No you don't. He's neither of those things. He's always been cooperative and non-violent. And he's never been sexually deviant. Ever!"

They got nowhere with her. Denials all around. They quizzed her on her own whereabouts as well as Tino's on the night of Billy's demise, but again got nowhere. They told her they'd be in touch.

On the way to the car Stroud said, "Boy is she built." Then he hesitated for a moment and went off on a riff. "Trouble is when you fuck her your dick's gonna fall off because her pussy's like a freezer and your dick's gonna freeze solid so when she moves one muscle, she'll break your dick in three different places. It'll just break and fall off. And don't think she doesn't know it. She's probably done it to guys all her life. It's part of her nature. Then she probably saves them. Just go and open her freezer. Dicks—all over the place. Lined up. And not only that. The worst is when she's doin' it to you. Then she'll make you wait—she's gonna let you know with that spooked smile of hers that she's about to move the muscle surrounding your frozen, brittle dick. And then she moves it and snap, goodbye dick. Gone!"

Grillo was laughing. "Steve, now I've got one for you. Did you notice she said 'ever' instead of 'never'?" He didn't wait for an answer. "It was when she said Tino was 'never' sexually deviant. Then she emphasized it by saying 'ever.' Well, ever means always, doesn't it? And, are you ready for this? She said, 'murder!'"

* * *

Once again I was flooded with all kinds of feelings about Sebastian's plight as well as Billy's death—with no relief in sight. I had to wait, to be patient. What had started out as an urgent sharing of information with Danny about Sebastian's life in the 15th and 16th centuries and my need to get Danny's input, turned into Danny's telling me about his very turbulent inner life in the here and now. So my meeting with Danny didn't do it; he was too overwhelmed with his own stuff. That's why I had to wait even though I still needed a real debate with someone regarding Sebastian's fate in order to vent my own anger. I also wanted to talk over a possible format for a conference on Sebastian. I decided that the someone for a debate was Vlad. I could work out the conference format with Jean, but the urgent business had to be with Vlad—theologian, interpreter, Christian. Of course it had to be a Christian. I was always able to vent with Vlad because he knew that although I could attack a philosophy or a religious tenet, I treated individuals individually. Elie Weisel doesn't believe in collective guilt, but I think I do. I believe an entire culture and people are indicted in any genocide, but there are always individuals who resist, desist, or escape—or, of course, die.

I wanted to talk to Vlad as soon as I got home, but first I had to take care of several things. Check messages, call Rita and review my schedule. I knew, of course, that my schedule included a talk that night at the institute on group process and psychoanalytic group psychotherapy. The audience would be composed of postdoctoral students, faculty, and invited guests. I also began thinking about plans for the Sebastian conference, and then I remembered that I had to check the date for my presentation on symptoms. I also had Doubled-Over in a couple of hours. But most immediately, I had to set a date with Vlad. So I call him. Not in. I leave a message on his machine asking him to call me.

When you feel the need for closure, you should know that what you are really seeking is empowerment. Getting what you want when you want it—that's the need for closure. And I had it. But now I had to wait for Vlad to call me. More waiting. So I couldn't have closure and that meant feeling disempowered. So I know I'm also a little angry because disempowerment always invites, invokes, elicits, evokes, provokes, or basically, causes anger—in any person.

And then before I could get comfortable the phone began to compete with my wishes of the moment. Everything always seems to interfere with what I want at the moment. When that happens, I, like everyone else, feels disempowered. And now, more so. Then we all reach for our ever-present anger dictionaries, lexicons and glossaries, and we begin to find the words we use to disguise the anger. We feel frustrated, dissatisfied, annoyed, inconvenienced, impatient, and the best one of all—upset. All code words for anger. But really, it's the anger that's there. And that leads to the question I asked Danny about the main task of life. And the answer is: THE

MAIN TASK OF LIFE—IS TO MANAGE YOUR ANGER. And here the phone call was interfering with even my contemplation of deprivation. I think it had me a little frustrated, dissatisfied, annoyed, inconvenienced, impatient, and yes, upset.

*   *   *

It was Rita. She had a whole litany of names, places, dates, patients, colleagues, friends, meetings.

"Rita, stop. Hold it. It's too fast. I only want to know my schedule for today and tomorrow. I know I have the group talk tonight. Also, has the conference on symptoms been confirmed and will there be discussants?"

She became more deliberate. "George Fletcher tonight at six. Mr. Fletcher has already called twice to see if the appointment is confirmed. I think he's a bit hysterical or obsessive, it's hard to tell which. Jean has called, and about the symptom conference, Dr. White says he wants you—I wrote it down –'To present your theory and technology for implementing the theory as a single author presentation and not as part of a symposium.' He said that at the end the discussion would be open to the audience. There are no discussants on the dais. You're the only one doing the talking. Drs. Seymour and Jenkins asked whether they might invite students of theirs."

I told her I was happy that students would attend and thanked her, adding that as soon as Professor Strebonovich called, she should put him in the number one slot and to ask him to call me at the office right away.

Now I had to prepare for Mr. George Fletcher, whom I had originally dubbed Doubled-Over. I was amused by Rita's analysis of him. As a result of working with me all these years, she started using clinical lingo. Her diagnosis of hysteric versus obsessive would be amusing for most clinicians, largely because these are just about opposites.

Another call. This one was from Gail Forester, Kruger's secretary. She had never called me before and now there she was calling me at my private office, in my other life, not my hospital world.

"Dr. Kahn," she started, and a flood of information poured out. "I know this is unusual for me to call but, well, Dr. Kruger is not being himself and I don't know what to do. I've talked to my husband about it, and after I told him that you and Dr. Gersh are people I could talk to, he suggested I do just that. What's happening is that I've been coming to work each day and I just sit at my desk with nothing to do. I mean, there's a stack of papers waiting to be processed, but I can't get Dr. Kruger to give me any instructions. He keeps saying, 'not now.' Either he's searching the property office building or he's in the library. That's it. He spent the last day in the library, and is now scouring the property building basement."

* * *

In the basement of the property office building, there was a series of small storage rooms, with the hospital's arsenal of bins and receptacles holding literally tons of goods—material possessions of patients. And Dr. Siegfried Kruger was actually going through each storage room, bin by bin. He was in a frenzy, and an obsessive one at that. Convinced that Billy Soldier had been ingenious in figuring out where to conceal the record books, Kruger, at this frantic point, and for the first time, believed that Billy had some ulterior, insidious, and yes, profit motive that led him to hijack the records for himself. In other words, Kruger actually felt that Billy, whom he himself had labeled retarded, was operating a highly worked-out scheme that even after his death was outwitting the great doctor. So there he was in a flurry of activity, in a dimly lit basement, not even having removed his suit jacket that was already covered with dust and soot, searching every item in the bins. Hour after hour.

* * *

"He makes no secret about it," she said. "He's looking for the records Billy Soldier kept, but they're nowhere to be found and he's frantic about it. I'm calling you to get some advice. Do I just sit here and wait for him to suggest where I should start on the papers, or, uh, just wait for him?"

I was also waiting for the right pause, and then I jumped in and told her that yes, it was perfectly fine for her to call me and that I could see why she was concerned.

She said she was grateful that I understood. I then told her that it probably would not be a good idea for me to intervene and that I felt she should just wait it out and do whatever she could to handle any work not necessarily requiring Dr. Kruger's immediate attention.

Sitting at my desk contemplating the phone call, I fixed on Kruger in the library. Very uncharacteristic. In all the years we worked together, I'd never once seen or heard of Kruger in the library. I called Tommy Gersh.

"The library?!" he simultaneously asked and exclaimed. "Why?" I told him I couldn't imagine why, but I asked him to try to find out. I wanted him to head over to the library at that very moment and ask the librarian — a volunteer — to give him a rundown of the latest material anyone at the hospital was reading. He was to tell the librarian that we were doing data collection on which subject matter was being read week to week. She was not to mention our study to anyone because we didn't want to influence the findings.

Tommy liked the idea. However, I realized that I wasn't sure I liked it. And I knew if Tommy thought more about it, he wouldn't like it either. I could tell he just liked the spontaneous sense of adventure this caper offered. But spying on someone with respect to their intellectual pursuits or anything else for that matter made me uncomfortable — like Kruger was me and I was him. He's the one who snoops, yet here I was doing it, too. But I also knew it was highly unlikely for Dr. Kruger to be in the library. Although Kruger reading in the library might look innocent, I was guessing it wasn't. And then again, I also knew that it was I who was involved in the Sebastian manuscript-hijacking, and the dread I felt about that was exactly how I felt about this. I was probably doing something wrong by shadowing Kruger, and I was suffering a little because of it. But, of course, knowing it didn't stop me from doing it.

At the moment, I guess, I was suffering even more over the collective fate of Sebastian, and Billy, and of course, underpinned by what happened to Katie, to me — to us. How to end this rumination? I decided to call Jean. I still needed her approval to call a conference, guilt-free, on the subject of Sebastian's discoveries, and at the same time I didn't want to destroy Jean's mole at the Vatican library by blowing his cover. I'd have to figure a way to keep him safe. My plan was to use the conference on my treatment of symptoms as a platform to unveil Sebastian and his contribution to the uncovering of various mechanisms of the psyche. Then I'd introduce Sebastian to American psychiatry at a later conference where, for the first time, the full paradigm of the circuitry of symptoms would be revealed and presented.

Richard answered. Jean wasn't home, but he told me that she had heard I was going to call a meeting with the heads of the American Psychological

Association, the American Psychiatric Association, and the American Psycho-analytic Association to prepare them for a momentous discovery concerning a 15th century manuscript uncovering the secrets of the unconscious. That was the rumor.

"Who could have possibly spread that?" I asked.

"I don't know," Richard said, "but Jean said it's all over the institute. She's afraid her contacts in the Vatican could be exposed and she was upset about it. She's due here in a half hour."

"Tell her not to worry. No such conference is planned. I'm not getting any heads of organizations together. I haven't officially planned any meeting whatsoever. It's in the thinking stage. Please tell her not to worry. I've got to talk to her about the importance of introducing Sebastian and his discoveries to the New York psychoanalytic community in a small meeting, and then we'll plan further. The material is too important to suppress. Sebastian's discoveries are vital for the alignment of the history of psychiatry. She's an important part of this picture and I want her to know it."

"I'll tell her exactly what you said. I'm sure she'll be relieved."

I was the one who felt relieved, at least to have touched base with Jean through Richard. I was sure she would cooperate and that we would find a way to present Sebastian without any personal or political fallout regarding her contacts. I put the receiver down and sat back trying to relax. I must have dozed because the phone rang and I awakened with a start. It was Tommy Gersh.

"Glenn, check it out. He's reading all about Dissociative Identity Disorder."

"Of course," I thought. "Dissociative Identity Disorder—he's doing 'multiple research.'" Gersh continued. "He took out your 'multiples' paper, Mitchell's paper on Mary Reynolds, the Prince study on Christine Beauchamp, as well as Bower's 'Therapy of Multiple Personality.' What in the world is he studying that for?"

I told him he'd done a great job, and that we'd talk it all over when we met. I reminded him not to share this little adventure of ours with anyone else, and of course I knew he wouldn't. Tommy Gersh was a blood brother. Again I put down the receiver and contemplated the whole thing. I knew the literature on multiples well so I was familiar with the works Kruger was reading. It was all about doctor/patient treatment in the uncovering of the personality phenomenon first referred to as "demon possession," then later as "alter personality," then as "split personality," and only later as "multiple personality." And now, its latest designation was "Dissociative Identity Disorder." It all really means "split."

This history includes some classic studies. Mary Reynolds, a woman who lived in the late 18th to mid-19th centuries, was treated by a Dr. Samuel Latham Mitchell, who reported that Mary Reynolds had two distinct personalities. One was shy, the other outgoing. Another classic case, Christine Beauchamp, was described by Dr. Morton Prince in the early 20th century. This woman had several personalities that would come and go. The Bower book Tommy had mentioned was an attempt by the authors to outline a treatment technology for the multiple.

I began to wonder what Mary Reynolds, Christine Beauchamp, and the cases I described in my own paper on multiples had in common. Headaches were typical in the cases I reported, but that wasn't it. Then I knew. It was sleep. That was it. Usually, but not always, the transition between personalities needed to pass through a period of sleep. It could be a twenty-hour sleep like that of Mary Reynolds, or one of a few minutes like that of Christine Beauchamp. In my own paper, however, shift of personality occurred in two out of three cases without the intervening period of sleep.

I was sure Kruger was checking on specific constituents intrinsic to Dissociative Identity Disorder. But why? Then it hit me. Plain as day. "Oh my God," I thought, "Kruger's treating a multiple! Probably at the hospital." And parenthetically, I thought, "Grillo's an intuitive genius. And the multiple Kruger's treating must be having all the classic signs—headache, amnesia for the alter personalities, innocent host, and so forth. Tino!"

Grillo and Stroud weren't in. I left a message for them to call me. I was revved. But at the moment I needed to shift gears away from detective psychology, as with Billy, and into psychological detective. Next stop, therefore, was my private office and my meeting with Doubled-Over, Mr. George Fletcher. And I felt a little like a split personality myself. How do you be, so to speak, a relaxed, calm and dignified practitioner when your insides are screaming at you to gain some closure on things in your own life? In this case, a murder, a heist of some protected manuscripts, a vain attempt to rescue a 15th-century Jewish monk, a shooting of a statue at the clinic, some violent attacks as well as exhibitionistic episodes at the hospital, and the major tragedy of your personal life. Very difficult. Very, very difficult.

I got ready to leave for my office, and while I was preparing to leave, I couldn't help pondering Kruger's pursuit of Billy's records and his research into multiples. But time is a healer, and Doubled-Over, Mr. George Fletcher, began looming large. Here I was, as Katie would say, "collecting characters." She always said I loved idiosyncrasy. And this guy was a trip. I liked him. His whole routine in the corridor at the clinic was hilarious—the business about breasts versus tits. I retrieved some notes from my study, collected my papers in a folder, and left for my office.

*   *   *

Doubled-Over was all smiles. He regaled me with his history of ruminating large breasts. He also mentioned he was lonely and was talking to himself in the street. But, it wasn't solely the loneliness. He was also feeling disempowered because his wish to have someone—to have a relationship—was thwarted, and thus he was distressed, disappointed, dissatisfied, frustrated, annoyed, rejected, bored, and, of course, upset.

His psychological education would have to include a growing understanding of how his wish for companionship was gratified by talking to himself and how his wish to possess the woman was realized by doubling-over. This latter symptom would be more difficult for him to understand. How does doubling-over in pain satisfy the wish to possess the woman? We would try to accomplish this little piece of work together and through the analysis I would follow his stream of consciousness and listen for connections, paradoxes, conflicts, projections, denials, identifications, displacements, and the other varied and sundry products of the psyche.

This stream, if followed carefully, would, I was sure, lead us to breasts, or tits, as he put it. Prevailing wisdom is that breasts represent the nurturing wish. However, in this case such prevailing wisdom is pure psychobabble. It's not about his mother or the mother's breast or mother's milk or mother's presumed or even ostensible abandonment of him. So what was it about? Well, he and I would have to discover that together as we proceeded in the analysis. Yet, I did have my hunch. I didn't think it was about breasts at all. Breasts, large ones, constituted his bread and butter symptom, but the fixation on large breasts was really just a symbol. Nothing more, nothing less. Emblematic of what was the question? I was betting the answer would turn out to be something regarding the size of his penis. How about that? This man was doubling over in pain probably because of something to do with large breasts but, possibly, really because of his perception of the actual size of his penis. I believed that that's what would be revealed.

When I would begin to ask him about it, I was betting he'd readily admit to feeling powerful and adequate because he considered his penis to be large. I was also betting that this man suffered, from time to time, with the thought that his penis also was too small. Or, if not too small, then not large enough. So that we might have had a paradox on our hands. How does someone simultaneously agree that his penis is large and small? Or adequate and inadequate? Or large enough and not large enough? And I believed that that was where we would ultimately work. In his crotch!

If he possesses a woman with large breasts, then he becomes adequate because the large breast represents the large penis. Possessing her means he's got the prize—the large one. Thus, his wish not to be inadequate is achieved. However, when he can't possess her large breasts, then the symptom appears. Ergo, in such a circumstance where he can't possess her, it's not his penis that is inadequate, it's just that his stomach hurts. This is the meaning of the "displacement upwards"—that is, penis to stomach. The job we have is for Doubled-Over to straighten up, and not be doubled over. His painful symptom told me that his wish was cast in a negative direction; that is, his wish was focused on his concern that his penis might be too small—which of course meant that his problem was fueled by his sense of inadequacy. Gaining greater self-esteem and beginning to value himself more, and not displace these concerns onto his penis, and then further onto large breasts would be the aim of the therapy. Then his Lerovitz hole will be filled—and sealed!

I had to contemplate the road ahead because I knew what we needed to do, the amount of time it would take, the ups and downs, and the sideways. I suggested that we meet twice a week, explaining why the work is more accelerated that way. He instantly countered with five times a week. My first reaction was that his over-eagerness possibly signaled a premature quitting. Yet, stepping out of his Damon Runyon stance he soberly said, "I'm worried."

* * *

Tommy Gersh really contributed to the process of getting the whole thing underway. Without anyone's permission, Tommy brought a suitcase of toys and doll figurines into the treatment room on the autistic ward. His idea was, in a non-intrusive and casual way, to interest Edward in playing with the material. And he succeeded. He timed it so that Velma, Tino, and two other attendants were on their hour-long lunch break, leaving only one attendant on the ward.

Tommy was pretending to count the toys and log them in a book. He was not attending to Edward in the hope that Edward would feel free to do whatever he wanted with the toys. And Edward went right to it. It was play therapy at its purest.

Edward took a little tin container over to the sink, filled it with water, and kept drowning a little super-hero doll by repeatedly inserting it head-first into the water-filled container and then just as quickly pulling it out. And all the while he was repeating the same mantra: "No, no, no, no."

Gersh called me immediately with the news. He was sure Edward had witnessed Billy's death. And, he was equally sure that in Edward's play, Billy was being rescued because Edward kept undoing the drowning. First he would replay the event by drowning the doll, and then he would undo the drowning by saying his "nos" and pulling the doll out of the container. No retardation there!

I told Gersh that I thought he should immediately contact Stroud and Grillo and tell them what he had just told me.

So the fog was beginning to lift. Edward, most likely, was a witness. Billy's death was not the perfect crime. It seemed that an unraveling process possibly had begun. Perhaps, just perhaps, everyone's acting out was beginning to fray at the edges. From a psychiatric standpoint, all acting out would be defined simply as behavior, frequently delinquent behavior, as in the drowning of Billy. But from a psychoanalytic perspective, the general definition of acting out concerns any behavior used as a way of doing something rather than knowing something: a way, therefore, of fortifying repression—keeping yourself from knowing it—whatever the "it" is. So if whoever drowned Billy acted it out impulsively, then the motive would have been to satisfy some other emotional, unconscious agenda—thereby fortifying its repression. But it's a big if, because, in fact, it may not have been an impulsive acting out. It may have been premeditated. Maybe yes, maybe no.

There was a lot of acting out going on both at the hospital and at the clinic. And whoever was doing it was doing it in order not to know certain things about the self. That's really the gist of it. Not wanting to know—keeping it all unconscious.

· 15 ·

FRIENDS

The message was from Grillo. He asked if I could meet Stroud and him at the clinic, where they would be occupied for the rest of the afternoon. They were there to gather more data, specifically on the shooting of the statue, and were scheduled to meet with Kruger in the conference room on the seventh floor—the floor where the statue was violated. Grillo said he figured it would take only a half hour, but he wanted me to clarify certain aspects of my papers on the multiple. He'd already seen my paper *Multiple Personality As Symptom*, and now he was referring to another one entitled *Multiple Personality Disorder: Release Levers and Side Effects*. It was really simple. The reference to "release levers" defined, more or less, the state of the personality during the time of the metamorphosis—one personality to the other. The reference to "side effects" concerned a description of how the person felt after the personality changed back to "host." Headaches and/or unexplained fatigue were examples of this sort of side-effect experience. In the case of release levers, sleep, either prolonged, or light and quick, as in even a momentary trance, comprised most of the mediating phase, the metamorphosis of one personality to another—between Jekyll and Hyde.

I found them in the staff lounge. "Look," I said hesitatingly, "Dr. Kruger is in fact researching the multiple literature. He's spending time in the hospital library looking it up. Don't ask me how I know. I just know. And it's unbelievable to me why you would focus on this split personality business. It seemed to come out of nowhere." Then I immediately thought, "No, nothing's out of the clear blue sky. He had his reason for pursuing it." "So, Detective Grillo, I need to know why you were fixed so strongly on the split business rather than on something else. I know there's a reason."

"Right," he easily answered. "You see, I believe that in any investigation when something pops up, even though there may not be a direct link let's say, still, something shows itself. Know what I mean?"

I knew exactly what he meant. He may not have realized it, but he was a devotee of free association and stream or sequence of consciousness. We were definitely like-minded.

"We were asking everyone what other people's specialties were and everyone seemed to know that you were an expert in symptoms. One of your colleagues had two of your articles in his shelf and we, you might say, uh, requisitioned them. Right then what popped out wasn't the overall deal about symptoms. What popped out was the one example of what you called the symptom of the multiple that, I think you said, swallowed up the person or the whole personality. Right?"

I nodded. "Well, that was it," he said. "It was reading that first article on this kind of split personality that gave me the feeling that that was interesting. Then I also read the second one on side effects and stuff—not that any of it was easy reading—lots of technicals. So, on this point, what do you make of Dr. Kruger reading about multiples?"

"Well," I said, "I thought he, uh, well, must be treating a multiple." I almost couldn't get the sentence out. "And," I continued, "since he's doing the research at the hospital library, my first thought was that he's treating someone at the hospital, either in one of the therapy rooms, or could be in his own office—the director's office."

"So you think there's a multiple at the hospital?" He didn't wait for an answer. "Do you think it's a patient or someone on staff?"

"At first I was assuming a hospital patient, but…"

"Flash," he said. "That guy, 'T,' the attendant, has been visiting headache clinics. Suspect number one. I'll give you odds the good doctor is treating him. What do you think we should be looking for if it's a multiple in terms of the personality of the guy?"

"I'm not sure," I answered, "but the obvious could be an aggressive personality alternating with a sexual one. As you know, the multiple can't integrate the personalities so she acts out the wish to be a whole person by becoming three people instead—the host original-self and two others. Ingenious, right?"

"You said 'she.'" He was right. I had been aware of it immediately. "The reason is, that the literature is full of multiples who were women," I said. "Even in the popular literature there's *The Three Faces of Eve* and the other one, *Sybil*. Both women."

They were interested. "You know," I said, "multiples have been identified in the psychiatric literature now since about the mid-17th century. We're talking about the Middle Ages. I've noticed a real paradox in the diagnosis of the multiple. First of all, they're very rigid like the obsessive. You can't convince them even to try to get in touch with the other hidden personalities because (a), they won't recognize the possibility that there are others, and (b), they get that peculiar awkward almost-smile when you talk to them about it, and you can tell that there's no attention span there. It's like a person with a delusion. Logic or reason doesn't work.

"So there you have it: multiples are reluctant, very reluctant, to hear any suggestion by the doctor to even look at the problem. On the other hand, I can show you some cases in the psychological literature where the doctor reports that even by the wave of his hand—almost like a post-hypnotic cue—the multiple will obey the command and change into another personality on the spot, and then with the wave of the hand, change back again. And the doctor can do this at will and for long periods, and the other personalities will be popping out left and right with every wave of the hand. The subject will not even be going through sleep transitions. I think it's because the effect the wave of the hand has on the person indicates that that person is in a highly suggestible state—like in an intensified hypnotic or hysteric trance. It's a switching phenomenon."

"You're kidding," Stroud said. It was the first thing he had said.

"No, I'm not kidding. So, you see, the paradox is in the fact that at the same time that we get a rigidity in the multiple that resists suggestion, kind of like the personality we see in obsessives or paranoids, we also get a slither of the personality that is nothing but suggestible, like in the hysteric." They were both looking at me. Grillo said, "Let's sit." We all sat. Then Grillo took it and blew open the case. "What we have here is the possibility that the murder was committed by a multiple. The guy, I'm assuming it's a guy—Billy was too heavy for a woman to carry—well, maybe the guy was being treated by Kruger and maybe not; but the guy either may have acted alone or, and this is the new wrinkle, he may have been influenced, like you say, suggested into it by someone else. It's either the patient alone, or the patient influenced by the doctor or it's the patient, the doctor, and a third person doing the influencing, or it's the patient and the third person without the doctor. That's the way I see it. Of course, the one who did it could also be either the doctor or the third person. But I don't feel that that's it. The guy who did it was influenced by either one or both of the others, the doctor and/or the third person. We have our suspicions. We're getting a history on that Tino guy."

Grillo was way ahead of himself, but he was dangerous. Whatever he said always carried weight. As far as Kruger was concerned, well, with Kruger, you could never tell what was what. But I knew he was not to be trusted. Things always happened around him. He may not have been directly responsible, but you could be sure he was connected. In any event, both detectives made me feel that indeed an alliance of threes was happening: in the actual case, patient, doctor and a third person; in terms of the investigation, Grillo, Stroud, and me; and, of course, the multiple with three personalities.

* * *

A message from Vlad: He wanted to meet the following afternoon for an early dinner at the Top of the Tower restaurant, one of our favorite dinner spots—not so much for the food as for the ambiance, the out-of-the-wayness, near the U.N.—atop a residential hotel overlooking the East River on the east and the glorious nighttime lights of Manhattan to the south, north, and especially west. In the spring, summer, and early fall, we would have dinner outside on the penthouse. Inside, we had our favorite table near the piano, a bit to the northeast side of the room.

The elevator opens directly into the restaurant, no vestibule. Vlad was already there when I walked in, and we immediately spotted one another. He had arrived forty minutes early and was just hanging out talking to our favorite waiter and sipping Scotch. It was late afternoon and the place was practically empty.

"I'm buzzed. My second Scotch. Now what's this about some great medieval text but that you're also disturbed about a murder at the hospital and a shooting at the institute. Three things, eh? Danny called me."

I told him what had happened but didn't go into detail because I had been so primed to talk to him about Sebastian. He picked up the cue almost instantly. "It's the Sebastian thing that's upsetting you, right?"

I nodded. "It's really something. I told Danny about it but you're the person I need to rail at."

"What do you want from me?" Vlad said, smirking, and then giving me his stock jibe. "I didn't kill Jesus!"

Before I had a chance to respond he preempted me. "But the astonishing finding of a newly translated Coptic text called *The Gospel of Judas*, states that Jesus told Judas to do the deed in order for the preternatural teleological process to occur—meaning that Jesus would leave his corporeal life so that, in a word, the entire process existed for the Father's final purpose, and that therefore, Judas was essential to the process corresponding to the apocalyptic prophecy. It's simple Christian eschatology. How about that? And it's going to turn everything right side up."

Vlad said it in such a meaningful way that my Jewish secular outrage, about to confront him was mollified. As usual, he was always there with some epiphany.

I had introduced Vlad and Danny about five years earlier and we all got along. They liked each other but never met unless I was also part of the plan. We were all like-minded with respect to loving cultures and people. So without skipping a beat, Vlad continued with what was at hand.

"What was wrong with your meeting with Danny? He must have been interested in the trials of Sebastian. No?"

"How'd you know it was trials?"

"C'mon Glenn. It was the Middle Ages. You found some manuscript of a surviving Jew who had been threatened with death, yet survived, and now you've got some evidence of his scholarly work and maybe even something about his tribulations."

Here I was, thinking I had some great secret, some great unearthing, and Vlad blithely describes it. Then I began the story from the beginning, starting with my uncovering of the citation that led me to Sebastian's material. He knew that part because he was the one who originally suggested I speak to Jean about it. But he knew nothing about what transpired after that. I filled him in, A to Z.

"The Vatican," he said sourly. "Rigidified." The stories I know would set your teeth on edge. I believe there's still a cardinal there who was and still is a member of Odessa." He was referring to the well-financed underground railroad for wanted Nazis—transporting them all over the world so they could escape prosecution. These were Roman Catholic priests—Franciscans—doing the transporting!

Vlad continued. "He still might be operating, and if so, the Pope knows it. The politics of the Vatican can make you sick."

"Vlad, the truth is," I said, "that I can agree with Christian ethics—your kind. But in the light of the Inquisition, pogroms, the Holocaust, The New Testament bible with its direct denigration of Jews and provocative Jew-hating language, well, man oh man. And you should hear how Danny analyzed the church as containing a basic split-personality infrastructure. But first I gotta fill you in on the whole Sebastian thing."

We discussed various aspects of the manuscript and Vlad, avoiding the Christian business, continued to ask a number of questions about the details of Sebastian's theories and discoveries. By the time the food arrived we were about to launch into the diary. I wanted to talk about Sebastian's loss of Ester and Alba and his agony knowing that Alba was probably alive but also probably in sad condition—shrouded, uncared for, perhaps in abject despair, perhaps even brutalized.

Just then the elevator doors opened and out stepped Danny. He saw us instantly. I was totally surprised. He obviously had called me at the office, and Rita must have told him we were here.

"Hiya, guys. I'm breaking in. Couldn't wait till next week. Glenn, I need to talk more about Cindy."

We reassured him and Vlad waved to Quincy, our waiter. So there we were, once again the three of us. Without caring at all about what Vlad and I were discussing—actually, without thinking about or considering the possibility that we were discussing something important—Danny launched into his story with Cindy. He knew, of course, that Vlad had no idea at all that there ever was a Cindy.

"It was an obsession, Vlad," Danny said. "Maybe still is. It's a young woman. I don't know if I should even call her a woman. She's in her mid-twenties. I told Glenn all about it yesterday, but it's still on my mind."

And before you know it, Danny summarizes the whole thing for Vlad as if he'd been open about it forever. I guess telling me had released him. And as Freud said about things that are not spoken (and heard) being reenacted instead, Danny was at the point where he was fed up with his obsessional reenactments. Now, for the first time, he didn't want this reenacting to become his fate. Of course, he trusted Vlad completely and probably felt that the three of us comprised a nucleus whose collective sensibilities could solve any problem. And if he didn't feel that, I certainly did.

"Danny, you give new meaning to the word loyalty," Vlad said. "Ruthie's a fortunate person."

"You're telling me," I chimed in.

"Yeah, Glenn said I was uxorious. Whatever the hell that means — too loyal. But, let me tell you, I'm really able to say things to women that are very intimate. You know, I'd like to tell Cindy that her lips are shaped so perfectly that I would almost give my life to kiss her long and passionately — softly, medium pressure and hard. And then I would vary it. It would be a kiss that lasted maybe twenty minutes. You know what it means to be sated, fully sated so that you feel simultaneously alive and drained, calm but disoriented, sober but drunk, completely achieved, like possessing what you've wanted all your life and to the fullest satisfaction, and with the knowledge that she loves you, and is there for you, and would do it again, and again, and again — and *will* do it again and again — because she's yours? You see, I lived on those thoughts. They got me through the day. It's better now. Anybody here ever have that kind of obsession — and acted it out? Actually achieved it? I lived this way through my secretions, guys. Through my feelings. Know what I mean?"

He looked at each of us. "Yeah," I sadly said. "It's like living on your fictions about yourself." He didn't answer, and they both avoided looking at me. Then Danny picked up where he left off.

"I would think of Cindy and this good feeling would begin to melt in me, through me. This is how I lived — feeling good through my thoughts. The ugly side to it is that my anger at her came out in the same fantasies I've had about Ruthie. They die in the fantasies. I don't kill them, but I get them somehow dead. Then I'm freed. But then again, whenever I felt desolate I would think of Cindy and that kiss."

There was silence at the table. Danny was in his own reverie. He was seeing it all. He knew exactly how it and she would feel. He sensed every nuance, in detail. It was almost as if he didn't really need it to be real. His rapture was so intense that you could see she was in him. He swallowed her whole and she filled him up. And although I've seen many obsessions over the years with scores of patients, and perhaps had a few myself, nothing

I'd ever seen compared to this. I could see that Vlad was feeling awkward because of Danny's reference to Ruthie's and Cindy's fantasy-death and how that reference might be affecting me. Surprisingly, it wasn't affecting me at all. At least not that I could tell.

"I know how it must sound," Danny continued. "You guys are stable. Nothing like this is devouring you. Except of course, you, Glenn. But even with what you're going through, including our discussion at Rock, you're a normal person. I mean you're stable in the face of catastrophe."

"Detached," I grimly said. "I don't let it devour me because my wishes get to be stronger than reality, or I should say, ostensible reality."

"But it actually began devouring me," Danny answered, accenting the "*me*." "It was devouring me until I began to actually live it through in my mind—like it was real and I could visualize kissing her, holding her. For the longest time I couldn't visualize having sex—actual penetration. But recently, in my mind, I started making love to her, and I realized how it would be. For the first time I could see her face at the point of intercourse. I could tell how her face would change and how it would look in the midst of passion and love—how it would be if she were in it with me and in love with me like I was with her, and in her." He paused. "Believe me, guys, it's finally good to say 'was' and 'in.'"

Vlad looked at me and then quickly focused only on Danny's saying, "was."

"It's like this, Vlad. It's Ruthie," I said. "The thought of Ruthie didn't permit him to see Cindy in a sexual way because he was so damn loyal that any measure of disloyalty would be an abandonment of Ruthie. And that he couldn't take. It would depress him. He might even feel he'd have to confess to Ruthie to shake the guilt. Danny's always needed to be pure, the good boy." I looked at Danny—"Right?"

"Exactly," he said. "Exactly. My obsession with Cindy was interfered with by my obsession with not giving up on the relationship with Ruthie. Going ahead with an affair would be acknowledging failure, but more, maybe even breaking the bond. I think that scared me. Now, I think I could have the affair. The fact is, I now seem to be able to entertain the whole fantasy of loving Cindy sexually. I'm free. If I had had the chance with her, I would have done it. Without any hesitation. Isn't that a blast? Most men would look at me like I'm a lunatic. 'What's the big deal? Just do it!' But it's not that easy for me. I have all these standards and obsessions with perfection. I think I'm getting over it, though. Maybe I am."

Now we were all in Danny's reverie. He broke the spell.

"Nothing like this at the Yale Theological Seminary, eh, Vlad? What you've got is peace and quiet. I envy it. Believe me. It's a blessing not to have been tortured by some impossible obsession. But not you, Glenn. You've got the Katie thing. She loved you and sex went with it. Your heart felt loved. Remember Sebastian's stuff?"

And just at that point Vlad stopped it cold.

"Okay, it's my turn. Not like yours, Danny. My own brand of secrecy. Maybe sin. That's right, sin!"

He was serious. Danny and I turned to him in surprise. His appearance called for silence. He was about to confess something. Something neither Danny nor I knew anything about. Vlad had shared what I thought was most of his life with me, but apparently this was something new. And I could tell it was going to be a beaut. I thought about how difficult it is to really know someone—how people usually have something they can't talk about. People feel ashamed about things, feel others would be disappointed in them if certain information became public. Yet, under the right conditions, all of these personal inhibitions and secrets can dissolve.

The secret was about to dissolve.

* * *

Siegfried Kruger, in his frenzy to find Billy's books, had painstakingly investigated every corner of the property office building, covering the basement and lobby floors, first and then the second floor. Billy's books had to be there but they weren't. His hiding place obviously was a secret. The only place Kruger hadn't scoured was the utility room. "What the hell," he thought," might as well." Up to the second floor again, to the end of the corridor, to the utility room. He waded through every item in the utility room. It was a jungle of wires, tools, broken chairs, cleaning fluids of all sorts, floor-waxing machines, and so forth. Finally, he looked in the last large tool box located under a table. He placed the box on the table, lifted the upper removable tray, and froze. There, two rectangular notebooks were fit neatly into the base of the toolbox. One was entitled **To Veronica***, the other,* **To Jericho***. His heart sank. These were not Billy's books. But he knew he had discovered something valuable—two alter personalities, Veronica and Jericho, writing to each other.*

Secrets were about to dissolve.

Kruger, of course, knew both writers. He'd already experienced Jericho's primal nature: Anger in its purest form. As for Veronica, her basic nature was sexual. She only wanted sensual and sexual pleasure, real or fantasied. And now Kruger had diaries that Jericho and Veronica were writing to one another. Anger talking to sex and sex talking to anger.

Kruger quickly browsed through the notebooks. It wasn't his particular interest at the moment, but the material was still irresistible. Maybe a first. One component of a multiple triad speaking to another component while the host personality knows nothing of the conversation.

Leafing through Veronica's notebook, Kruger's eye caught the phrase, "I need power." He started to read.

"Jericho," Veronica wrote, "my wish is for Velma to see my big dick and then to want me. I need power over her Then she will want me and then I can have her."

Ah, Kruger thought, **that's** what the exhibitionism is all about. Veronica just wants Velma to want her. Then what Tino has wanted all his life will be achieved. He then quickly leafed through Jericho's notebook, stopping when he caught the word, "kill."

"Veronica, I hate helplessness. I'll kill to escape helplessness." And farther on in the notebook Jericho says, "Veronica, do you realize that you can only exist when I don't? It's only when Tino can't feel me that he goes to you. Everything, Veronica, depends on whether I exist, and then, when I exist."

Now it dawned on Kruger—he felt he understood the basic nature of the multiple personality. His research of the multiple had alluded to it, but now Kruger could see it in the flesh. Something about where there is anger there is no libido, and where there is libido there is no anger. But Jericho clarified it even better, indicating that anger is the power lever. Apparently, Tino was so saturated in his wish for access to Velma and so frustrated in this quest, that his reaction generated vast episodes and eruptions of anger within. So Jericho, in Tino's projection, is a bundle of continuous episodic angers seeking explosive avenues to behave aggressively, to fulfill his nature as Jericho—anger personified. And here it was that Dr. Siegfried Kruger, ironically, could probably have been the first person to have ever discovered two basic emotions, with respect to their core identities, talking to one another, and for sure, thereby also supporting the proposition that each basic emotion has its own disposition, its own distinct nature.

Jericho had revealed that an emotion can have a personality. Thus, Jericho's personality profile of anger was composed of an attack proclivity, an explosive *potential, an aggressive drive, a confrontational inclination, an entitled frame of mind, and its nature, therefore, acted as a characteristic empowerment.*

So Kruger had the rare opportunity to see directly within, inside the mind of the multiple, right down to the demarcations between the personalities, down to their primal differences of nature, motives, emotions. But was that what gripped him—witnessing the very insides, the infrastructure of a scientific phenomenon? No! Rather, what gripped him, obsessed him, was the search for Billy's books. That was all he could think about. Yet, he took the notebooks to his office, duplicated them, and then, returning to the utility room, replaced them in the toolbox. Preoccupied, and staring into space, he pensively walked out of the room.

* * *

Staring at the table, Vlad started. "It began in 1960. I had been in this country about four years, was thirty-two and in seminary. One day, I was on the subway heading for Columbia University to hear a lecture by none other than Martin Buber. At Fifty-ninth street, the doors open and in come five nuns and they sit directly opposite me. Among them was a slightly plump young novitiate with the most beautiful rapturous face. She was obviously entirely devoted to her calling and was reading a bible. The others were just sitting quietly. Five nuns all lined up and only one of them reading. My eyes were fixed on her. She must have sensed it because she looked up and directly at me. We both knew that some ignition—maybe from a higher force—had sent an electric current at the speed of light from me to her. Her body was ripe—succulent. Her eyes glistened with love of life. I felt she was desperate, love-starved, but that she didn't quite know or understand it. She quickly looked away, averting my gaze, and tried to become entirely rooted in her reading. But in a few seconds she again glanced at me. I was staring at her, almost sadistically staring, making it patently clear that I wanted her, even though she knew I knew that such desire was off limits for her. Our unspoken connection was already beginning to cause her untold misery. She was fighting with every fiber of her being not to have this wonderful romance with me even if it was only for another five minutes or so. But she was losing. I, of course, was already a goner. The minute I laid eyes on her I needed her. It was the single most urgent experience of my life. Then they all stood and moved toward the door."

For the first time, Vlad looked directly at one of us, right at Danny.

"Like you, Danny, I could sense exactly how our love would be. I knew it exactly. We were meant to be in each other's arms in a powerful, tender, passionate embrace. She knew it, too. Anyway, the doors opened and they all exited. The next thing I knew, I, too, was on the station platform. I actually followed them out without quite even knowing what was happening to me. I just couldn't let her get away. She turned and saw me standing and watching them all wait for the train on the opposite track. The train arrived — going to the Bronx. They got on. I got on. She knew I was there. I had the advantage because I already felt this was destiny. Here I was on my way to becoming a theologian and here she was already a nun. But she couldn't tell who I was. I mean I wasn't wearing a collar or anything that would tell her that I was kindred. As it turned out, age wise, I was five years older."

Danny and I then realized that somehow Vlad had established contact with the nun. But neither of us said a word.

"I followed them to the Bronx and walked a distance behind them. They arrived at the intersection of a street labeled Claremont Parkway and Webster Avenue. On Webster Avenue, into a church they went. And, of course, into the church I went.

"It was *Our Lady of Victory*, a little Catholic church servicing that area of the southeast Bronx. The parishioners were mostly ethnics and Hispanic and black. I sat in the last pew at the farthest side away from the door. It felt as though I was possessed by some demon deep within my soul. A Dybbuk. But it was a love Dybbuk. And what it needed superseded all other considerations of propriety or even morality. I was not knowing what the next moments would bring. The nuns disappeared into the rectory. I was sitting there daydreaming about how nice it would be for her to just arrive — to walk up to me, sit next to me, and help me talk to her. As I was feeling the deep wish of this thought, believe it or not, she emerged alone from the rectory, walked up the long aisle to the side where I was seated and actually came up to me and sat down. I immediately told her that I was a student at the General Seminary down in Chelsea. I wanted her to see that despite my not being Catholic I was not a kook and that it was okay for us to be together, to talk, to walk together, to be friends or lovers or like you said, Danny, devourers of one another. I could barely keep my hands to myself. She was so full-bodied and round. I had the impulse to get under her habit and kiss and caress her thighs, and arouse her by caressing her breasts so that she would not be able to put me off."

Vlad stopped at this point. Danny and I still didn't say a word but we were both dying to know what happened. Danny was also obviously identifying with Vlad, seeing Cindy as the nun. Danny wanted them to do it right there! So did I.

"So, gentlemen, I did it. Right there in the church. Before she knew my name or I hers. It was dark and we were the only ones there and we were in a corner in the back. We fell into each other's arms. I felt her body, top to bottom. Her thighs felt exactly as I had imagined. Her breasts were everything I had dreamed. We didn't have sex there, but we were in an impossible rapture, in an impossible place, under impossible personal restrictions. And yet, there it was, she a Catholic nun, and I an Episcopal almost theologian."

Vlad paused and Danny finally broke in.

"Vlad, I feel like cheering. It's important to me. Did you two follow through with it? I mean afterwards. You know?"

"This was 1960," Vlad again said. "We were together after that for ten years. In mid-1969 she was diagnosed with breast cancer, and she died almost a year later. They caught it too late. Well, actually, she had not been going for checkups on a regular basis although she'd been diagnosed with suspicious cells. She'd let it go for years at a time. At first, when we began, we had these, you might say, furtive assignations. But then again, sometimes we would meet near her church on the other side of the park—it's called Claremont Park—and we would, how shall I say, perambulate all the way back down to Webster Avenue where the church was."

Vlad picked up his drink, which had been neglected through all this talk, looked at it, then put it back down.

"You're the only people I've ever told. We worked out a way to see each other. But we knew she would be disgraced, so we lived a cloistered existence. At times I thought it was abnormal. Sometimes I thought it cowardly. But never was it immoral. I'm no longer sure which adjectives apply. No matter. Anything anyone would have said, we had already said. My faith was actually more permanently etched because of this miraculous event that led me into Carmen's arms. We were together for those ten years and we were inextricably coupled. There was no question in her mind or in mine that our union was blessed by God, and no judicial or priestly body of any sort could have persuaded either of us otherwise. And that's it. I still miss her. When she died I thought I would never survive it. But I did. Sorry to bring it up, Glenn."

After that we sat nibbling, but not saying much. Of course, I felt it was my story. Carmen was Katie.

Reading my thoughts, Vlad said, "Glenn, you've got to talk about Katie."

*   *   *

"There are all kinds of stories to tell," said Kruger. Tino was listening and waiting. It was the day that Kruger had discovered the notebooks of Jericho and Veronica. Now all of them were in Kruger's office for Tino's therapy session. Seeing Tino was probably the only thing that could distract Kruger from his obsession with Billy's books, as he knew that Tino, Jericho, and Veronica would all have to think about the proposition he was about to present.

"So, Tino, if by any chance you come across Billy's books, remember, I have a trade to offer you. Because, you know, Billy's books tell a story, and there are certain other books that have come into my possession. Yes, I've copied them and have them in a safe place. These other books written by two very important people also tell a story. It's a story that could put certain people in a tough position. A lot of explaining would be done to certain detectives. But never mind, I know you're not aware of any of it. I'm just talking out loud so that my point won't be missed by any interested parties."

"Dr. Kruger," Tino said, "sometimes you tell me things that I can't make sense out of. But when you say 'interested parties,' I think you mean that other stuff and it upsets me."

Kruger immediately began doing damage control, trying to placate Tino. He wanted no part of Jericho, and he could see that Tino was getting mad.

"Tino, I've been doing research on your type of headache. I'm making progress. We're going to cure them and get rid of the demons once and for all. Imagine, Tino, your life free of those awful poundings."

It worked. Tino was immediately mollified. He forgot all about his upset. It dissolved in the face of Kruger's promise of relief.

"Dr. Kruger, I just want to have everything turn out all right."

"Tino, I know what you mean. You don't want to have any headaches like you've been having and all you want to do is keep living with your mother so

that the two of you can keep looking after one another. Isn't that right?" He didn't wait for an answer. "I mean she does love you very much and I know you feel the same about her. So you protect each other. You would do anything for each other. Right, Tino?" Again, he didn't wait for an answer. "But remember, Tino, if your mother has Billy's books, it's very important that you tell me. Then I can trade those books for the ones I've found. In that way, you and your mother will be better protected. Doesn't it feel good when I talk about how both of you can be safe and protected? So, Tino, tell me."

*   *   *

Both Vlad and Danny waited. Vlad's voice was like a distant echo. "You've got to talk about Katie, Glenn."

There was silence at the table.

"Okay, I'll start this way. I don't steal, I don't cheat, I'm not an alcoholic, I don't overeat, don't take drugs, don't lie. Don't, don't, don't. What do I do? I work hard, and I try to help people. But I like to win and I try my best at things. Like Danny, I can actually take failure, but not if it's unfair, and it's the kinds of random-negative events that are not fair—those are the ones I can't accept. So my wish to gain the ascendancy, so to speak, gets to be so strong that it begins to compete with reality, and then I create my own reality.

"It's not psychotic. That's what I told my shrink. Rather, it's my way of not yielding to a life where I'm permanently tragic. Tragic is not for me. I've been thinking for a long time now that in each person's life, there's kind of a last train out. The question is, do you get on that train or not? Vlad, you were literally on the train and got off. It means the same thing, only the metaphor is inverted. And you, Danny, seems to me you couldn't get on, except when it was just about too late, and of course, the train pulled out. Then you were ready. For me, Katie was life. I got on the train immediately. Didn't hesitate for a second."

I paused and thought a bit, not realizing they were watching and waiting for me to continue.

"It's that I hate the feeling of helplessness, and always did everything in my power to avoid it. Now I'm helpless. I need to know how to get her back. We were planning to have a baby. No time. There was no time. Now my relationship is with—is with a ghost. It's hard for me to admit that, and even to say that 'g' word. People tell me things like, 'I'm so sorry.' Sorry for **what**, I feel like saying? Because to me she's not gone. People mean well, but hardly anyone understands. I don't want to hear the words or phrases like: 'killed'; 'you'll eventually have some closure'; and things like that. Would you believe, some even say: 'Oh, you'll never get over it.' Can you believe that? They're not even talking about, thinking about, or considering me. What they consider as wisdom is really a cliché that reflects their own personal anxieties. Of course, they mean well, but wisdom it's not. It's the opposite—whatever that is. I have an equivalent cliche: "It's all about them." I guess I paused for a few seconds. "Ah, forget it," I quickly recovered. "Sometimes I fulminate—my protest becomes a rant. It's especially when I detect that people are really only interested in themselves. Actually, maybe I'm no different.

"Anyway, Katie's all I cared about. So now, I keep talking to her. And I know what she would answer. You know, I hear it. But it's not over because I've got this need to go to L.A. to look for her. No, it's not a delusion. Maybe it was someone else in the accident and Katie's there somewhere. Maybe somehow she lost her memory and even her sister whom she was visiting, doesn't realize it. It's sometimes called *The Madame Butterfly fantasy*—a wish for the loved one who has disappeared to return. That's what's got me. It's urging me on—inside—to go to L.A. and find her."

Again, I paused.

"You know how you said you perambulated with Carmen, Vlad? In that park? Well, I do it with Katie. Whenever I get to my office, there's a certain chair that I've kind of assigned to her. I embrace the perimeter of space that I imagine forms her configuration in that chair. I lean down a bit, and I embrace her. I'll kiss her—usually on the lips and on both cheeks. I'm really kissing air. And there's more. Before I leave for the day, I'll say: 'Okay, Katie, let's go.' And I imagine she rises slowly because she's recovering from the something that happened to her. And then I walk slowly out of my office in a way that suggests she's accompanying me—as though she's there with me. When I'm in the street, the drama disappears, and I just go. But once or twice when I was halfway up the block, I realized that I left her walking slowly. I quickly returned to her, and then slowly escorted her for another block or two. The drama always ends, and I go on my way. It ends because I drift—begin thinking other things."

Silence at the table. "Okay, guys, did I say enough, because right now I desperately need to discuss Sebastian, not my history and not my craziness.

But I can't seem to get to it, and at the moment that's what's making me feel helpless. The point is that underneath, I must be raging. You know, helplessness breeds rage—always, in everyone. But consciously, I only feel frustrated, and also miserable." I looked down at the table and then at them. "If I keep talking about Katie, I'll get choked up, and at that point I'll be finished for the day."

"I know," Danny said. "It's my fault. I've been so focused on Cindy that I couldn't relate to much else—even Katie, or even the persecution of Jews."

"I know, I know," I said. "But I've got his diary. It's never seen the light of day except for the translation close to a hundred years ago. This guy, this Jewish monk, was high up in the Spanish court and wound up exiled. He lost his only child, a daughter, and his wife was probably burned at the stake. I've got the murderer by name. I know how Sebastian escaped, where he went and how he got there. The entire history of the Inquisition is laid out in detail. The workings of the court, the deals, the hoax of royalty, the insidious role of the church in murder, in theft, the hijacking of all wealth by the nobility, and finally, the conscious scapegoating of Jews implemented by a corrupt Christian power structure. The abject disempowerment of the Jewish population—women and children tortured and murdered—and it all reflected church mentality at the time. Like you said, Danny, a split-personality of the church."

Vlad deftly side-stepped what I was saying by waving to our waiter, Quincy. Scotch for Vlad—his third—rye for Danny, and bourbon for me.

Vlad picked it up. "I'm sorry, too, Glenn. Everything we talk about seems to refer to Katie, either directly or by implication. As far as you're concerned, Glenn, you're interested in signs of life, not death. That's why you talk to Katie, and also want to cure symptoms, and go to L.A. to find her. That's why Sebastian's fate affects you, and why such things always reach you. Sebastian was given signs of death, not life. You want to bring him back just like you want to bring her back, and just like you want to bring those six million Jews back. And you won't acknowledge a God until that's done. The topper is you probably think you can do it."

"Just Katie, Vlad. Just Katie. Maybe I can do that. If I only could do that!"

Vlad was right. I do want them all back. I rail at those forces, those circumstances that marginalize people, that oppress them, render them helpless. Even people racked with symptoms are rendered less viable. Wasn't Billy Soldier less viable and then not viable at all? And Edward, isn't he very much less viable? "Oh, Katie, don't be less viable," was my fleeting image. I could almost see her.

I thought, "I'm in a thrall with spirits, with ghosts."

With those musings about spirits, and ghosts, and my relationship with Katie, and with Billy, and Edward, and no less, with Sebastian and his ordeal, I flashed on the multiple personality, the person marginalized because his fractured three-part nature is less than the whole. And then again I knew for sure that Grillo was an intuitive genius. There *was* a split at the hospital. And here, one moment I was focusd on Katie, and then on Sebastian, and then on Billy, and even on a fractured statue. What I had was not what would be called an anxiety-free condition. Talk about split!

*　　*　　*

After the session with Kruger, Tino was relieved. He felt the euphoria of the anxiety-free condition that always developed when he sensed that he and Velma would be safe. And that's just what Kruger had promised. Safety.

The next sequence of events was a blur. It was nighttime, about 11 P.M. Dark. Tino was walking to the utility room of Kruger's building carrying a small package. He used his master key and entered. Up to the second floor and to the utility room. He went straight for the tool box. Both notebooks were intact. He opened the package and proceeded to change into his outfit: blouse with falsies, leather skirt, kerchief around his neck, and, of course, heels. However, his feet were so big that he couldn't slip into the heels and needed to wear his own shoes. He carefully applied his makeup, ending with a generous amount of lipstick that challenged the natural perimeter of his lip line. On top went a coat. Furtively, he exited the room and the building and headed a hundred yards or so to the hospital post office. There on the night shift was a Ms. Migdalia Rivera, whom he had been eyeing for weeks. When he first saw her he could have sworn she was Velma's double. Rivera had the same body type, and from the back, and especially in their uniforms, it would be virtually impossible to tell them apart. Ms. Rivera was both full-bodied and just as tall as Velma, and, like Velma, she was perfectly configured by that form-fitting uniform: tight at the waist, straining at the ample bustline. It was the first time in his life that he felt as drawn to another woman as he was to Velma.

Veronica now waited for Migdalia Rivera to leave the building. She knew her shift ended at midnight. A few minutes after midnight, Migdalia Rivera walked to the front door. She stopped to get her key from her bag, to exit the double-glass entry door, which needed to be locked and unlocked when both entering and leaving. She unlocked the door and, as she was about to step out into the night, abruptly hesitated, and fully stopped in her tracks. Standing half in the building and half out, she spotted the figure of a tall, strong woman, suspiciously positioned just beside the oak tree directly outside the building. The woman was hooded with a kerchief partly covering her face. The dim light from the lobby provided just enough illumination for Ms. Rivera to make out what was happening.

Veronica shimmied her leather skirt up, and there she revealed a very large penis in full erection. Ms. Rivera didn't move. Veronica gripped her penis with one hand at its base, and then while adding another grip to the first with her other hand, she broke the silence and transformed everything from fantasy to reality. Veronica audibly whispered, "See, there's still room almost for one more grip." Migdalia saw clearly that Veronica was right. Despite both hands wrapped around that penis, starting at the base, one grip adjacent to the other, the large head of the penis extended further from the end of the second grip. It would take somewhat more of an embrace to cover that entire penis. Migdalia, silently gasped.

Veronica kept whispering: "It's over ten inches long and it's thick." Migdalia kept staring. She knew she could, in an instant, step inside the door and lock it without this exhibitionist making even a first step toward her. Besides, there were other men in the building who, she knew, would protect her. So she wasn't at all frightened. Rather, she realized she was interested in seeing it all, and she knew it. She was absolutely clear about that. Veronica started to notice it, too, realizing that Ms. Rivera was staring — that she was waiting to see more.

Veronica grew bolder. She stepped to the side in profile, so that Ms. Rivera could appreciate this phenomenon from a better point of advantage. Seeing that Ms. Rivera was seeing it all, Veronica removed both hands from their grip and turned to face Migdalia, now considered by Veronica to be a willing participant-observer. Veronica continued whispering, thinking that if she kept up her bold but quiet patter, something could happen, some compliance, some acknowledgment of Ms. Rivera's desire.

"I need to hold you and feel you," Veronica audibly whispered, ecstatic because Ms. Rivera had not panicked. Rather, it seemed to Veronica that

Rivera seemed willing to hear that declaration of love, of lust. So Veronica continued: "I want you to love me." Just then, Veronica, in an inopportune moment, couldn't sustain her excitement and in an involuntary peak sensory-shudder, orgasmed. She exploded in a great premature ejaculation. In addition to several missile-burst gushes of opaque semen, more translucent and less dense semen also discharged, streaming and trailing from the tip of her penis to the grassy earth below.

At that point, Veronica quickly took a second kerchief from around her neck and used it to wrap her penis. With her partially erect penis tied in the kerchief, she pulled down her leather skirt and took a last look at Migdalia Rivera, who was still motionless. Veronica, with bowed head, respectfully expressed her utmost reverential appreciation to Ms. Rivera, and then receded into the darkness and disappeared.

Veronica was now tied to Migdalia. She would have to see Ms. Rivera again. But for the moment, her libido was sated.

It was clear. Veronica and her compatriots were distorted, contaminated. They certainly were less than one whole person.

* * *

Vlad was right. I wanted people to be whole. I said so. "You're right, Vlad, I want those people whole—in one piece and not decimated because of accidents or ideological rationalizations and obsessions with purity of blood. The Inquisition, the pogroms, it didn't matter. It was ethnic cleansing coexisting with a diabolical heist in the stealing of the possessions of its genocidal victims. It all means, or perhaps meant, that the closest synonym for the church is, or was—sin!"

Vlad was about to answer me but I preempted him. "But wait, Vlad," I said. "The church has another favorite activity." I stopped. "Okay," Vlad said, indulging me: "What?" Without skipping a beat, I answered, "Molesting children, young boys—what else?" Danny laughed, then looked at Vlad and quickly stopped. "Not you, Vlad," Danny said. "Not you."

I saw Quincy approaching with our drinks, so I lightened it all up by saying: "Even with the ongoing horrors of the world today, like mine, like slavery and genocide in the Sudan, and Islamic fundamentalist lunacy, at this very existential moment, here we are having dinner and drinks—at a penthouse restaurant, no less."

I timed it so that as I said, "no less," Quincy arrived at the table.

"This discussion is tabled," Danny announced. "I declare it in the name of friendship, secrets shared, obsessions obliterated, lives reconstituted, and justice for all people. How's that, Glenn?"

I got on board. "Okay, Vlad," I said, "you do the toast."

He agreed. "Here goes. Danny, here's to a Nobel and here's to Cindy and/or Ruthie, one or both. Glenn, here's to Katie, to reconstituted lives, the absence of helplessness, to fairness, and justice. And to me, as always, to the memory of Carmen, and, of course, to Jesus, the true Christian."

· 16 ·

GROUP

Vlad always points out that during the Inquisition Christianity also attacked Islam and Protestants. It wasn't just Jews. And we know that all over the world all kinds of people are attacking all kinds of other people. Seems injustice, rage, and then retaliatory rage are both epidemic and endemic. In this sense, at the lecture, I planned to present the idea that the basic nature of groups, in its core, is the need to blame.

I'm also part of a group. The difference is that my group is called *The Rectifiers*. I've always known that when there was an injustice, I was never satisfied with apologies per se. Vlad is exactly right. I want all those people back. All six million. And only literal rectification can bring them back. But we know that can't happen. They are Gone! Erased! Ghosts!

And yet I'm not willing to say that about Katie. When I boil it down psychoanalytically, it takes me directly to my regression, and I think that perhaps I may be having a temper tantrum. Imagine that, a temper tantrum! And because I can't accept injustice—even with respect to the frequent phenomena that occur by the random events of life—I find myself insisting on rectification. Things need to be fair! In my so-called adult life I know this wishing appears in the form of a denial of the event, of the reality of it, of her absence. I then feel a kind of righteous indignation—as though because of the injustice of it all, and because things need to be fair, I actually might be able to retrieve her. So, I'm constantly trying to see her, to find her—and at the same time I'm completely defeated. But I won't be defeated. I'll go to L.A.

When I talk about wishes—especially about the grandiose facet of wishes around which everything revolves, I immediately think of exploitative Kruger, who brought opportunism to new heights, who was responsible for positioning people so that the whole person could no longer be seen. Only shadows. Whenever I had contact with any patient of borderline intelligence that he had tested, I generally felt they were slightly higher in I.Q. than the scores indicated. I was never sure if this was because of my own bias or whether Kruger was, well, actually warehousing people. If it was true that he was warehousing people—keeping them in the hospital when they should have been discharged—I couldn't, for the life of me, understand his motive. But if indeed he was actually doing that, then these patients would be consigned to live in the hospital indefinitely, essentially incarcerated unjustly, not living a real or viable life. Phantoms, helpless phantoms. And in many, many cases, no one was trying to retrieve them.

I was careful to always keep in mind that I had a negative bias where Kruger was concerned. But I wasn't alone. There were rumors over the years that he was exerting control over the lives of those in his charge who were I.Q.-challenged. But nothing had ever been proven, and it would have been difficult to know even where to start. If in fact he was warehousing such people, he would have to alter the scores on the I.Q. tests to just below the cutoff necessary to consider release from the hospital. That way, if the patient was at some point retested by another staff member or by an outside consultant, Kruger's handiwork would cancel any visible significant discrepancy between the scores on tests, as for example given to Billy at different times during his so-called tenure at the hospital.

I realized, of course, that I could never accuse Kruger of any specific wrongdoing because I had no evidence and perhaps also because I didn't want to sound vindictive or even paranoid—especially to Grillo and Stroud. I could imagine Grillo quizzing someone about my suspicion that Kruger manipulates scores on tests and then getting answers like, "No, I don't know anything about that," or "No, I've never heard that." Then Grillo and Stroud would come back to me, and Stroud would look down at me and say, "Dr. Kahn, no one knows what you're talking about." Then Grillo would take over, and in his seemingly innocuous, yet informally determined, even covertly ominous style, he would say, "Dr. Kahn, in your multiple personality article you mention that when splits are not acting out any of the other personalities, they can get dramatic and exaggerate stories. Know what I mean?"

No, I didn't mention my suspicions about Kruger to Grillo and Stroud. But now that I think I know why, I'm going to.

*　　*　　*

About fifteen miles from the hospital, on a winding road in a rural area off the main highway, there were trailers dotted here and there on the sides of the roads. They cast an anonymous and at the same time ominous shadow. Best not to stop and ask for directions. Also, hope that you've recharged your cell phone. And you'd probably not want to be changing a flat tire there in the wee small hours.

This particular smaller white trailer with chipped green trim around the windows and door was located about 100 feet from an overgrown wooded area, through which one could still see an abandoned railroad track. This was the makeshift domicile of Nurse Secora and adopted son Tino 'T' Vescaro. Mother in her 50's, adopted son in his 20's. The inside was one rectangular room that included a kitchenette with a table at the far end and a bathroom adjacent to it. A sleepaway couch, two chairs, a TV set, and that was about it. It was a makeshift domicile because it had the feel of people who didn't expect to live there forever. It was obvious. These were people who would be on the move. No permanence here. An old beat-up 1990's Chevy was parked on a grassy area closer to the trailer and further from the woods, with the nose of the car pointed directly toward the road.

"T', we both know what happened."

"I didn't do anything," he said.

"In other words, you're not aware of it?"

"I didn't do anything," he repeated.

She thought she believed him. She thought that there was a much better chance that it was Jericho who killed Billy. But she wasn't sure. She was suspicious. She knew she'd better not probe. Yet, she couldn't resist the need to actually do it. She decided to ask him the difficult question.

"What about the others, did either of them do it?" she asked.

Tino held it back. He didn't get violent. He began repeating, with a pained bent-over posture, red in the face, "No, no, no." Over and over. Then he stopped. He remembered. The "no nos" reminded him of Edward. He abruptly ran out of the trailer. Velma shouted for him to return, but he was gone. She knew she'd been chancing it. If she even implied criticism of him, he took it as a scolding. This time he seemed to become furious but he wouldn't let her, or maybe even anyone, see him get angry. Most importantly, certainly, he himself would not want to know he was angry. He would run away first. Yet, Velma noticed that indeed, he was angry—especially with respect to his tone and expressive postures during his "nos."

The problem for Tino was that at least in the past, and as far as he was concerned, there weren't any others. He always denied it. But, of course, she knew better. She'd seen it often. No matter what kind of treatment he got for it, nothing helped. That's why she came to Brentwood. She had learned that Brentwood once had a program for the treatment of multiple personality disorder. So she managed to get both of them jobs at the hospital. Her plan was for Tino to be treated by Kruger for both his headaches and his unusual sleep or trance episodes.

Despite Velma's power over Tino, she was unable to eliminate his headaches. As a matter of fact, it was her poking into his psyche that caused these headaches in the first place. In order to cure them, she would have to, at least, relinquish her probing. For her own reasons, Velma couldn't tell 'T' that the headaches were a function of his multiple-personality disorder.

In Kruger's office, 'T' was crying. This tall, dark, strong, and handsome man was crying. He had run from Velma directly to Kruger's office, looking for relief. But it was not to be. Kruger asked him the same question.

"Did you do it?"

So now it was Kruger's turn to grill him. Again, Tino denied it. "I didn't kill Billy!" Of course, Kruger didn't completely believe him. Kruger knew it had to be either Tino, Jericho, or Velma. He knew he didn't do it. Kruger had been compromised by Velma, and it was in both their interests to keep information to themselves. The compromise happened when Velma discovered Kruger's property office scam and that Billy was the one who kept all the books—the information about value of items, receipts, and how and where the stuff was sold. So Kruger reasoned that it had to be either Velma, Jericho, or 'T' himself who killed Billy.

Velma discovered everything when Kruger and Billy had been counting money in the condemned, forbidden part of the building in the early morning hours. She had several times seen Billy going in and out of the room but couldn't find anything of significance when she herself entered it. She never touched anything. She was too smart for that. She simply looked around. But she knew something was up when Kruger came to the ward to speak to Billy. That was unusual because Billy always went to Kruger's office. She decided to spend some time in the empty, dark entry closet within that forbidden domain. With the closet door slightly ajar, she could see and hear everything. As luck would have it she got to the closet with only about ten minutes to spare.

First, Billy entered. Edward was there with him and took a seat on the wooden rocking chair. Edward was gently rocking and feeling comfortable as Billy's devoted companion. Billy sat on the covered couch and waited. Kruger entered a few minutes later, and he and Billy pushed the fireplace frame away from the wall. They removed a large case and started to count money. Billy would note the amount in his book, carefully printing each notation. Then they replaced it all and left.

Velma hadn't surprised them. She waited until they were gone. Then she herself, hands covered with nurses' gloves, pushed the fireplace frame away from the wall, removed the case, and counted the money. There was five thousand dollars in the case. "A small amount," she thought. She paused for a split second, and then with certainty recounted half the amount and placed that half in the large pocket of her nurse's smock. She returned the other half to the case and pushed the fireplace frame back to the wall. When she got home, Tino was asleep on the open convertible couch. She sat at the kitchen table just adjacent to the couch and began writing:

> Dr. Kruger, I know all about Billy and the fireplace and the money. I was there last night and I saw the whole thing. I took half of the $5,000 but I left half of it for you. Like this we can be partners. I know there's going to be a lot more of this so I want to be fair about it. Is it a deal? I also sent a letter to my lawyer telling him to open the letter if something should happen to me. Do you understand what I mean? Are we partners? I need a yes or a no. Now.

Velma put the note in an envelope but didn't seal it. She called it a day. She disrobed, slipped into a nightgown, and then into bed next to Tino.

The next morning after Dr. Kruger had made his rounds and was about to leave, Velma asked to speak to him. She handed him the envelope.

"Please read this while we're standing here, and just tell me 'yes' or 'no.' Then I want the note back."

Kruger instantly knew this was something to be worried about. He stared at the unsealed envelope for a few moments and then removed the note. As he kept his head buried in the note, Velma could see his eyes were practically burning a hole through it. She didn't budge—was entirely focused on him. After some seconds, he lifted his head and looked directly at her. He handed her the note.

"Yes."

*   *   *

Rita's message was for me not to forget my talk on groups. In fact, I was quite focused on the talk. I was thinking I'd have to talk about how groups can affect the lives of people, both in good and bad ways. And talk about blame! I would iterate and reiterate that groups tend to have a basic blame nature. Political groups and religious groups can be the worst—especially when they unite. Because they will begin to figure out who you are. And they don't get confused or bewildered. They know there is a *who* and they know it's you!

At some point I'll ask the audience a rhetorical question concerning the basic motives of groups. The answer will be that the nature of well-defined groups, the basic motive, is to exist indefinitely. If it were possible to ask a group, "What is your purpose?" the answer would be "My purpose is to stay alive." In other words, groups resist becoming ghostly. Then I'll talk about educational and therapy groups where neurotic or self-defeating behavior becomes rectified and members try to discard any pretense, always attempting to deal with frustration and then anger—that key emotion. I'll call these the self-adjusting rectification groups. I had the thought that Sebastian, Grillo, Billy, Tommy Gersh, Rita, Jilliana, Danny, Vlad, Sully Polite, my lawyer, Mark Terra—and Mrs. Forester, as well as other special ones I know like Katie, all comprised such a group: a virtual federation of individuals with the same purpose in mind—try to do good work, be conscientious, honest.

Further, I'll indicate that the human organism is a wish-soaked creature constantly looking for objects—that is, people to blame for all sorts of unanswered, frustrated, and thwarted wishes. And Sebastian—genius that he was—sensed that in fact, there did indeed exist a psychology of blame.

He felt that suppressed anger and the resulting feeling of disempowerment, was the ultimate emotional culprit in the construction of this need to blame.

My thoughts shifted away from the lecture and to the hospital. I considered the possibility that Billy's killer would be one who blamed him for some sort of thwarted wish and then killed him.

The phone again. This time it was Grillo. One of his intermittent, yet consistent phone calls. He got me just as I was about to leave my office, and he practically assaulted me with a lot of "we."

"You'll never guess what we've come up with—or rather what we haven't come up with! We've been checking Tino's background. Can you believe it, he never went to school! No school records anywhere. So we checked with Velma. Guess what? She stalled but finally admitted she gave him home study because he was afraid to go. How about that? He never went to school. No friends. Just Velma. Looks like she was the only one in his life." He paused. "You there?"

I'd been listening. He was talking full tilt.

"Yeah, I'm here," I said. "I'll tell you," I continued, "it could be a recipe for more pathology down the road if he was completely isolated. Home schooling is okay as long as it doesn't lead to complete isolation. If it's only the two of them, that really constitutes an exclusive group—like they're sealed off from the rest of the world. And usually, that kind of situation produces a we-they, or an us-them mentality—a true partition of the two of them from the rest of the real world. I would call it psycho-social inbreeding. On the other hand, if the kid had a school phobia, it would mean that on top he was afraid but deep down he was angry—and at someone. Guess who?" He didn't answer so I continued. "I mean, I'm not saying Tino's responsible for anything. Don't get me wrong. I'm just making a general clinical assessment. Something tells me it wasn't a simple school phobia. I think it probably had more to do with Velma."

"Man," he said, "that Velma really had this kid locked up. And he keeps insisting he's normal. But if he's a split, he's in the dark. Right?"

"Yes," I said, "the whole thing is strange."

*   *   *

Tino kept insisting he didn't kill Billy and Kruger did what he had so often done before. I'm sure he first learned about it from my paper wherein I referred to the "hand-wave," and then he confirmed it through his library research on the multiple when he found the relevant reference. It was in the 1993 book by G. Greaves entitled "A History of Multiple Personality Disorder." Greaves cites the famous example offered by Eberhardt Gmelin of a multiple personality case Gmelin had treated in the late 18th century, in 1791. As a result of a movement of Gmelin's hand, this twenty-year-old woman would suddenly shift into a different personality. One personality was that of a French woman, the other, that of a German woman. It was then that Kruger tried it with Tino. It worked. Tino was definitely susceptible to the hand wave. Kruger was amazed. He had control of a multiple. Tino would trance briefly, then the aggressive personality would come forward first. Jericho would always be first.

"Fuck you, Kruger," said Jericho. "Sure, I know who did it. But I'm not telling you shit! So suck my dick! I'm not afraid of you at all. I fuck you where you breathe. How do you like that?" Kruger remained silent. He was actually frightened because this belligerent, crazy, and very strong guy was, so to speak, in his face. "The most I'll tell you," Jericho asserted, "is that it was either Tino himself, or it was me, or it was Velma. And of course, I know what Tino thinks. He denies it was him, but he might be lying. And I'm not going to tell you which is which. How do you like that?"

Jericho's objective was not so much in taunting Kruger as it was in disrespecting him. The taunting was just the vehicle of the disrespect. Perhaps not the most original method, but definitely effective.

"But if Tino's not lying," Jericho continued, "then he thinks it was really Velma who killed Billy and he's trying to protect her. He doesn't think it was me because he doesn't believe in me." And Jericho smirked, loving his own logic and, of course, his control over Kruger—as long as it lasted.

"See, Kruger," he persisted condescendingly, "you have no influence over me and I couldn't give a shit about your psychiatry bullshit!"

So here it was. Who killed Billy? Kruger agreed it probably was Jericho or Velma or Tino. On the other hand, Jericho claimed he actually knew who killed Billy, and one would have to assume that he was telling the truth when he implicated himself along with Velma and Tino.

When Kruger saw that Jericho was becoming more and more belligerent and out of control, he waved his hand and Jericho immediately tranced. Suddenly, and with hardly a transition, Veronica appeared. Impulsively, Kruger waved again. He had no interest at the moment in talking to a cross-dressing, exhibitionistic, libidinous hedonist named Veronica. Kruger knew Veronica hadn't killed Billy; aggression was not in her genes. Veronica tranced to Kruger's hand wave and then Tino himself emerged.

One could count the number of relationship-permutations that existed between these particular personalities—probably only four: Kruger and Tino; Kruger and Jericho; Kruger and Veronica; Jericho and Veronica. You couldn't count Tino and Jericho, or Tino and Veronica because Jericho and Veronica were strangers to Tino—strangers existing together and thereby invoking the law of physics regarding any two objects occupying the same space at the same time. In this case of relationship congruence, it was three objects occupying the same space at the same time—Tino, Jericho and Veronica. Three objects and only one relationship—Jericho and Veronica.

And talk about relationships? Several investigations of Billy's murder were being conducted simultaneously. Everyone was sure it was someone who had a relationship with Billy. No one even considered the possibility that the culprit was a random person. Obviously, Grillo and Stroud were trying, full-time, to figure it all out; in his own way, Kruger was trying to get at it, too. And Velma had her own reasons to watch it. Finally, I was trying to understand it all psychologically.

Tino was the centerpiece. Most people were looking at him as the culprit. Kruger couldn't help but think it a strong possibility. Grillo and Stroud knew that 'T' was being treated for headaches, and they also knew that headache in a multiple could be a side effect of the transformation from one personality to the other.

Everyone needed closure. Everyone wanted someone to confess. Everyone wanted to understand the key relationship. Everyone wanted to locate blame.

* * *

And here we'd come to it. The examining of relationships. With that in mind, I'd ask another question at the lecture: "What is the basic model of the therapy group; that is, when sitting in a circle, what does the group resemble?"

I then would focus on my discovery that the underlying group model was not at all what had been accepted for more than five or six decades—that the basic model of the group is that it represents one's early-in-life nuclear family of mother, father, siblings, and any others living in the household. I am now absolutely sure that that is incorrect—at best superficial. Rather, how one behaves, and feels in the group is the key to understanding how one is, behaves, and feels in a primary relationship, such as marriage. In fact, I'm going to propose that the role one plays in the group is an exact reflection of the role one plays in his primary relationship. One of the main keys to a successful adult primary relationship is the presence of autonomy in each partner. That means that each needs the freedom to bring an independent sensibility to the table. In the absence of such autonomy, such courage, partners begin to feel isolated. Since the basic model of the group is the adult primary relationship, then the level and nature of difficulty experienced in the group will be a good index as to the level and kind of difficulty that would be experienced by that person in a marriage. In physics it's called isomorphism—in scale, an exact one to one relationship.

Thinking about this brought me back to Billy. His primary relationship people were: Kruger, for whom he worked in the property office building; Velma, who was chief nurse of his ward; Tino, who was the attendant on the ward; and, Edward, his autistic friend. This was Billy's nuclear family, his group. As far as anyone knew, Jericho, the attacker, and Veronica, the exhibitionist, were not in the mix with him. This was the unifying issue that began to focus my thinking. Billy's killer was someone he knew—someone in his group—someone with whom he had at least the rudiments of a primary relationship.

* * *

Stroud and Grillo distributed questionnaires to all personnel on the hospital grounds requesting information about any strange relationship, violent act, threat, or unusual behavior of any kind, that anyone may have witnessed. They were hoping that someone who perhaps had seen something would show up. And they did, in fact, get a number of responses. However, everything reported to them became public almost as soon as the questionnaire was completed. For example, when it was discovered that a strange man was loitering near the hospital grounds, word spread immediately that the police had a stake-out going on just outside the grounds. In another instance one of the nurses expressed her suspicions that one of her patients might have been involved in the Billy killing. Immediately after this revelation, she also reported feeling that she was being watched by someone. A paranoia seemed to be sweeping the entire hospital.

This paranoia was precisely why Migdalia Rivera decided to call Stroud and Grillo rather than to fill out the questionnaire. It wasn't that she lacked courage. Quite the contrary. How many people would have stood there as she had while the exhibitionist did his thing? No, it wasn't a lack of courage. Rather, Ms. Rivera was a realist. She knew the rumor mill could be trusted so that anything she wrote on her questionnaire would quickly become public. So she made it a personal contact.

After Migdalia Rivera described in detail what had happened, Stroud and Grillo decided they would not reveal anything about the event. They decided to shadow Ms. Rivera, assuming that because she had been such a willing observer the first time, it was almost certain that the exhibitionist would try an encore. Rivera also readily admitted to getting a real eyeful and having been fascinated by the whole experience. Realizing that Rivera was no prude, and trying to be a man of the world, Stroud said, "Well, no big deal, you've probably seen bigger and better." Without missing a beat, Rivera answered: "Perhaps better." She then added: "I think he has premature ejaculation problems."

The bottom line was that the detectives felt they could rely on Rivera. To others it might appear that she had been stupid and even reckless to stand there and watch the whole episode in the first place—that she, in fact, encouraged the exhibitionist to elaborate his act. But Stroud and Grillo didn't care about her motive. They knew they had someone who was going to cooperate with them, just as she had with the exhibitionist. And they were excited that she had the courage to do it.

Talk about the psychology of courage in relationships. Tino confessed to Kruger in one of their sessions that when he was twelve years old Velma scolded him about his interest in one of the girls who lived down the road. She told him:"I'm the only girl in your life. No others. Do you understand? You're too young. They'll make you do things. Do you understand? No others except me. Only Velma." And Tino kept nodding Yes with every one of Velma's 'Do you understand me's.' "Only Velma," she said. So, even though he was afraid of her, he was also secretly excited by it. Yet, beneath it all, and more fundamentally, he must have been very angry.

No doubt that she was controlling him, and that's what would be making him angry. But in his heart of hearts, he also desperately wanted her, so that instinctively he understood that having her also meant being dominated by her and he accepted the inevitable. Thus, already, at that young age, Tino was becoming psychically arranged so that it wasn't a failure of courage that prevented him from rebelling, rather, it was a capitulation to his own wishes. Then the process of controlling him began to get more specific; Velma didn't permit him to be angry, and now she was beginning also to control his sexuality. No friends, no anger, no sex. Actually, he felt it was a good trade. He wanted Velma, and in terms of this trade-off, he reasoned that he actually had her. He would obey her and she would be everything to him—the complete relationship.

But now, since Billy's death, 'T' noticed he could actually feel sexual as well as angry. Not too much. Just a little. He definitely began to notice it. The demarcation, the membrane between compartments, was becoming more permeable. Jericho and Veronica were bleeding ever so gradually into his consciousness. But he never told Dr. Kruger. He couldn't chance the possibility that Kruger might tell Velma. He knew there was a good possibility that in such a case, Velma might/would abandon him. Plain and simple. So that shut him down. But he also knew that the headaches and the difficult sleep remained intractable. He was still suffering. So silence it would be. He needed Kruger, but even more, he needed to remain Velma's primary partner—nothing else would do.

"Only Velma!"

*   *   *

I kept going over my talk. The group is the marriage, the relationship. I thought of Tino and Velma as primary partners. Sick. Then I flashed on one of Sebastian's proposals of what he called five roles of marriage. These roles were spouse, lover, friend, parent, and child. I thought: "Did Tino and Velma fill these roles for one another?" In terms of my talk, I tried to remember which of Sebastian's five was the crucial role—spouse, lover, friend, parent, or child? Which role, if missing in a primary relationship, would contribute in the most significant way to the demise of the relationship? I then recalled that Sebastian said it was the role of the parent, or more specifically, the good parent. He said something like: "When the good parent disappears as a factor in the relationship, then the lover component soon also departs."

I thought about Velma and Tino. I was sure that in order for Tino to be attached to her, he had to feel that she understood him. That would be the key to their relationship. She would have to give him the feeling

that she understood his primary need and then she would be able to manage him. If she'd be the good parent often enough, he'd be compliant. It
occurred to me that if Tino's a multiple, then his nuclear group consists
of: himself, the product of a tyrant; Velma, the tyrant herself; Jericho, the
attacker; and, finally, Veronica, cross-dressing exhibitionist. Since the idea
of blame is associated with the basic motive of groups, then whom does
this group blame — this group of Velma, Tino, Jericho, and Veronica? And
since how one acts in the group is an exact replica of how one acts in a
primary relationship, then in Tino's case, he's a victim once with respect to
his relationship with Velma, and twice, with respect to his relationship to
himself; that is, he can't hear or listen-in to his other inner voices. He can't
even say "Who is — 'me'? Where is the 'I' in 'me'?"

· 17 ·

THERAPIST

So, I knew Deborah would be it. I knew none of my core group could take it. They were all involved in their own stuff. I flashed to Katie. She was the one to whom I could tell things—the one who would listen. On second thought though, I realized that as soon as I would begin to lay out the bare bones of Sebastian's story she would surely stop me. Katie couldn't tolerate violence, bloodletting, cruelty of any kind—especially descriptions of helplessness. So any discussion over the fate of Sebastian, as well as the story of the death of an autistic boy at the hospital, would be too much for her to let me continue. So, I thought, "Even with Katie, I guess I wouldn't be able to tell my story."

But Deborah let me talk. And she had no need to justify her presence by making interpretations, or even saying anything at all. If she sensed that I had a need to talk, she wouldn't interrupt me. This time, we had a conversation. Deborah had been a supervisor of mine at the institute when I was in training. She was one of those special people you meet now and then in your life. I knew it the first day. She was an exceptional analyst. So Deborah it was.

* * *

"This is a very complicated story," Deborah said. "You mean you have these documents and you've digested all the material but you don't know anything about the events that took place to get the documents to you? At the same time a murder is being investigated at the hospital and you have some residual, remote idea that you've not been fully cleared of suspicion?"

I nodded.

"So?" she said.

"So with Sebastian, I'm not able to get through two main things. The first is his wife's apparent death and also his child's disappearance. The second is the abject slaughter of people in the name of Christian purity infused with an intense desire on the part of these Christian authorities to steal everything in sight. Vultures and velocorapters. Nothing less. So these two factors—the wife and daughter and the purge—are simply killing me. And, of course, this thing about the kid at the hospital, Billy Soldier, is terrible. He must have died such a helpless death, and I think he understood what was happening. He never hurt a fly. He was such a good kid. And of course, it all boils down to, to—"

"To Katie," she preempted me.

"Right. And I keep going from one to the other. Now what strikes me and also kills me is that when Sebastian was ten they murdered his father. The same sense of helplessness is invoked in me about Katie and how I'll forever wander trying to find her. And Billy's death is also plaguing me, and it's about Sebastian's helplessness as well. So I think I'm walking around perplexed on top but very angry beneath.

"Talk about trauma? Sebastian lost his father to the Inquisition—murdered by a relative of this guy Ferrer and his army of cretins. He was struck with such a psychological trauma that he wasn't able to sleep for the next decade; a *decade*, for crying out loud! He spells out his trauma and his analysis of it, which he finally made years later when he was twenty. He remembered mourning his father for all those years. His agony about his father was shattering."

With that I pulled out the diary from my briefcase and began to fill Deborah in on the background leading to Sebastian's recording of all of these signal events in his life.

"Here on page forty, he states that his father was killed by a band of Jew haters who then looted all the family possessions. And they were singing, 'Hail, Ferrer!'

"When I first read it I thought, 'No different from Heil Hitler.'

"His mother then sent him to a special tutor for the study of languages and they relocated in Malaga on the Mediterranean coast. He says in the diary that his mother and father always planned for him to study languages. Now this occurred in 1452. That's when he was ten." Taking this note from my briefcase, I read to her:

> When I was told my father was gone I wept but I could not talk. No word sounds would emanate. Only sobbing. This I could not control. This well of tears only abated when I was twenty. I would continue to repeat: "Father, father, you can't be gone, you can't be gone. You must be somewhere. I will find you."

"Let me tell you, Deborah, I understand that only too well! He goes on to report his feelings of needing to hold onto his father and to see him. He laments not being able to talk about word derivations—what he called his and his father's special etymological pastime. His father apparently would tell Sebastian that the boy had a rare gift for words and language. They were very close. Always talking to one another. His father was his lifeline and Sebastian's world was obviously animated by the presence of his father. Talk about role models!" I further fumbled through my papers.

"Like here, listen to this. Sebastian's talking about his father:

> And suddenly he was no more. It was only at twenty that I was able to erase this unbroken decade of misery. It came to me in a dream. I was shouting at him. 'Why did you leave me? Why did you leave?' I was angry. And in a most unbelievable moment, I realized it was my father toward whom my fury was directed. The dream was an incubus and it awakened me. I lay there in bed and gradually, a lucidity arose in me. I began to understand the fitful nights and my lifelong fixation with his disappearance. Before that, I felt I could never have a farewell. I simultaneously sensed the importance of angry feelings that are not, and cannot be in one's awareness, and it was also then that I sensed the power of the psyche. It occurred to me that the psyche had rules to follow. I knew that anger and fury were somehow not acceptable and therefore the psyche was perhaps culturally instructed to

conceal such feelings, to develop a place to conceal them, and probably also to develop mechanisms to ensure that they're kept concealed.

"See, Deborah, as soon as he understood that he was angry at his father, he had worked out something, and the instant he worked it out, he was able to focus his attention on the intellectual task of understanding the process: his agonizing obsession, and the emotional sense of loss and its ultimate hold on him. On top of that, he somehow knew intuitively that there was a cultural imperative here that informed the psyche and gave it rules for functioning. It rings true to me. And wait, here it is. He says:

> I knew with this incubus, with my shouting at him, that something was loosed. I now knew, beyond any doubt, that I was angry with him for abandoning me. Nothing mattered, not even, and I am horrified to think this, that he was murdered. His leaving was an emotional fact and that was what mattered. The additional fact that I had vengeance in my heart, was most definitely a secondary consideration to his physical absence. He was gone. That was all that mattered in my immature subterranean mind. And my poor sleep and my ruminations were all manifestations of this suppression, designed by my psyche to keep me from knowing my raging soul. So for ten years I had symptoms of an illness that no one could cure because it was not understood.

"And that was it, Deborah. Talk about Freudian insight! He was curing himself by lifting his repression about his anger, and he had the 'who.' It confirmed for him that anger is the salient emotion of everyday life — the linchpin of the personality."

"So, Glenn, what are we talking about? Do you feel better?"

"Yes and no. Yes about Sebastian because I'm happy he was able to help himself. But, no, because it's occurred to me through Sebastian's analysis that I'm probably angry at Katie. I'm trying to see if I can feel it — you know, somehow get in touch with it. But also, another difficulty is the loss of Alba. I can't seem to take it and I can't seem to shake it. A precious little daughter—loved, valued, innocent, friendly, trusting. What the hell could have happened to her? I'm stuck with a kind of unrelenting agony as though I'm the father of this child probably held in strange hands. Man oh man, what Sebastian must have felt. I think I have a need to find Alba for him and bring her to him—in America!"

"Glenn, you're going to make me cry again."

"Well, someone should cry. The whole world should cry."

"What eventually happened to Sebastian?"

"I've tried to trace his escape by piecing together fragments from the diary. It seems that he escaped to Malaga where he used to live, and from there he made it to the island of Ibiza, then to Majorca and Minorca, then to Corsica, and finally Tuscany. He was running, escaping. Livorno was his region and he became known as Sebastian of Livorno. He's got it all scattered here and there in the diary. So he wound up in Italy constantly trying to return but not being able to. No money, no influence, nothing. Even though he spoke all those languages and was accepted as a monk, he never actually spoke—never actually uttered words vocally. He wouldn't and perhaps he couldn't. It looks like they burned his tongue, or what was probably part of his tongue. He worked on illuminated manuscripts for the rest of his days, and as far as I can tell only from this one diary, he never saw or heard of Alba again. That one's hard for me. I'm hoping that in his other diaries he'll report finding her. I doubt it, but I hope so. As I think of it, I realize there are literally millions of stories like this that happened during the Holocaust—just as shattering, just as devastating."

"That's how you feel—devastated?"

"Absolutely, but I think I'm also feeling motivated to work on whether I'm angry at Katie—crazy as that may seem. Possibly, in a way that might help me. Although the truth is, I don't want to be helped. I'm not going to be helped to feel that she's gone!"

* * *

I walked out of a tunnel. I was weary. I left Deborah's office on the Upper East Side and began to walk—East End to York and then south on First. I hit the 70's. Before I knew it, I was at Rockefeller. The guard waved. I walked up to him and we chatted. Decided not to walk the campus. Didn't want to bother Danny. He'd insist we walk and talk. Kept walking south. Hit the 50's and then headed east, over to Beekman. It was early afternoon and I had some time before my lecture on groups. I hit Beekman and felt like I was in another world. I walked slowly, looked into windows at the exquisite architecture, the well-appointed rooms, carefully examined the embassy homes, searching for the mood I usually get on that street. I felt myself decompressing. It started in Deborah's office, continued as I was walking south, and now, on Beekman, it felt as though I had escaped the persecution and made it to the other shore. All the while I was thinking of Katie. Then I passed Charley's office. I could see his light from the street. He was seeing patients.

I think I felt soothed even though I decided that I was actually feeling a little angry at Katie. That was a hard one to face. I also knew I wasn't a suspect in Billy's death, but then thought that even if I was, it was okay because I simply didn't do it. Decided to walk down Mitchell Place. I passed The Tower and headed over to the U.N. and up to Tudor City. Then I headed over to Lex and walked down to Gramercy and to my office. It was better to walk. I didn't want to be in a vehicle. I was tired. That was close to three-and-a-half miles, six or seven centuries, and a significant probe of my psyche.

* * *

What I didn't know was that my search for someone to listen to me was coexisting with another search. It was the stakeout at the hospital. It was all set. A deal was struck with Ms. Rivera and she seemed excited about it. On paper the stakeout was perfect. Rivera helped them understand the geography of the hospital grounds, especially with respect to the particular path she took from the parking lot to her building. There must have been a half dozen detectives scouring the grounds. They were perched here and there, high and low, peering through windows to the outside from dark offices on the inside, and also stationed in places on the grounds that gave each a wide scope of the buildings and terrain of the hospital.

Stroud and Grillo had gotten reports that almost nightly someone else reported seeing a man lurking. Some of those who made the reports were vague, but others were absolutely sure. The detectives considered the sightings valid and that this was not group hysteria. It was really happening, and they were determined to get him.

But it turned into something like the Keystone Kops. They almost had him. One of the detectives who was ducking around a building ran smack into him. It was about 10 P.M. Dark. He didn't see the guy's face, but the impact of the collision floored the detective. The lurker took off like the Road Runner with the detective slowly getting up off the ground and then starting the chase while two of the other detectives, bringing up the rear, joined in. But the distance between the lurker and the detectives was dramatically increasing, and he disappeared into the woods at the far end of the hospital grounds. He was gone.

Grillo tried to console Stroud by reminding him that at least it wasn't complicated; they'd confirmed it was a big guy.

The very next day Grillo and Stroud drove into the hospital grounds, parked outside the main administration building, and, unannounced, entered Dr. Kruger's well-appointed office. Kruger was surprised by their visit but abruptly ended the meeting he was having with his personnel director and asked what he could do for them.

"Billy Soldier was drowned twice," Stroud said. Grillo was carefully watching Kruger's reaction. "According to the final path report, he was drowned first in water that had hardly any chlorine content, probably a bathtub, and then in another place, obviously the hospital pool, where the chlorine content was concentrated."

Kruger listened but didn't show any sign of concern. "So," said Stroud, "where are the bathtubs in the hospital?" Kruger shrugged his shoulders as though to say, 'Are you kidding?' "They're all over the hospital. Every patient building has several tubs; there are even huge vats that were originally designed for hydrotherapy. Even the administration building has a tub. The doctors' quarters all have tubs. We have more than a dozen full-time nurses, psychologists, social workers, psychiatrists, and so forth, in these apartments. Each has a bathtub. As you know, this is a very large institution."

And he stopped. Kruger had them. If Stroud expected Kruger to be caught red-handed, this new information didn't seem to faze him.

"Obviously," Stroud said, "Billy was drowned in one of those tubs and then carried and dumped into the hospital pool, where heavily chlorinated water soaked him inside and out. And there were bruises around his nostrils and mouth. We're convinced he was forcibly drowned. Why he wasn't bopped on the head and knocked out first, only God knows. Maybe a sadist or something."

Kruger still wasn't shaken. He said, "Do you want a list of all the bathtubs on the grounds, by building? I'll be happy to supply it immediately. I'll call maintenance and have it all tallied."

The detectives agreed. Kruger called, told the head of maintenance what needed to be done, and asked him to put everything aside and to personally supervise the count and location of each bathtub in the hospital.

On the way to the car, Stroud said to Grillo, "Whatya think?" Grillo answered: "He didn't do it. Not a trace of recognition. I don't think he's that good an actor."

*   *   *

Rita said my call-sheet count was in the twenties and that I needed to do a lot of catching up even though she would take care of at least half the list on the basis of purely administrative requests. She reiterated that I had to make some calls. I then checked messages on my private machine. Hung up, dialed, pressed retrieve. It seemed like a lot, but actually, I only had six. Three were from patients and two were hang-ups. The last one was from a Dr. Bernard Barrett, a well-known psychopharmacologist, who was a consultant to the major pharmaceutical houses. He always had his radar up for any new approach to the treatment of anger-related disorders. He had written an article on the subject of suspected anger-related diseases, and both he and I were invited to participate on a panel at the International Association of Psychological Consultants. He wanted to discuss the panel with me in order to coordinate our presentations.

It was a welcome distraction from my obsessional focus on the cruelty of life. I called him immediately because I had already begun to work out a system showing that anger could be neutralized or controlled so that before it gets repressed it goes into a kind of suspended state; or, on the other hand, it could be surfaced, or even calibrated. CALIBRATED! The idea of anger being calibrated really got to me. In theory, then, determining the management of anger, having control over it, being able to calibrate, neutralize, or even nullify it, would have a tremendous influence on controlling, adjusting, or even eliminating psychological and emotional symptoms.

Just think of it. People would be spared the torment of panic attacks, anxiety attacks and obsessions that can torture you, and hysterical conversion reactions such as paralysis, and irritable bowel syndromes and migraines and hallucinations and delusions and dermatological horrors and impotence and premature ejaculations and frigidity and all sorts of intrusive, agonizing thoughts, and on and on. Is this possible? Yes, but it hasn't been done yet because no one knows the entire circuitry of the anger-to-symptom syndrome. But I believed I had it and that perhaps Bernie Barrett could confirm this circuitry by detailing it through the chemoneurobiophysio substrate.

That's what I'd been waiting for. My two or three courses in graduate school on the physiological and neural bases of behavior were not going to help me now. I needed an expert, and he was it. He, too, was convinced of the importance of anger in the entire symptom-disease process, but he didn't have the psychological understanding necessary to put him in the right place with the right code for the right anger-to-symptom process.

Some weeks later when we met on the panel, I only hinted at what was underlying the symptom complex. I hadn't yet fully integrated all of Sebastian's work, and my understanding of the anger-symptom complex crystallized only gradually even though I was already using the code in treatment. It was like living in a house during its construction.

I also noticed that Bernie was hinting at things at that conference that had a remarkably familiar ring to me. He was beginning to examine the same kind of relationship — the one between the experience of anger and physical disease. I too had been thinking that if the repression of anger could cause psychological symptoms, then what could the same process do to the appearance or even the genesis of physical diseases? We all knew that overall stress was a factor. What wasn't realized is that stress develops when wishes are threatened, thus starting the journey of anger into repression. My take on it is that stress is actually another code word for anger.

"Glenn, I'm glad you called." It was Bernie. He got right into it. "I've been thinking about the problem, but I haven't worked out why anger should play such a role in the disease process. It's really not about the fact that anger is disorganizing. I mean so what? Just because it's disorganizing doesn't really tell me why that produces symptoms. Right?"

"Exactly right," I said.

He continued, "I'd like to talk to you about it some more. There's something here that no one really knows about. If I could figure out the 'why' then I could be on to something. Perhaps we can collaborate?"

My first thought was: "It's the 'who,' not the 'why,' Bernie."

I liked Bernie, and in fact, I often collaborated on projects. But this was different. It was true, I needed a consultant who knew chemistry, biology, neurology and overall brain physiology. But to wire up a co-authorship on this project was not something I believed was needed. I already just about had the code.

*   *   *

The detectives had wired Migdalia Rivera for sound. And they agreed upon a code. A simple one. She was to whisper that he was there. That was it. For this particular operation, ten other detectives were now stationed at various points and latitudes, each with a view of the hospital post office where Rivera worked.

No one had considered that Veronica would enter the post office building at about 3:45 P.M. and go straight to the staff bathroom. There, she waited in one of the stalls, sitting on the seat, with the door latched. Everyone on the outside was on the lookout for the lurkerr from 8 P.M. on, when it started to get really dark. That was the official time of the stakeout, the thinking being that they should all be in place after dusk had descended and then morphed into a stark darkness.

Now it was nearing midnight and Rivera was about to finish her shift. Veronica looked at her watch. 11:50 P.M. She'd been waiting for about eight hours. She was a man with a purpose. The amount of time waiting meant nothing to her. Veronica discarded her heels, took a pair of boots out of a plastic bag and put them on. She hitched up the same leather skirt and let her penis, at half-mast, suspend out in the open. Quietly opening the door a crack, she looked up and down the corridor and then spotted Ms. Rivera all alone in the sorting room which was visible at a short distance from the bathroom. The sorting room was enclosed mostly by glass so that whoever walked down the corridor could see everything that was going on there. As Rivera began collecting her personal belongings from the sorting table, she also checked the mini-microphone in her blouse. Then she suddenly felt that she was not alone. She froze for a moment, then slowly turned toward the door. Veronica, hooded, with her face mostly covered with a kerchief, was standing there in all her glory. Whispering, Veronica said, "I just wanted you to see me when I'm not completely all the way up. See," Veronica continued to whisper, "it's still big." With that, her penis grew to its full erect length—about ten inches—more or less flirting with the length of a ruler. Veronica turned off the lightswitch next to which she was standing so that the only illumination was from the lamp on the table. She was too close for Rivera to whisper those powerful two words: "He's here." For some moments, Migdalia Rivera was mute. She had tried to scream, but nothing came out. Veronica instantly noticed Ms. Rivera's terror, so she whispered, "Please don't worry, I just want you to let me hold you so we can be close. I know you want me to."

And with that, Veronica's bolt shot into another kerchief that she was holding in her hand. The stimulus for Veronica was to utter the need she felt about wanting to hold Ms. Rivera. That was enough. Merely saying it out loud was enough for Veronica to have that sudden release. Veronica's release was then apparently the stimulus that Migdalia Rivera needed as she then let loose with blood-curdling shrieks. In that split second, Veronica bolted again, but this time out of the room. Within some moments, the detectives were swarming all over the place.

They tried to calm Rivera while she clutched onto Stroud. As she calmed down she was able to explain that when Veronica had been outside the building the distance between them was far enough that it hadn't been really scary. But now, at such proximity, the whole thing was terrifying.

They combed the building. No Veronica. Vanished. They knew one thing for sure– the exhibitionist had not exited the building. Hospital security were the very next group on the scene. Grillo shouted to one of them that the exhibitionist must be in the building because they had it all surrounded. The head of security shouted back that they should check the underground tunnel.

"Undergound tunnel?" *Stroud exclaimed incredulously.* ***"What underground tunnel?"*** *Of course, by this time, Veronica was gone. Out through the underground tunnel leading to Building A, about 50 yards across the hospital quadrangle.*

"Detectives," the security guy said, "all the buildings have underground walkway tunnels that everyone uses during cold weather. All hospitals have them."

Stroud looked at Grillo. "Slipped right under, and out."

* * *

I had fifty minutes before my talk on groups, so I had just about enough time for a snack. On the way to the restaurant I began to think numbers. But in wondering why I suddenly wanted to think of numbers, of things to count, I realized that I needed to distract myself because whenever I walk alone Katie immediately comes to mind and I begin talking to her, and thinking about what happened to her. I do all sorts of things to distract myself. Sometimes I'll think about sexual things. Sometimes I'll try to hum a popular song I know. This time I guess I decided to count — to think of numbers. So, I started.

I remembered Sebastian's five roles in marriage and five criteria in choosing a mate. In my groups I always find one person who doesn't realize that when he or she talks, everyone else fades out and drifts. So my admonition to such a person is to count. I'll say, "When you talk in the group your job is to count — to see how many people are listening and how many are not."

And when I'm treating a married person who is having an affair and the marriage is about to break up I'll say, "Be careful, two usually equals zero." The patient will probably lose his wife and girlfriend, or her husband and boyfriend, or one partner of another.

Or I'll say to a couple I'm treating that when trying to repair an argument: "The aggrieved one needs at least two or three approaches. All rejections work the first time."

Or when someone talks about the nature of time, especially when they're operating with the defense of denial, I'll say, "Every blink is ten years."

Or when someone is sensitive to criticism I'll say, "Don't make it two against one." This means that you shouldn't ally yourself with the accusation and make it the accuser and you, against you.

Or I'll tell people, "Be a first among equals." This means that you have to consider yourself to be a valuable partner in any primary relationship, and hopefully your partner will also feel valuable so that both of you can be firsts among equals.

When working with a patient on his very difficult marital relationship, I will repeat what Sebastian postulated: "In a primary relationship a plus multiplied by a minus always equals a minus. It's like algebra. Even though the plus believes in the power to elevate the minus, it's always the minus that drags down the plus." The message there is to be careful not to go on rescue missions when falling in love. Sometimes it's necessary for everyone to have his own problems, and for you not to take on the problem.

And when each partner of a couple states the hopeless truth that neither can really completely change their personalities and therefore each spouse feels they will always be disappointed in the other and so the marriage can never work, I usually ask how much percentage change does each have to register in order for the relationship to indeed shift? Invariably, with both men and women, the answers I get never go below 25 percent. Most estimates fall between 25 and 75 percent, and some go as high as 100 percent.

The correct answer, in my opinion, is about two to three percent—certainly less than five percent. The truth is people can't really change their spots more than five percent. Personality becomes etched very early on. But people can learn to struggle better, control impulses better, become more relaxed, more spontaneous, less shy, less withdrawn, happier, and so forth—about two to three percent shift. That's all we need. Personality-wise, this two to three percent is an enormous change because personality configuration is the strongest substance in existence—certainly stronger than most other substances, including that of steel.

I'll sometimes say, "Second or third best is frequently better than being first." It refers to not always insisting that you're right and your partner is wrong. Or recently, I've added Sullivan Polite's wisdom: "Your job is to lose." The gist of this little bomb is that sometimes very competitive or obsessive types can do much better when they're not hanging on so tightly to every little point. Let go. It's okay. The universe won't dissolve. It's a matter of looking at it from another vantage point. Even if you do insist most of the time on your point or position, and if because of this you're not liked by everyone, so what! It's okay. It enables you to know where the other person leaves off and you begin. You retain your individuality.

Or, when someone is hopelessly ambivalent, I'll point out that ambivalence is not democratic. One side is Yes, and the other is No. The problem in ambivalence is that the No gets two votes while the Yes only gets one. Thus, in ambivalent moments, the No is pulling on you more than the Yes.

So on my way to the restaurant I recited numbers.

"Two equals zero. Five roles in marriage. Five criteria in mate selection. Every blink is ten years. Every rejection works the first time while it takes about three approaches to repair a breach. Never make it two against one. Count. Second or third is frequently better than first. Lose—even to zero. A plus multiplied by a minus equals a minus. A two to three percent shift is a significant change in personality. Two votes for the No and only one for the Yes. Always be a first among equals."

My stream of consciousness suggested a final number. Katie, and Sebastian, and Billy, and the circumstances surrounding their lives came to mind. I thought: "Anger knows no civilization. The world is got to be, at best, a C minus."

BOOK 3

EVENTS

· 18 ·

THE CONFERENCE

"Human nature has a genetic foundation." I would begin my paper with that statement. The conference was all set. *The Psychological Contributions of Sebastian Arragel: A 15ᵗʰ-Century Monk*. That was the conference title.

Some time had elapsed after the notices announcing the conference were mailed. Five hundred people had finally responded to the mailing and would be jamming an autditorium that seated three hundred and fifty. The uncovering of a body of work by a fifteenth-century monk on the unconscious, the formation of psychological symptoms, and the nature of relationships, had apparently intrigued this sometimes jaded psychoanalytic and psychiatric population. Speakers had been invited who could shed light on various aspects of the psyche; libido theorists would discuss implications for population biology, and Danny Margolis—who I decided could make more easily visible the biochemistry, neurophysiology, and brain structures implicated in the operation both of pleasure generally and libido and anger specifically—would appear. After the program committee read my paper at a pre-conference meeting, an ethicist and philosopher were also invited to participate as discussants.

A week before the deadline for the printed program, I called Bernie Barrett. I had decided my work didn't need a collaboration. However, I was definitely interested in consulting Bernie on the pharmacological implications of the management of anger and its effect on the libido. I was worried that he would be disappointed about my decision not to collaborate, but as it turned out, he was already at work for a new biotechnology startup company and any memory he had of our previous discussions had receded in the face of his excitement about his new position.

What I was hoping could be developed was a tablet that would either keep anger in a virtual state, erase it altogether for untoward circumstances, or calibrate it so that its power would remain just under the potency threshold. I liked the calibration idea, best. Thus, it would be a little tablet, designed to control psychological/emotional symptoms, and perhaps also dilute physical problems such as hypertension and relieve the effects of depression including sleeplessness, eating disturbances, impotence, frigidity, and so forth.

I was going to present the idea that the psychological disease process is set off by the thwarting of a wish, by the corresponding emotional reflex of anger towards the offender, and by the repression of that anger. I was planning to propose the kind of research implementation that would be necessary for the development of a pharmacological agent designed specifically to short-circuit the psyche's emergency process ultimately implicated and encapsulated in the form of the transformation of the thwarted wish into a symbol—a symptom. Help people not suffer. That's really what it was all about.

If I'm successful in the development of this tablet, we would see a decrease in the population of those people who get subtracted from themselves, who get compromised because of their crushing symptoms, and who, because of these symptoms become a little bit like ghosts. Instead we will now see a population of symptom ghosts—that is, symptoms that are no more. Symptom ghosts rather than people ghosts!

*   *   *

Velma Secora went to work early that day in her civilian clothes, planning to change into her nurse's uniform on the ward. 'T' arrived shortly after Velma. Having taken the tablet, Buspar, Edward was better, more whole, not suffering. His best, his only friend in the world, was gone. Dead. Finished. And here was Edward, sitting calmly, and apparently not grieving. But he wasn't rocking in his chair. Just sitting still. On second thought, "No, Edward is grieving. He's not rocking in place. It's like the life in him is stilled."

Changing into her nurse's uniform barely inside one of the linen closets, Velma removed her blouse and skirt. She was in her bra and panties, visible only to Edward, 'T,' and other autistic patients who were wandering around the ward. She knew that the doctors, nurses and other attendants weren't due for another half hour. She lingered, put her leg on an adjacent chair and rolled up her white nurse's stockings.

Edward began to rock. She was unnerving him. She noticed it, but didn't seem to care. Edward could rock or not rock all he wanted. He didn't matter to her at all. He really wasn't a person anyway. 'T' tried not to look, but couldn't help taking furtive glances. He was in conflict. Don't look, look; look, don't look. Velma was now fully dressed — white stockings, white tennis shoes, white smock with the large square pockets, no hat. Then, having observed T's sullen mood, she scolded him for all to hear. But she didn't care because who was 'all?' Autistic children? But 'T' still felt embarrassed. To him, his scolding was, in fact, witnessed by the children, autistic or not.

"Tino," she said. "I can change my clothes all I want, when I want, and where I want. Do you understand? Anyway, you've seen it a million times. Being in a bra and panties is like being in what?" she pointedly asked him. "Like in a bathing suit," he complied. "So," she reminded him, "you don't have to sneak looks."

Tino didn't look at, or answer her, but he seemed glazed at being publicly scolded. He knew he was leering at her and what that meant. He couldn't take it. What he didn't at all get was that this woman, his so-called mother, was nuts, that her behavior was totally inappropriate, and that she was basically and unabashedly exhibitionistic and seemingly quite consciously seductive. Poor Tino — showing him her body but making it clear that she was the one in charge of the touching department; sleeping in the same bed, but again warning him to unfailingly wait for a permission cue — keeping him on the edge and in a state of subservience, controlling and dominating him. His dominatrix. Nothing more, nothing less. He couldn't show anger and he couldn't react sexually. Both were taboo, and he was always in torment about it, whether he knew it or not. The problem was that beneath, unconsciously, he wasn't just angry — he was furious — and, in addition, he was not only sexual, but in a constant state of libidinous over-stimulation whenever Velma, his so-called mother, began showing him her body. And that's what she did, show it to him. And that's exactly how he described it to Dr. Kruger in their sessions together.

"I can't sleep alone. I know it's different with other people, but we've always slept in the same bed. And she's so beautiful."

"I know you see her naked," Kruger stated, of course raising the subject once again.

"Only sometimes," Tino said, and then volunteered, "All my life it's been like this. Most of the time she's only in panties and bra, and then she stands, puts her leg on some chair and rolls up her stockings. When she rolls them up she stands a little bent over. Then I can see her breasts through her blouse. That's when she's not wearing a bra, just some top. I can see all of her then. Her breasts just filling the whole blouse. Sometimes she'll ask me to go to the closet and get her some clothes."

"What do you do then?" Kruger followed.

"I get them and bring them to her."

"In other words, you always do what she says?"

"Yes, of course."

"And then?" Kruger eagerly asked.

Tino went blank, again glazed. Kruger repeated the question, but was met with silence. It was obvious what Tino did. Whenever Velma scolded him, Tino would trance. Tino would become the angry Jericho, but occasionally a shift would take place and he would change into women's clothes, acting out his cross-dressing sexual impulse—especially when she was seductive. When that happened, he would disappear through the illicit door into the netherworld of the condemned part of the hospital building.

Now it was 8:30 A.M., and here he was already dressing in the dark: leather skirt, stockings rolled up just as Velma did them, bra stuffed with more stockings, tight sweater. He became a she, but didn't bother to apply lipstick. Leaning against the wall, she rubbed her penis through the leather until she climaxed. Relieved, she stood there trancing, went to the bathroom, washed, changed back to the attendant's uniform—teal pants, teal shirt, black tie, black socks, black shoes—went for the door, peeked out to see if the coast was clear, and reentered the real world—in the autistic ward.

One thing for sure, Tino's multiple personality wasn't genetic. If Velma seduced him, his sexuality was sparked. However, this was entirely dependent upon the absence of his frustration and subsequent anger. The essence of the *whole thing came down to Tino's capacity, or rather, relative incapacity, to manage his anger.*

* * *

At the conference not only would I try to demonstrate that it is the anger and the management of that anger that really determines what happens to the person and personality in terms of symptom formation, but I would also try to show that ego and coping strength, potential success in relationships, and even maturity, depend upon how anger is managed. Of course, I understood that this management of anger is also the key dynamic in the very genesis also of the multiple personality — that fractured identity.

One of the problems is that cultural forces make it frequently impossible for people to ever know they're feeling angry in the first place. As a result, people seek ways to keep such inclinations of anger out of awareness. Other than using anger code words to refer to the feeling of anger, the most frequent mechanism of the psyche that permits this unawareness to exist is the operation of repression. So when anger, the attack emotion, is directed at the self, the anger is repressed and as its nature dictates, attacks — in this case, attacks the self. In cases where such anger is a rage, an implosion can take place. The anger can explode inwardly. The problem is that once such anger is imploded, how does it get harnessed before it pervades the entire personality? How the debris is contained once the bomb has imploded is the issue.

My solution was to develop a medication regimen that would put a perimeter around the debris. My objective at the conference was to carefully explain how all this would be possible. I had to present material on the relation of the wish to the overall pleasure principle; that is, I would point out that people are guided by the need to feel gratified — to be satisfied. I needed to explain that the wish is the pleasure principle's agent, disciple, messenger, reflector and most derived representative. Then I needed to show that when the wish is blocked, the person, at that moment, feels an absence of sufficient control over his life. In the face of this absence of control — in the form of either impotence, weakness, helplessness, overall disappointment or disempowerment — exploding with anger is frequently experienced as the only way to reconstitute one's sense of self, one's sense of pride, dignity, and self-esteem. That's what is known as re-empowerment. So the key is that when one is disempowered, anger is frequently the only re-empowerment available.

Next, I'd have to hook up the wish and the symptom. I'd tell them that when Freud pointed out that no wish will be denied he formulated another of the greatest discoveries ever made about the psyche and its dynamics. When a person experiences a symptom, the symptom represents the wish gratified, albeit in disguised, or what I call perverse form. All of it operates according to Freud's hydraulic system of the drives; repress something like anger or sexuality and you build up pressure. This shows us why people really love their symptoms, even though consciously they may believe they hate such symptoms. People love their symptoms because the symptom represents the wish — the symbolic psychically gratified wish. The formation of all emotional/psychological symptoms, *without exception*, follows these rules of the psyche. That's the main point I would need to emphasize.

I had it all rehearsed this way. But I was going to have trouble convincing anyone that this synthesis is really what happens. My job at the conference and the real trick would be to carefully and gently inform the audience of the possibility that when the circuitry of anger can be calibrated and controlled, then a great deal of misery, symptoms, and diseases exacerbated by accumulations of repressed anger could be eliminated. My ace in the hole would be to cite Sebastian and Freud as indispensable to the uncovering of the code. Then perhaps people would listen.

"Eliminate misery? Isn't misery a premise of the human condition? Anxiety can't be eliminated!" That's what the philosopher would say. The ethicist would agree. My answer would be that of course that's true, but also that we are on the edge of a new light source, that is to say, an evolutionary leap. Now with the realization of the Genome Project and a technology that could control repressed anger, much could be accomplished in the management, or even the elimination, of psychological symptoms.

*   *   *

Kruger was sitting in his office. It was late, and only the night-shift people were around. The office was dark except for the lamp providing light on his desk. He was poring over the Jericho/Veronica diaries. This time he was fascinated. Veronica was always either talking to, or answering, Jericho.

*"Jericho, I don't understand you. You're always angry. I know what that is because I can tell it's very different from what I'm always trying to get. I just want to be happy. That's all. It's what I understand. So I do it my way. You get me, Jericho? I know that I do certain things because Velma doesn't like me to be with other women. So to get with women, I dress like one and then put my own clothes back on over the woman's clothes. This makes me feel good because then Velma won't be able to catch me thinking of women. My man's clothes hide it all. I feel safe that way. Then when I feel safe, I can show my thing. It's like I have a weapon. It's strong. When they look at it I get great pleasure. I think they **like** to look at it and that then they want me. I can never get that from Velma, so I do it this way. See? I can get around very easily dressed this way. Sometimes the man's clothing gets me close to women and sometimes the woman's clothes gets me close. It doesn't matter to me because all I want to do is show it. I learned that from Velma. But sometimes I just want to watch them like Tino watches Velma. When it can be dangerous and I think I could get caught, then I just watch. Jericho, you know, you're the only one I can talk to. I have no friends. But I always find a way to feel good and I feel good writing to you. You're my only friend."*

Kruger put the diary down on the desk and contemplated Veronica's contemplation of her experience. Then Kruger picked up Jericho's notebook.

"Veronica, I'm always mad because Tino can never get what he wants. So I'm always boiling. That's why I'm around more than you. You're only around sometimes. Every once in a while when Tino's very hot and underneath it all his sex is kind of touched, then he changes into you. But that doesn't happen much. Most of the time Velma makes him so mad that he calls on me because I don't care about anything. I'm not afraid of Velma. I can hurt people who bother him, and that's why I'm always around. But I never get mad at you, Veronica, because I only attack real people, and like me, Veronica, you're not a real person."

Kruger closed the notebook. He turned off the lamp and sat there in the dark.

* * *

The ethicist and philosopher at the conference would be there because the committee felt that in discussing control over anger and sex I was entering the domain of human nature. They weren't sure that I was the right person to do what I was doing. Maybe they thought there was no right person.

My biggest job would be to sketch the biogeneticneuroendophysio-chemical anger systems. What would become clear would be the identity of the major switches for anger around which the whole bio-smorgasbord is arranged. After that I would point out the connection to the solar plexus, the location of that little brain called the enteric nervous system in the field called neurogastroenterology, where intuition lives. Finally, I would propose the DNA key to the whole shootin' match — the evolutionary key!

The first problem I'd have to face when detailing these levels of biological interaction would occur the moment I mentioned the words "prefrontal" — as in prefrontal cortex, and "lobe" — as in temporal lobe. Everyone's going to think: "Lobotomy!" And that would be a natural assumption because prefrontal lobotomies were a relatively commonplace surgical procedure, especially during the 1940's. And what was that all about? It was about controlling anger. And it was one of the most horrible, misguided, high-handed and autocratic dictates of the psychiatric power structure.

However, anger was indeed better managed. The problem was that accompanying this better-managed state of anger was the new condition called "vegetative;" these lobotomized people were now sitting and staring. Lobotomies interfered in the color of emotion, so anger was more or less dead. But so was pleasure and joy.

This was the legacy I'd have to face when discussing the calibration of anger through some Big Pharma. The ethicist and the philosopher would surely call for my head — whole — not just my lobotomy. The irony is that I'm the one in the forefront — the frontal — of the opposition, because when I think of the thousands of lobotomies that were performed, I scare myself. When this pharmacological agent that I'm proposing is finally developed, as I thought it would be, I had no doubt that it would in fact calibrate anger better. I believed there was no doubt that people would feel better and that certain disease entities such as psychological and emotional symptoms could even vanish in the same way that most conversion hysterias vanished in the 20th century. But what my detractors were also certain about was that when anger is attenuated then libido is likely to be unhinged, and then the experience of pleasure would be getting more experience-time than ever before in the history of evolution. "Anger," they would say, "would no longer be a control over libido. And what would that bring?"

It's actually a good question, the answer to which cannot really be a certainty. If the answer wasn't good, then how do you stop that proverbial freight train — the one carrying the feel-good pill? My hope was that this new step would really just eliminate the deleterious effects of rage. But I also reasoned it this way: If anger is calibrated down, it would necessarily mean that in order to become re-empowered, people would need to find ways to struggle better. They would need to put their ingenuity to work, and not be so dependent on some impulse — some reflexive, convenient, and expedient response like anger or rage, or symptoms. Rather, because rationality begins to be more necessary, people will need to make better distinctions between major and minor wishes. In turn, they will have to be motivated more by the prospect of useful aims, and ends, rather than experiencing incentives that are determined solely by wishes, pleasure, immediate needs for gratification — even profit.

The mutational event here is the unlikely marriage between Adam Smith and Karl Marx: determined individual struggle pollinated by a contributory work ethos. How's that for an evolutionary mutational biological event with effects in behavior, philosophy and culture?

Of course, I would have to state my case strongly — that I believed culture would triumph over genes. I felt that such an anger-calibrating tablet like I was proposing would be designed only to prevent intractable symptoms so that people can work on their problems in the absence of pain.

How that would help me personally — meaning also financially — was not at all lost on me. So despite my fears, the positive idea of empowered people and the sense that science can create conditions of positive evolutionary acceleration appealed to me.

*   *   *

It was Stroud on the phone. "Just keeping you informed, Dr. Kahn. Everything's accelerating. We've discovered that Tino Vescaro and Velma Secora may be a couple of grifters. They were dismissed from a hospital in Wyoming for unusual circumstances involving something about consulting fees from a nursing home. We're still working on getting the whole story. We're bringing them in for questioning as we talk."

· 19 ·

THE COMMITTEE

Velma and Tino were escorted into the precinct and met by a committee of two. Grillo stood by while Stroud led the interrogation.

"We know your last jobs at Silverado State ended with a truce. The hospital was not going to press charges of theft, but you were to leave immediately. I think you got off easy. And you, Tino, you were being treated for headaches by the staff doctor. They also caught you in women's clothes. Now what about that?"

Velma interrupted with a non sequitur. "Tino carries his father's name. Yes, he sometimes cross-dresses. It's not a crime. It's a psychiatric problem. It's not illegal."

"Now look," Stroud said, "there's been a murder and the patient murdered lived on your ward. It looks very bad—don't you think? We've also been told that Dr. Kruger is treating you, Tino."

Velma interrupted. "Any conversations in therapy sessions are protected. They're private—confidential and privileged." And looking at Tino, she said, "No need to answer questions, Tino. We need to speak to a lawyer."

"Yeah, yeah, you need a lawyer like I need another personality," Stroud impulsively said.

As Stroud's comment reverberated, Grillo interrupted. He wanted to reassure Tino. "Look, Tino, we're just collecting information. No one's being charged with anything. But we'd like to know, you know, maybe at times you've felt dif-

ferent. You know? Kind of like you weren't yourself? You know, we know about your dressing in those other clothes and things."

Tino, this tall, handsome man, was sitting there, tears in his eyes. Both Grillo and Stroud saw it.

"Well, Tino," Grillo persisted.

"I don't know about those other things. I'm only me. Everyone's trying to tell me these things about me. But they're not true. I get headaches and that's what Dr. Kruger is treating me for." Though seemingly vague, at this point he knew better.

"Is the treatment working? I mean, are the headaches better?" asked Grillo.

Tino couldn't say that the headaches were better, and no matter how many ways Grillo or Stroud tried to allude to Tino's alleged multiple personality, Tino evaded all such attempts. Velma similarly stonewalled everything. At that point, Dr. Kruger was ushered into the room. Kruger looked around. He knew everyone.

"Dr. Kruger," Grillo said. "We're trying to do this informally. No one's being charged with anything. We've asked you to come down here because we're trying to see whether Chief Nurse Secora and/or her son Tino, are in any way implicated in wrongdoings at the hospital, but not necessarily connected with Billy Soldier's death. And you can help us if you will."

Kruger acknowledged Velma and Tino and sat in the chair offered by Stroud.

"Look, detectives," Kruger said. "I'd like very much to cooperate, but I have no knowledge of Nurse Secora's activities outside of the hospital. Of course, I'm sure you know that I'm treating Tino and that such treatment is strictly confidential. So my hands are tied. Regrettably, it doesn't seem that I can help you."

Then Stroud, in an attempt at frontal emotional shock therapy, and without regard to Tino's presence, said: "Look, Dr. Kruger, we could challenge that position and you could be vulnerable to jail time for refusing to reveal potentially important information in a murder investigation. You know? Now the plain truth is that we're suspicious about Tino. Quite frankly, we think he may be suffering with, you know, a split personality. And if that's the case and if he's involved either directly or indirectly in Billy Soldier's death, and you know about it, we're talking serious jail time. You know?"

Kruger wouldn't budge. He took the high ground, which also gave him the appearance of total innocence. "No," he said. "Jail or no jail, I cannot and will not reveal any information obtained through psychotherapy sessions. I've taken an oath." And in a page from Stroud's book, Kruger added, "You know?"

Then Tino, in a moment reminiscent of Edward's "no, nos," began to wail: "I'm only me. I'm only me." He was crying.

It seemed that everyone was trying to pry something loose from everyone else, and even though the detectives were onto something, they couldn't quite break through the psychological barriers.

*   *   *

Waiting to interrogate me on the other committee was this well-known ethicist that I had never met. He had the reputation of being ultra-conservative in his ethical excavations and quite liberal in his social agenda. He was wary of new-fangled inventions that purported to have salubrious effects for the future of mankind. His name was Dr. Thomas Rex, and people referred to him as Thomas the Rexonator. Some called him "T-Rex." I had the thought, "Here it is again, another 'T.'" I was thinking that after Dr. Rex read my paper he would see my proposal as genetic engineering leading to some plot to make people happy and smiling all the time, when the state was enslaving, exploiting, or otherwise controlling them. What worried me even more than the Rexonator was the fact that I agreed with him. I was more worried about the implications of my project than he could ever be.

Thus the presence of the Rexonator was not going to be an ambush. Whatever his objections, they would never be as troubling to him as they already were to me. I was thinking of Dostoevsky's *Grand Inquisitor*, where freedom is exchanged for security and bread. So the Rexonator had nothing on me with respect to checking and balancing, especially with Dostoyevsky, not to mention Huxley and Orwell, shadowing my every thought, my every move.

Nevertheless, I pushed ahead. The audience would have to suffer a mini-lecture on basic DNA structure. The anger pill would be based on this DNA structure. Thus the answer of how to control anger does not lie in interventions along the anger highway of the bioneurophysio-brain coordinates. Rather, the answer lies in the non-toxic, non-invasive, respectful alliance with the DNA dynamic and its constituent lexicon — histones, the wrapping of DNA, and the bending architecture of DNA. This microscopic gala and how it gels is what would lead us to the calibration of anger.

Of course, as soon as I raised the issue of the smoothing out of the anger response and the predictable increase of libido as the remaining dominant pleasure response, I was certain our population biologist would explode with urgency. He would ask what I was also asking. In anger calibration, symptoms disappear or cannot crystallize. The person then feels better rather than worse because libido and sexuality should be more available. Such availability of libido would necessarily lead to more sexual liaisons, and most likely, an increase or maybe even an explosion in the birth rate. Of course, as soon as the population biologist got wind of this possibility, she would hit the roof. I was sure she would predict an impending Malthusian supernova. And this was where her greatest ally in opposing such experiments was me.

This population biologist, Dr. Darcy Walden, was a known opponent of increased population growth and was one of the founders of the organization known as *Zero Population Growth*, or *ZPO*. Her main position was simple and one to which I subscribed. In the event of a serious outbreak of exponential population growth, serious shortages of food could lead to famines around the globe, which could in turn also lead to conflicts and wars and the increased probability of plagues, atomic attacks, atomic fallout, nuclear pilfering, and massacres. This scenario would be the basis for our mutual argument for the discontinuance of any undertaking even resembling my proposal. She would argue that it is far better for civilization to continue on its snail's pace of suffering symptoms, agonies, and known diseases than to pursue an alternative route that could result in massive and cataclysmic population eruptions which could create permanent political destabilization. And I agreed. Still, I felt myself moving ahead in my vision of an agony-free emotion universe. Even if what I was suggesting couldn't totally erase agony, it could effect *some* elimination of agony, *some* reduction of helplessness, *some* modification of a segment of dis-ease and disease, and thereby perhaps even immeasurably improve the human condition without any of these hypothetical downsides. What then? Maybe these envisioned horrors were just that—envisioned, not really real. If that were the case, then not pursuing this program would be horrifying. My hope was the idea that the only thing the smoothing out of anger would do would be to enable people to feel better about struggle and therefore to be authentically more in pursuit of greater goals. So in light of this positive implication, and on faith, I pushed ahead.

*   *   *

In addition to Dr. White, who would introduce the speakers, and Dr. Siegfried Kruger, who of course would side with everyone against me—and in my paradoxical position would side with me against me—the only other participant would be Dr. Shelby Simmons. Dr. Simmons is a philosopher who I thought would want to dissect what we might call my "split personality"—go ahead with the project, don't go ahead with it. He'd put my dilemma in a philosophical context. The discussion would center on the age-old argument of what defines personality. Is it actually what you do during defining moments of your life, such as developing this little tablet, or is it your thinking, overall ideology, ethical position, and moral stance regarding the possible implications of the project that determines who you are? That sort of question interested me.

I figured I'd see contentious opposition to my proposal that might eclipse the Sebastian introduction. I already felt that the conference was being usurped. I wanted it to be simply an introduction of Sebastian and his work, with a discussion about what I believed to be direct implications of his work for the relief of psychological/emotional symptoms. Instead, I expected Kruger to try to turn it into a polemic about ethics and morality. Kruger would be morally correct, unrivaled, even morally transcendent. He would create a straw man out of me and what I considered to be my important presentation. Then he would try to knock me down. Not knowing him, the conference participants could be taken in by him, allying themselves in a false all-or-nothing battle, one that would create a real polarization of the participants where none needed to be.

I asked Dr. White who on the committee had requested the additional outside panel members. White said that while he himself agreed that it was important to broaden the scope of the discussion (given the implications of my paper), nevertheless, it was Kruger who had raised the question of those implications. White admitted to not initially recognizing those implications and thought that Kruger had a good point in suggesting that scholars of other disciplines be included in the discussion.

Most of the other committee members didn't see the introduction of other conference participants as an anti-Kahn move and readily agreed to the expanded format. While I understood Kruger's real motive, I couldn't confront it because it would make me seem paranoid. My only hope was to keep the conference divided into two parts: the first would introduce Sebastian and his work; the second would then be devoted to what I considered the implications of his work, as well as my suggestion for the development of a psychopharmacological agent for the recalibration of any kind of anger that could get repressed as a result of people becoming frustrated — the operative terms here being "recalibrated," and "repressed."

I also realized that the economics of this project needed to be disclosed and discussed. I knew that even if I was the one to introduce the issue, Kruger would use it against me and maybe rightfully so. But if I was right, many people would get very rich as a result of the success of the project. The anger pill could become the rage of the psychopharmacology industry, and I stood to benefit the most financially whether or not I wanted to. I did indeed recognize that.

So my job was to navigate the potentially treacherous maze of the conference while maintaining a stance of open, unalloyed, and honest inquiry. It was one thing to register my own doubts and quite another to capitulate to them. After a while I wondered whether those at the conference would see any positive side to the anger pill at all. I needed to get Vlad and Danny back to the tower restaurant so the three of us could also dissect the whole moral dilemma, work out the arguments for and against, and weigh them all. The one thing I had to make clear was that the pill would not eliminate anger as an emotion. Rather, it would calibrate the repression of anger. It would calibrate the mechanism of repression with regard to anger. That was it!

Thus, sorting out the implications of this little tablet would be a task for three people sitting at a penthouse bar/restaurant: one a psychoanalyst, drinking bourbon and soda; another, a biochemist, drinking rye and ginger; and, the third, a theologian, drinking Scotch and water.

· 20 ·

THE ACCUSATION

Grillo and Stroud had spent the remainder of the day, believe it or not, navigating the maze of buildings housing bathtubs at the hospital. The head of maintenance provided lists of tubs and their building locations, and the detectives were quickly moving from staff apartment to staff apartment—tub to tub—and ward to ward in each patient building. So far they'd checked about thirty tubs, and there were other lists to go. They tried to establish when these tubs were used. They found that since Billy's death all the tubs had been used repeatedly. This included the bathtubs in the medical wing of the hospital reserved for patients with physical problems. All the tubs were dusted for prints, and all the people who were interviewed were also fingerprinted.

When they finally arrived at Billy's building, where Edward lived and where Nurse Secora and 'T' worked, they quickly examined the two bathtubs on the ward, thinking that because it was Billy's ward and because Velma and Tino were essentially in charge of the ward, they would find the smoking gun there. But that wasn't to be, and they couldn't face another minute of tub search. They told the maintenance chief they would continue the next day and asked him to be available. As they were preparing to drive away, Tommy Gersh saw them and ran up to them excitedly.

"Detectives," he said, "did you hear about it? Edward keeps repeating something about Billy getting drowned and he keeps saying: 'Billy in the water. Billy in the water.' Everyone's telling everyone else about it. It started happening

about twenty minutes ago in the cafeteria. He's still there repeating it and people are all around him."

The detectives asked Gersh to accompany them to the cafeteria. "He saw it," Grillo said to Stroud. "Could be," Stroud answered.

Sure enough, there was Edward, surrounded by a crowd of people at the end of a long cafeteria table, repeating, "Billy in the water." Rocking and saying it. When he saw the detectives he stopped.

* * *

As I walked into my office at the hospital, a message on my machine from Tommy Gersh told me that he was going to look for the detectives because Edward was repeating that he saw the killer drown Billy, or something like that. I ran out of the office and onto the walk outside the building. Two nurses passing by told me that practically the whole hospital was down in the cafeteria. Something about Edward confessing to the crime. Man oh man, I thought, rumors can really take off. I immediately rushed over to the cafeteria. When I arrived, they were all still there. Tommy saw me and waved me over. Like everyone else, I watched. Edward was, in fact, repeating the line about seeing something. The detectives led him out of the cafeteria, out of the building, onto the walk, and over to their car. It was no use. Whatever they asked him, he kept silent.

Detective Grillo motioned for Gersh and me to follow him. "What do you guys think?" Grillo said to us. In fact, I had a definite thought about this new development.

"I think you can't leave Edward alone," I said. "The implication is that he may have witnessed it. He may now be vulnerable to the killer."

I realized later, of course, that both detectives knew that before it ever occurred to me, and indulging me, they readily agreed. Grillo again asked what I thought.

"I do have an idea," I said. "Have you ever heard about 'facilitation' for autistic patients?" Both Grillo and Stroud motioned no. "Okay," I said, "here it is. A new technique has been presented in recent years that claims to help the autistic person communicate more or less normally. It's a little typewriter keyboard that the autistic child or adult, types on with another person holding either the person's wrist, or elbow, or even shoulder of the hand that's typing. The gist of it is that the person gets a kind of focus this way, or that a different part of the brain is invoked, and somehow, an aphasic-like obstacle, I mean an obstacle to expressive communication, as in talking, is circumvented. What this means is that these kids then come out with complete sentences and thoughts and even whole compositions in reasonably good linguistic form."

Of course Grillo pounced first. "Well, is it real? I mean how do we know who's doing the typing? Maybe it's the person holding the typist's hand."

"Well, that's the ongoing debate," I said. "Some swear by the method and others call it fakery, an unconscious acting out wish of the one holding the writer's wrist or even in some cases a conscious manipulation of the writer's hand."

"Geez," Stroud stated. "How the hell do you get around that?"

Grillo didn't wait. "We spread the word that we're bringing in, uh, what is it?"

"A facilitator," I answered.

"Yeah," he said, "someone like that who can make Edward speak normally through this typing. That'll challenge the killer. Then we slip Edward out, and wait."

Grillo and Stroud, ready to set the wheels into motion, said their good-bye's and promised they'd be in touch.

*   *   *

And now I, too, at the conference, would have to defend the challenge to my character on a whole host of moral as well as ethical issues. I knew the wheels had already been facilitated regarding potential attacks on my research credibility, on what is called the nomological network—a fancy phrase for the internal consistency of one's theory—of my work, including, now, the additional ethical implications of that work. That led me to think about summarizing my entire theoretical hookup in simple sentences more or less as I eventually worked it out, as a sequence of fifteen points arranged with reference to four successive phases reflected in the symptom code. I set them down.

Phase 1
Before the Symptom Forms

(1) The pleasure principle of life starts it. We want what we want.

(2) The chief example of how the pleasure principle works in everyday life concerns the drive that people have, to realize their *wishes*. When that happens, we feel empowered.

(3) When a wish is thwarted frustration is experienced.

(4) The result of a thwarted wish and its subsequent frustration, is a feeling of helplessness or disempowerment.

(5) The natural reflex to disempowerment is the response of *anger* which in itself is a pleasurable alleviation of frustration. This anger reflex is natural because when someone is disempowered anger frequently becomes the only way to feel re-empowered.

(6) The need to repress the anger is based on social and psychological injunctions against aggression.

Phase 2
Formation of the Symptom

(7) As a natural by-product of this *anger-repression*, psychological/emotional symptoms appear because the nature of the anger is that it is an attack emotion. When the anger is repressed it takes the self — attaches to the self, and the self is then of course, attacked.

(8) Freud discovered that no wish will be denied. Thus an actual denied wish becomes apparently achieved in the symptom and *as* the symptom, albeit in perverse form. Therefore we love our symptoms because they *are* the wishes gratified, though disguised.

(9) Because of this sequence of repressed anger leading to perverse wish-fulfillment in the form of the symptom, the axiom is formed that where there is repressed anger not only will there be a symptom but there *must* be a symptom, and, ergo, where there is no repressed anger not only will there not be a symptom, there *cannot* be a symptom.

Phase 3
The All Important *Who*

(10) All emotion must take an object in order to be realized as an emotion; the *object* always refers to a person.

(11) Thus, the reaction of anger is always about a person, a *'who.'* The emotion cannot just hang there suspended in mid-air. The emotion seeks the *who*.

(12) At times, when the other person — the object — is absent, or for whatever reason cannot be targeted with a direct expression of anger, the self becomes the substitute target of the anger so that the self becomes the object. Thus, the emotion still has a person to attach to — the self. This then is the process identified as the anger attacking the self.

Phase 4
The Lifting of the Symptom

(13) When the object of the anger, the *who*, is identified, and the anger toward the *who* becomes conscious, then the strength of the symptom is challenged and the symptom may instantly lift. Thus the principle that "consciousness is curative" is validated but only if it is the emotion of anger also targeting the *who* that becomes conscious.

(14) The symptom, however, will be challenged more decisively if, after the *who* is identified and the anger becomes unrepressed, the subject then actively engages the original circumstance involving the wish with the object (the other person, the *who*), so that that kind of *doing* implementation will, for all intents and purposes, ensure the erasure of the symptom.

The Exception:
Resistive Symptoms

(15) When the symptom results from a major implosion of rage so that anger debris pervades and permeates

the entire psyche, or when the symptom represents
a chronically encrusted condition, then the symptom can only be defeated through the use of psy-
chotropic medication.

That was it. It was just lying there like a puzzle waiting to be assembled. If one understands that we are all hard-wired this way, and the all-
important point that it's possible to understand this wiring, then the next
step is recognizing that with some intervention, symptoms—all symptoms—could be neutralized, nullified, erased, held in abeyance or in virtual state, diluted, weakened, or even deleted—eliminated entirely.

"And," I thought, "did I have one of those resistive symptoms?" I mean,
this sort of question, and this sort of endeavor that I was starting—this
cure of symptoms—took me away from my obsessions, my demons, and
put me in a another universe, in a different life. In this other universe,
I realized that my anger was relieved—probably also my anger towards
Katie. I think I truly believed that because even though I wasn't actually,
or fully, in touch with any anger towards Katie, nevertheless, it was obvious to me that she was the *who*. Thus, because I had this obsession, this
obsessive symptom of bringing her back, it was also obvious to me that
I necessarily must be angry at her. It's why I don't mourn in the normal
manner. I don't feel the anger because I won't let her go. So, what does that
mean? It means she's not gone—that's what it means! So, if she's not gone,
then why would I feel any anger at her? I wouldn't. What I *would* do is get
involved in some miracle cure. And that's exactly what I find myself doing.
Spinning and spinning, trying for it not to touch me. Running away from
it. Running. Or, running to catch it!

But I wasn't the only one running. It seems that everyone was running—on the trail of curing symptoms. All over the place, chemists and
pharmacologists, epidemiologists and endocrinologists, medical research-
ers generally and genetic engineers specifically, were all racing to develop
the pill! The first generation of such a remedy had been there now, for a
decade. But here we would be going all the way and the question would
be: Was the whole thing possible? Was it possible to improve upon four
billion years of evolution by marshaling knowledge, experiment, understanding, and insight, and then intervening in the basic dynamic of DNA
and its effect on the brain? Could we be smarter, quicker, more efficient,

and craftier than the life span of four billion years of evolution? Harvard's molecular biologist, Walter Gilbert, has even suggested that by virtue of new insights, perhaps evolution can become more efficient than ever before, or even than ever imagined.

* * *

As far as life span, and being gone and not being gone was concerned, those questions were an abstraction to Jericho. He knew he could be erased forever if only Tino could resist Velma. Jericho's existence was very much based on Tino's willingness to suffer extraordinary deprivation at her hands. It had been going on for years, and it was always on Jericho's mind. He even spent some time telling Veronica, in his notebook, that her existence wasn't as important as his and that Tino needed him far more often than he needed her. This was not a slap at Veronica; it was merely Jericho's stark truth-telling usually without considering what anyone felt. And although he knew that Velma could end his existence whenever she wanted simply by freeing Tino so that Tino could be one person, he was sure she never would. Jericho had been through this deliberation with himself many times. Yet, he recently, and surprisingly, seemed to notice changes in Tino.

Jericho again was walking directly to the utility room. Into the building and up the stairs he went. He unlocked the door and made a bee-line directly to the toolbox. He was angry and he was determined. He took out his notebook entitled **To Veronica** *and started to write.*

> *Veronica, everyone thinks that I killed Billy, but of course I didn't. We know that. We know who did. And for sure it wasn't me, and of course, we know it wasn't you. They're all liars, Veronica. Velma, Kruger, and even Tino. They're all liars, except for you and me.*

Jericho felt better knowing that Veronica wouldn't be disappointed in him. He was reminded that out of the perverse union of Velma and Tino, others were born—he and Veronica. Jericho knew that everything about the Velma/Tino connection was contaminated, distorted, even evil—mother/son evil. His only catharsis was in either accusing Velma of this evil, or in being violent.

Jericho couldn't but help be allied with Veronica because he knew that, like him, Veronica was controlled by the same controlling forces, and that they both shared knowledge of Tino's fractured personality. They wrote to each other because that was the only way they could communicate. Whenever Jericho couldn't express the full extent of his rage, his only catharsis came from writing to Veronica. Then his frustration subsided. He didn't have to feel like a failure, and could then gradually evaporate, become derealized—back to Tino.

But before his morphing, he quickly replaced the notebook in the toolbox and then left the utility room. He ran down the flight of stairs two at a time, and exited the building. He strode surely and directly back to his place—as Tino, in the autistic ward with Velma. And then, as Tino, Jericho became anonymous.

*   *   *

The accusation came. It was an article published in a national periodical distributed to scientists and clinicians. There it was, a headline story on the front page: *On The Nature of Evil.* It appeared as a long letter to the editor, with the byline: *Anonymous.* In it, the author considered the two main elements of evil in the modern world, both discussed interchangeably and in no particular sequence. The two examples were serial killing and scientific arrogance. To the issue of serial killing, the author cited actual serial killers and tried to critically assess their evil deeds, motives, and general psychology. To the issue of scientific arrogance, the author cited the work of three scientists and one clinician, all by name. I was his designated clinician:

> Dr. Glenn Kahn, in the guise of calling a conference on the psychological work of an obscure 15th-century monk, is actually planning to present his own project at this conference. This project consists of the development of a pharmacological agent that will seize the pleasure centers of the brain, control dissatisfaction, enhance sexuality and keep all people in a relatively happy state. A renowned ethicist has been invited to appear at the conference in order to control Dr. Kahn himself. Here we have an example of an attempt by certain forces to begin to introduce the idea of an exchange: happiness for control. The evil is revealed in Kahn's obvious temerity. He has decided to take God's work and make it better.

Of course someone will have to be in charge. 'Dr. Kahn, might the one in charge be you?'

Again, I thought of Dostoevsky's *Grand Inquisitor* in terms of the moral trade-off of accruing security but sacrificing autonomy. But more than this, the Grand Inquisitor is a reference to Torquemada, the Hitler of the Spanish Inquisition. And here I was trying to honor Sebastian Arragel, a prototypical victim of that same Inquisition. Had Sebastian's Inquisition followed him to the twenty-first century—right into my hands?

So I felt placed in the category of potential victim, directly in Sebastian's line of descendants. Thinking about it that way actually felt good. Nevertheless, I was flabbergasted. It felt as though I'd been shot by a sniper.

I thought of Kruger at the clinic but dismissed the thought. So if not Kruger, who? I didn't have a clue and was stuck with the fact that a few thousand professionals were now seeing my name connected with a discussion of evil. I thought about calling my lawyer and trying to get the name of the author from the publisher and then suing for libel. Then I did some therapy on myself and realized that I felt helpless and therefore furious. But I knew toward whom I was furious. In identifying my anger and its source, it seemed that I didn't repress anything, so I was fairly certain I would not develop a symptom like a headache, or a homicidal impulse towards Anonymous. And I didn't.

Then I thought that Anonymous did in fact have malice and evil intent toward me. Yet, I was betting he wasn't born with an evil gene. The idea of a gene for evil was absurd to me. Sure, the first sentence in my speech at the conference was going to be, "Human nature has a genetic foundation." But that doesn't mean that evil is inherently etched in the human makeup.

Evil must emanate from compensatory drives to elevate the self in any number of ways. That's what Sebastian referred to when describing Modesto Ferrer. Ferrer's compensatory drive to purify himself, enrich himself, and empower himself was Sebastian's idea of Ferrer's ignition for evil. Thus Ferrer indeed enriched himself, and his evil could be related to his empowerment through Sebastian's illegal disempowerment, achieved of course, immorally. That could surely be an example of evil.

* * *

Thinking about Billy Soldier, again I thought he had to know what was happening to him. He couldn't ignore the killer. He was experiencing the evil. But I also realized that Velma couldn't have done it. She wasn't strong enough to carry Billy to the pool.

Grillo and Stroud came to this conclusion as well. They were trying to rule out certain possibilities and rule in others. So Stroud, in one of his famous unsubtle moments, came up with a question that stunned me. "Doc, Joe and I, you know, we've been considering all kinds of things, and we thought there might be a possibility that even if it's a split guy, that the guy maybe could be a serial killer also. Whatya think?"

All I could think of was that both Stroud and Grillo had read the article. "I'm amazed you say that because just a few days ago I, along with other scientists, was accused of being evil, akin to serial killers. So I have to tell you, I'm a little spooked by your bringing that up about serial killers."

"Forget that, Doc, we know you're not a serial killer. Right?"

"No, no," I answered, "I wasn't even thinking that. I'm just flabbergasted that you brought it up exactly when I'm preparing to deal with just that subject at a conference. I can't explain it any better. It just amazes me."

"Okay, Doc," Stroud said, "just tell us your opinion. Could the guy have been a serial one? You know? I mean, yes or no?"

"Splits aren't usually serial killers," I said. "They're not, you know, underhanded and involved in plotting. Probably the word is insidious. They're not insidious.

"In splits, what you see is what you get. The angry personality is angry, the sexual personality is sexual, and other alters are what they are, and that's it. Unlike splits—you know, multiples, or rather dissociative identity types—serial killers have integrated their anger, their violence, into the personality. It's total control of the victim, total focus by the victim on the killer, and total validation of the killer. The killer's psyche is not split. He knows what he wants to do at all times. Serial killers are always planning. You know, in terms of the psyche there's always full employment. We're all focused on what we wish for and that goes in spades for the serial killer."

Then Grillo spoke for the first time. "So the serial killer wants to be noticed."

"Exactly," I said. "The wish of the serial killer is to be completely focused on, and this gives him the feeling of empowerment. He wants that victim to focus on him, and of course you know that nothing focuses the mind so much as one's impending death. So the killer places the victim in a position of disempowerment—either drugged or in some other state of complete helplessness." They both nodded for me to continue.

"In terms of personality," I said, "the serial killer feels an absence of selfhood; he feels incomplete, inauthentic. And yet the person may be smiling, pretending, while inside is the hollow person who wants to be somebody but is furious about feeling like nobody.

"It's different for the multiple like we have here who only wants to be left alone. I can imagine the multiple in his or her normal state, saying something like: 'Leave me alone. That wasn't me dressed in ladies' clothes. That wasn't me being angry and shouting. Leave me alone.'

"Of course, in the other two personas, the angry one just wants to strike out and settle scores, and the sexual one just wants to be sexual. On the other hand, the inner soliloquy of the serial killer, showing how evil and depraved he really is, might go something like, like, uh, let's say something like this:

> "I felt like nothing. Now you feel it too. Now you can't ignore me. I know, without having to worry about it, that I have your full attention. Now you are unwhole and I am complete. You have no power and I have all the power. And to prove it, I'm going to kill you. I can do it in a number of ways. All of them will be cruel because the cruelty only reflects the agony and cruelty that I've felt being nothing! I'll leave you in a shallow ditch, in a river, dismembered in plastic bags, or if I'm still not satisfied with our power discrepancy—if dead is not enough—I will need you to be more disempowered then just dead. I will eat you, and only when I excrete you, only then, will I feel that you are truly nothing and I, everything. Or you will just remain inside of me and then I will forever have your attention. The fact is that henceforth you will remain temporary, or if I excrete you, you will soon dry up in the woods or be washed away by a sanitation truck. That will be your fate, your destiny. I will then be everything and you, nothing."

After a moment of silence, Stroud said, "Did you do that off the cuff, Doc?"

"Yes and no," I said. "I've been doing a lot of thinking about the subject since I was accused. Actually that sort of person feels dead inside so the killing keeps him excited and feeling alive—like a psychopath who needs endless external stimulation because inside it feels so deadened. So these killers find themselves in a continuous desperate state of emptiness. Like anyone else, they really need community. So serial killers—and here's the killer—form their own community. A community of dead people. It's a community of dead people scattered here and there, so that the idea of geography as an objective map of the world is obliterated. Actually there is no geography. There is only roaming, scanning, planning, and killing. This becomes the killer's very own idiosyncratic and necrophiliated community. So, you know, it's like serial killers are always in the process of creating their own sociology. They populate their lives and their memories with this very dead community—a perverse support system. Imagine that?"

Again, a few moments of silence passed, and I noticed that they were both observing me still in my reverie. Then Grillo gently eased me back into the conversation and asked me about Jericho in this regard.

The gist of what I told them was that, in my opinion, this was not the personality of Jericho. He wasn't out for money or any hidden advantage. He was not power-hungry or interested in conquest. Jericho probably was just avenging a hurt.

That was about as far as I would speculate. And although they tried to pry more out of me, I couldn't add anything else. As a parting comment, Grillo said:

"Doc, I really love how you do these things."

* * *

*The actual truth was that Velma had begun to attract Carl Emory's attention and to conquer him gradually—his will, his needs. Only then did Jericho feel murderous. The blow was intended to go **through** Carl's head and was not merely aimed **at** his head. But the execution of the blow did not quite succeed. The fact that Jericho could have such an extreme need to kill someone, even though it was based on Tino's irrational and extreme jealousy, indicated just how psychologically unhinged they had become.*

Clearly Velma had gone too far. She held the reigns too tightly and deprived Tino in excruciating ways, dangling her seductive incestuous temptations until they became impossible to bear. Jericho wasn't born condemned with a malicious nature—just with an angry one. And certainly not with evil. If anyone was evil, it was Velma.

*   *   *   **

Meanwhile, the chief of maintenance at the hospital was reviewing the lists of tubs he had given to the detectives. Then it hit him. The condemned part adjacent to the autistic ward, also had a tub, and although it was no longer in use, it was in theory still a usable tub. He just never gave that part of the building any thought. He immediately went to the ward, and with his master key unlocked the door adjacent to Nurse Secora's station that led into the condemned domain. He switched on the lights and looked around, then ran into the bathroom exploring the room visually. He moved toward the bedroom and suddenly stopped in his tracks. Leaving the room abruptly, he locked it and sprinted out of the building. He drove up to his maintenance office building, rushed inside and called the detectives.

"I'm sorry," he said, "but when I was there I realized I should have called you first so I immediately ran back out."

"Jesus," Stroud said. "That's it! We'll meet you at your office. We'll be taking prints. No one enters," he ordered. "Recreate your movements, exactly. We'll be taking prints, and when we find yours, we'll have to compare them with what you say about where you were. Understand?"

· 21 ·

THE INVESTIGATION

The place was a madhouse. Cop cars, marked and unmarked, in front of the building. Inside, Grillo and Stroud were off in a corner of the room talking privately to the maintenance chief. The lights were on for the first time in who knows how long, and the place was nothing but dust. Whatever you leaned against, or sat on, left its dust swath. Prints could practically be seen with the naked eye. Identifying the prints would be easy, but that didn't necessarily mean the person identified was the killer. It did mean, though, that that person could be in big trouble.

Another group of lab guys was in the bathroom. One of them called out:

"Looks like it happened here. Steve, Joe, come on in here." Stroud and Grillo entered the bathroom. "Look here," the lab guy said. "Print marks, scratch marks on the dust all over the rim. I'll bet anything it's the kid's prints. Water stains on the drain rust here, but not on the faucets. I'm sure of it, but the lab'll confirm it. Whoever did it, man, was not a professional. There's no attempt to cover anything up. Either the guy was stupid or scared. And the tub works! Water just pours out."

"Okay," Stroud said, and told him to get the prints of everyone who worked on the ward—patients, personnel, and visitors, and in addition, he wanted prints of doctors Kruger, Kahn, and Gersh, and of everyone in the maintenance department. He also wanted a list of visitors to the ward the week that Billy was drowned. "Get to it."

* * *

Rita called from the clinic and informed me that mail responding to Anonymous' attack was beginning to pour in, and it was less than a week since the article had appeared. The first letter she opened was from a biologist who was outraged by my project. His professional affiliation was an independent think tank called "Population Control," whose mission was not hard to figure out.

I asked Rita to give me the gist of some of the other letters.

"The crazy ones are starting to come in, too," she said. I braced myself as she started. "You deserve to be fired from your job. How dare you release more sexual energy in people. This is not God's work. Your plan is Satanic and must not be permitted to succeed."

"Something else," Rita said. "A letter came from the patent department in D.C. They're informing you that an inquiry was made regarding your patent application."

I was stunned. How did anyone know that I had sent for an application? I guessed it was the mail routing at the clinic, which I knew was not tamper-resistant, and could be controlled by others—read, destroyed, or both. My motive in sending for an application had been to protect the intellectual property of my discovery. I was also seeking copyright protection. Apparently, someone was monitoring my activities. I felt that it was the same person who had tampered with the cab reservation, making Jean, Richard, and me, miss our Kennedy/Vatican airport connection. Then I knew. It was the letter on my desk to my attorney, who was handling it all for me. Someone read it.

Rita had asked where the request originated and the reply was Rome, Italy. That little piece of information hit me right between the eyes. Someone at the clinic was directly in touch with someone at the Vatican. And this little cabal had knowledge of the disappearance from Vatican 'protection' of Sebastian's manuscript and diary. I knew that the Vatican wanted Sebastian's material to remain unseen, under lock and key. But I also reasoned that surely they must know that the knowledge, the information, was now out—seen. So what did they want with me? There must be something else that I wasn't aware of, that I wasn't getting. Something in Sebastian's material. But I thought: "The Vatican hates it also because the aggressive homicidal part of its split-personality is about to be exposed."

When I got to the clinic, Jean and Rita were both waiting for me at Rita's desk. Jean looked sober, concerned.

"I was just informed that I'm part of an international criminal investigation of major proportion. I think you'll also be implicated in accusation of theft."

"Sebastian!"

"And how!" she said. "But I think they're making it bigger than that. They're claiming that people inside the library have been stealing valuable church manuscripts and art objects from their vaults. The Vatican lawyers are implicating people all over the world as couriers or receivers. We've been identified as individuals who have received and utilized stolen manuscripts. I believe we'll be deposed by these Vatican legal people. I've already called my lawyer."

Now I knew. It had nothing to do with a code within Sebastian's writing. It was really a larger Vatican issue about Sebastian's material escaping their maximum security. I was shocked by the accusation because Jean and I always thought of our little adventure — really escapade — as a moral mission. Academic freedom was the issue, not thievery. The materials were sent back. We never had any intention of keeping them. However, I never had any intention of not copying the materials, even though we were told not to. And it wasn't just academic freedom that was the underlying assumption of our involvement, but also freedom from the antidisestablishmentarianists. We were clearly anti-antidisestablishmentarianists. This was like a caper that college kids feel triumphant about because it defeats injustice. I guess that's how we felt.

Jean's lawyer had told her that the Holy See took the position that Sebastian's work — what I had read, plus eight or nine other volumes — contained occasional diatribes against events of church history and policy, and that the church saw no reason to publish or distribute any material that in any way vilified or profaned its body. They claimed ownership of these vituperative materials and stated that they never permitted release of such materials either by written word or oral agreement.

Although all of this should have alarmed me, I didn't call my attorney. I thought it strange that such an event should start a theft investigation. For one, I knew we were not the first ones to have had access to Sebastian's work. Aldo Fiscali, the Italian psychiatrist, had also seen it. In fact, I first learned about Sebastian in that particular citation by Fiscali. I don't know quite why, but what stayed with me was that Fiscali referred to the Greek philosopher Artemidorus with respect to Artemidorus' work on dreams which Fiscali compared to Sebastian's work on stream of consciousness in Sebastian's analysis of his own dreams.

Obviously, Fiscali got the material either directly or indirectly from the Vatican library, either through normal channels, in which case a precedent was set regarding the distribution of Sebastian's material, or by other means. In any event, we knew that the material had seen the light of day at least once in the twentieth century before we saw it.

Intuitively, I felt the Vatican was bluffing since it surely wouldn't want to be accused of censorship. What kind of public relations would that be? Yet the Vatican had already officially informed Jean that she was a suspect in the case, and the phone call to the patent office in Washington was no accident. Still, I remained unalarmed. I felt that mine was a sense of rightness, and in this case also of anti-censorship. The challenge by the Vatican, those direct descendants of the Spanish Inquisition, raised my hackles.

And while I was in my fighting stance, a phone call from Dr. White struck me down. I couldn't believe it. White said letters were already going out to the entire mailing list informing them of the cancellation of the conference and promising to announce a replacement date in a later mailing.

The phone rang again. It was Jean.

"The conference is canceled. Dr. White and Dr. Rivers have received official notice that the clinic has been implicated in the theft of valuable documents belonging to the Church. Allegations have been made that the documents were housed at the clinic library reference room for several days." She was breathless. "I was named as one of the conspirators and your name was mentioned but not stated as having been charged. Actually, no one has been charged and my lawyer says that that's a good sign. What they've done, he says, is threaten to throw a hand grenade into the room. They simply want to scare everyone to death. He thinks they will make official charges later, depose everyone concerned, including you, but then drop all charges for some promises and apologies. He doesn't think they want too much publicity."

I felt much better hearing this. "Jean, the whole thing is ridiculous. Ours was an important mission. Do you care if there's a trial? Because I don't. Right now I feel good and angry at those hypocritical bastards."

"One more thing," she said. "My lawyer said it might be best for me not to communicate with you and that you should get your own attorney—that we should be delinked legally. I told him I wouldn't stand for any of that, that I was going to call you, and that we would continue to be associates and friends just as we have been."

"Terrific. If or when I get an attorney for this, I'll say the same. We're going to stick together. You know they're going to try to pin it on you through your librarian contact at the Vatican. Do you realize that?"

"Yes, I know. But it doesn't matter. He's been identified. They're charging him with theft. I happen to know he's been sending classified church documents to scholars all over the world for at least the past three years. And the former librarian who selected him for that particular position was also a mole for openness. It's an old story and that's it."

Jean explained that there are those in the church who recoil at the suppression of material. They find themselves engaging in this academic espionage, liberation of documents—an underground scholar's railroad. If one is not against the underground railroad that spirited African-Americans from the South to the North, out of slavery, then one would be hard-pressed to oppose freeing of the written word.

Now I felt fortified with righteousness—even looking forward to the next day's meeting. Those bastards—forcing us to cancel the conference.

* * *

The stakeout at the hospital was still going on almost a week after the detectives had, to no avail, chased the mysterious, tall stranger in pitch dark through the hospital grounds and into the woods. But now he was at it again, challenging them. He was wearing all black, and he was stalking. He was looking forward to it.

Detective John Hamil was also tall and strong, and it was he that the lurker chose to attack first. Hamil went down with one blow, as he heard the echoing voice proclaim:

"I AM JERICHO!"

Jericho was evidently determined to get them all. He had attacked Hamil with a hammer. Could have killed him, but it didn't seem to matter to Jericho. Next came Detective Neil Waller, who was smoking a cigarette cupped in his hand to conceal the ember. He had just called the coast clear into his cell phone. He was in the moat, the sub-grade second entrance to the building, on his toes peering up at the top of the walk, with a clear view of everything around at ground level but where no one could have a clear view of him.

But apparently he still missed that figure. With one motion Jericho vaulted into the moat. On the way down, as he cracked Waller on the head almost killing him, Jericho remarked, "No smoking."

Detective Robert Mays was stationed in the corridor of Building 22, which housed the hospital laundry and the agricultural supplies used on the hospital farm, and was located about thirty or forty yards from where detective Waller had been stationed. Jericho circled the building and entered through a street-level window in the back. Quickly, and with knowledge of the building layout, he deftly made a bee-line for the corridor perpendicular to where Mays was standing. The place was dimly lit. Mays was intent on scanning the grounds through the window with his binoculars. This time without a word. Crack! Mays was down, bleeding profusely from the head.

When neither of the three was heard from, it began to dawn on the other three that something was wrong. An ambulance took them to the hospital emergency ward, which was in the opposite direction, about thirty or forty yards from Building 22.

All three detectives survived, although Mays was badly hurt. The following day Stroud and Grillo spoke to all personnel connected with the stakeout. No one, not a soul, could identify the assailant and not one of them even heard him approaching before he struck. Grillo said it.

"This guy's smart. Nothing scares him. But he's nuts. No doubt about it!"

* * *

Stroud wanted lists of all male personnel on duty that night. Grillo, on the other hand, wanted a personality profile on someone who would do something like that. With that in mind, he called me, didn't give me details, but asked me to do some guesswork.

"I don't want to tell you exactly what happened, but I need you to give me some kind of personality profile on a guy who would attack cops on a stakeout in the middle of the night, and who didn't really care if he killed them or not. Oh, yeah, and the guy used a weapon like a hammer or something deadly like that. I don't care how much guesswork goes into it. Could you try that?"

I told him I would try it, but I'd have a better shot at it if I knew some details. He told me not to worry, he would tell me the details later, adding that he was actually more interested in my guesses. That was Grillo. It was apparent to me all along that Grillo put his trust in the kind of knowledge embedded in intuition. Again I felt he truly believed in the brain in the gut.

I told him I couldn't do it right then because I was due at an important meeting at the clinic within the hour, but that I would call him when I had something for him.

* * *

We met in the Board Room on the ninth floor, a large room with a huge, oval, shiny mahogany table. Chairs jammed around the table to seat twenty-five people. This was a huge table that went almost the length of the room.

"Let's get on with it." That's how I felt. "Let's get the hell on with it!" I knew I had to be careful because when I got like this, not only was I ready to fight, but I wanted to. That righteous indignation thing. I glanced at Stan Rivers, our executive director, who nodded to me. Dr. White and his assistant, Dr. Beth Rothstein, were there. White stood and extended his hand. That made me feel good, but it also didn't. I wanted the entire room to be against me.

My next disappointment was to be warmly greeted by the institute's attorney, Eric Lessing. I began getting the feeling that rather than the expected Inquisition against me, this could turn out to be a rally of support. Perhaps most of the people meeting there shared my feeling of outrage over the suppression of scholarly material.

Finally Jean and her lawyer entered, followed by Mr. J.T. Meehrling, who was the CEO of Music Anthologies of America and an influential member of the board.

As usual, Dr. White opened the meeting. He described the situation and made it clear that the conference had to be canceled based upon the advice of Jean's lawyer and Lessing. They didn't want to further antagonize either the church authorities or their attorneys. Dr. White apologized to Jean and to me for the abrupt cancellation, and indicated that he abhorred the accusations that were being made. As it turned out, only Jean and the institute itself were accused in the indictment, although I was mentioned as a possible conspirator or receiver of stolen goods.

As the board representative, Mr. Meehrling indicated that he could understand how Jean and I had found ourselves in this chain of events and that he, too, was in favor of scholarly freedom. However, he also made it clear that we had no justification for using the physical plant of the institute to receive and house the crates for the several days that they were there. Having said that, he also felt he needed to announce that he was a practicing Catholic. Clearly, it didn't matter. Meehrling was a fair guy, no question about it. Both lawyers agreed that it didn't look as though the case would go very far. It seemed to me that they either didn't quite believe the story of the Vatican theft-scam that had allegedly been taking place on a continuous basis, or they actually approved of it.

"Ladies and gentlemen, I have another piece of news," White announced. "Yesterday afternoon, Manuel Roland and Tyrone Thorpe, both of our custodial staff, were accused by Rachel Zismoor in Records of tampering with her mail. Apparently, she sent an authentic scorecard of the New York Yankees pitcher Don Larson's no-hitter, World Series game, to Larson himself on the off chance that he might sign it and mail it back. The envelope was addressed in big bold letters by her ten-year-old son and the handwriting was obviously that of a child. To make a long story short, she had taken it with her when she left home for the clinic yesterday thinking she would mail it from here. She says that she instantly regretted doing so, ran down to the mailroom to retrieve it, and it was gone. Two other pieces of mail that she had sent along with it were there, but the scorecard envelope was gone. Manuel had picked up the mail from the outgoing box, so she started looking for him. She entered the store room and there he was, along with Thorpe, looking at the scorecard. The envelope was torn open and lying on the table. Rachel says they seemed excited about their find. She demanded they hand her the scorecard, which they did. They were stunned. She then came to me."

Stan Rivers immediately indicated that there would be an official discussion with both men and they would be written up. He would then send a request to the union that they be fired based upon this incident.

"This is an easy one," he said. "Let's hope the Church situation will be as easy."

And then Dr. White dropped the bomb. "Wait. This situation has created another one. Within ten minutes after Rachel left my office, both Manuel and Tyrone appeared at my door. They were visibly shaken and told me they knew that this jeopardized their jobs, which they couldn't afford to lose. They begged me not to pursue the matter. Then they confessed that they had opened mail from time to time for years now because, and I hesitate to even say this, because Dr. Siegfried Kruger had given them special tips when they permitted him to look at mail. When I asked what kind of tips, they said, 'money.' I didn't ask how much money or how frequently this occurred, but they also said that at times they would offer him supplies from the supply room. But what he took was inconsequential, like pads and pens, all sorts of inexpensive items. They once offered him an electric pencil sharpener and he took that, too.

"So, in an effort to come clean and repair the Rachel situation, I believe they've gotten themselves in even deeper, and, in addition, seriously implicated Dr. Kruger in what looks to me like psychopathic juvenile nonsense. What in the world does Dr. Kruger want with someone else's mail, or pads, or pencils?"

Dr. White turned to Eric Lessing and asked what the next step would be. Lessing thought that before anything official was done, Dr. White and Stan Rivers should meet with Kruger unofficially and discuss the matter. With that, I interrupted.

"Jean and I have suspected for some time now that mail has been tampered with here. I've had some difficulty with the mail—things have disappeared. Once, an important book review of my first book, and then, when Jean and I were working on Sebastian's materials, there was a foul-up in the arrangements we made to get the crates back to the airport. It looked like tampering. There've been other subtle and not-so-subtle indications of tampering. Jean knows I've suspected it because we've discussed it a number of times. It's just that I've never had any hard evidence, nothing substantial, so I kept it to myself. I did suspect someone, but at this point I'd rather not mention who." I paused. "But there's more. As you know, there's been a drowning of an autistic patient at Brentwood. Well, it's already been declared a murder and everyone connected with the hospital has been questioned, including Dr. Kruger as well as myself. I believe neither Dr. Kruger nor I have been fully cleared of suspicion. I just thought I had to bring this in now, and I assure you that unlike the Sebastian situation where I was heavily involved, I had absolutely nothing to do with the event at the hospital."

Everyone was supportive and encouraging. Dr. White actually stated that to suspect me of that sort of thing was absolutely ridiculous. Without even noticing it he didn't make that disclaimer for Kruger.

Kruger, that overachieved, undereducated, ambitious narcissist had clawed his way to nowhere, only to descend from there. Now he was probably going to be charged with petty theft, certainly fired from both the hospital and institute, and as far as criminal proceedings are concerned, who knows? And he was still a suspect in Billy Soldier's death. The more I discovered about him, the more I was becoming convinced that he actually should be a suspect in Billy's death.

As Dr. White was about to end the meeting there was a knock on the door. Rita entered, excused herself, handed me a note, and promptly left. I read it quickly.

"Ladies and gentlemen, a message. I've just been informed that I will have to appear for deposition on the case: The Catholic Diocese of New York representing the Holy See against Dr. Glenn Kahn. The subject: receiving stolen goods."

· 22 ·

THE DEPOSITION

A civil suit. I was sure it was going to be a criminal suit charging theft. But what we faced was called a replevin order—an order from the judge instructing the sheriff to take possession of whatever goods were purported stolen. My attorney explained that since the Vatican had what's known as "superior possessor interest," it gave them the right to replevin the goods. The order was the Vatican versus Jean and me together. Apparently, after the Vatican got the replevin order, it then submitted proof of theft and the FBI was called in. Having secured a warrant, the FBI was able to search the premises of the institute, Jean's apartment, and mine. The objective was to seize property wrongfully taken from the plaintiff. One of the problems here was that in a replevin order, the defendant did not have to get advance notice of the seizure plan. I could only argue against the order after the seizure had taken place. And the prospective deposition would be a chance for the plaintiff—the Vatican—to ascertain where the alleged stolen materials were located. These were the technicals.

The searches were difficult. Even knowing they were coming, when they did arrive their knock was deafening. Imagine the FBI arriving with a warrant to search. Even if you're innocent, you feel guilty.

For me it was a full day. I wondered what the odds would be that I would have my fingerprints taken as part of a murder investigation at the hospital the same day that FBI agents came to search my house for a completely different case. But that was the day detective Grillo called me in advance and told me not to worry because the prints were necessary to make a thorough investigation. At that point I also told him about the civil suit. He didn't seem affected by it.

The search at the institute was formal and at first it was all quite conspicuous. Several agents arrived. Dr. White was paged and personally escorted them to his office. He invited them to hang their coats in his closet and had his assistant accompany the agents wherever in the building they wanted to go.

They all came wearing trench coats—four tall, austere-looking men. There was nothing to find because none of Sebastian's material remained. Still, the four of them thoroughly searched the library knowing exactly where to look. They zeroed in on the back room, where I had spent hours reading Sebastian's manuscript and where we had photographed and transcribed it all. They searched the three trash baskets under the three desks in the reference room. Nothing was found. They asked to visit the lounge and the bathrooms and they also searched the mail room. No one really cared because patients, faculty, therapists, and secretarial and administrative personnel were all over the place, coming and going. It was a good thing White had them hang up their coats. Four men in those trench coats wandering around—that would have been a sight—but four men in tie and jacket didn't attract any attention whatsoever.

The search at Jean's house was also thorough. Jean said it was horrible. Two agents were assigned to her apartment and even though they were polite, they looked into all the things in her bedroom and bathroom. There was nothing to find. My house was searched by the same two agents. I answered all their questions without hesitation, even though I thought that the answers could be incriminating. I didn't care.

* * *

In the meantime, Kruger had been sent a notice by Dr. White that outlined the accusation against him and instructed him to appear at a meeting that was scheduled with the ethics board of the institute. Kruger then made a preemptive strike. He sent a registered letter resigning from the institute. He'd been a member of the institute for decades, and a senior one at that, but here he was in a bloody mess. His resignation made unnecessary his appearance at any ethics hearing, and unless the institute board of directors wanted to press charges against him for petty theft (which was unlikely), this matter at the institute, as far as Kruger was concerned, was at least unofficially over.

But Kruger's two conspirators, Manuel and Tyrone, later confessed not only to the opening of mail but to other things as well. Dr. White related all of it to Eric Lessing. the institute's attorney. Lessing then met with Manuel and Tyrone and directly told them that they were both be in trouble and that their jobs could not be protected. It was then that Tyrone spilled.

"Sir," Tyrone said to Lessing, "that's okay. We'll leave, but not jail. Please." Manuel visibly nodded in agreement. "We decided to tell the whole truth about Dr. Kruger."

Tyrone started blurting it out. "Dr. Kruger shot the statue outside the elevator. He has a gun. He showed it. He knows how to use it. Something about the war, but I don't know about the war."

"What?" Lessing exclaimed, cutting Tyrone off. "He, himself shot the statue? Kruger has a gun?"

Tyrone repeated it. "Dr. Kruger also tells us whose mail to get. Mostly Dr. Kahn's mail and Dr. Fiske's mail. Sometimes he has us seal it again and deliver it and sometimes he keeps it."

"Dr. Kahn's mail and Dr. Fiske's mail?" Lessing repeated incredulously.

"Yes, sir," they both nodded. "And he gives us money for it."

At this point, Kruger's notion that everything at the institute was over was exactly the opposite. It was just beginning. Everything was about to unravel. Lessing discontinued the meeting at that point. Tyrone and Manuel were excused after apologizing and continued pleading to be let off.

After Lessing described it all to him, White referred to Kruger as "apparently a psychopath." Then without giving it a second thought Lessing suggested that White call Stroud and Grillo with the news and ask when they'd want to meet. White agreed and said, he also wanted to tell Glenn Kahn about it, and Lessing okayed it.

*　*　*

We met in the interrogation room at the precinct. I wasn't being interrogated, but it was the only private place in the precinct where several people could sit and talk quietly. There were five of us: me, Grillo, Stroud, and the two detectives who had been collecting prints from everyone on the ward at the hospital.

"Listen, Doc," Stroud started. "Two things. First, the psycho that's been wandering the grounds at night hammered, and I mean hammered, three of my men who were on stakeout duty." Grillo, looking at me and interrupted. "That's the detail that I didn't tell you about." I nodded as Stroud continued. "One's in serious condition. We've been keeping it quiet. All three of them, knocked out. I thought you should know that. Only ones who know are the emergency room night staff."

I thought, "First, how'd they keep that quiet in this rumor mill, and second, why is he telling me?" I wanted to say, "I didn't do it," but what came out was, "Jesus, really?"

"Yeah," he said, "and whoever it is could've killed any one of them. Cracked them on the head, it just didn't matter to him. You know, when you hit someone like that you can't know how to make the shot only knock the guy out. You just slam the guy and whatever happens, happens. In this case no one's dead, but one of them was close. Pure luck. So if it's a split in his aggressive personality, then this guy can kill and you said they don't kill. Right?"

"I take it back. What I should have told you was that it's rare for multiples, but it doesn't mean it's never happened. Like anyone else, multiples don't usually kill. I mean even in the aggressive state they can be involved in killing but usually as a result of a moment of passion. So I apologize for my abbreviated interpretation. My explanation wasn't complete."

"No, that's okay," Grillo said. "We're keeping the stakeout going but with teams of two. Now let's see him try it. Obviously, we know it's not you. Right?"

"Right," I directly and decisively answered.

"Okay," he said. "Here's number two. Detective Johnson here doesn't get it. None of us do. We've never seen anything like it. The killer just left his prints all over the tub without caring about it. He didn't wipe anything. What the hell is that? Because the truth of it is that we can't figure it out unless if it's a patient who's nuts, let's say, then the guy wouldn't be thinking in a clear way—obviously. Right? Know what I mean? But Steve here thinks it could be the split guy in his aggressive stage so that maybe he doesn't think in that logical way when he's crazy like that. You know, he doesn't think about coverups and such. See?"

He stopped. They were all looking at me. "Yeah," I said and I pointed my finger at them as though to say: 'Wait a second, let me think about this.' "As you suggest, it could also go along with someone who cracks someone on the head without caring about the difference between knocking him out or killing him. Right?"

"That's right," Stroud said. "Now, like Joe asked you before, we need you to make some guesses for us." He stopped and Grillo jumped right in. "Doc, what could it mean psychologically speaking? I mean, for example we're ruling out mental retards and others who are totally disabled—like, nuts. So we're asking you, who or what kind of person should we be ruling in?"

Now I had to get specific and think about diagnosis. That's what he wanted.

"Okay," I said. "Here goes. First, generally speaking, acts of violence, like at your men, are not random. The only kind of person who would engage in random violence like that would be some kind of organically brain-damaged individual who sometimes strikes out of an uncontrolled impulse, or a bipolar type in a catatonic-like excitement. In this case I'm eliminating those as possibilities because the attacks were too planned." I looked at them as though to say: "Is that right?" and they nodded. So I continued, "Furthermore, seemingly random violent acts can also be acted out by individuals with various forms of what we might call classic schizophrenia, but hardly ever with respect to some planned intricate goal. So, I guess I'm saying it's not about randomness. This was all aimed. I would say, again, in a general way, the motive could be wanting to hurt those who he feels are trying to control him, in this case the cops. Psychoanalytically speaking, the basis of the angry motive would be "transference"—the guy is probably controlled by someone in his life and the fact that he needs to comply with this control makes him furious. Or, has been over-controlled by someone at an earlier time in his life and is so damaged by it that the only way he feels he can rectify the situation is by knocking someone out or even killing. In such a case, you would be right. It would probably not matter to him whether he killed the guy or not. But I'm not sure if that's the case here. The more likely possibility is that he's in a struggle with someone in his life now, and that he wants to show you that no one can control him. As a matter of fact, he's showing you that he's controlling you. My hunch tells me he could have killed every one of your detectives if he wanted to. But the fact is that that was not his motive. He didn't kill any of them even if he did get close. His motive was simply to express his rage, to show he was in charge.

"Further, I would say again, in the parlance of psychoanalytic lingo — I'm sure you're going to think of it as psychobabble — the guy has what we call a 'thin stimulus barrier.' This simply means he can easily get provoked to anger, especially when his needs and wishes are frustrated."

I paused. There was momentary silence in the room, and I preempted Stroud, who was about to say something. "Also, I could give you a thumbnail sketch of various diagnostic syndromes and tell you to what extent I think they may apply to this guy."

I went back to Stroud. "Did you want to ask me something?" "No," Stroud replied. "Do what you just said."

"Okay," I continued. "Now about the fingerprints. Here goes. Let's start with paranoids. I think paranoids are entirely too guarded not to wipe away their prints. The same for obsessives. So these, I would say, are out of the question. So we need to go over to the opposite side of the diagnostic spectrum — the hysteric side. It would have to be someone like a hysteric or some variation because such people can get confused with too many details and throw up their hands leaving the scene in a way that we might call unattended. It also could be someone who, in the past, we would call the inadequate personality type. The inadequate type is an innocent who can get caught up in some accelerating situation, some accelerating complication, and would then find himself in a momentum, one that's probably not premeditated. It would be a situation that unexpectedly hooks him in so that the momentum is too much to handle and he can't stop it. It's a possibility, but I would say an unlikely one — he's inadequate."

I stopped. "It's good, Doc," Grillo said, "keep going."

"Well, let's take dissociative, identity disordered types like the multiple. It could be a deranged multiple in the aggressive state who is so enraged that he doesn't give a damn. Yes, I would say that that's a possibility. A little dramatic, but possible." Then I paused and kept thinking. No one interrupted. "Of course," I then again continued, "there are several psychotic and anxiety types. Also, there's the pseudoneurotic schizophrenic who is in partial or even full life-long remission and who only shows anxiety — meaning the anxiety contaminates everything the person does. That kind of person might try to wipe off the prints, but if so, would leave new prints while wiping off the first set. Know what I mean?

"I think the bottom line here is that it's either a deranged multiple, as you were thinking" — I looked at Grillo — "a hysteric, a pseudoneurotic schizophrenic with high anxiety, or a high-functioning inadequate type with an innocence about him." I stopped for a moment. "Wait, I've got another obvious one. It could be what's known as a borderline personality, a person who can have strong rages at minor frustrations and also at unexpected times. Although on second thought I don't really think so, because to be able to plan how to lurk in the hospital and to be able to withstand the pressure of stalking and waiting and watching — I don't know if a borderline could have the patience to do it — neither would an irritable bipolar mood disorder type in a catatonic-like excitement, who has piss-poor judgment — know what I mean? So I guess we'd have to consider these as lesser possibilities unless it was one of these high functioning mood types."

I was thinking that all of my choices were possibilities — that I wouldn't at all make a good police or forensic psychologist. Then another diagnosis hit me. "Wait. Of course, I can't forget our garden variety psychopath, or sociopath. Whatever the diagnosis, under it all we have here an example of psychopathic behavior. I think that's about it. If I think of others I'll call you but I think I've covered it."

"I followed it, Doc," said Grillo. "You think you could list them in order, like the best odds to be the guy to the worst odds?"

"Let's see now," I said. "I would say that's a hard question to answer. For example, the hysteric could be overwhelmed with the details of it and possibly therefore not wipe off prints, but such a person, I don't think, could carry off a drowning like that. Same is true for the pseudoneurotic type. Might not wipe prints because of all that anxiety, but it's hard to picture such a person drowning someone. The anxiety would be too great. The psychopath, I believe, would definitely purge the prints. The borderline, probably no. A high-functioning one maybe would wipe off the prints. I would say all of these are less likely — except for the psychopath. The bipolar one is more likely, but, well, and now, I'm sure this is not going to be lost on you, Detective Grillo, that leaves the multiple. And that's actually a good possibility. A multiple personality either in the innocent state or in the aggressive persona. You see, in the aggressive persona we can have a combination of an indiscriminate borderline rage operating as a low-level psychopathic pathology with grandiose notions of power. Leaving prints becomes meaningless, but hammering someone to display power over them can seem relevant.

"So I'll rate them. Let me think. Okay, the best odds, I guess, would be the dissociated type like the multiple. Joe Grillo, you're making me a believer."

I was about finished when it suddenly hit me. "Hey, wait a minute. In such a multiple, the intelligence and ingenuity of both the aggressive and sexual personas make a strong contrast to the so-called normal host, one who, compared to them, comes across as," I hesitated.

"As inadequate," Grillo pounced. "Innocent," he practically shrieked it.

"Tino Vescaro," Stroud blurted out. "No doubt. An innocent and a multiple."

After this diagnostic excavation, the question became whether a person in the innocent so-called normal state of a multiple triad could be convicted of criminal behavior, when the crime was perpetrated by one of the other personas, in this case, apparently, the aggressive one—if it wasn't the innocent host himself who did it? .

The question became should I take the fifth on the deposition? The other side was sure I would take the fifth, and knew that my attorney would insist on it. If I didn't, I could be subject to a criminal prosecution and a possible jail term.

Mark Terra, my attorney, said: "The replevin order can put you on the spot. If you take the fifth in a civil case, it then can be used against you in a criminal action, in which event they'll probably get the goods back. The court is allowed to draw adverse inferences in a civil case from a party's refusal to testify. If you refuse to testify, then you can't defend the civil action and you lose by default. Then they've got you."

I couldn't really follow him but in any event, I was determined to testify. I was going to defend Sebastian, come hell or high water. I was going to answer it all.

"Well," he said, "in that case their next tack will be to get the testimony sealed. They'll be shocked that you've decided to testify. That much I'll tell you."

I thought for a moment and then asked him if he had a plan. I shouldn't have done that because he began rattling off all sorts of legalese including something about testifying in a civil case puts someone in jeopardy, or something like that, and then he completely buried me with something about needing to stay the civil case so the criminal one can be done first. I couldn't stop him because he immediately continued with something about "without prejudice in the civil case," then something about "an injunction," which I think he referred to as a TRO or "Temporary Restraining Order." He returned to the replevin order and something about a "confidentiality order," then something about something being "filed and sealed," and that violation would mean jail time or fines and injunctions, and something about First Amendment questions being raised, and something about the First Amendment not restricting speech but having the right to enforce criminal laws. He also mentioned "prior restraints"—whatever the hell that was—and by this time I was a goner! He even added as a postscript that The Pentagon Papers was an illustrative case.

At that point, I laughed, and said: "Mark, the whole thing is a jumble to me. All I know is that their aim is for Sebastian to be silenced again, and I'm not going for it."

"No, Glenn. Just listen. I know you're going to need to go over this many times, and I'm going to give you material to read. When you read this material you'll also review this little preamble I just gave. I'll have it all written down for you. Okay?"

I nodded. Did I have a choice? It occurred to me that Stroud and Grillo must have felt somewhat the same way when I was speeding through all that diagnostic stuff.

"I'm kind of looking forward to seeing how it all turns out," he said.

He smiled, but it didn't last long because I gave him another little jolt.

"Mark, by the way, you know that drowning murder at Brentwood, well, I'm a suspect—remote suspect—in the investigation. I'm pretty sure the detectives doing the investigation know it wasn't me, but nevertheless they've taken my fingerprints along with everyone else's."

"Are we okay?" he said, meaning that we both knew I didn't do it.

"Absolutely okay," I reassured him.

"All right then, let's forget it for now. If something comes up, call me. And don't answer any leading questions without calling me first."

Well, that was my attorney's take on both situations—the civil case and Billy's case. And his take was usually what it turned out to be. As far as the Sebastian case was concerned, he was sure from the beginning that it wasn't going to be a criminal trial. He smelled a rat and felt that the real deal here was that the Vatican wanted to shush up the whole affair and at the same time continue suppressing Sebastian's material. I had explained to Mark that Sebastian's scientific material was not really critical or pejorative towards the church in any overt way, nor was it even concerned with the church. So it had to be his diary they wanted to suppress. I described to Mark what Sebastian had gone through, and Mark agreed. They wanted to kill Sebastian's science in order to hide church sins that were described in detail in the diaries—at least in the one that I had: virulent anti-Semitism of the Spanish Inquisition, along with homicide and its accompanying larceny. And here they were—at it again.

I wondered whether anti-Semitism was so engraved in church consciousness that it more or less characterized the essential nature of the church? Even in modern times, when Pope Pius XI produced the Encyclical against anti-Semitism, the committee writing it couldn't prevent their anti-Jewish poison from seeping in. Because of this, the Encyclical was buried for fifty years. Essentially a Pope wanted the church to apologize and the church writers made a stab at it, but they simply couldn't do it. The anti-Jewish genetics of the church was just too strong. And what about Pope Pius IX who was head of the First Vatican Council when it convened in 1869? At the time, an enlightenment was happening all over Western Europe, and rights for all people was gaining the ascendancy. The exception was that this Pope was preaching that Jews be kept in confined areas we now call ghettoes, and of course, religious freedom for Jews was out of the question. Along with that, he kidnapped a Jewish boy whom he never released despite widespread protests. This caused a scandal that is sustained to this day. And in the face of this, even now, in the new millennium, Pope John Paul II was seeking *beatification*, no less, of this inhumane nineteenth-century atavistic pope. To add insult to injury, Monsignor Carlos Liberati, another church fellow-traveler, who is overseeing this *beatification* process, has actually stated, in terms dripping with obvious, yet coded anti-Semitic allusions, that: "The church does not use scales like a pharmacist or a gold-smith." How about that!?

I thought: "If you are what you do, or even did, then the church is in huge moral trouble. The new tradition that is gradually developing in the church—mostly in urban areas—holds out some hope for the church. It's called—Christianity. And, of course, Pope John Paul already apologized for historical church anti-Semitism.

As I was both thinking this and ranting to Mark about it, I realized that Mark was right there, all the while carefully observing me. Mark was an intuitive type, like Joe Grillo, and believed that the law was founded on the logic of fairness. He knew that no matter how many variables existed in a conflict, the law searched for the best balance of justice, and this balance revealed itself in the process of going through the legal complex of variables and their vicissitudes and permutations. Of course we both agreed that truth trumps any ideology, every time.

Despite his enthusiasm for the complexities of the case, I knew that he would tell me to take the fifth and try to settle the matter. He'd told me that he would try to get permission for at least some of Sebastian's material to see the light of day, even after the quid pro quo. But I wanted to testify and answer every question truthfully and I didn't care about consequences. Here was our first disagreement. What made it difficult was that Mark had never once sent me a bill. "Phone calls from you don't count, Glenn," he said. "You're not on the meter that way."

"But this is much more than phone calls," I said. "I want to answer everything. I have a chance to help Sebastian speak. Then I have a chance to get him some justice."

Mark then wanted to know about Sebastian. He was interested in Sebastian's diary more than the scientific stuff of the manuscripts. I could tell he was becoming conflicted about contributing to the suppression of Sebastian that had gone on for all these centuries.

"In that case," I said, "I'll need to familiarize you with a project I'm proposing on the development of a pharmacological agent to deal with psychological symptoms. There are ethical and moral underpinnings to the whole thing. I've already been accused in a journal for conduct considered to be evil. I think you should read that article."

He thought for a moment and said, "Give me a one-sentence hypothetical book title for your project. Can you do that?"

It occurred to me in a flash. "*The Calibration of Anger Through DNA and Its Control of Emotional/Psychological Symptoms.* How's that?"

"In other words, you've hooked up the relation of anger and symptoms to DNA chemistry and there are implications to it that are causing tremors among certain people."

"Exactly. And I'm the number one certain person feeling the tremor."

"You mean you're concerned about implications of your work."

"Right."

I gave him a thumbnail sketch of my theoretical network regarding wishes, anger and symptoms. I described my discovery linking the calibration of anger to DNA chemistry and then shared my fears and doubts about the whole project—the same fears and doubts for which my detractors wanted my head. He asked me for examples of how the symptom gets unlocked, and I spent the next twenty minutes describing Josh's bottles under the bed, and the body watcher. He pondered it all for a few seconds and then asked a fundamental but brilliant question. It was the first time anyone had taken the next step to ask such a question. He wanted to know why some symptoms gave people a good feeling and other symptoms produced pain, and he wanted to know whether his question was relevant.

"Very relevant," I told him. "The same question occurred to me when I was working out the details of the cure. The answer is simply that if a person's wish concerns a positive outcome, that is, cast in a positive direction, then the symptom would produce relief." Then I explained some cases. An example of that was Josh's bottles. He wanted his father to love his mother—a positive wish. Of course, there's a negative side to it. He was angry at his father for what he believed was his father's not loving his mother. But the focus Josh had was not on the negative. His wish was solely to get his father to love his mother—a positive. When he put medicine bottles under his father's side of the bed, the purpose was to cure his father, and therefore his father would now love his mother and thus the family would remain intact. So when Josh put bottles under the bed, it gave him a good feeling, dissolved the funny feeling in his stomach, and permitted him some relief. Voila, a positive wish and a symptom process that is relieving. On the other hand, if the wish is a negative one—a wish to avoid something, like a wish negatively cast, then the symptom will be painful as in Mr. Dunbar's migraine. Sully Polite described it to me; it was when Sully and White interviewed Dunbar. Apparently, never in his entire life could Dunbar tolerate his hearing and speech impediment. He sought compensatory activity that made him feel worthy and normal. When he felt he would no longer access these compensatory activities, he developed the killer migraine. He didn't want to face what he felt was his inferiority. A wish like that, with a negative focus like him not wanting to relocate his entire life to his wife's sister's home in the South, will produce a painful symptom. In either case—positive wish and relieving symptom, or negative wish and painful symptom—the person falls in love with the symptom because the symptom satisfies whatever the focus of the wish, positive or negative, albeit in perverse form."

Again Mark was staring at me, his head slightly cocked, with a trace of a squint and a faint smile. He was enjoying what he heard.

"By the way," he said, "when I spoke to their attorney, the one who has the personal contact with church authorities here, he kept asking me about this specialty of yours. He obviously knew about it. I guess they've researched you because his queries about you were very much targeted to symptoms. He was indirect, but I had the distinct impression that he was interested in you above and beyond this case. I'm not sure if he was fishing for himself or for one of the church people. I could be wrong, but his conversation was interspersed with the kinds of questions you get from someone who basically doesn't want you to see what he's getting at. At the moment it really has no central relevance to the situation at hand. Let's just keep it in mind. Right now, we need to prepare for the deposition. They're going to try to rattle you."

"They can rattle all they want," I said. "I'm going to answer truthfully. I never considered Sebastian's material to have been stolen. From our point of view, it was borrowed material. We fully intended to keep our word and get the manuscript and diary back to the Vatican according to the time-table set for us. We put everything back to normal. The real problem, and this will probably come out in the deposition, is that I had the material copied, even though I knew that was definitely not part of the deal."

"Glenn, remember," he said, "copying or not copying has no relevance here. It's not about confessing. The authority challenging you was not involved in any deal to transfer material whatsoever. Those who sent you the material are the ones really in trouble. Forget about the copying." Mark wanted me to understand the entire case and then we would work out how to proceed. I was thinking about what it was that I really wanted everyone to know. If I had my wish, what would it be?

*   *   *

Stroud and Grillo had Kruger in custody. Apparently, Kruger was refusing to confess to any theft of property at the hospital, and kept insisting he had nothing to do with Billy's death. He was also stonewalling Manuel and

Tyrone's claims. What a fool, I thought—involved in nonsense at the clinic, in robbery at the hospital, and who knew what else. Now I was practically certain he was warehousing patients: keeping them incarcerated longer than necessary, thus dashing their wishes for release, and then stealing their possessions. I was sure there was more. Maybe Billy, but if not, then other things.

When I got home that night, I found two letters—one from Tyrone, the other from Manuel. It seemed that they didn't have the means to retain lawyers and were just plainly overwhelmed with the entire mess. All they wanted was to tell the truth in the hope that all the trouble they were in would disappear. Each of them apologized for any inconvenience and invasion of privacy. They swore they were paid by Kruger to go through the material on my desk, and to intercept mail sent to me. They pleaded for forgiveness and said they needed the money Kruger offered. They said they were feeling miserable.

Katie would have immediately said: "You're going to help them, aren't you?"

"Without a doubt," I answered audibly.

* * *

The materials Mark sent consisted of First and Fifth Amendment summaries, civil cases, criminal cases, and abstracts of articles dealing with much of what he had described about the possible ramifications of the case. Alone in my office, that night at home, and the next day over breakfast before a clinic staff meeting, all I was doing was reading and trying to understand what I was reading. The material was dense and initially confusing, and I needed to handle it paragraph by paragraph, often sentence by sentence. Gradually, I began feeling the confusion lifting.

Mark asked me to try to create a metaphor that could readily be understood so that my work could be appreciated by a lay audience—like in a courtroom. I had anticipated him and so I was prepared. I would say that the infinite number of psychological symptoms is analogous to an infinite number of different locks with each lock requiring a different key—its own key. The staggering fact was that I had discovered the one key that could open all the locks! A master key. How valuable is that? How important is the elimination of symptoms—pathological emotional/psychological symptoms?

I'd tell Mark that I wasn't going to claim anything at the deposition that could be interpreted as inappropriate. But I would tell him privately that even though modern man, that great oxymoron, is only one hundred thousand years old on a four-and-a-half-billion- year-old planet, and even though DNA in earliest life forms has been dated back three and a half billion years, the bald fact of the matter is that with this key, it was possible that we could make an improvement on the design of DNA that might otherwise take natural evolution who knows how long to reach on its own, if at all. The level of current research was years behind in understanding the phenomenon of anger in all its guises, and perhaps even farther away from understanding how to decode and cure symptoms. Should we wait for this when we have it now? If useful to him, then Mark could apply this question as a guide for the entire inquisition.

I felt good about having an inquisition. It gave me the sense that now, when I said my piece and defeated the church goons — those perpetrators of the real Inquisition — I would in some way have alleviated Sebastian's suffering, indulged my deep sense of indignation, and perhaps exacted a certain kind of victory. The church, in its zeal to again quash Sebastian, was now involved in another Inquisition. But this time I was going to force them to confront the issue!

I did have all of Sebastian's material copied — that was the thing I considered unethical. We were told not to have anything copied, but we did and I was the one who arranged it. That was where I crossed the line. It was untrustworthy and probably compromised other people. I rationalized it by thinking that there was a greater issue at stake. Yet, even though Mark reminded me that it wasn't legally relevant, nevertheless, it continued to bother me. I did it because not doing it was making me feel helpless, and I guess I rather wanted to feel triumphant. It was to revitalize Sebastian — to bring him back. And of course the idea of 'bringing back' is what obsessed me. That kind of endeavor hit me right where I lived, where I was hopelessly obsessed. So to be victorious would give me at least some rendition of the hope I needed.

* * *

Victory was in the air. Billy's prints, Edward's prints, 'T''s prints, Velma's prints, and Kruger's prints were all over the room. And, apparently, even Velma was careless. One of her prints was found at the fireplace. Stroud and Grillo told me all of it the next day. I was in the clear. They determined that I'd never been in the room.

They had thoroughly dusted the living room, the bedroom, closets, and bathroom. Kruger's prints were found only in the living room, mostly around the fireplace. They also noticed that the fireplace frame had been moved away from the wall, and when they moved it they found the cache and money. Of course, Kruger refused to say anything without his lawyer, but he did vehemently deny having killed Billy, lawyer or no lawyer. And the evidence seemed to bear him out. There was not a trace of Kruger's prints anywhere in the bathroom or around the rim of the tub.

But Tino was in trouble. His prints were all over the tub. They found Tino's female garb. His prints were also on the leather skirt and on the fireplace frame. Then when Kruger was confronted with the evidence of his prints, he abruptly dropped his ethical stance and spilled his guts with a lot of "Yeses."

Yes, Tino was a true multiple personality. Yes, he was a transvestite, and Yes, in one of his three personalities he acted out sexually. And yes, his other personality was hostile and aggressive. Yes, Tino's hostile personality was named Jericho, and the sexual one Veronica. Then he claimed that Tino never mentioned killing Billy, but that he believed it was either Tino or Velma who had done it. He said Velma was a scam artist.

It looked to me as though Kruger and his just deserts were surely due for a rendezvous. Kruger ended his accusations by saying that he didn't know whether Velma and/or Tino were in possession of Billy's books. That was a clever ploy. Of course, he knew those books were gone and that it was highly improbable that they would ever be found. So he told the detectives that whoever had the books also had all the evidence and a host of other information about unsavory doings and, perhaps, deals undertaken by Velma, and perhaps Tino as well.

Now Stroud and Grillo would have to apprehend Velma and Tino.

* * *

Talk about deals? My office intercom rang and Bishop Falkner—the church spokesman for the Vatican leading the fight against me—was on the other end of the intercom. He asked if he could see me. I didn't know quite what to do. I instantly felt lines were being crossed, so I needed to speak to Mark and get his okay to see this man. Yet I was confronted with the fact that I would have to play this one by ear. Would this contaminate the case? But if it did, wouldn't it contaminate their side of it and not mine? I didn't pay him a visit—he paid me one. I didn't ask to see him—he asked to see me. Maybe this was a ploy? While I was thinking these thoughts, I rang him in.

I offered him a cup of tea, which he accepted. He was portly with a big stomach that needed to be on a much larger man. We sat in easy chairs at right angles to an end table that held a lamp, a plant, and still had room for our cups. I used this seating arrangement for non-patient meetings.

"You have a beautiful office. All these paintings and photographs. Are you an art-maven?"

He used the word "maven" meaning expert. It's a Hebrew word used in Yiddish. Its more precise meaning is connoisseur. Was he trying to pander to me?

"Not really," I said. "I just love art. My wife was—uh, my wife's paintings. That large abstract there is hers and so is the one with the three faces."

"You're an honest man, Dr. Kahn. We know that. And I'm sorry about your wife. I've been told. Perhaps I shouldn't have mentioned that. We've compiled an entire dossier on you. The only person willing to besmirch you is under a cloud now for petty theft at your institute as well as for a number of other things at his hospital."

And there it was again, out in the open. Kruger!

"Quite frankly, Bishop, he has been, is now, and most likely always will be, a misanthropic pygmy. And I hate to say that only because I truly have nothing against pygmies."

"Well, I can tell you for sure that it was he who linked you and your librarian friend to the ostensible theft at the Vatican library. You notice I say 'ostensible.'"

"Look, Bishop Falkner, I'm not sure what this is about, but don't you think a line is being crossed here?"

"The answer is yes." He paused. "And no. It's been decided to short-circuit the civil action. Obviously you did nothing so terrible, and it's clear to me that the Holy See simply wanted to restrain you from publicizing Arragel's tirade against the church."

"Wait a minute," I instantly and almost pugilistically said. "Arragel's tirade is exactly Christ's agony. Not one iota different. The church, in many respects—not some, but many respects—remains the anti-Christ.

How do you like that? And I don't mind telling you this in the face of what the church might call my apostatized state. Now, if you want to know what a tirade is almost like, that might be the start of one."

"Easy, Dr. Kahn. I take it back. Arragel did not engage in a tirade. Of course, you're right. It's true, the church has been historically always at the root of anti-Jewish feeling. And this latest attempt to coopt you and prevent you from publicizing Arragel's diaries is an infantile attempt at best, and an irresponsible, and I would even say hateful, attempt at worst, to retain control of the public relations of the church. It's a disgraceful attempt at damage control. But it's a moot point because of Pope John Paul's apology, also in theological terms, for the church's contribution to the historical persecution of Jews and for residual anti-Jewish sentiment. And as you know, Pope John Paul released closed and even sealed files regarding church responsibility for a whole host of egregious programs and acts against others dating from the mid-sixteenth century to the very early twentieth century. Joseph Cardinal Ratzinger, who was head of the *Sacred Congregation for the Doctrine of Faith*, and, of course, is now Pope Benedict XVI, is working on further opening of these archives."

I took stock of his revelation but was struck by the dates. After a few seconds, I saw what I thought might be the insidious nature of this whole church confessional enterprise. Maybe I just couldn't give the church the benefit of the doubt. In this case what hit me were the dates. On one end they avoid the Spanish Inquisition and ongoing Inquisitions of the late fifteenth and early sixteenth centuries, and at the other end, they avoid the role of the church in twentieth-century horrors such as the Holocaust. They were ducking the two big ones.

My hypothesis was challenged when the Bishop said, "And His Holiness has also decided to open the Inquisition files."

I thought: "We'll see!"

"Look, Dr. Kahn," he said, "it appears that the leak of the Sebastian papers has reached all the way to the Pope. And I see what you mean. The implication was not lost on me as it was not lost on you. I, too, believe that in order to quash the spectacular nature of the diaries, the Pope and his advisors first decided to bring the civil suit, but then crafted the better plan of disclosing other anti-Jewish church policy. I guess it was better to put the onus on the church with respect to a wide array of horrors spanning about three centuries—and, yes, framed on either side by the Spanish

Inquisition and the Holocaust—while omitting both of those evils from view."

His point was a good one. The Vatican brain-trust had probably envisioned that even if Sebastian's diaries did surface, the sheer volume of material emerging from official declassified Vatican releases spanning more than three hundred years would swamp Sebastian's papers so that these papers would be lost in the shuffle.

"Quite frankly," he said, "you've got yourself to blame. I believe that your decision to go full steam with the truth regardless of consequences reached the powers and in record time. The upside is that because of this the world has you to thank at least for these impending church confessions."

He paused and I thought: 'This guy's got a sense of humor and I think I like him.' He continued. "I've instructed the attorneys to create delaying mechanisms until I'm forwarded official word canceling the depositions and the entire civil suit. As soon as that happens I will see to it that all of Arragel's manuscripts and diaries are in turn forwarded to you. I'm sure that with you they will be treated in the manner they deserve. Also, I'd like you to know that originally, I believed everything about the theft—that it was acts of trafficking in stolen goods. I never considered, never had the slightest idea, that an important revelatory process was about to emerge. Otherwise I would have at least asked for a dispensation and recused myself—even possibly vocally opposed the entire enterprise. So if you wish to speak to your lawyer, please call him and we can reschedule this visit. But I would very much like to, rather, I need to speak to you as soon as possible—please."

This man was so obviously sincere that I felt somewhat embarrassed that I had jumped at him about the tirade remark.

"Okay, Bishop, I take your word for it. How can I help you?"

"Well, my research assistants singled you out as someone who understands the true nature of symptoms. I followed up and was told that you actually cure them. Would you say that that is reasonably put?"

"I believe I understand symptoms, and yes, I can cure them. I guess others can, too. But there's a big 'but' here. Sometimes conditioned responses become obstacles in the rapid elimination of the symptom. And sometimes the person's diagnosis is so severe that the symptom actually vanquishes the personality—takes it over, kind of like the kinds of symptoms the church uses exorcisms for."

"In other words, you're saying sometimes the symptom disappears quickly, at other times it gradually dissipates, and in other cases it never disappears?"

"Exactly. But your diagnosis, I can see, is not of the severe type." I could see he was an intact, normal, neurotic personality. "The main point is that if we decode the symptom and understand its various components, then, whether more quickly or more gradually, the symptom will disappear. The other possibility is that the feelings you harbor may have imploded, so that the amount of emotional debris can render any talking cure ineffective. In that case I would recommend medication."

He nodded.

"However," I said, "I doubt whether this last qualifier applies to you, although I could be wrong."

He thanked me and said: "I'd been to another therapist for about four months last year with this same symptom. It was starting to plague me. But nothing changed so I terminated my sessions. I've been waiting and trying to avoid the symptom, but it's gotten worse — much worse. I'd like you to treat it and me as your patient with all payments and implicit obligations of the treatment relationship, including, and most especially that of confidentiality. I need to pay your regular fee for this service."

"I'll be happy to help you. I hope I can. My fee is three hundred dollars for each forty-five minute session, but I'll treat you only if you agree to a flat fee of one hundred dollars for each session. But I have another agenda in mind. I have a request to make, the answer to which has no bearing on my willingness to help you with the symptom."

"Yes, by all means, please state the request."

"I've been thinking of establishing a Sebastian Arragel chair at the psychoanalytic institute. This chair would be occupied by a distinguished theoretical psychoanalyst whose stipend would be solely dedicated to study and research. I believe we would need approximately one and a half million dollars to endow the chair, and I believe it would be fitting for the church to make the first donation to the endowment in the amount of twenty-five thousand dollars. Let's call it an oblation. Can you do that?" And I quickly added, "I don't consider this to be extortion because, in any event, I will treat you and for the one-hundred-dollar fee. I also don't care whether one would think this is unusual pressure or unethical. I'm telling you in advance that no matter what your answer, I will try to cure your symptom. I just think it's fitting for the church to be the very first donor to the Sebastian Arragel chair."

Without thinking or blinking he said: "I believe that could be arranged. And, of course, not contingent on whether you will cure my symptom. I can see that your fee for me is also your contribution along with mine for the Arragel chair."

"I'm astonished that you can so quickly consider that amount of money," I said. "Bishops must have a lot of power."

"It's true. Bishops do have power and are able to, as you say, consider large sums of money—of course for causes that benefit mankind. And I believe Sebastian Arragel's horrible experiences need to be aired. I know that you, too, believe that his scientific and clinical contributions need to be made known. In that spirit and in the name of the church, I respectfully promise to raise the first twenty-five thousand dollars."

I then asked him whether even the reduced fee was doable and he assured me it was, especially since he hoped a short-term treatment would achieve our goals.

So, I thought: "The truth of the matter is that there really are Christians in the world. The church is totally schizophrenic. On the one hand, you have a church-body full of primitive-minded individuals, and on the other you have Falkner and Vlad types who would die for you."

"One more thing," I said. "Do you know how Arragel's papers managed to get cited? I was writing a book on dreams and nightmares when I first came across a reference to his work in a bibliographic compendium."

"That's it," he said. "Bibliography. One of the research associates at the Vatican library—a man who has worked there for twenty years—was secretly including all kinds of materials from classified files in outgoing bibliographic compendia. Arragel's work was not the only classified literature to have been cited this way. For example, they had uncovered scholarly work regarding charismatic Judaism of which Jesus was a major proponent, and who was preceded also by Hanina ben Dosa, another charismatic Jew. Apparently, there were many of them. This flight of materials had been the route taken for all sorts of documents for the length of his tenure. He and two others at the library spent years translating all of the materials, also in the spirit of others before them who had done the same kind of clandestine translations, and especially with the advantage of more modern language usage. The three of them have been dismissed, although no official charges have been brought against them."

So there it was. Jean and I had sort of guessed it, but now I had it, more or less, firsthand. I thanked him and started. "Okay, tell me the symptom, please."

"Fine. But first I would like to give you some good news."

"Uh oh," I thought. "Good news in church lingo usually means some sort of Gospel, or that Jesus is here, or something like that."

But I was wrong. He said, "In Washington D.C. the Catholic colleges have now been sponsoring a program called *Bearing Witness*. Students visit the Holocaust Museum and study documents of the Nuremberg Trials. It's an attempt to introduce a moral lesson against anti-Semitism, racism, and oppression into church curricula. It's actually becoming popular with church students. I thought you should know that." He didn't wait for me to respond. "And by the way," he continued, "I was very moved by Cardinal O'Connor's apology to Jews. If anything was ever heartfelt, that was it. Did you read it?" "Yes, of course," I said, "and you're right, it was especially moving."

And that was a natural conclusion to our mutual introduction. "Can we count this as the first session?" he shifted. "We've been here for fifteen minutes. Do we have another half hour?"

"We can have the session, but we'll count forty-five minutes from now. Okay?"

He nodded in a way that said thank you.

*   *   *

"I have what my former therapist called an intrusive thought. It involves another person, a woman. You know bishops have all the weaknesses of any other person, and sometimes I feel my weaknesses, are in fact, stronger than most."

"That's funny," I said, "because I feel the same way about my weaknesses."

He laughed and thanked me. "This woman. She's thirty-five years younger than I. I'm seventy, she's thirty-five."

I instantly thought of Danny's situation. Older men with younger women. It seems to be an epidemic. He continued: "Well, I'm beguiled by her. She is wholly beautiful and I've been tortured with ideas about her. They include leaving the church and marrying her, which I know is not possible. Nevertheless, it's a compelling thought. She is positively the only woman in my priestly existence who not only has tempted me, but because of my obsession with her I have destroyed any personal dignity I ever entertained. I've known her now for ten years. When I was rector at St. Joseph's she was one of the parishioners, and when I saw her, I was instantly smitten, and in that instant, she took my life away. Took it away!"

That hit me like a mule-kick in the guts. It's exactly how I felt about Katie. She took my life away. Yup, it took an instant, and I was smitten. That word again. Everyone is always being smitten.

He continued. "Over the years, we'd gotten to know one another, and she often stopped by to say hello and just chat. She never confided in me or sought me out for advice or confession. She never flirted, but she frequently acknowledged with appreciation my positive feelings about her. I sometimes told her how special or how very unique she was. It was I who tried, in my feeble manner, to flirt. I did it so subtly that I was never sure if she got it. And then I would think: 'What am I doing? This is insanity.' Yet, it gripped me and I couldn't ignore it."

I was about to ask him what the actual symptom was, and he anticipated me.

"You're probably wondering what the symptom is. Three years ago she married another parishioner. They have no children. I say that because in my mind she's still a virgin. I can't bear to think of her in any conjugal relationship. To me she is saint-like, unsullied. I actually think that she married only for companionship and that the marriage is asexual or abstinent. I know this is nonsense, and at times I visualize her face in ecstasy as she's having sex with her husband. Then I feel myself sink into nothingness, and I can't bear thinking about it. Some time after she married, I noticed I was having this strange thought. And here is the symptom or I might say, intrusion of thought."

He leaned back and closed his eyes.

"I see myself with her."

He then opened his eyes and leaned toward me.

"And now it gets embarrassing. The thought is so primitive and strange and embarrassingly personal. It's beyond me, and it's not a dream. It's all a conscious fantasy." He paused. "Well, here it is. In the fantasy she tells me that she has scores and scores of cysts and little sores like pimples that get popped and extrude pus. They're all on her back and they look like little craters: red around the edges with pus accumulating at the head. She tells me they are painful and that she cannot permit any doctor to puncture them because the slightest pressure on her back can cause severe pain. Well, no, not exactly. I think what it is in the fantasy is that she says she hasn't found the doctor with the right touch. Yes, that's it. It's not that the doctors can't do it. It's that the doctors can't do it in a way that avoids pain. She says the pressure on each of the cysts has to be just right, and in my thoughts I get the impression that I will be the one to put exactly the right amount of pressure to each cyst on her back because I'm so in need of her, I so empathize with her, that I can sense exactly what it is she needs.

"And so we're in her bathroom or in her bedroom—it changes in my mind from time to time—and I'm not sure how it transpires, but I begin to persuade her to let me try. I just begin to try and she permits me. Then different things happen. For one, there's a scene where she is partially disrobed but holding her blouse or sweater against her breasts. I tell her that that's not important now because we're concentrating on more important things. So, she drops the clothing and leans over. I see her breasts. They're modest, but merely seeing them is not what makes me happy. Because it's not about sex at this point. It's about my happiness in helping her and in her permitting me to get this close and intimate with her. It's about spending time together. She's giving me her time and sharing with me—and only with me—her most personal concern. When I've helped her and broken all the cysts and thus when I'm successful with her, we then get even more intimate—but still not sexual—and in my fantasy, I then run a hot tub and gently lower her into it. You see, she has to soak so the cysts will continue to drain. The cysts are full of pus and they keep draining. Because of that she's in my hands and we need to be together, working on this problem and curing her, purifying her, emptying her of all that pus. Then the fantasy switches to another variation on the theme. Shall I continue with the variation?"

I nodded.

"Well, as I said, it changes. At this point I've made a template of the scores of cysts and pus-sores on her back. At first the template is on paper which I've placed on her back in order to trace the exact location of the sores and cysts. Then I somehow transfer the paper template to a large board that now contains the exact map of the sores and cysts on her back, with respect to size and circumference of each and the distance of one from the other. If you place the template on her back, all the sores will peek through their respective holes that I have already poked open. See? Then in the fantasy I place her on what could be a massage table and the template-board for her back is the surface upon which she lies, so when she lies down, all the cysts and sore-like pimples will fit directly into their respective holes. The weight of her body pressing down begins to naturally pop the array of eruptions through the holes. Under the template are balloons attached to each hole so that when pus drains from each site, the pus then collects into its own cyst balloon. None of it is wasted. It's all collected.

"Then when that's done, I sometimes have her soak in the tub for a time while I stand at the tub and watch her soak. I'm slightly bowed looking at her and we're talking. She's naked in the tub and she's becoming accustomed to me seeing her in her nakedness. The fact that she becomes accustomed to me seeing her like this is also very satisfying. It means that she is relaxed with me even though she's naked. Therefore she is more intimate with me than with anyone else. Oh, yes, I also pop the cysts with my hands and I wear like those surgical thin rubber gloves in the fantasy. I'm never doing it with bare hands. Then I have her stand, and I go to work again because after soaking in this hot bath, more pus has collected, and then I finally push the rest out by pressing my fingers against each cyst. This time even more pus is emitted and the final amount gushes out of each cyst, giving her tremendous relief as if pounds of weight have been lifted. Then, out of sheer love for me, she falls asleep naked in my arms, in bed. This part of the fantasy then sort of fades, as though I'm spent. It's not like an orgasm or a sexual feeling, but it's a feeling of relief and a satisfaction that I get. Yes, it's like a satisfaction. At that point I no longer need to continue the fantasy. I find that I then go about my life until another time when the fantasy returns and I go through the same thing again.

"That's it."

He stopped and waited for me to say something.

"You know," I said, "I can imagine that you feel this is extraordinarily unusual, but I can assure you that your symptom — this intrusive thought, this obsession — is no different from any other symptom, and we'll try to understand it. Tell me again, when did you first notice the thought or the fantasy?"

"I believe it started after she married and it continued to worsen over these years."

I asked him about anything recent that might have happened and he quite easily continued his story. It was all about her.

"I recently heard that she was in touch with another parishioner and they had an extended conversation about the church, but no reference was made to me. She never sent her regards. It made me sad."

"And angry," I added.

"Yes. Well, could be. Even though I haven't seen her for the past year, I've begun, for the first time, to actually think of her having sex with me, or I should say not that she's having sex with me but rather I'm having sex with her. I broke through a barrier there. Yes, I've begun to fantasize sex with her. It's the typical missionary position and we are in passionate sex. I see her face is quite sexual and her expression is that of a woman in the throes of an orgasm. This is when I feel she is mine."

I instantly thought of Danny. Very similar. It took both Danny and Falkner a while before they could permit themselves to imagine actual penetration sex with their respective fantasy partners. So I said to him, "It sounds like the fantasy has been getting more energized. You raised the stakes."

"Yes, I would say so. As a matter of fact, the problem is that the fantasy about the cysts is getting the best of me. In the past several months it's been out of control. I now think it all the time. Every day, sometimes several times a day. It's obsessive. I can't figure out when it will appear or why, and it has me worried."

The intrusive thought, the symptom out of control and flooding the psyche—I thought: "It's either understand it and work it out, or it's medication."

"Isn't this strange?" he said. "Why am I thinking of cysts and pus? And I should tell you, I have never had sex—although from time to time, I do masturbate."

Quite a confession. At that point I knew that he was, under it all, angry with this woman. Otherwise there could be no symptom. The wish to have her love him is cast in a positive direction, so the symptom gives him relief, not pain. The wish is truly gratified by the extrusion of pus, and that's an important point. She permits him to accomplish his aim and he feels relieved; that she gives him access to her naked body is not the central point though it is a contributing factor in his gratification through the symptom. The relief only comes when the aim is accomplished—when he finally gets all the pus out.

I decided to share my thinking with him.

"Okay, the obvious symbol of the surgical gloves could relate to the idea of absenting yourself from contamination and to protect you from commitment. But this symbol of protection, either way, is probably secondary to your wish to keep her pure. We're not going to tackle that yet. We know you're angry at her—at least, I think so—and we know your perverse wish is satisfied—extruding pus and saving every drop of it in balloons. Don't be worried about the word, 'perverse.' It really means, like, neurotic. I'm tempted to say, neurotic is normal. I'm sure you know what I mean." He nodded. "So what's the wish?" I continued. "Obviously the wish is for her to give to you. It's not anything you don't realize. You want her to give to you. So the question is, what is one process through which a woman gives? Or another way of asking it is: What is one way a woman can give both symbolically as well as in reality? The first clue is that you're angry with her because she deprives you. Deprives you of her what? That's the question?"

He looked at me with anticipation.

"You see, Bishop, in psychoanalytic understanding, things are sometimes symbolized backward or opposite; in dreams, up can mean down, in can mean out, young can mean old. So, too, with symptoms, sometimes the law of opposites kicks in to disguise the meaning of the wish. In your case I believe that's what's happened. I believe that her back means her front, so that all the pimples or sores or cysts on her back are really on her front. And what do such configurations look like? You said they're crater-like and red, and have a head to them where the pus accumulates."

He instantly interrupted me and practically shouted, "Nipples, it's nipples. I'm thinking about her breasts."

"Yes, I believe that's right. The question is why? Why are you thinking about her breasts?" He was considering it, pondering actually. "Hint. You've been constantly deprived by her. You've been wishing she could be giving to you. Giving of herself."

"The breasts give milk," he said excitedly. "That's it. The pus is the milk. Of course." He said it as though he was discovering it. And he *was* discovering it. It just came over him. "That's why I collected every drop—it represented her milk. That's when I felt most satisfied—when it was being all collected. It was her giving."

"So when you got all the pus out, that's when you felt relief—when she yielded all her milk to you and only to you."

"She only permitted *me* to get it. Not the doctors or anyone else. Only *me!*"

"Right. That's the symptom of the exploding and extruding pus that gratifies your wish and relieves you. You're right, it's not about sex. It's about acceptance. You just want her to accept you as an intimate. That's the first step."

"Wait a minute," he interrupted. "Then I feel I'll be able to have sex with her. In fact, I've recently been able to fantasize about having sex with her because the intrusive thought has been giving me the sense that she does need me, and want me, and trust me, and want me alone with her in the bathroom, naked, just the two of us, and then naked falling asleep in my arms in bed."

"Yes, I believe that's it," I said. "You can't have your wish in real life—all this proprietary interest in her in real life—so you have your wish in fantasy in the form of a symptom. An obsessive, intrusive thought that gets a profound grip on you. That's why you couldn't shake it—it was already shaking you. And the scores and scores of cysts and pimples represented a multitude of nipples reflecting the true desperate nature and magnitude of your yearning and need for her. I congratulate you on a most ingenious symptom."

He started to smile but said, "Wait a minute, I remember a dream. She and I were together somewhere talking and she said—I remember her comment verbatim. She said: 'Well you just have a hunger for me.' I awakened. Now I know it means just that—I have a hunger for her.

"The fact is I've gained forty-five pounds over a three-year period. My appetite knows no bounds. She married three years ago also. It's got to be related. I was never this heavy. At five feet nine inches I usually weighed a hundred and sixty-five pounds. Now I'm two hundred ten. I look at myself and I'm horrified."

"You might have had two callings, Bishop. Good connection. Good insight. I think also that in your heart of hearts you've given up the ghost. You've decided it will never be, so you're eating as a way of not being empty or alone. Because empty means alone."

"Yes," he said. "I always want to feel full and bloated."

"That's right," I said. "Your bloated feeling signifies that she's with you. If you're full then, so to speak, she's in you. You possess her. You're actually afraid to feel hungry because that would be an admission that you're without her. You know, you said it yourself—you hunger for her. The wish is for you to have her. You're bereft that the wish to possess her is thwarted, so you feel angry, you repress the anger, and then eat. Feeling full is the wish gratified, albeit neurotically. You'll do anything but admit to yourself that you're really angry at her for ignoring you and, in fact, leaving you. That's the reality. You don't face it because it would mean that you don't have her and perhaps never will. You feel fatalistic now, that it's not to be. And *that* you cannot bear. If I'm right on all counts—symptoms, cysts, appetite, and stomach—then, for sure, neither the symptoms of cysts nor the appetite will have the power over you that they've had. One other thing. The symptom becomes more readily dissolved when at this point there's something you actually do—some kind of work product that in some way is related to the relationship-wish you had with her."

"That's easy," he said. "We were involved in the cataloguing of gifts to the church for our rummage sale. It's a very large event with loads of materials, gifts, and all sorts of items. She and I were in charge of collating and cataloguing. The problem was that when she left, I really couldn't finish the job and for years now, the cataloguing has been haphazard. I have no motivation for it. Do you think that that should be something I could do? Would that be something like what you mean?"

"Could be," I said. He quickly continued talking as if he was afraid the session would end. At that point I flashed to Billy. Cataloguing! Billy could do it easily. Then I thought that the fantasy Falkner had, and all such idiosyncratic fantasies that people have, are usually so very personal that they can seem autistic. He interrupted the thought.

"I'm still thinking of my eating orgies. Let me give you an example of this gluttony. Last night I ate a large rib steak with French fries and garlic whipped potatoes. Two kinds of potatoes! I like the taste of both. I was never like this. On top of that I had pecan pie and regular coffee with four sugars. Now that's disgusting!"

"Well, no," I said. "I'll simply call it a symptom. And by the way, all your weight is in your belly. Otherwise you look a bit stout, not really obese. You're big boned and you carry weight well. Except for your stomach. And that means something special."

He kept looking at me, waiting for more. I knew I could use profanity with him, but I asked him anyway.

"The best way I can express this is by using some profanity. Is that okay with you? Would you be offended?"

"No, of course not. It's fine."

"I think it means that you've been fucked. You feel you've been fucked by this parishioner—the woman who has deprived you all these years. That kind of deprivation and the circumstances surrounding it amount to, colloquially speaking in the negative sense, getting fucked. So what happens when you get fucked? You get pregnant! Now your big belly is your pregnancy. You're carrying the product of your lady friend's essence—what you want—in your stomach. Thus you're carrying your wish, albeit in perverse form, in your stomach. Your gluttony is the perversion. It's the pleasure you want from her but can't have, so you have it another way. Furthermore, you're actually acting out the pregnancy by experiencing food cravings. And here we have what we call a symptom-content shift, that is, a shift from the internalized object—her—to food. You see, Bishop, in the psyche, wishes never get denied. You are very careful about not having an empty feeling in your stomach because that would mean your wish is denied—that she's gone. So you have food cravings and your wish is not denied. Then, symbolically, you do not have to face life without her. Of course, in bleak reality, you actually don't have her. What you have is a big stomach."

I paused but not as if I was stopping. He waited. "The thing to remember is that you're basically very angry with this woman because she is the source of your deprivation, of your perhaps never-to-be fulfilled unrequited dreams. Because she has, or better yet, because you have given her the power over your wishes, then, of course, she has tremendous power over you. And you've been helpless in the face of it. You need to remember that powerlessness generates anger. And you need to know that your supressed anger toward her is what keeps her incarcerated in your psyche. That's how you continue to possess her—by harboring the anger. Now I know that if she suddenly appeared the anger would instantly disappear. But so far that's not happening. You're left with an intense wish in the face of severe emotional deprivation, and yes, abandonment. Believe me, Bishop Falkner, I understand such feelings personally.

"I believe the intrusive thought will now evaporate," I said, "especially also if you engage in a 'doing' activity regarding the cataloguing. But we'll see."

I went to my desk and retrieved my appointment book. We scheduled five more sessions for the following two weeks, including one more that week. I told him I was going to alert Mark to the imminent dissolution of the civil suit. He sincerely thanked me.

I said to him, "Bishop Falkner, it was discoveries by Sebastian Arragel that helped me understand these principles of the symptom complex."

"Thank God," he said. "Thank God."

· 23 ·

THE MAKING OF GHOSTS

Grillo was sitting at his desk. Stroud came in. "It's here. Finally. Officially on forms. Listen to this: 'Prints confirmed. **Living Room**—*Tino Vescaro, all over. On fireplace mantel and frame, on both doors, on arm chairs and on leather skirts. Also on materials found in fireplace vestibule.* **Living Room**—*Dr. Siegfried Kruger, all over. On fireplace mantel and frame, on both doors, on arm chairs, on materials found in fireplace vestibule.* **Living Room**—*Chief Nurse Velma Secora, prints on fireplace and objects.* **Living Room**—*Billy Soldier, all over. On fireplace mantel and frame, on both doors, on arm chairs, on materials found in fireplace vestibule.* **Living Room**—*Edward Sedgwick, only on entry door and arm chairs.* **Living Room**—*Dr. Glenn Kahn, no prints anywhere.* **Living Room**—*Dr. Thomas Gersh, no prints anywhere.'"*

Stroud looked up from the report and said, "Okay, here's the **bathroom**. *No prints anywhere for Dr. Siegfried Kruger, Nurse Secora, Dr. Kahn, Dr. Gersh. Repeat, not a trace of prints anywhere for Kruger, Secora, Kahn or Gersh. Also, maintenance guy's in the clear except for his print on the light switch. "Now it comes.* **Bathroom**—*Only three sets of prints. One: Billy Soldier, all over rim of tub, on bathroom door—front and back, some pressed down hard so that they're bold, while some smeared across the door typical for holding on but being dragged away. They match the prints all over Billy's room. Two: Prints of Tino Vescaro, all over rim of tub, on bathroom door, both sides. No evidence whatsoever of attempts to wipe prints in any of the rooms. Three:*

Prints of Edward Sedgwick, on faucets of tub but not on the rim. So that's it. Tino definitely did it, either with or without Edward. A sweet guy like that. Maybe it's what Kahn said. You know, the innocent inadequate type who's in a momentum and can't stop."

Grillo, tight-lipped, stared at him. "How do ya figure it?" Grillo wondered aloud. "He's a nice guy, but ya know, I'll bet it was his other personality, the angry guy. Another thing," Grillo said, "would he do anything without Velma's permission?"

Stroud didn't care which. "Okay, let's pick him up — and Velma — and that Kruger, he was there. Oh, man, was he ever." Grillo concurred but said, "You know, Steve, I feel sorry for Tino. He's a split guy. No doubt about it. He's like a poor soul — babe in the woods. I never got the feeling he was tough or mean or anything like that. Just always seems a little scared like he'd rather not be seen. Emotionally the guy's poor. Even where they live. That trailer we found. He never had a chance. Living poor, inside and out. He can't even have one whole personality."

Stroud wasn't concerned with the pathology of it. "Let's get em' all."

* * *

Bernie Barrett had been calling, trying to get me to meet a James Wyeth, who was the CEO of the new company Barrett had joined. In fact, the same day Bernie called, I received a formal invitation from Wyeth himself, who asked to discuss the feasibility of working on my plan for the symptom-tablet. Apparently, Bernie had been keeping abreast of my work, and just about tantalizing Wyeth with my discovery.

In the note, Wyeth asked to have the meeting at his home in Palm Springs. All the major players of the company would attend. It was an abrupt wrenching away from everything that was happening with the Billy Soldier case, and with Sebastian's material. Nevertheless, soon after Wyeth's invitation, I found myself, with my lawyer's okay, on a corporate jet heading for Palm Springs.

Before finalizing my plan for the trip, I was concerned that detectives Stroud and Grillo would try to reach me. After all, they had been in intermittent, yet uninterrupted touch with me ever since their investigation of Billy's death began. I wondered if they would see my departure as suspicious. Terra laughed. "Are you kidding, Glenn? Go! There are no charges against you whatsoever."

Being on a private jet could get to be habit-forming. All the amenities one could ask for. A charming flight attendant was on constant call and made sure we were always comfortable. "We," meant Bernie, two executives of Biogene Inc.—the new biotech company that this was all about and that Bernie was consulting with—and the chief biochemist of the company.

On the way, I discovered that Wyeth was an entrepreneur and speculator. Rumor had it that he was going to hook up Biogene with one of the companies involved in the Genome Project. Bernie kept assuring me that Wyeth was quite interested in my work and was willing to part with a huge sum of money if I were to sign with Biogene.

So here I was, possibly entering the culture of wealth: a corporate jet, no less. Actually, I was told only Wyeth used it, so for all intents and purposes, it was really a private jet—his. I was reminded of the books on poverty I had read over the years: Frank McCourt's Irish, Michael Gold's Jews, Oscar Lewis's Mexicans. And since I, too, come from a culture of poverty—parents were shtetl Jews from Ukraine—and despite the fact that I, myself, had become reasonably affluent, nevertheless I naturally identified with the disenfranchised poor.

Bernie distracted me from my ruminations of poverty. He told me he had read the article about arrogant scientists (meaning me) and serial killers. He laughed. "It must have troubled you, Glenn, but you must admit, it's hilarious. Whoever wrote it needs your pill." John Springer, the chief biochemist at Biogene, was the one who had first showed the article to Bernie, who in turn told John that he knew me. He and John began talking about my decoding of the symptom complex and the feasibility of my anger pill. That's when John decided to take it to Wyeth. They had a meeting with Wyeth that same day. Wyeth made some inquiries to ascertain the legitimacy of the work and then, apparently satisfied, insisted on seeing me.

The plane landed in Desert Springs. We were escorted to a stretch limo and got in. Seated in the limo, Wyeth greeted us cordially. He seemed to be in his mid-sixties, graying at the temples, tall and trim. Central casting couldn't have done it better.

"Dr. Kahn, I am so pleased to meet you. Many thanks for making the trip. I'm hoping you'll not regret it." He continued, rapid-fire. "I wanted John and Bernie to let you know just how interested we are in your discoveries. Bernie has briefed me to whatever extent he could, but I need to hear it from you, and I'd like John Springer, our chief biochemist, to sit in. The plain fact is that Biogene is searching for a product that could catapult us up there with the big boys. But most importantly, something that could make a real difference in the lives of people."

He got me with that one. Then he began filling me in as we headed out to Palm Springs, launching into a review of Biogene and its financials. He was not shy and frankly and openly discussed his wealth and the potential of Biogene. I was duly impressed, partly because of his straightforwardness and partly because I had never been so close to such abundant wealth. The limo pulled up to a spectacular spread. I couldn't call it a house. It was a hexagonal sculpture. We exited the limo and Bernie and the two execs made a bee-line for the front door. Wyeth took my arm and waited.

"I know it's gorgeous," he said. "A Frank Lloyd Wright contemporary, Sidney Elton Filmore designed it. A bona fide original. I paid 25 million for it about ten years ago and lord knows what it's worth today—probably almost triple. It's not boasting, Dr. Kahn. I'm just taken with it the way anyone would be. I've never really considered it mine. I'm only borrowing it. As far as I'm concerned, I'm living in an artistic vision that belongs to the architect. I'm only borrowing it. So I talk about it as though I'm a visitor admiring it and I'm not shy about it. Come, let's follow the others," he said.

Of course, what I didn't say was that I knew perfectly well what it was like to live in an artistic vision. But before I even had a chance to ruminate further, in we went. The outside transformed inside into a softly-lit elegance. We sat in the study, just the two of us. We were served shrimp and champagne. He began by trying to articulate the central notion of what I'd discovered.

"The agent—this pill—goes to the source, affecting the machinery of DNA first. You see," he said, "I know Bernie told you that we're looking for exactly that sort of agent. Do you really think it can work? I mean, do you really think such an agent will eliminate psychological symptoms?"

"Yes, I do. I can do it verbally in an office session as well, although there are enough individuals—actually many—who are unable to access much emotion or who are ego-deprived, or who, for other reasons can't approach the problem, and so can't get it done. These are the people who need such an agent."

"You're a psychoanalyst."

"Yes, I do conventional psychoanalytic treatment with patients — you know, patient lying on the couch and I'm sitting behind the couch. I'm also, about half the time, treating patients in what's considered simply, psychotherapy — like the patient sitting in the chair. The work is different in each case."

He smiled. "I always thought I could do that — I mean as a patient."

"You'd probably do well," I said. "The thing is — and all clinicians know it — that the symptom is sometimes so pervasive, or intense, or severe, that the symptom takes ages to reach, if ever. This little pill will reach it immediately. That's the idea."

"And I know you feel that this agent can also affect certain biological disorders and contribute to their cure," he said. "Is that right?"

"Yes, I think so. I believe this agent may also do that — contribute to the alleviation of any number of stress-related biological problems. But that's a hope."

"Well, what we're looking for is symptom-cure and Bernie says he would bet that you've found the method, the technology to do it."

"You know," I told him, "my attorney suggested I think up a metaphor for the whole thing. This is it: Symptoms are locks and each lock needs its own key and each key is different because each lock is different. What I've put together, what I've found, is the master key — the one that unlocks all the locks, even though all the locks are different."

I could see he was taken with it and understood the image. So whatever test I had been taking, I obviously passed because he then felt it was his turn. Yet, I wasn't trying to impress him, or persuade him, or even interest him. It's just that I was so taken with the image myself that I found it exciting to repeat.

He then took a folder from his briefcase. "Here's my story — my various companies and amount of wealth I've amassed. You know how? I enjoy pursuing good ideas. And yours is not just a good idea — it's — well, I don't want to say just how good I really think it is. By the way, please call me Jim."

"Good, call me Glenn."

"Okay, Glenn, here it is. I'm going to make you an offer that will make you a wealthy man. I've decided I believe in you and in your discovery. I'm not someone who throws money around, and I'm not pitching you or trying to seduce you by appealing to ego. I'm just telling you how I feel. I feel you are onto something gigantic. And John and Bernie concur. I want to be part of it, I want Biogene to house it, and of course, I want you to sign with us. I know you'll be getting many offers. I want to be there first and try to be there with the most. Whatever the others tell you, please remember that I've done it before and I can do it better, and I'm going to do it again—I hope with you. I think my experience will be invaluable here. We will give you carte blanche with respect to research facilities, staff, administrative personnel, budget, and whatever else is needed. You can set up the work in New York City or you can work here at the Biogene Labs. It would be entirely your choice."

This was all new to me. Everything up to that point had been speculation. My work with patients on symptoms was real. But the sense of mobilizing this entire project, of actually proceeding with the implementation of it—developing a big pharma—was still a pipe dream to me. And here was Wyeth telling me, no, it's not a pipe dream.

Wyeth continued to fill me in. It was obvious that he was a billionaire. At one point he paused in his story, then rushed on because, as was evident to me, he was just below the threshold of feeling suddenly conspicuous, and almost blushing about it.

"I'm telling you this because you need to know everything. To start Biogene, I raised four hundred fifty million dollars on Wall Street on the first day. Those who invested knew my track record. The company is now about to be listed on the NASDAQ to open at about seventeen dollars per share. We have sixty million shares outstanding. Our net worth is okay and we have a lot of cash available. We'll be adding a dot com to the company to multiply our marketing by some factor."

He looked at me and without changing his expression an iota said, "You saw me feeling embarrassed."

"Yes, I did," I answered.

"It's the damnedest thing. I can't help it. Never could. Did I get red in the face?"

"Only a touch," I said.

"Okay doctor, cure me."

"You want the short answer or the long one."

"The short one."

"You want people to look at you—you *want* to be noticed."

"The long one," he said.

"The long one is that at some point, earlier in your life, you must have felt ignored, or at least not sufficiently attended to, or, you were essentially prohibited from expressing any pride in personal achievement. So, when you want to express pride in something you've done, you can't. Then you get angry and instantly repress this anger. Thus, you're not even aware that you're angry. When that happens, the blushing symptom appears but only because your anger is repressed. The blushing is the wish gratified — that is, your need to be noticed becomes realized in disguised form, in the blushing. You blush and people see it. Voilá, the wish not to be ignored, rather to be seen, is met. Getting red in the face gets you seen."

"Interesting," he said. He studied me for a moment or so, and then he made the offer: signing bonus, stock options, percentage of profits. It was a multi million deal.

I told him that I thought I had understood it, but was, quite frankly, flabbergasted. How was I going to grasp all of this — to metabolize it?

"There is something you should know," he said. "Biogene will probably invest somewhere in the neighborhood of eighty to a hundred million dollars to test the product. We need many, many trials with a wide array of subjects and we need to meet all sorts of government standards, regulations and procedures for this type of research. At any time during the trials, results could be so questionable that we would have to shut down the entire process. Despite that possibility, your deal will still hold but only with respect to the signing bonus and the stock at market price. So even if nothing happens, you'll be many million dollars richer. The good news is that I'm looking forward to getting off the ground. I have a strong hunch about this one. Then he stated his long-term projections.

Everyone has symptoms," he said. "So the product will keep selling — year after year, decade after decade — worldwide. Forever. We could be talking about — in a cumulative sense — a multifactored trillion-dollar product."

He didn't emphasize it. Just said it and I knew I was in a new universe.

"It's all very unreal to me, to tell you the truth," I said. "I mean, I believe everything you say, but I didn't expect this to crystallize so soon and so acutely. I think it's going to mean a life change, and I need time to think about it."

I then told him about the civil suit and that it was being cancelled. I also told him I'd have to discuss the whole issue of intellectual property, copyright, and patent law with my attorney. I further told him I had established ownership but my attorney wanted to discuss setting up additional structures supporting the ownership.

"You know," I continued, "my discovery feels to me the same way this home feels to you. I really don't think I own the discovery even though I made it. The discovery and its fruits really belong to all people. I'm not sure I deserve to be rich because of it."

"I know what you mean," he said. "But remember, even though I really feel like a privileged guest in this gorgeous domain, I do live here and others don't. And that's a fact. No matter how I turn it, I own it. I'm humble about it because of my deep respect for the architect's vision. But at the end of the day I live in it. And I own it. Your discovery belongs to mankind. Yes. But without you there is no discovery. You did it. You made it happen. It's yours."

I thought about it for a few seconds, but it wasn't sitting right with me.

"You can't patent the laws of nature," I said.

"Yes," he said, "but you can patent a method of surgery. That's what we're going to do. We're going to develop a method that utilizes laws of nature to turn the wheel. But the method will be ours, and *that* we can patent. Ask your lawyer."

*   *   *

I had a lot to think about. I was in it. The forces moving ahead weren't big, they were huge. All the talk, all the speculation now seemed like child's play. Wyeth was making the deal. It was clear to me that sooner or later when the code of symptoms eventually revealed itself to some other scientist—whenever that would be—the James Wyeths of the world would develop and distribute it and no discussion would be able to stop it. I guess it's all about what the market wants. That doesn't necessarily make it good, and perhaps it doesn't necessarily make it bad, either. Yet, I was nagged by the thought of what that great theoretical mathematician, G.H. Hardy, said. It was some profound comment about scientific developments usually accentuating the gap between the rich and the poor—making the rich more rich—and in addition, moving humanity closer to destruction. He said something like that. Chilling!.

*   *   *

Wyeth's private jet took me back to New York. John Springer and I were the only passengers. It was obvious that John wanted me to discuss the mechanism by which DNA is engaged, and the molecular manipulation that would be required to calibrate anger. My immediate problem was how not to reveal the key but still engage in the discussion.

He started by talking generally about DNA. He mentioned that the DNA molecule was about a hundred-thousandth of an inch across and we marveled at that. "I never fail to be amazed," he said, "that there are a hundred trillion cells in the body. A hundred trillion! And another amazing fact is that the DNA molecule is constructed by an unbroken string of billions of nucleotides—and the heredity of each person in the genome is like a resource book with three billion letters etched right into the molecules of DNA."

In one or two long breaths he referred to billions and trillions. He was talking about the molecular alphabet. He didn't realize it, but he was really reciting big numbers as though he was Wyeth.

He continued with the big numbers. *The Human Genome Project*—now that's really something—billions of dollars in research in order to decode all three billion nucleotides of our DNA. I mean, doesn't it boggle the mind that we function with no less than a trillion neurons—fifty billion in the brain alone—and here's the big one, the really big one—maybe fifty to a hundred trillion interactions between all trillion of them."

After getting to know him a little, I liked him. He was enthusiastic. I could have gotten him off the nosebleed numbers by talking about the four pairs of histone proteins that form into a single—one—octomer particle, and the strand of one hundred forty-six bases—DNA subunits—that are wrapped around the octomer twice (a low number)—to constitute the essence of the chromosome called the nucleosome. I didn't, because I knew he would instantly ask, "Well, which one is implicated in the calibration of anger? Is it the nucleosome, the bases, the histones?"

He would, of course, get very focused on histones because he knew that histones are conductors of gene activity as well as packagers and benders of chromosomes, and he would probably guess that histone architecture was the issue. In other words, histones are the band that plays the music so the DNA knows whether to tango or waltz. But John Springer wasn't interested in four/four time or three/four time. He was mesmerized by big numbers — only big numbers. So, I decided not to say that often, big things come in small packages — in this case in historian DNA packages. I did, however, offer him a different way of considering DNA.

"DNA is really software, John," I said. "Think of it as software."

We sat silently for a while — he apparently contemplating my comment. I, on the other hand, drifted back to the deal. Millions of dollars? As much as I was embarrassed by the trumpeting of it all, nevertheless I realized the possibility that other than some medication eliminating disease entirely, prolonging life indefinitely, or curing cancer, a little pill that calibrates anger and eliminates emotional/psychological symptoms would be, without a doubt, just as Wyeth had said, one of the biggest pharmas of all.

I needed to talk it over with Mark. I'd depend on him to set up the financial advisors, patent lawyers, copyright experts, accountants. It was definitely the culture of wealth that I would be entering. It's different from McCourt's Irish, Gold's Jews, and Lewis's Mexicans. My heart was with them — all of them, and I would be leaving them. I began to notice that I was no longer agonizing about the real possibility of rescuing Sebastian by plucking him, Ester, Alba, and all the Jews out of Spain and magically bringing them to a safe America. I guess I was now in a different reality, perhaps the real reality. But, of course, the only one I wanted to tell it to, was Katie.

* * *

Waiting for me when I got home was a letter — an official invitation from the court to provide expert testimony on the psychology of Dissociative Identity Disordered Multiple Personality. Then a court clerk called and repeated what was in the note — whether I would be available to do a psychological evaluation on a split personality disordered person, should the need arise.

I wasn't opposed to court appearances or to being an expert witness, but it always seemed like a lot of work and usually took days. Also a lot of sitting around and waiting, a lot of postponements. Nonetheless, I accepted the invitation, also advising them that it might actually be a case in which I was also involved.

It was this invitation from the court that brought me back down to earth, knowing full well that first, I would have to talk the whole Wyeth thing over with Mark. Then, I would be back with Billy Soldier, Grillo, and all of them. In addition, Sebastian was always lingering there in the recesses of my mind. I had decided to write a book with Sebastian's scientific contributions as the relief centerpiece, along with the Spanish Inquisition and Sebastian's persecution as the backdrop.

But first, Mark Terra. I called Mark and filled him in. He knew of Wyeth and said Wyeth was a serious business man and that it was all real. We scheduled a meeting to discuss the entire issue of fortifying the intellectual property of the symptom code. It was only then that I called the detectives.

I told them that I'd been away and now I wanted to hear about any new developments in the case. Grillo gladly accommodated me. He welcomed me back and then gave me a blow by blow—a full, richly textured account of all the interrogations that had taken place with Kruger, Tino, and Velma.

Apparently, Velma was brought in first and Stroud confronted her about her prints. She denied any wrongdoing and pointed the finger at Kruger. She accused him of tampering with Tino's personality, claiming that it was she who was only trying to protect Tino from Kruger himself. According to Grillo, she called Kruger a thief and said he was poisoning Tino against her. She further claimed that all she did was follow Kruger and that's when she discovered the secret room. In order to protect Tino, she told Kruger she would call the police unless he promised to really help Tino and not to manipulate him.

And Velma stuck to that story—that she was innocent. She was protecting Tino and essentially blackmailing Kruger to keep him honest with regard to Tino's treatment. She insisted she had not been stealing anything, and most importantly, she vehemently denied knowing anything about Billy's death.

Then Grillo said that with Kruger it was different. He wouldn't talk without his lawyer present, so Stroud had Kruger call in his lawyer. Stroud told the lawyer that they had Kruger dead to rights. They revealed that they had confessions from Kruger's henchmen detailing Kruger's shooting of the statue at the clinic. Stroud then offered that to the lawyer as a gift—meaning he was starting to make a deal. He told the lawyer that they had Kruger's prints all over the secret room, and that they were sure he was involved in theft of property at the hospital and were in the process of collecting evidence to prove it conclusively. And he assured the lawyer that they would indeed find Billy's books.

Neither the lawyer nor Kruger answered. Later, the lawyer insisted on Kruger's innocence in Billy's death, took them up on the gift about forgetting the clinic statue shooting, and asked for no jail time whatsoever if Billy's books were found, even somehow if they implicated the doctor in questionable activity. In return, Dr. Kruger would reveal what he knew about Billy's death and who may have been the killer, and would testify to it. Perhaps it was Tino, the lawyer implied. In any event, Dr. Kruger held the key to the whole case. Was it a deal?

Grillo told me that he and Stroud looked at one another and without conferring, Stroud said, "Deal."

* * *

Although it would still take some time for the trial to get underway, it appeared to me that Tino was about to be indicted for Billy's murder, and yes, they wanted me to deconstruct his psyche, to open it up and lay it out so that the court could really see what was going on in there. I was thinking that I would probably need a session or two with Tino in clinical interview, and another session to administer psychological projective tests. If I could have that time, then after another two or three hours of analyzing the data, I would try to develop a picture of what they wanted: the nature, arrangement and functioning of Tino's psyche. This picture would then make clear the workings of whatever personas may have been inhabiting that psyche. Assuming he was truly a multiple, how in his personality did these personas develop and what function did they perform? The opportunity to examine that sort of psyche was rare, and I was definitely interested in the prospect of it. Tino's responses on the projective tests would peel off the cover of the story. It was impossible not to be especially curious as to what his responses would be to the ink blots, and when asked to draw a person, what kind of person he would draw. What was it that would surface from beneath?

* * *

An undercover detective in an attendant's uniform was working on the autistic ward, keeping an eye on Edward's door. Inside Edward's room another detective was stationed behind the door, not visible from the window. He was sitting in a chair, reading and waiting. Edward had been transferred to another location and was accompanied by a nurse and a detective. The nurse came equipped with tranquilizing medication, just in case. Of course the concern was Edward's unpredictability.

More or less at the same time that Edward was leaving the hospital, Tino was brought into Stroud and Grillo. They sat him down and explained the entire situation to him.

"Tino," Grillo said, "it looks serious. We've got your fingerprints on the tub where Billy was drowned. Only your prints and Billy's prints were on the tub. We know you did it, and we want you to tell us about it. It's gonna get serious and there's gonna be a trial. Do you understand? Your mother's going to be involved as well. Do you understand?" Grillo repeated. "She's been implicated by Dr. Kruger."

That did it. At first Tino seemed to be stonewalling it, although in a way he was, really only blank. But when Grillo mentioned that Kruger had gotten Velma involved, Tino snapped.

"Okay," Tino said. "Velma had nothing to do with it. I can't say I killed Billy, but I know she didn't. You can't blame it on her. Maybe you can blame it on Dr. Kruger. Velma says he was stealing from the property building and selling everything he could. Velma said he kept all the money in the fireplace in the room. She had nothing to do with it. He had Billy figuring everything out and writing everything down. Billy was his slave. It had nothing to do with Velma."

"But what about Billy?" Grillo continued. "Billy was killed. Were you involved? Or maybe it was someone who kind of takes over when you're like asleep or something, like something that happens with your headaches." He didn't wait for Tino to answer but still was especially kind and sensitive with him.

"You know, Tino, when this goes to court, Dr. Kruger will testify that your headaches are related to another problem you have that makes you not know certain things that are happening." And like Stroud, Grillo said, "You know?"

Tino listened but acted as though nothing was registering with him. Then he said: "Edward knows. He saw the whole thing. He was there looking into the bathroom and he was rocking and crying and he started to yell." Then Tino became silent.

Grillo pulled up a chair next to Tino's. "How'd you get him to stop crying?" Grillo gently asked. "Edward went into the ward and ran to his room," Tino answered. Again, Grillo casually eased into it. "And how do you know all of this?"

With that, Tino had a peculiar smile on his face as if the logic was inescapable, but still he couldn't or wouldn't answer the question. Then Grillo raised the stakes.

"Tino, maybe even though Edward was watching, you held Billy down in the tub while your mother kept his head under the water."

But before Grillo could barely finish that sentence, Tino shouted, "No! That's not it. She wasn't there. She had nothing to do with it. I told you before. She had nothing to do with it."

Whatever the approach, whether from Grillo the gentle detective or Stroud the tough guy, Tino would not confess to the murder. But he did finally say:

"I always liked Billy and I gave him extra things—even food. One day I went into his room to leave some cookies on his bed and he was there. I didn't knock because he was supposed to be with the occupational therapy group for the morning. But he didn't go. He was sitting on his bed with a whole lot of medical forms and a calculator—one of those that you hold in your hand. He was very upset and then he just told me." Tino then paused.

"And then he just told you what?" Stroud interjected.

"He told me that Dr. Kruger was cheating on the Medicare and Medicaid treatments of his private patients. He was charging for more patients than he could ever see. It made me feel that Billy was mad at Dr. Kruger and was finding out things about him. Or something like that. He said Dr. Kruger cheated on a promise."

Tino wasn't given a chance to pause because Stroud was right there.

"And," Stroud demanded, "go on!"

"Billy was counting the number of hours for each patient and showed me how he calculated Dr. Kruger's charge for each patient and said he knew Dr. Kruger was cheating the Medicare and also the Medicaid. He said Dr. Kruger would have to work twenty-eight hours a day for a ten-day week in order to account for all that money coming in from the Medicare and Medicaid. You know, Billy was very smart with math. He told me not to tell anyone."

"Well, did you?" Stroud stridently asked.

"Only Velma."

They couldn't get anything out of Tino regarding the murder, but now they had something more on Kruger that had to be investigated. They would have to get hold of the Medicare and Medicaid statements for the past few years and compare them with time sheets and Kruger's records.

They held Tino for the murder of Billy Soldier, and he was led away. Then they called off the watch on Edward's room. Edward would soon be back on the ward.

Stroud looked at Grillo. "Joe, here's how it went. Tino told Velma about the Medicare and Medicaid stuff. Velma blackmailed Kruger into who knows how much hush money." Grillo agreed, but said, "I don't know, Steve, maybe Velma helped Tino kill Billy, maybe not. Maybe Kruger knew about it, maybe not. We know Edward knew about it. That's what he was babbling about in the cafeteria. He actually saw it go down. But what good is it? Edward can't communicate."

"You know," Stroud said, "I think if Velma was there, she would have killed or had Tino kill Edward, too. To me that means Velma wasn't there. Just Tino.

"Or," Grillo said, "maybe Tino himself, who is basically nonviolent and doesn't know enough to cover his tracks did it, but pities Edward and wouldn't want to hurt him. It would be the same Tino who wouldn't think of wiping prints off the tub, like the kind of diagnosis Kahn told us about." Then it hit him. "Oh, here it is. I got it. If Velma was there, for sure she would have taken care to clean that mess up. There would have been no prints left at all. That's it. Velma wasn't there."

"Right," Stroud said. "Velma wasn't there, so what it boils down to is the possibility of two suspects. Either Jericho did it, in which case Tino has no memory of it, or Tino himself did it. One or the other!"

*"Wait," Grillo jumped. "Unless Velma didn't clean up the mess because Tino's become too much baggage. You know, that Jericho guy is completely out of control. And it looks like, out of **her** control."*

*   *   *

As a postscript to my meeting with Wyeth, Bernie Barrett called to say that Wyeth had agreed that my plan to control psychological symptoms via DNA intervention reminded him of the Kandel project that was being developed as a method of memory erasure. Eric Kandel was the scientist who had recently won the Nobel Prize. Over many years he had been working on erasing painful memories through DNA manipulation. The fact was that the work on memory modification worried me because when memory is erased, the emotion attached to the memory would possibly not follow suit. The point is that in the brain emotion is largely rooted in the amygdala while the processing of memory is associated with the hippocampus. And although there is interaction between these brain structures with respect to how emotion and memory function together, still, one is not identical with the other. Ergo, memory erasure possibly could interfere in the elimination of symptoms. For example, imagine an erased memory, pried loose from its attached anger-emotion. It could mean that a symptom can no longer be cured because the *who* is gone (memory erased), and the anger will now, by default, only go to the self; this could result in permanent symptoms because the link between memory and emotion is severed. Now the self becomes the permanent *who*. I didn't mention it to Bernie, but I was picturing the anger forever in a futile search of its intended.

The making of ghosts!

CODA

EXTINCT AND EXTANT

It was the Medicare/Medicaid fraud that finished him. Dr. Siegfried Kruger's career as a psychiatrist was effectively over. Stroud and Grillo couldn't stop it. That kind of fraud wasn't in the deal. And it was Billy who had done it. Kruger made a huge mistake. He wanted to take Billy's precious books away from him. Billy was beside himself and he kept screaming till he was beet red. "No, no, no, no." Over and over. As Kruger gradually backed down, so did Billy. His indignation gradually became a whimper. Kruger promised that Billy could always keep the books, but that was the second promise he was backing away from. Billy very well remembered that Kruger also betrayed the promise that the amount of their account would start with zero, and never reach the one-hundred thousand amount. Now because of Kruger's lies, his untrustworthiness, Billy felt entirely disregarded. That's when the cascading began and his momentum took him to his calculator. He began calculating Kruger's ledgers. Billy had suspected it and followed through. And that's when Tino, bringing Billy some cookies, happened to be there. Then in an episodic rage, Billy sent it all to the F.B.I., along with a letter on hospital stationery in which he pointed out the fraud. And all he did was address the letter: **FBI, Washington, D.C.**, *and sure enough, it reached its destination directly.*

Yes, not only was Billy not retarded, but in certain respects he was quite intelligent. In letter writing and in math he was definitely a high-functioning Asperger. His letter then started an escalating process of investigations. The authorities tallied the number of patients Kruger claimed to have seen, each for a full regular session, and the fraud immediately revealed itself.

And now, with Billy as the only material witness to Kruger's fraud, Kruger again became a high-list suspect in Billy's death, despite the absence of his prints on the rim of the bathtub.

* * *

I received a letter from the District Attorney's office regarding materials recovered from Kruger's papers. The police had discovered a series of files he kept on various people, and the letter also enumerated items taken directly from his file on these people — including me. One item I had never received was the review of my first book. So what I originally suspected had actually happened. Kruger had stolen it. Gradually, over the months, more and more was revealed, and Kruger emerged as a true psychopath in whose wake was littered a continuous path of illegalities. His overarching symptom was his zeal to acquire power. This explained his single-minded attempts throughout his professional life to strive for prestige. I understood it as his need to assuage inferiority feelings and as an expression of his grandiosity. He needed to have those around him see him as, if not superior, then at least as a man of achievement. And I was certainly one of those around him. So I could imagine how enraged he must have been when I bested him at the hospital Grand Rounds on the subject of symptoms.

Now, his madness was out in the open. It was the confessions of Manuel and Tyrone of the mailroom staff at the psychoanalytic institute that finally sealed it. Not only did they accuse Kruger himself of shooting the Freud bust, but they claimed they were always perplexed about what he wanted with small stuff, and offered Stroud and Grillo the example of the airline fax that disappeared from my desk.

Manuel and Tyrone further confessed that it was Kruger who canceled our reservation for the trip to the airport, and they admitted to trying to get at the crates in the locked library room. They swore that Kruger had given them specific instructions to focus on my mail and on the mail addressed to Franklin Fiske, Chairman of the Board of Trustees at the institute. I didn't know whether to feel deflated because I wasn't the only object of Kruger's madness, or to be honored that I was the only other person in the company of Fiske. Apparently, over the years, Kruger would either destroy Fiske's or my mail or steam mail open, read it, reseal it and have it returned.

More and more revelations unfolded in the tabloids. Even though Kruger was still a suspect in the drowning at the hospital, the tabloids were reporting first things first and so the public was reading more about the Medicare/Medicaid scam. The newspapers were predicting a jail term for him. As it turns out, for all the time I knew him, he was a serial liar, schemer, and thief, and who knows what else? Perhaps even a murderer. But I tended to doubt that. Untrustworthy, unscrupulous, yes. Murderer didn't ring a bell. Although, I also remembered that he did own a pistol.

Further, in the tabloids, it was reported that according to his billing statements the case against him was proven beyond a shadow of a doubt. They had him dead to rights. It was reported that according to his billing statements, the government calculated a twenty-six-hour day as the minimum needed to justify his claims, but this twenty-six-hour day would need to occur seven days a week. Billy had based his figures on one year, while the government calculated the number of total years of the fraud.

So much for physician/psychiatrist Siegfried Kruger's concern for his patients. I remembered that at one point I was beginning to feel sorry for him, thinking that what he did actually didn't physically harm anyone. But now I knew that because of his pathology, he had personally eclipsed the lives of many patients — rendered them invisible. And when I thought of the arrogance of it all, the pervasive absence of any empathy, the self-indulgent megalomaniacal narcissism, and his puffed-up chronic pose as some God-like authority figure dictating the fate of all these people while they were literally abandoned and languishing for decades in back wards, I felt personally and inconsolably disgusted.

When detective Grillo called, he told me about the original deal they had offered Kruger. It had finally boiled down to a quid pro quo — information about Tino's personality issues, in exchange for information on Billy's participation in Kruger's property scam as well as setting aside the statue shooting incident. But at that time they had no knowledge of the Medicare/Medicaid business. Therefore, the D.A.'s office had no reason to make a deal. So Kruger was cooked. And while there was still the implication that he wasn't fully in the clear on Billy's death, Grillo confided that it was almost certain that Tino did it and that it was doubtful that Velma was present or participated. But she also was not yet entirely in the clear.

I wasn't sure what to believe. But I did think that whatever Tino said in court to incriminate Kruger in any wrongdoing would be nullified because Kruger's attorney would claim that because of Tino's split personality, his testimony could not be accepted.

I was not at all surprised by Kruger's willingness to reveal Tino's private therapy conversations to Grillo and Stroud. Making a deal for himself would be typical Kruger opportunism. But what he tried to do later on at the trial of Billy's killer revealed again that Dr. Siegfried Kruger was an habitual self-serving villain.

* * *

I assured Jean that the case against us was being dropped, though I didn't reveal how I knew. I said I wanted her to take it on faith and that I would be able to complete the story in a day or two. We began once again to develop an agenda for the conference on Sebastian, and I told her that I had it on good authority that we would be getting all of Sebastian's material—manuscripts as well as diaries.

Mark wanted to set up a series of appointments with a specialist in intellectual property law along with one of his own partners, a patent lawyer. He also suggested convening a meeting of venture capital people who he felt would be able to tackle the large amount required for the development of the entire project. Of course I knew Wyeth could capitalize it by himself, but Mark felt that others needed to be included.

What was less than clear to me was who else to bring in. I knew Danny was in, and I was going to make Vlad an offer he couldn't refuse. Danny predicted that Vlad would donate all of his end to the church. That almost stopped me dead in my tracks, but I realized that if that were to be the case, Vlad's donation would be carefully tailored for true Christian charity and good works, sort of like an oblation. In my own musings, I was also planning to give shares to all of my relatives, close friends, and favorite charities.

I had one more theory to share with everyone involved—Wyeth in particular. It was ultimately the only one that mattered. It was a glimpse down an evolutionary tunnel of "what-ifs" that might be selected once we embarked on this DNA anger-calibration project.

Here's the gist of it. If you control the calibration of anger, you then effect profound change with respect to personality. And if you change personality, you control mind. If you control mind, then way down the line of more intervening steps I could see how immune system imperatives — that are part of this personality chain — could be affected. Basically, the implication here concerns ultimate evolutionary survival; that is, which series of links, which of the personality types will survive and which won't. The synthesis of the system — personality, emotion, mind, immune system type, and the effect of the calibration of anger — comprises, in my opinion, not merely beautiful prismatic effects; because of its ultimate implications, this synthesis constitutes an awesome mosaic.

It's a matter of extinct and extant. Some will recede while others will not. But there are all kinds of reasons for receding. Not everything is evolutionary selection. And I went down the list. First, of course, Katie — a catastrophic life-ending traffic collision. I shouldn't have said that — I take it back. Again, out of no fault of their own, Sebastian, Ester, and little Alba receded — genocide. And Billy receded twice. Once because of his genes, and second — murder. And Edward also receded. His was genetic — cerebral anomaly. And Kruger was gone — self-destruction. Now it was Tino's turn — fractured. Velma Secora, designated a material witness — sick. The making of ghosts.

*   *   *

Strangely enough, Dr. Kruger's trial and Tino Vescaro's trial were both set to begin the same week and were being heard in the same court building, in adjacent courtrooms. Some of us who were called to testify were occasionally shuttling from one courtroom to the other. Kruger for Medicare/Medicaid fraud; Tino for murder. Of course, Kruger was called to testify in Tino's case and to confirm that it was he who was treating Tino in psychotherapy for headache, fugue state, and dissociative identity disorder or in its historic/commonplace form — split personality.

Whenever a conflict arose, Tino's trial took precedence. Everyone was eager for Kruger's testimony because they wanted to hear about this split personality that was headlined in the daily newspapers.

Kruger's strategy immediately became crystal-clear. After he was sworn in, his lawyer put it to him directly.

"Dr. Kruger, would you say Mr. Tino Vescaro, the defendant, is a stable person?" The state objected but was overruled. Kruger was sober and deliberate in his response, assuming his most authoritative stance. He was good.

"Mr. Vescaro is not stable," he said. "He is plagued by a host of problems and serious symptoms. They fully compromise his personality and make him, in effect, and at times, not responsible for his behavior, not responsible for his judgment, and not responsible for even his own opinions."

The obligatory objection was made and again overruled. It was obvious to all of us that Kruger was trying to disqualify Tino as a potential witness against him. Kruger knew that Tino was aware of his partnership with Velma and that Tino would want to protect her. But just in case the seal of silence around Velma dissolved, he realized that to eliminate Tino as a witness offered extra protection in his own case. So he began to paint a severely pathological picture of Tino as a classic split personality. Ironically, it may have been a rare instance of Kruger in a truth-telling moment.

The judge, a woman in her sixties, had the reputation of wanting a witness to tell his story with the minimum of interruptions, so she overruled almost all objections.

"Mr. Tino Vescaro is a multiple personality," Kruger said. "This means he has what has been commonly known as a split personality or is now referred to as dissociative identity disorder. It has been also termed in the past as multiple personality. Different personalities can emerge from this man and when they do, he himself does not know of their existence."

His lawyer asked him to elaborate.

"Well," he said, "Mr. Vescaro essentially houses three personalities. One is the man you see here, Tino Vescaro. The second and most dangerous one is named Jericho, a foul-mouthed, hostile, malicious and dangerous person. The third is a woman named Veronica, who is a sexually promiscuous, exhibitionistic transvestite cross-dresser seductress. She roams the hospital grounds at night where both I and Mr. Vescaro are employed, and tries to attract whoever is around, either hospital patients or staff. Veronica is only interested in seducing through exhibitionism. Tino, as Veronica, exhibits his penis. With respect to cross-dressing—that is, a man dressed like a woman –Veronica's psychology contains the impulses of the transvestite, but then she cross-dresses as a man."

A look around the courtroom would tell anyone that Kruger had a hundred percent attention/interest score with that one. But Kruger was frustrated. He was annoyed that whenever he wiped his brow or brushed aside his hair with his hand, Tino was averting his motion, refusing to look at him. No matter what Kruger did, Tino wouldn't look. And then Kruger had a scare. It was obvious to all in the courtroom. He was almost sure that on one occasion he caught Tino's gaze precisely in the motion of the hand wave but Tino didn't trance. He thought Tino saw him, but then again, he wasn't sure. What everyone saw was Kruger's consternation because when Tino didn't trance, Kruger practically rose from his chair and unselfconsciously pointed, as though to say: "What's wrong? You're not doing it." At that point Tino looked directly at Kruger, who in turn, and in an obvious gesture, waved his hand. Tino did not respond. Did not switch.

I knew that Kruger was aware of another Billy. It was the case of Billy Madigan, who raped a number of women on a college campus and was ultimately found not guilty by reason of insanity. Of course Kruger wanted to pin our Billy's murder on Jericho. Then Tino would be found not guilty by reason of insanity, and incriminating statements made by Tino against Kruger would be nullified. That was why Kruger was wiping his brow and brushing his hair aside. He wanted Tino to catch the wave of the hand and then to trance. Kruger knew the first personality out after the trance was always Jericho. He also knew that Jericho couldn't care less about authority or punishment, and would arrogantly and defiantly confess to the murder right there for all to hear. In fact, he might even tell the judge to go fuck herself. As far as Kruger was concerned, it was Jericho who killed Billy. He was really counting on Jericho to nail it down. Once Jericho did that, Tino was off the hook for murder by reason of insanity, with the Madigan case as a precedent, and Kruger was spared a hostile witness of the first magnitude.

It was late Friday afternoon and despite everyone's anticipation, the trial was recessed till after the weekend.

* * *

And Mark was also eager. He was counting on it. He had been at his law practice for decades, and I had the impression that despite his expertise and renown, he was involved in a lot of routine stuff—a lot of sameness.

So a new project could feel life-giving to him. In view of the fact that because of the numerous legal, scientific, and strategic details of getting the project underway, thus keeping the weeks flying by, nevertheless I knew that Mark's motivation was humming right along. I could tell he thought this was really *it*. I could see it was all getting set off with discernible momentum and literally into an unstoppable process.

Despite my tendency to want to go it alone I also kept thinking of Wyeth. He engendered trust. I felt he had integrity. With our conversations we had seemed to bond. We certainly did not see eye to eye on various subjects, yet we both came away with mutual respect, and neither was afraid of the other. I felt there was something more real about the entire enterprise with Wyeth in the picture, but if he was going to be in it, it wasn't going to be in the way he originally planned, and probably not the way I conceived it either.

I decided we would work it out with Wyeth. I wanted him involved almost to the extent to which he wanted, but again, not quite completely the way he had envisioned. I would direct the research team. The Board of Directors and the positions of President and Chairman of the Board would be set up in such a way that my leverage would equal his. I didn't want this to fall apart because of his power or mine.

Mark agreed. After our phone conversation, in which I outlined all of my concerns, Mark informed me that a meeting had been set up with the attorneys and venture capital people. I asked him to invite Wyeth. When everyone finally met at Mark's office, it was a sight to behold. It was apparent that all of us realized the importance of this project and were all grateful to be involved. Some for the money, some for the fame, some for the money and the fame, and some for the sheer, once-in-a-lifetime excitement of contributing something to the world that would be a first and, hopefully, have lasting value.

Then I shifted gears, called Dr. White and told him that the case against me was being dropped. I also told him that we needed to replan the Sebastian conference for later that year because, if my source panned out, I would be receiving all of Sebastian's manuscripts as well as his diaries and needed sufficient time to have it all analyzed.

The thought of receiving all of Sebastian's manuscripts was both a relief and also a burden. At last, Sebastian would be free, but I wouldn't. I would need months to go through the manuscripts and diaries. I needed to form a committee of scholars so that the material would be considered from a variety of vantage points. There would be plenty of material to go around. Vlad should be on the committee along with other first-rate scholars—historians, psychoanalysts, theologians, and linguists among them. We would rotate the material so that everyone on the team would be able to examine every document, every manuscript page, each diary entry. The conference could be scheduled at the end of the first go-around, and it would be devoted solely to Sebastian's work.

White got on board immediately. Then he gave me his information.

"Did you hear?" he said.

"No. What is it?"

"Dr. Kruger. They're predicting three to five years based upon a probable guilty verdict on all counts of Medicare and Medicaid fraud and theft. They say he's also going to owe a ton of money."

So the bets on Kruger's verdict were in. Much later we all learned that Kruger had indeed been using the hospital as a holding pen for those patients who were without families, and then also stealing whatever these patients were getting in government subsidies. Then he was selling their possessions, to which he had complete access.

White continued. "It's said that because he has no prior record, he possibly could be released in much less time than his full term would demand. Are you there?"

I was. I felt a little sullied by the association I had had with Kruger over the years despite the fact that I always considered him to be superfluous to anything I was doing or thinking. In the end he was a person without character. His self-serving behavior was also exemplified in his testimony and psychiatric evaluation of Tino's personality which, in turn, convinced each juror beyond a shadow of a doubt that Tino was a true multiple. Whatever Tino could say to implicate Kruger, therefore, was not going to mean much. While that may have effectively eliminated Tino as a hostile witness in Kruger's trial, it apparently didn't matter. The government had an air-tight case against Kruger, and everyone was thinking the jury would convict him.

But now it was Tino's turn, and even though it was Tino who was on trial for murder, Velma and Kruger were not off the hook yet as far as Billy's murder was concerned. It all depended on what Tino would say and whether the jury would take him seriously or dismiss him because of his personality pathology which the court, of course, would consider as insanity.

* * *

"I did." Tino was answering the first question put to him, "Do you know who killed Billy Soldier?"

"I did. I killed Billy."

There was a cumulative gasp in the courtroom. All gazed directly at Tino. He repeated it.

"I killed Billy Soldier. I drowned him in the bathtub."

Kruger stood straight up out of his chair as if some force had lifted him and declared in protest: "That's not possible. You cannot be violent. Only Jericho can be violent." And with that he waved his hand directly at Tino. No trance. Nothing.

"Dr. Kruger, control yourself," the judge commanded. Kruger slowly sat back down. All attention was returned to Tino. The prosecutor asked:

"Mr. Vescaro, are you telling us, confessing to the murder of Billy Soldier by way of drowning in the Brentwood Hospital bathtub in the condemned building?"

"Yes."

"Could you explain it to us, please?"

In a monotone and without any sensationalism, Tino told his story.

"Billy was angry with Dr. Kruger and with my mother, too, because he said they were stealing money from patients. It was true of Dr. Kruger but not of my mother. I tried to reason with Billy. I told him my mother had nothing to do with it. But Billy didn't listen. He wouldn't stop saying that he was going to get them both. He said they were going to take his books away from him. But he said they couldn't because he had put them in a secret place."

"Where were you both when you were having this fight, or discussion?" the prosecutor interrupted.

"We were in the secret room in the dark part of the building. Dr. Kruger had a hiding place there behind the fireplace. Edward was there, too. Edward always followed Billy around. He liked Billy and Billy would never mind that Edward was there. I liked Edward, too. I liked Billy, too. And Edward was in the bathroom. He had turned the faucets on and the tub was filling up. He was just watching the water. We went into the bathroom because we didn't want Edward to flood the place. So Edward left the bathroom. Me and Billy stayed there and talked more. Then Billy got mad and started screaming: "I hate them, I hate them—Dr. Kruger and Nurse Secora." He was getting louder and I didn't know what to do. I begged him to stop mentioning my mother, but he wouldn't. Then I pushed him and he fell into the tub. He tried to get up and now he was screaming: "Dr. Kruger and Nurse Secora, I hate you." Something like that. He wouldn't stop. I didn't know what to do and I just got angry. I pushed him into the tub again, but he only fell halfway in and that made it worse and he was getting more upset."

Again, Kruger interrupted, stood straight out of his chair and pronounced: "That's not possible, you cannot get angry. It's a lie." Then looking at the judge, Kruger said, "He's protecting his mother." The judge ordered the bailiff to escort Kruger out of the courtroom, and that was the end of Kruger's presence. The judge then instructed Tino to continue.

"I needed to keep him quiet so I forced his head into the tub. His whole body was out of the tub and he was leaning over I think from his stomach into the tub. I had his head in the tub under the water. I held it there. Then he stopped struggling. I kept it there for a long time. Then I knew he was drowned. I had to hold him up because he was on his knees and after he drowned his knees bent more so I had to hold him up to keep his head in the tub."

Tino stopped. Velma was in the courtroom, her head stooped.

"How long did you keep his head under water?" the prosecutor asked.

"I don't know. It was a long time. Then I carried him out. Edward was staring at me from behind the chair. He saw the whole thing. I left Edward there and carried Billy in a fireman's carry out of the building and to the pool. I opened the gate—I have keys—and figured I would just slide him into the pool, which I did."

He stopped.

"What about Edward?" the prosecutor asked.

"I have nothing against Edward. Edward is a good boy—and so was Billy."

"But they were going to bring in a facilitator to talk to him," the prosecutor said. "Didn't you hear about it? Didn't that bother you?"

"No, I don't know what that means. It didn't matter."

Open and shut. Tino did it. No accomplices. At least no one saw any, and there was no proof that another person had helped Tino in the drowning. Tino was in trouble, but Velma was in the clear. Whether Velma was there or not, no one would ever know. But Grillo repeated to me the epiphany about Velma that he had originally told Stroud. He reasoned that if Velma had been there, no prints would have been left on the tub unless, because of Jericho's increasing delinquency, she finally just wanted to scuttle Tino — she may have wanted out.

No one believed Kruger that Velma was in on his property scam, even though her prints were found on the fireplace frame and on other objects. Velma claimed that she came into the room, which directly abutted her ward, and following the sounds, she came across Kruger and Billy and tried to retrieve the materials they were holding, all the while scolding Kruger for obviously involving Billy in some secret business. There was no evidence to convict Velma, beyond a shadow of a doubt, of anything. So Velma did not only avoid indictment, she was also cleared of all wrongdoing.

*　*　*

Of course, Tino would be committed to an institution. That was certain. But for me it wasn't over. The prosecution had retained me as a diagnostic consultant and Tino had consented to the assessment. So in the previous several days I had met with Tino. The assessment was wholly uneventful. Tino was his unmalicious natural self and was fully cooperative. My report was almost half written when Tino had confessed. Nevertheless, I was called by the court to present my findings. My testing of him had consisted of interviews, a detailed examination of his history with particular focus on his relationship with Velma, psychological projective testing, and an examination of Dr. Kruger's notes.

When I was sworn in, I was asked to identify myself and my title and to state the circumstances under which I became a diagnostic consultant in this case. I indicated that I was a psychologist/psychoanalyst and that I had written books on psychopathology as well as published papers on multiple personality. In addition, I stated that I was recognized as a specialist in symptom cure, that I was a consultant at Brentwood, a colleague of Dr. Kruger's at both the hospital and at the psychoanalytic institute/clinic. Finally, I said I had known both Velma Secora and Tino Vescaro because we worked at the same place and couldn't help but casually know each other the way all staff members become familiar with one another. Otherwise, I had no other contact with them. I also added that the court had provided me with Dr. Kruger's notes. I was then asked to read my report while the judge followed my analysis with a copy. I stated my name as author of the report, indicated my degree credential, and read the title of the report. I began:

The Psychological Organization Of Mr. Tino Vescaro.
*A Case of Multiple Personality/
Dissociative Identity Disorder,
Formerly Referred To As Split Personality*

by Glenn Kahn, Ph.D.

I consulted on two separate occasions with Tino Vescaro, a twenty-four year old man with a classic case of multiple personality. Mr. Vescaro is beset with three separate personalities. The first is Mr. Vescaro as you see him every day. The second is Jericho, a mean, hostile, and entirely corrupted individual. He can be dangerous and would not hesitate to physically attack a person he identifies as an enemy. The third personality is a woman named Veronica, a transvestite/cross-dressing exhibitionist. There is no evidence in the data of any organic brain deterioration that might imply the brain disease called frontotemporal dementia. A person with such a brain disease can show distinct alter personalities similar to what the split or multiple personality shows. In the case of Tino Vescaro, testing shows that his disorder is entirely psychogenic—that is, psychologically determined and not based on brain deterioration.

In the etiology, that is, the development of the multiple personality, it is generally agreed upon by experts in the psychiatric field that discrete personalities emerge in such cases because a deeply etched imperative in the core of the psyche does not permit the integration of the alter personalities into the so-called normal or host state. Thus the psychological solution of such a person is to create separate personalities in order to be one whole person. Therefore, instead of one, there are three or even many more alter subunits. In the case of Tino Vescaro, there were three.

It is usually the case that in the early history and in the development of this sort of personality, as for example in this case, an authority figure has made it impossible for the developing child to express or own aspects of his personality. In this case, anger and sex were forbidden. The subject then goes about creating a hidden life, in fact creating these hidden personalities, each one becoming a perfect embodiment of the emotion that is being concealed. In the case here, the personality of Jericho was the angry one and the personality of Veronica the sexual one. The presence of these alter personalities connect specifically to the particular adult authority who prevented the expression of these emotions in the first place. In Mr. Vescaro's case, it is my opinion that that adult authority was his adoptive mother, Ms. Velma Secora. His need for her along with her discipline—or the requirements of that discipline—created the ground out of which this ingenious, yet emotionally debilitating symptom picture, developed.

I'll begin with Jericho, the aggressive personality. In Dr. Kruger's notes, he indicated that he, quote "used the hand wave to create the transition to Jericho." It's a simple wave of the hand, and with it, Tino tranced and in a few moments, Jericho emerged. Jericho was nothing but belligerent. "The first thing he said to me," according to Dr. Kruger, was "Fuck you, Kruger, you've got nothing on me. Your big-shot position doesn't scare me one bit. So go fuck yourself—you and all your scumbag psychiatrists."

In Dr. Kruger's notes, this kind of response is typical of Jericho. He has no respect or tolerance or any shred of good feelings toward almost anyone. I do have evidence from my projective testing, however, that Jericho does harbor some cautious feelings toward Velma Secora, Tino Vescaro's adoptive mother, and that he does, in fact, seem to have at least a benign and even protective feeling toward Veronica, his cohabiting alter personality. Jericho knows that Velma can keep him from existing simply by indulging Tino's wishes. In that respect, Jericho knows that Velma has considerable power. And so in Tino's psyche, there is a power struggle that takes place between Velma and Jericho. Tino is an innocent bystander in this power struggle, while Jericho is surly all of the time. In the psyche of Tino Vescaro, Jericho's aim is to avenge the frustration that Tino feels—especially that of feeling frustrated by Velma with respect to Tino's wishes. Jericho is Tino's rebellion, albeit on an unconscious level. His choice of the name Jericho was his unconscious drive to reflect his "battle" with Velma.

Veronica reflects perhaps the more interesting dynamic. Veronica is a transvestite. But the catch is that Tino Vescaro cannot permit Veronica to be a public persona. The reason for this prohibition relates to Veronica's serious concern that she will be visible to Velma and therefore that Velma will see that it is really Tino's unconscious wishes that are embodied in her; that is, that Tino is interested in women—generically speaking. This is a conflict for him because he understands instinctively as well as consciously, that Velma forbids such generic interest. So when Tino dresses as Veronica with leather skirts, tight blouses with large false breasts, and is made up with lipstick and so forth, she then must don men's clothing over the female garb she is already wearing in order to conceal her femaleness. Her exhibitionistic impulse acquires its seductive nature apparently by imitation — what is known as the mechanism of identification with the same-sex parent figure — Veronica as Velma.

My psychological testing of Tino has revealed that his relationship with his adoptive mother constitutes an example of a classic psychological phenomenon. It is almost an example of a folie à deux or double insanity. The issue here is that both adoptive mother and adopted son share one pathology — that is, that these two people who are closely associated are infected with a reciprocal psychological contagion — that of one person influencing the other. The qualifier here is that Velma's influence is direct and of course Tino's power only exists indirectly — through his alter personalities. How it works is that in the mind of Tino Vescaro exists a warning — a flashing light. The warning says: "No other woman. No other woman." In other words, because of the influence of his mother, Tino cannot permit himself to have a relationship with any woman other than his mother. So he tries to transcend this injunction against relationships with other women by actually projecting one into the world, and without even knowing why, names her Veronica, with the letter 'V' as the connection to Velma. However, he needs to conceal her presence from his mother's pointing finger that is ever vigilant in his mind. So he, in fact, does indeed conceal Veronica by dressing her as a man. In the end we have a man dressing as a woman, dressing, in turn, as a man — a rare picture of transvestite/cross-dressing. And this of course best explains the nighttime sightings by patients and staff alike of a sometimes lurking man or sometimes lurking woman, both of whom acted out exhibitionistically and were clearly sexual. It was Veronica on the prowl — a sexual, exhibitionistic, seductive prowl.

Veronica's aim was always to exhibit her penis — an attempt to invite adoration and admiration of something that she possesses; this in the hope that the observer would then see her value and accept her in both a figurative as well as in a literally physical embrace. It was Tino's attempt in this rather indirect and opaque manner to look for mother substitutes so that through the exhibitionism, Tino, a.k.a. Veronica, would then symbolically melt Velma's willpower so that she would see him as desirable and want him as much as he wanted her. Thus, we can see the operation of a highly devious and intense process of incestuous desire and its consequent pathology. It needs to be said however, that this intense desire on Tino's part for his mother's accessibility was, in all likelihood, nurtured and carefully promoted by this self-same mother, in an obsessively tyrannical attempt on her part to completely control Tino's psyche.

In his host state, Tino feels compelled to be the good boy. He has been educated to the fact that if he is a good boy, then, and only then, will he be able to be close to Velma. Because he so desperately wants her approval, his pathology exists as an incestuous oedipal wish to possess her. In fact, and in keeping to the oedipal theme, because of his mother's mandate, Tino can have no woman other than her and no other woman but her. Clearly, the incestuous power is in her hands. This mother, although highly seductive, never, or almost never, permits Tino to be sexual. His desire for her is the lever that she uses to control him, to guide him, to instruct him, and to do whatever she wants to, or with him. Tino is so invaded, even branded with the imperatives of his oedipal wish, that he projects this imperative as a steady product of his psyche. Thus Velma has entirely occupied his psyche and is in almost complete control of his emotions. I say "almost" because Tino's psyche has obviously devised a method, unconscious though it is, to conceal parts of himself so that his mother has only limited access, if any, with respect to her possible influence on the parts named Jericho and Veronica.

Because of this division, Tino can, through Jericho, for example,release his rage, and through Veronica, assert his intense needs for acceptance and recognition from mother-like figures. This is what is known as a transference phenomenon. That is, Veronica's exhibitionism is always unconsciously considered by her to be exhibiting to Velma. Tino therefore achieves psychological recognition from his mother whenever Veronica exhibits her penis. Veronica's hope is for this act to invite a response. In this kind of roundabout way, the symptoms, meaning the presence of Jericho and Veronica, gratify the wish that Tino can, through Jericho, actually angrily protest being deprived as well as controlled by his mother, and at the same time, through Veronica's successful exhibitionism, possess his mother.

One might say that Velma held tight control through a bodacious, exhibitionistic display of breast-power. She would dress and undress in full view of Tino, although not ever be completely uncovered. She would wear sheer nightgowns and parade around their trailer in a bra that loosely held and visibly showed, her considerable endowment. Tino witnessed this display over many years, and was kept in a constant excited sexual state, desperately wanting physical contact with her. Velma then fortified this incestuous seduction by having them sleep in the same bed, although ostensibly actual sexual intercourse never occurred. The objective of the mother was to keep Tino in a state of sexual desire and duress, with a vague implicit promise of some physical contact as an eventual reward for his good behavior. And of course good behavior meant obedience and compliance. Yet Velma's positive reinforcement for Tino's compliance was only intermittent, and of course intermittent reinforcement is always stronger than continuous reinforcement.

More or less, these are the dynamics and analysis of Tino Vescaro's psychopathology. Technically, the mechanisms of psychological defense that are employed to permit the psychic construction of his three separate personalities are called repression, disassociation, and compartmentalization. These mechanisms of defense keep the personalities segregated from one another, and I will not define them here because of the technical details such definition would require, including explanations of acting out that concern doing things as a defense against knowing or realizing something; implications regarding the nature of impulses; the psychology of dependency and why and how it generates rage; in this case the effect and influence of sexuality on the latency phase of development; an explanation of the basic nature of certain emotions; and, how all of these factors function in the formation of the multiple personality—dissociative identity disorder.

Now a word about why Tino did not trance in the courtroom, even though he did see Dr. Kruger's hand wave. In the past, Tino was susceptible to a wave of the hand and would trance into Jericho whenever Dr. Kruger waved. The unfortunate truth is that the moment Tino broke loose with rage and aimed it at Billy, and of course did it on his own in the absence of Jericho, at that precise moment, Jericho allegedly lost his grip. His role of representing Tino's anger, at best was erased, but most likely only became weakened. Because of this, Tino had for the first time expressed rage and acted on it himself. It was no longer necessary to have a surrogate do it for him. Unfortunately, it was a moment that led to the death of Billy Soldier, most likely because Tino thought he was protecting Velma. The irony is that it was Velma's handiwork that created Tino's split personality in the first place, and also it was concern about Velma that perhaps has finally undermined it. I assume that what Tino has not yet realized is that Jericho's weakening also signals Velma's ultimate decline in her influence over him. Thus, the tyranny that controlled him is now weaker. In my opinion, Tino's multiple personality structure, although undermined, will still take time to perhaps entirely disappear. Although weakened, I am certain that Jericho still exists.

If Tino's anger is actually and smoothly integrated into his personality—which would have to occur first—then it is likely that sexuality will follow. The principle is that where anger is smoothly integrated in the personality so that the person is no longer always in a rage, then libido or sexuality can finally be permitted. In that case, Veronica will also disappear. It would signal the possible birth of a genuine psychological separation from mother in place of his separate personalities. The tragedy here is that the germ of cure occurred through a violent act. It is my opinion that this violent act was not premeditated and was based on impulses entirely out of Tino Vescaro's control or awareness. To say he was not in his right mind would not be an overstatement.

The hidden issue here was Tino's anger toward Velma. Tino was not even aware of his rage. He experienced Velma's withholding as unrequited love. Sustaining his multiple personality structure ensured that his anger toward her would remain repressed. In this sense, it kept Velma imprisoned in his psyche. In the end therefore, in such a pathology, even though she had him, he also had her.

In summary, Tino Vescaro is also a victim. He was subtracted from himself just as Billy Soldier was. Billy languished all of his life. He was less than he could have been. Certainly, the same can be said of Tino Vescaro, especially since his three was less than one.

* * *

The trial was over. When I left the courtroom, I was spent. Grillo and Stroud met me at the foot of the stairs.

"We heard it," Grillo said. "Great. Now guess what?" He didn't wait for an answer. "You were always right about Billy's intelligence. For sure, no retardation there. We found Billy's books. Well," he qualified it, "we ourselves didn't exactly find them. The cat did. The cat that Billy fed scooted into Dr. Kruger's office and attacked Kruger's oak floor to ceiling bookcase as though it was a scratching board. A couple of detectives were in the room and tried to get it. Instead, they found Billy's books on the lower shelf of the bookcase looking like any of the other hundreds of books. I guess we can say that as Billy was drowning he knew he was sitting on the information, but still he wouldn't give it up. Maybe it was happening too fast."

I thought about it and said, "You know, guys, cats are kind of autistic. They only do things they want to do. Just like Billy's Asperger's autism or Edward's real McCoy. It's come full circle. A somewhat autistic creature conjured the plan, and a somewhat autistic creature revealed it."

They wanted to know about Velma. "Could you imagine," Grillo said, "how she just sat there without moving a muscle or changing her expression, even when you explained all that sickness that she perpetrated. What's gonna happen to her?"

"Well," I said, "it's going to be interesting. If the neurosis is really broken between them, she could feel no need to hang around and could disappear—only to try to find another Tino. I mean, the fact is that physically, she can't live with him now and do her sick stuff—at least for a long time to come. And she *needs* to do her sick stuff. The other possibility, and it's a real one, is that the whole thing turns around and Tino now becomes the controller. She stays around and visits him and supplicates herself to him and starts to feel in need of him. The psychological literature cites cases like that. It's kind of like a reversal of the sado/masochistic relationship. A third possibility is one I hate to think of. It's that Velma sticks around, the craziness with them is really not resolved, not by a long shot, and she visits with him each week and just continues the torture. And I haven't got the slightest idea which of the three it'll be. Quite frankly, I'm not even completely convinced that Tino hasn't protected her. Some thought, huh?"

They both paused and stared at me. "Nice to have met you, Doc," Grillo said. Stroud nodded.

* * *

Sebastian was not out of my mind by a longshot, but I was consumed by the courtroom drama. And I didn't have time to wind down because Wyeth flew in from the West coast—his turn to fly to see me. We spent several hours before the meeting talking about Tino's trial. It was all over the news. Then we talked about my plan for Biogene. I tried to persuade Wyeth that it was not avarice that made me suggest this particular arrangement of forces, but that I needed to have more power to guide the project. I felt it would be in the best interest of the project and its ultimate success that we do it this way. Surprisingly, Wyeth agreed to it all. Maybe not surprisingly. He was a consummate forward-mover. Biogene would indeed have a large part in it all.

As it turned out, Wyeth's presence at the meeting was important. Whenever he said something, everyone deferred to him. He made it all seem possible. The venture capital company, represented by two of its principals, also pledged to come on board. The meeting largely centered around setting up the legal structure of the enterprise and then arranging for more financing than even Wyeth originally planned. We all sat there from lunch till dinner time. Everyone was educating everyone else about the distribution and trajectory of the work. The first draft of the contract would be prepared by Mark's office. A second meeting was scheduled in ten days. In the meantime, each of us had assignments to accomplish for that next meeting.

Wyeth and I shook on it. We did indeed like and trust one another. Time would tell. I was ready to leave, going to a quiet dinner alone. But no one else budged. Then Mark asked it. He wanted to know about the implications of the theory, especially about the connections among DNA, brain, mind, and personality, and the relation of it all to the calibration of anger. Apparently, the others were also interested, and there were questions coming at me from several of them.

I quickly outlined for them the differences among character diagnosis, symptom neurosis, and psychotic conditions. I ended it by pointing out that there were only a few basic diagnoses that underlie all clinical conditions. I asked them to take it on faith that each diagnostic pattern contains its own chain of personality variables reflecting every level of personality, such as: levels of defensive organization, emotions, personality trait formation, behavioral mode, dream and nightmare type, personality conflict-forces, psychosomatic systems, cognitive thinking style, and immune system implications. I promised I would have Rita forward each one of them the two-volume set I had published entitled *The Personality System*, where many of these ideas are detailed.

That ended the meeting. Everyone said their goodbyes, and exited. Wyeth and I again shook on it. Mark asked me to wait. Then he went right to it.

"Great going, Glenn—and it can all be shifted by the calibration of anger?"

"Yes," I said, "and *only* by the calibration of anger."

"So I guess this is just a tad bigger than symptoms."

"Yes, and no," I said. "Discovering the code for unlocking symptoms tied all of it together. So it's bigger than symptoms, and then again it isn't. Without Sebastian's work, I couldn't have gotten to it. It took Freudian understanding, my own clinical formulations, and Sebastian. So Sebastian finally gets to speak again. Wait till the world hears what he has to say."

"Glenn, you've done something important for Sebastian."

"I hope you're right. It would mean a great deal to me if that were true. But the real truth is that I've had what we might call a magnificent obsession about rescuing Sebastian. I think I was actually feeling relieved with the fantasy that I could bring him here to America where he would be safe, that I could undo the past. And of course because that's not possible, I was suffering with what I would call profound helplessness. Thankfully, I think I figured it out. I was the *who* toward whom I was angry because I couldn't do the miracle in the present, which despite everything I also knew couldn't be done. Looking toward the future is what needs to be focused on. That's why my focus on this little tablet of ours—our contribution to fixing the world—has maybe freed me a little of my rescue obsession regarding Sebastian, but," I said, "not Katie. I don't think anything can shake my rescue thoughts there—about her in L. A. Maybe not even our little tablet. Nevertheless, I think I'm possibly empowering myself and looks like everyone else, too—with our project. So now Sebastian's discoveries help everyone." And I thought: "Rest in peace, Sebastian. Rest in peace."

But I knew I couldn't say that to Katie.

* * *

Mark paused, and squinting pensively, changed the subject. He shifted to what I considered the ultimate question. First, he said I had convinced him that the calibration of anger was indeed the power lever. Then he said: "Glenn, you know how the whole thing is tied together? I mean DNA, brain, personality, mind, those diagnoses, immune system type, and the calibration of anger? You know which personality lines of descendency are on a survival course and which on an extinction one?"

"No, I don't," I answered. "C'mon, Glenn," he continued, "I mean, you know which lines are being ciphered, becoming ever so gradually subtracted from existence?"

"No, I don't," I repeated. "Not completely, not really, and not yet. But in one way or another, people are under pressure and they get subtracted from themselves. So I guess that means that people need to be willing to fight. They need to fight those forces that want to diminish them, and they need to fight so that they also don't diminish themselves by basing every single thing on self-interest. They need to fight the dying of the light!"

"But, Glenn," he said, "some compromises can't be helped. You know that."

"Of course," I answered. "But still, you've got to fight. It's about self-respect."

He stood there looking at me knowing I had an unfinished agenda. So he added, "What about L.A.?" His question was a challenge and he was right on it. I answered him the only way I could.

"Retrieval and rectification, Mark—without that, injustice rules and it becomes, well, you know what it becomes. When injustice rules, there's no way to prevent it from becoming the making of . . . you know."

*   *   *